The OTHER SIDE of NEVER

DARK TALES FROM THE WORLD OF PETER & WENDY

Also available from Titan Books

DARK TALES FROM THE WORLD OF PETER & WENDY

The OTHER SIDE of NEVER

Edited by

MARIE O'REGAN
and PAUL KANE

TITAN BOOKS

The Other Side of Never
Print edition ISBN: 9781803361789
E-book edition ISBN: 9781803361796

Published by Titan Books
A division of Titan Publishing Group Ltd
144 Southwark Street, London SE1 0UP
www.titanbooks.com

First edition: May 2023
10 9 8 7 6 5 4 3 2 1

A CIP catalogue record for this title is available from the British Library.

Printed and bound by CPI Group (UK) Ltd in Great Britain.

Table of Contents

Introduction

MARIE O'REGAN & PAUL KANE

Even before we had finished working on the anthology *Wonderland*, we were thinking about which popular mythos to tackle afterwards giving it that same, darker spin.

Just as we are both fans of the Alice tales, looking back on our childhoods provided a clue about what to turn our attentions to next. The original book *Peter and Wendy* – which began life as a play in 1904 – has always been as much a part of our lives as eating and sleeping, just like it has for so many generations. It has already inspired such a huge amount of work, from other plays (like the musical *Neverland* and also *The Terrible Tragedy of Peter Pan*) to radio (Dirk Maggs's 1995 production for the BBC, for instance), from TV shows (including ABC's popular series *Once Upon a Time*, which featured Colin O'Donoghue regularly as Hook), comics (*Peter Pan – The Graphic Novel* by Stephen White,

Cheshire Crossing by Andy Weir) and books (*Hook's Revenge Series* by Heidi Schulz, *Peter Darling* by Austin Chant, *Son of Neverland* by Cal Barnes) to films, of course: most recently, the movies *Pan*, *Wendy* and *Come Away*.

But, as with our previous undertaking, we wanted to do something just a little different. Grown-up tales inspired by the legend of a boy who *never* grew up. Once again, we assembled a group of spectacular writers to help us with that mission, providing stories that are *definitely* not for children. And thankfully, each and every one of them has risen to the challenge.

In here you'll find the supernatural, in Laura Mauro's and Muriel Gray's stories in particular, while A. K. Benedict and Cavan Scott take the idea of shadows and run with that. Robert Shearman focuses on a fear of the subject matter in hand, just as A. C. Wise, Kirsty Logan and Guy Adams put a very modern spin on the material. Edward Cox is deep in dystopian territory and Lavie Tidhar gives us a thoughtful piece to ponder over, both revolving around that all important question of "what if"? Rio Youers and Gama Ray Martinez use a certain famous hook as their jumping-off points in very different ways; Anna Smith Spark and Claire North give us, in turn, historical and social commentary; Juliet Marillier provides a throughline from Classical mythology to the original adventure; and there are also tales that deal with the "lost" in various ways – just look at Premee Mohamed's, Alison Littlewood's and Paul Finch's contributions to find examples of that.

A stunning range of interpretations, by a stellar line-up of writers. All of them providing a glimpse of more thought-provoking or ominous alternatives…

The *Other* Side of Never.

Marie O'Regan and Paul Kane
Derbyshire, September 2022

Foreword

JEN WILLIAMS

When I was at art college, I spent a lot of time in the campus library, browsing all sorts of art books for inspiration purposes (or, more often, procrastination purposes). On one of these slow days, rain pelting against the windows, I came across Paula Rego's Peter Pan illustrations. Rego is celebrated for her dark, uncompromising and even uncomfortable art, and her Pan pictures pull no punches (try saying that three times quickly after a flagon of pirate grog). If you've never seen them, I encourage you to seek them out: you could hardly find a Peter further from the animated one many of us grew up with – except perhaps within the pages of this excellent anthology.

The image that particularly stuck with me was Rego's buff, split-tailed mermaid, her muscular arms holding Wendy under the water, a fairy-tale sky crammed with stars wheeling overhead. It's a shocking image, but on a deeper level I wasn't entirely surprised by it. J. M. Barrie's story is a timeless classic intertwined with the nursery, with story time, with faeries and adventure, but I think we instinctively know there is more to Neverland than that. We know darkness is just under the surface, like a crocodile waiting in the sapphire waters of the lagoon. After all, we know what it really means to "never grow up".

These stories, expertly gathered by Marie O'Regan and Paul Kane, explore every facet of Neverland and the Peter Pan mythos. From the catastrophic fallout of losing your shadow to Lost children of all varieties; from the dark origins of Peter himself to the frankly terrifying spectre of lads who refuse to grow up – the short stories collected in *The Other Side of Never* offer the same creeping delights as Paula Rego's alarming illustrations. Terror and magic, murder and monsters… We know there are teeth waiting for us under the water, but the pixie dust is just too tempting. So I invite you to step into these pages and discover all the surprises Neverland unleashed has to offer. You already know the way.

Jen Williams
London, January 2023

A Visit to Kensington Gardens

LAVIE TIDHAR

Pitter patter Peter pipers pans across the tended green. Here's a statue, here is Peter, here are parakeets preening green.

"The parakeets," a man in faded jeans says nervously, addressing a group of young adults, "are said to originate from a pair that escaped the set of *The African Queen*, starring Humphrey Bogart and Katharine Hepburn, in 1951." He twists a silver wedding ring nervously. The students look bored. "The statue to Pan is also a Pokéstop," the man adds, helplessly.

Pitter patter, Peter pipers, here across the changeless green. Here's a statue, made by Frampton, all in bronze – it looks nothing like him.

No one pays any attention to the little boy in green. Demon-baby riding goat, that's how Rackham drew him once. How he loved to torture fairies! Pull their wings, collect the dust!

How he loved to sail his nest-boat, all across the Serpentine. Then the fairies lost their fear and found him friendly, baby Peter playing pipes. How he loved to watch their dances! How he loved to love his life.

Long-term memory is fleeting, Peter lives in *here* and *now*. Fairies die, and when they do he forgets them, but sometimes he remembers little bits of his life.

There was a girl, he is almost sure of that. She was going to be his wife. He isn't sure what "wife" is, but he knew he wanted one and there was Maimie, but she went back to her mother. Years later he would still find little gifts and letters from her hidden in the shrubbery. He tore the letters and the goat faded away in the end, but still. They always left him in the end. They always grew up.

The man is still talking. He is balding on top. He says, "For your mid-term assignment, I'd like you to write your paper on Peter's relationship with either Charles Kingsley's *The Water-Babies* or with Mole and Rat's visit to Pan's Island in Kenneth Grahame's *The Wind in the Willows*."

The students look confused. One girl raises her hand. "How many words?" she says.

"Two thousand," the man says, "and please—" with a long-suffering sigh "—don't forget to cite your sources and use a bibliography. Remember, Wikipedia is not an appropriate source for academic citation."

The *water-babies*? Peter remembers *them*. Poor lost souls, drowned in the river. He used to pal with them from time to time. There was a young woman, too, a sort of mother to the little ghosts. Harriet, was that her name? She wore leaves in her hair and recited poetry. He had liked her. But she, too, faded away after a time.

The city, every time he comes back to it from the Neverlands, is the same but different. St Paul's is always there, brooding, and the Tower with its poor ravens who can't fly. The Thames and the Serpentine still sing to each other and gather the drowned into their watery depths. Once, Peter saw a lost whale come up the river. Later, its carcass washed up on the bank. He saw jumpers and those who were thrown. The rivers are Neverlands all of their own.

He thinks Barrie got it almost right, when he'd tried to tell him the story. A Neverland is always an island in a child's mind. The Neverlands change like the city changes. He vaguely remembers a man with a hook, a ticking clock. Then the rail tracks came and the trains, then all kinds of things that beeped and chirped and glowed white-light with screens. It doesn't matter to Peter. Peter loves *now*. The man with the students swipes his finger across the screen of his phone. "See?" he says. "A Pokéstop."

The students lose interest. Tourists feed the parakeets. The green birds fly down and peck seeds. Mothers go past pushing prams. Peter looks at the babies with hatred. His knife is always nearby. When did he last pull it out? On Wendy's baby girl. But he had been startled then, scared.

It's always confusing when they grow up.

Is Wendy there? Will she come today? He looks around him with hope in his eyes. It isn't yet Lock-Out Time so the fairies are not out yet. Humans wander through the park without a clue.

"Did any of you read *The Wind in the Willows*?" the man says, with that same defeated voice. Peter looks at the students. They are Betwixt-and-Between, not quite grown-up yet, not quite children. Will *they* see him? The same young woman from earlier raises her hand.

"Yes?" the man says.

"I think so?"

"You remember the chapter where Mole and Rat find an enchanted island where the god Pan lives?" the man says.

"Um, no?"

"No one ever does," the man says. "And Mole and Rat themselves forget, after they've been there."

He smiles hopefully, like he's made a joke somehow, but no one laughs. The girl looks to where Peter's hiding. Does she see him? She blinks. He waves, hope breaking in his heart. She looks away and hope dies. What did she see? Just bushes, grass, a squirrel squirrelling a bag of crisps? Or did she glimpse him, Peter; did she see the shadow of a child?

"The water-babies," the girl says, "they were dead?"

The lecturer brightens, the other students look at the girl as if to say they just want to go off. The lecturer says, "Well, it's an interpretation."

"Everything is an interpretation," the girl says. The lecturer gives her a hopeful smile. He glances to the side, where Peter is. Does *he* see Peter? He says, "Have you looked into the notion of the Edwardian enchanted summer and how it relates to inter-war depiction of fairylands yet?"

"Professor…" a boy groans, and the man catches himself,

startles, says to the girl, "Perhaps we can discuss this later, if you'd like—"

Something passes between them, but it is not a thing Peter can understand. Perhaps the man wants the young woman for a mother, just like Peter, who left his, keeps seeking Maimie – or was it Wendy? Or was it Margaret, or Jane? Who is it now? Are there still Darlings in London? Well, there must be, or something like them, for the Neverlands, though always changing, are still there; and so is Peter, and the first of the night fairies flies by his ear and laughs delightedly, the evening starts to settle on the park and the students are restless and the man says, "Well, we made it here with the old map from the book, so... Feel free to look around, and we'll continue this next week in class."

"See you, Professor," a couple of them mumble, then they scatter off, eager to find something else to do, children at their play, and Peter longs to play with them. The man and the young woman walk away, too, and Peter is left there by the statue, and momentarily at a loss, he waits. A girl will come, sooner or later, who could see him. And then he'll take her for a wife and they'll fly home; second to the right, and straight on till morning.

"Peter?" she says.

He turns to her. She lies in the bed. Her long white hair spread against the cold white pillow. The window open, the stars beyond. A double-decker bus goes past. Peter watches the people on the upper deck. A woman in a head scarf stares at her phone. Can no one see him?

"Oh, Wendy," he says.

"It is time, dearest," she says weakly.

"Darling," he says, and she tries to smile. "Me, or my family?" she says. Their old joke together. Jane's in Australia, they spoke to her on Zoom only that morning. John's hunting flamingos in Cyprus. Michael ran off to America with a showgirl, worked as a stagehand at first, moved through the ranks, directed a couple of films for Monogram Pictures, *Lost Boy* with Lugosi in '42, then *Hooked* with Karloff in '43. Wounded in Normandy and honourably discharged. Married, divorced, and married again. Drowned off the Santa Monica pier in '58. God damn it, Michael, Peter thinks. He misses him still, and every day.

"It won't be long now," Wendy says. She closes her eyes. She breathes so softly. "Do you still have some of that fine fairy dust left?"

He sprinkles it on her. She rises, light as a feather. She hovers above the bedsheets, which are stained with her sweat. Peter's fingers are messy with dust. He wipes his hand on his trousers.

"Must you go?" he says.

"You know I must." She looks at him trustingly. "I just need a little bit more. Just a little more dust."

He nods. He treads heavy. He goes to the cupboard that's locked. He turns the key and tries not to look at the tiny cages inside. He hears their tiny voices. He reaches in, blind, picks one, squeezes until the dust coats his hand. It doesn't matter, he thinks. He told Wendy's mother long ago. He forgets them when they're gone.

He goes back to her. She is almost at the window. The moon outside. Two stars in the sky. He sprinkles the dust. She rises higher. White as a sheet. White as a ghost. White as the moonlight that streams through the window. Another bus passes, but nobody looks. Nobody wonders at this slip of a woman, as white as an envelope, ready to go.

"There will be pirates there," he tells her, "corals and jungles and shipwrecks and more."

"I'll have my own tiny house," she tells him. "All to myself."

"I will come!" he says, panicked.

"Yes, yes," she says.

"You will mend my clothes?"

She doesn't hear him. "I left a meal in the oven for you," she says. "And a note by the washing machine. You must learn to use it."

"But I don't know how."

"You just put the clothes in and a capsule, and turn the dial."

"Must you go?" he says again helplessly.

She is half out of the window now. The wind could snatch her away at any moment.

"You know I do," she says. "It is time."

"Will you come back sometimes?" he says. "I will be here, waiting."

"You still have to grow up," she says sadly. "But I am all done growing."

Then she is gone. The wind takes her away. A bus goes past and she flies above it. On and on she goes, until she vanishes from sight; second to the right, and straight on till morning.

"You see," the balding man says eagerly over his glass of house wine, "in all the British books about fairyland, the worst thing you can do as a girl is grow up. Growing up is worse than death itself – it is a loss of *innocence*." He takes a sip of wine. The young woman watches, head inched. "Carroll *mourns* Alice at the end of *Alice's Adventures in Wonderland*," the man says. "How, if she just opened her eyes from the dream, the world would change to 'dull reality' and she will grow into a woman who could only dream 'of Wonderland of long ago'. Only kids escape into the Neverlands. Susan can't go back to Narnia. And so on. But for Barrie, it isn't Wendy who loses out on Neverland. It is poor Peter, stuck, forever infantile, while Wendy grows up as all children should. Do you understand?" He says it very earnestly.

"I think you're full of shit," the young woman says, and the man laughs. He is a little drunk perhaps.

"Lucy in *Dracula*," he says.

"What about her?"

"She lets Dracula seduce her and loses her innocence, so she has to be destroyed. The stake to the heart, again and again, and the spouting blood. It's very sexual. You see, they valued innocence, the Victorians, they made a fetish of it. I think the British still have it. The *Carry On* films—"

"What are those?"

"Old comedies," he says, dismissing them with a wave of his hand. "All the men are weak and fearful and the women are grotesque and domineering. It's the other side of the coin. The henpecked men lust for youth."

"And you?" she says.

"Your lips are red," he says. "Like Lucy's."

"And you are Dracula?"

Something in her voice. She drinks her wine and pushes back her chair. Stands up to go.

"Is this your Neverland?" she says. "Because it's shit."

He watches as she walks away.

"There are pirates there," he says, to no one in particular, "and coral reefs and shipwrecks and monkeys in the trees…"

He frowns. He finishes his wine. Then he walks alone to the tube station.

Peter tries to use the washing machine. The thing spins round and round and the clothes inside are wet. He goes back to the room and to the empty bed. He pours himself a glass of wine. He shakes some fairy dust into the wine and drinks.

The silence presses. Life goes on outside. The buses go past, faces in windows lit up by projected light from screens. Suddenly he can't bear the silence anymore. He drops the glass. It shatters on the floor. The wine soaks into the old, old rug. Peter bends down, picks up shards. He cries softly as one cuts his finger. The red of the wine, the red of the blood. The red of Lucy's lips.

He scoops up the rest of the shards and puts them carefully in the bin. He straightens, feeling the twinge in his back. He hears a rustle at the window.

"Wendy, you're b— Oh, it's you."

His shadow creeps in sheepishly from outside. Peter takes it. The shadow is wet from the dew.

"Have you been out all night in the park again? I thought I lost you for good."

The shadow says nothing. Peter shakes him to dry.

"Wait here," he says.

He goes to the cupboard. Gets out the old kit. The shadow waits patiently on the bed. Peter comes back. Peter sits down. He places the shadow beside him and opens the kit, takes out needle and thread. His fingers are clumsy but he threads through the needle. Silence settles again. A bus goes past outside. Peter darns. Peter mends. Peter sews his shadow back on, stitch by stitch.

Manic Pixie Girl

A. C. WISE

Light seeping between curtains the color of rust; cheap motel sheets tangled around my legs. There's a stain half-hidden beneath the melamine nightstand. I look at it for a long time, trying to pretend nothing's wrong.

Dee's going to be pissed. But I swear – this time, I really tried.

My legs wobble, all new-foal gangly when I pry myself upright and my head swims. I'm still high, starlight running through my veins, a little taste of another world.

Careful, careful, I tiptoe across the ugly carpet to the bathroom, making a game of trying to minimize contact between my feet and the floor. I almost lose my balance, giggling inappropriately for the situation. Thinking too many happy thoughts. I catch myself on the pedestal sink and manage to stay upright.

Looking in the mirror, it's Dee's voice I hear, and her face looking back at me with sad puppy-dog eyes.

Oh, Bell. What did you do?

I want to tell her it isn't what she thinks, but that's exactly what it is. I fucked up again. But just for the moment, I play pretend. I make believe I went home with someone nice; I'm waking up in their bedroom and not a shitty motel. Right now, they're downstairs making me breakfast. I can almost smell coffee brewing and bacon sizzling. I could eat a whole fucking pig right now, I'm just that starved.

Cold water splashes on my face, scrubbing away last night's make-up, applied like warpaint under the flickering light in the club's graffiti-littered bathroom. I turn off the tap. Light catches the glitter still smeared on my skin. That part isn't make-up. It never comes off.

Deep breath. Shoulders back. Chin up.

Time to face the music. I creep back to the bedroom, still wobbly, and survey the damage I've done.

The boy on the bed looks like someone carried him high into the air and dropped him a very long way down. Sunlight and shadow dissect him, a magician's trick separating him into boxes. See his limbs (bent the wrong way) over here; see his neck (never mind the angle) over there; look at his eyes (wide open in surprise) over there. Blink once to let us know you're okay.

See his lips (no breath passing them) and fuck me – he's smiling. Like he died the happiest boy in the whole damn world.

He's not really a boy, he's a man – old enough to know better, but choosing to behave otherwise. He took a woman he just met back to a cheap motel because he thought she'd be an easy fuck, he wouldn't have to try too hard, and just look what happened to him.

I swipe my phone off the nightstand, fingers clumsy because I'm still coming down, still reacquainting myself with gravity. I hit the last number dialed.

Please answer, please answer, please answer.

Then the sweetest voice in the world.

"Bell? Where are you?"

"Motel." I flick back the curtain, squint into the terrible glare of too much sunlight washing through the parking lot. I have no fucking idea. "By the highway? I don't…"

"It's okay. I'll use the app to track your phone." She doesn't sigh, but I hear it anyway, under the jingle of her keys and movement toward the door.

"It hurts, Dee." I sit at the foot of the bed, where the dead boy's feet are, think better of that, then slither down to the floor.

I hate it, coming back, coming down. I was flying, a million miles away, tumbling through a field of stars.

"I know, honey. Hold on. I'll be there soon."

When Dee hangs up, I scooch around to the side of the bed, let my fingers rest ever so lightly against the dead-spider curl of the boy's hand. Dee is too good; I don't deserve her.

"Sorry." I lean my head against the disgusting polyester comforter.

The dead boy hasn't earned my apology, but it's not for him.

Let me tell you a story.

Once upon a time, Dee found me shivering in an alleyway. She didn't know me, I barely knew me in that moment, but she asked me how she could help. I told her I remembered dying in a faraway land. I told her I used to have wings, I used to know how to fly. She didn't laugh, or call me a liar, or tell me it was all in my head. She took me to a diner and bought me breakfast.

I'm trying to be better, for her. I'm trying to pay her back, but I keep fucking it up.

Oh, Bell. What did you do?

Let me tell you another story.

After she saved me, Dee let me crash on her couch for a while. She's studying to be a social worker, but when she isn't doing that, she spins at the local clubs. I didn't know what to do with myself that first week she brought me home, so I went and watched her work.

Sweat-slick bodies, sliding against each other on the dance floor. Music thumping louder than a heartbeat. Colored lights flashing everywhere. There was a boy whose eyes picked up those colored lights and reflected them back, but seemed to have no color of their own.

Dee keeps a water bottle nearby when she works; it gets hot in the clubs. I watched the boy with every-color eyes slip something into it when Dee wasn't looking. I knew he wanted to hurt her.

And then everything went all...

It was like touching my finger to an electric socket, like holding a star in the palm of my hand. Incandescent anger, a dog with its hackles raised. In that moment, I thought I knew exactly what I was made for: protecting Dee, tearing that boy apart.

I took Dee's water bottle and I took the boy's hand. I made sure he saw in my eyes that I knew what he'd done, and then I drank the entire bottle down and smiled. His every-color eyes went all wide – a girl who would do that, knowing the water was drugged. It should have been a red flag, but it only made him hungrier.

I stole him away while Dee was working and taught him how to fly.

Dee yelled at me for a good solid hour when I slunk back home. She didn't know what had happened to me. She was scared. Didn't I know I could have been killed? Not me, Dee. Never me. I already died once – at least once – and look at me, I'm perfectly okay. I didn't want to lie to her, ever, so I told Dee everything. Then I made her waffles for breakfast.

The motel room door opens and I lift my head. Dee's father installs high-end security systems. He's a total nerd for locks. When they were kids, he made a game of challenging Dee and her sister to see who could pick a lock the fastest. Lucky for me, that means she's really good at breaking into motel rooms to save my sorry ass.

"Up you get." Dee's arm goes around my waist. "Can you walk?"

"Uh huh." But I'm not sure I can. There was too little gravity before, now there's too much.

Dee shuffles me outside, bundles me into the back seat of her car.

"He was so bright, Dee." She clicks her seat belt into place, starts the car like it will drown out my words. "Like starlight. He burned right up until there was nothing left inside."

Dee's apartment. Dee's bed, which smells of freshly washed sheets. I roll over just in time to be sick in the trashcan.

"Water." Dee enters holding a glass, puts it in my hand.

"Just let me die." Self-pity, complete with an arm flung over my eyes to block the light even though the curtains are drawn. "It's what I deserve."

I'm trying to make Dee smile, hoping she'll forgive me once again, but I mean it a little bit too. Can't stop. Won't stop. No matter how many times I try. The fact that I'm here, Dee nursing me back from the edge again, is proof of that.

"Do you hate me?" I lift my arm a little bit, sneak a look at her.

"Yes. Very much so." Her arms are crossed as she leans in the doorway.

Like call and response, this is what we do to find our way back to normal.

I've lost count of how many times I've woken up like this, Dee brushing fingers over my sweaty brow. Each time, I promise myself and promise her I won't do it again. Though sometimes I forget to say it out loud.

"What do you want to do with your life, Bell?" Dee has asked me more than once.

"I'm going to run away and join the circus." I evade, I avoid. "I'm going to be a famous rock star."

Dee just shakes her head.

"It can't just be this forever, Bell. You have to want something from life, something more."

My instinct screams: *no I don't*, wanting to stick out my tongue. As far as I know, I don't age. I have all the time in the world. This is what I'm good at, this is what I can do. Why does there have to be more?

None of which I say out loud, because I know deep down I'm avoiding Dee's question. I was never allowed to want anything before I came here, before Dee found me. What if I get it wrong? What if I try and fail?

Dee's mother is in data security. Between her and Dee's father, protecting people is literally in Dee's blood. But none of them could protect her big sister, so I know how even the best-laid plans can go horribly wrong.

Sometimes I'm afraid Dee only takes care of me because she couldn't take care of her sister. Wouldn't it be easier for everyone – for her, for me – if I could actually be what I project to all those sad and lonely boys who are just waiting for someone to tell them what to do?

Look at me – I'm charming, I'm available, I'm fun. I don't want anything at all from my own life, so let me be a supporting character in yours.

I could be that for Dee, except she's the one who's got her shit together, and I'm the one falling apart.

"Do you even remember his name?" Dee's voice brings me back to the here and now.

"Ethan. No. Evan? It was one of those, I'm sure."

Dee deserves so much better than a bad friend like me.

I hurry to catch up with her in the kitchen, sliding in front of her before she can reach for toast or a breakfast bar or something utterly boring.

"Waffles?" I give her a thousand-watt smile.

I see her wanting to be stern, to tell me off, but she relents and sits at the counter. It feels like a victory, even if I know it won't last. I pull out ingredients and line them up. She watches me cook. I'm pretty good, actually. My waffles are always perfectly fluffy inside, perfectly crispy outside. Dee even has a carton of fresh strawberries waiting to be sliced, like she knew.

Maybe that's something I could do? Scrounge together some cash and open my own bakery, an artisanal waffles-only food truck, a classic throwback diner serving nothing but breakfast, twenty-four hours a day?

Right, because bankers are just dying to give out loans to girls with no credit history who can barely make rent and can't even hold down a regular fucking job. Visions of rejection dance through my head before I've even so much as tried, bringing me to the edge of panic. I hate that feeling, as much as I hate that word, so I push thoughts of considering the future, wanting too much, making real plans, right out of my head.

I slide the first batch across the counter, hot off the iron, and try to look chagrined.

"Forgive me?"

"Always," Dee answers with her mouth full, so I can't tell how much conviction is in her words.

She cuts her waffles into methodical squares. I nibble – top left corner, right edge, bottom middle – like each bite is part of an arcane code.

"Are you going out tonight?" Dee wipes syrup from her lips.

She tries to sound casual, like she doesn't care, like it's my business if I go hunting, and nothing to do with her. I know the answer Dee's looking for, but I only shrug. She squints, like she's trying to bring me into focus. Does she see the shine on my skin, the outline of wings? Sometimes I want to take Dee's hand and ask her to run away with me.

Second to the right. Straight on 'til... You get the picture.

Except that would make me no better than *him*, the first boy who wouldn't grow up. You know the one I mean.

I want to be the person Dee thinks I can be. I can't fly here, and running away from problems never helped anyone.

"Just be careful, okay?" Dee looks like there's more she wants to say, but she knows it's pointless; it's all been said before. "I'm working tonight until at least one a.m."

A pointed look, an unspoken warning – *don't fuck up until then because I can't drop everything to come save you.*

"I need to shower now so I can hit the library before work." A not-so-subtle hint to leave. "Be good."

Dee squeezes my hand and shoos me toward the door. I smile for her, trying to mean it, trying not to make her worry. I promise, this time, I'm really going to try.

There's an open interview session at one of the local hotels, drop in anytime between three and five, résumé in hand. I figure what the hell. I could clean rooms. I could wash dishes. Everyone has to start somewhere.

The interviewer spends most of our fifteen minutes trying to suppress an active frown, looking at the space just above my left shoulder, like shifting me to his peripheral vision will make me less disappointing somehow. Yeah, well, fuck you too, pal.

At the end, I get a handshake and a coupon for half off one drink in the hotel's high-end cocktail bar. I'm not hunting, not really, just one drink to wind down and then straight home.

The boy glides up, smooth as a shark. Everything about him screams Finance Bro. His suit is a dead giveaway.

"Bourbon, rocks, and another of the same." He points to my glass, flashing what I assume is his perfected-in-the-mirror-panty-dropping-smile.

I angle my seat in his direction, letting him get a good look at me. Spiked blonde hair, bitten nails, lipstick chewed to the faintest smudge of color. Glitter shimmering on my skin. Combat boots and a strappy floral sundress – clearly I don't belong here in this fancy-pants bar. His impression of me is written all over his face: I'm "not like other girls".

I smile my encouragement. Look at me, I'm quirky, I'm available, I'm fun. I'm your supporting character, here to make your life more interesting. You don't have to try too hard with me, or even try at all. I'll just fall right into your arms and be yours, straight on 'til morning.

The bartender places our drinks on the counter, and to his credit, shoots me a look that asks *is this okay*? I give the faintest of nods. The bartender asked; the Finance Douche assumed. First of what are sure to be many bright red warning flags.

"Are you here for the conference?" He twirls a finger, indicating the hotel.

"Nope." I snag the orange peel from my drink and lick free the trailing drops of bourbon. "I just like visiting new places."

"Alone?" Smirk blooming from his smile.

"It's the best way to get to know a place, throw yourself into the deep end. No safety net, nothing familiar. Just close your eyes and fall."

I let my hand move closer to his arm without touching. I save that to punctuate my answer to his next inane question. The faintest brush, a little sprinkling of pixie dust. Think happy thoughts. All sense of reason and restraint flies right out the window, and we're off to never-never land.

Up in his suite, he tells me about himself, even though I didn't ask. He lets drop casually how he's tired of dating supermodels, how he wants something real. Ooh, yeah, Mr Finance Douchebag, neg on those high-maintenance girls to show me how down-to-earth you are. You don't care about looks. Bonus neg, to make sure I don't think I'm hot shit, then swoop in for the kill.

If he'd care to listen, I could tell him: nothing about this is real. I don't give a fuck about his emotional growth. I don't care if he's ready to move on from hot girl summer to girl with deep thoughts and a tragic backstory fall.

I'm here for one thing: to feed.

A little pheromone-based hypnotic suggestion and Mr Finance Douche is all over me, licking my skin, breathing the glitter-that-is-me deep into his lungs. Fairy dust is a fucking powerful thing. It makes kids leave their parents without a backward glance or a kiss goodbye. It pulls people out of themselves into another world and makes them believe they can fly.

The moment Mr Finance Douche gets me into his bloodstream, I'm a goner. The more he takes, the more he wants. The more he wants, the more I have to give. Like a kid eating candy until his stomach aches, he's all hunger, no satiation. What I am gets inside his bones and shakes all his inhibitions free. No consequences, just abandon. It's rollercoaster-drop-ice-cream-sugar-rush-favorite-song-blasting-wind-in-your-hair-best-damn-orgasm-ever all rolled into one.

A feedback loop, building like a storm inside me, setting me tip-to-toes on fire. Everything is fast and loud and bright, bright, bright. My eyes roll back in my head, my skin flickers with starlight. For one brief, beautiful moment, I lift off the ground. I remember how to fly.

It's like Mr Finance Douche is plugged straight into an electric socket. I see his bones through his skin. Feel the current jolt straight through me. Feeding me with his desire, with his gimme-gimme-grabby-fists-and-call-you-never. But just on the cusp of everything flying apart, when the bed is no longer beneath us and gravity need no longer apply, I stop. Which is something I've never done before.

And for one brief, beautiful moment, the world stops with me.

I lean over and catch a reflection of myself in Mr Finance's blown-wide eyes. Me in miniature, drifting against a field of stars. I remember how to find the second one to the right, feel wings spreading between my shoulder blades. I could keep going, chase that whisper of forever until he's hollowed out and burnt to ash if I wanted. He might even deserve it. But that's not what I want anymore.

Sooner or later, everyone has to grow up. I've seen firsthand what happens if you try to keep on running forever and never look back.

It catches me by surprise, but giving a shit, doing the work, and actually *really* trying this time doesn't sound so terrible anymore.

So what if I try and fail? I'll try again. Because when you've been given a second chance, that's what you do.

I promised Dee, and I really mean it this time.

I'm out and running. Not away, but towards, through the city streets, dodging puddles, because it rained while I was inside.

I stole Mr Finance's wallet on the way out. It's not like I'm going to reform myself all in one go. I left him half-hollowed, bruised and aching, but alive. Maybe just enough of what passed between us will surface from the haze of his mind like a dream that he'll think twice next time. Perhaps he'll see a girl who catches his fancy, and take the time to get to know her. Maybe he'll ask instead of assume.

If I can summon up some degree of hope for him, maybe there's hope for me too.

The idea of it, of having hope, terrifies me. And panic is there waiting to trip me up, to pull me down.

I see it in the puddle first. The bus idling next to the curb, waiting for passengers to load. *His* name in bright green, emblazoned across the side, accompanied by a cartoon logo that looks nothing like him at all.

A sob lodges in my throat, caught on laughter trying to claw its way up and out. My heart lurches and swoops all at once, rising and falling, just like flying. It's like he's holding out his hand, giving me one more chance to fall back into my old ways.

I could get on the bus. I could find a new city. I could start all over again in fresh hunting grounds where at least I wouldn't be hurting Dee. I could save her for good, by sheer virtue of not being stuck looking after me anymore.

But running away never solved any problems, and only those who refuse to grow up fly out the window without even saying goodbye.

I step back, put my foot down when it was halfway to the bus step and climbing aboard.

Stronger than the impulse to run is an impulse to go home and clean up my apartment. Invite Dee over to my place for once, and make her dinner instead of breakfast just to say I'm sorry. We could sit together with a blanket over our legs, make popcorn and plan to stay up all night watching bad movies, but fall asleep before the first one is halfway done.

I want so badly it hurts and my face aches from smiling.

Mr Finance Douchebag's wallet is over-engineered, with a catch that releases to spread all his slick, impressive-looking cards in a fan. I rescue the cash, and rifle through the rest, finding Mr Finance's business card. Turns out his name is Joseph. Who knew? Turns out he specializes in small business loans.

When he sees me again, he won't remember me, but something in the back of his head will linger – an itching sensation telling him I deserve a break. Telling him he owes me one. And if I really try this time, I bet I can put together one hell of a business plan. I mean, who doesn't like waffles, after all?

There's one last story. It's an old story, and it's about me. I don't know if it's true, but once upon a time, I died in that other land, the one I came from. But I came back to life there too because somebody believed in me. Here, only Dee believes in me, but she can be almost as persuasive as I can when she tries, and maybe, just maybe, it's enough to get me to believe in myself too.

I'm running again, so fast I'm almost flying. Escape velocity nearly achieved. I'm still grinning, thinking about what I'm going to cook for Dee when I get home.

Clap for Tinkerbell, children. I really think I'm going to make it this time.

Fear of the Pan-Child

ROBERT SHEARMAN

I

I once had a friend at school who'd got a pathological fear of
███████████. You might well share my disbelief that anyone
could be scared of anything as silly as ████████████, but there
you are. (You'll appreciate my caution in saying the words out
loud – it's clearly for some a sensitive issue.) Certainly with
this boy, you couldn't mention the words to him. He'd go
pale, or shake, or quiver – so much you thought there was no
way this could be real, he must be putting it on – sometimes
he would even scream. There's a word for the fear of children's
literature, they call it bibliopedophobia. But this kid wasn't
bibliopedophobic. He had no problem with *The Wind in
the Willows* or Enid Blyton, and he positively enjoyed the
adventures of Winnie-the-Pooh. You might think that would
be better, that his dread was focused on such a tiny thing, that

it was specifically limited to ▮▮▮▮▮▮▮▮▮▮, and ▮▮▮▮▮▮▮▮▮▮'s appearances in the selected prose and dramatic works of J. M. Barrie. But it wasn't better. His fear had no name. Fear is a lot more reassuring when you can put a name to it.

I say he was a friend. He wasn't a friend. I don't think he had any friends, actually. There was something so determinedly odd about him. Children can be very cruel to outsiders.

If you're scared of heights or spiders, that's easy – you just do your level best to avoid high towers with cobwebs. But when you have a fear of something that doesn't exist, where does that leave you? There'd be no relief to it, I think – and he'd be constantly terrified that at any moment ▮▮▮▮▮▮▮▮▮▮ might burst out of nowhere and drag him off to the NeverPlace. In class he always had to sit in the very centre of the room, at the farthest possible point from any of the windows. And the windows always had to be fastened tight shut, even in summer, even in a heatwave. He wouldn't thank us for that, of course, all we had to put up with for his sake. He'd be too busy darting his head towards the windows on all sides, looking for signs of danger like a frenzied meerkat. God, I think we hated him.

Children can be cruel, yes – and I don't say that to exonerate myself, but I wasn't one of the worst, and I don't say that to exonerate myself either. (But it's true, I *wasn't* one of the worst.) We called him a lot of names – he might have expected that, that was fair game. But it was a bit relentless. We probably made his life hell. And then there was that time when some of us – not me – held him down in the playground and forced open his mouth – not me – and we put mud in it, and leaves, and I don't know, anything we could pull up from the flower beds, worms, probably. I watched, but it wasn't my idea, and I wasn't the ringleader.

All in all it was no great surprise when one day the teacher told us he was dead. I mean, really, caught between us and ▮▮▮▮▮▮▮▮▮, what did he have to live for? The teacher told us there'd been an accident, and that she'd answer any questions we might have. Yes, it had been a horrible accident, he'd fallen out of his bedroom window. No, he wouldn't have suffered, she was sure of that, it would have been very quick. Yes, he'd fallen. Yes, he'd just fallen. No, there was no reason to believe he might have jumped, why would he have jumped, let's not jump to conclusions. No, he hadn't left a note. And at that point she looked a bit stern – why, she asked, would he have left a note? Why would I even ask that? Because, yes, I'd been the one to ask. I said I didn't know, I'd just wondered. No, she said, no note, no jumping, just an accident, a terrible, terrible shame. Should we get back to Maths? Or was there anything else we wanted to ask? Now or never – and she folded her arms, and we just sat there in the classroom, and she glared at us, daring us to come up with something. It was so hot in there. It was stifling. "Oh, at least we can get some bloody air in here at last," she muttered, and went to open the windows.

2

When Harriet died, I only wanted to do the best thing for our son. Some people said that my decision we move house was selfish – especially my in-laws, but I had never got on with my in-laws, and if there were any little benefit to Harriet's death it was surely that I could move far away and never have to see them again. The school had given Philip a counsellor. The counsellor advised me that what Philip needed most was a reinforcement of structure and routine. That I needed to offer recognisable stability and resist the temptation to cast all that aside. But he would say that, wouldn't he? That my son should stay at *his* school, that I should continue paying *his* salary. I asked Philip about it. I did – I said, are you happy at your school? Are you actually *happy*? And he shrugged, which I hardly felt was a ringing endorsement. So we moved. Away from Harriet's parents, and those dreadful Sunday visits every other month, and all that nagging, and all that grief. And went back home, back to where I'd grown up, back to *my* parents. It'd be a brand new start. Or not brand new, back to basics. Look, either way, I knew it would be good for him.

My point is, I gave Philip a choice – and if he'd *made* a choice, I would definitely have taken it into consideration. He wasn't a very confident child, even before his mother died so suddenly – the stammer was already there, and that way he wouldn't look at you when he spoke to you, and that way he'd hide so he wouldn't have to speak in the first place. Was it normal shyness? I don't know, what's normal for a seven-year-old? Had I been like that? I can't remember. I thought my parents would remember. I thought my parents might help.

And I did want help, I did. If it were selfishness to move, then all right, can't I be allowed a bit of selfishness? Everyone asking me about Philip, how poor Phil was bearing up, how he was coping, and giving him a counsellor – and no one asking me how I was, not very much, not in particular.

I hadn't seen Mum and Dad in so long, Harriet hadn't liked them much. Mum put her arms around me and I thought for one ludicrous moment she was going to say I'd grown, but she didn't, she said she was sorry, and I said there was no need, and she said she was sorry anyway, and I told her not to be. It was fine, it was all fine. Dad had his hands in his pockets. You doing all right, then? I said I was fine. They were shy of Philip, they didn't know him very well. So Philip was shy right back, which was a shame. Let's go eat, said Dad, at last; Mum said, let's eat, I've made you your favourite! And I thanked her, and I was a bit curious, I'd honestly forgotten what my favourite was.

It hadn't occurred to me that Philip would now be going to my old school! It excited me when I realised it, and that seemed to excite Philip too. The day we took a tour around and we met the headmaster Philip looked really smiley again, like it was an adventure! The headmaster was young and full of energy, and I liked his new teacher, Miss Collins, I thought she was sweet. I pointed out old classrooms – "I learned Maths in there!" I said. "You'll be learning Maths there too!"

And what about ███████████? Well, nothing, to begin with. That school counsellor had suggested that I try to comfort Philip by maintaining any bonds he had shared with his mother – had she, for example, ever read him bedtime stories? I asked Philip if she had; he said, yeah, sometimes. So I'd read to Philip most nights: a bit of *The Lion, the Witch and the Wardrobe*, a bit of *Harry Potter*. But we never read any ▮▮▮▮▮. There was no reason for that in particular. There are lots of other books to read.

The stammer didn't get any better. I said to Philip one day, "Look, if you ever want to talk about your mum. If you ever want to ask anything. I want you to know you can. Not necessarily now. I mean, not now. But sometime, that's okay." He looked a bit frightened, as if I'd caught him out not having done his homework. He said he'd try to think of something. "You don't need to try! Just if anything pops out. And if doesn't pop out, that's fine." He nodded, and I gave him a hug, and then we read a bit more about what was going down in Hogwarts.

3

When Philip came home with his news, I was pleased, and proud too, of course. The minute I came into the kitchen I knew something was up, he was grinning from ear to ear, and he could hardly sit still, and my mum and dad were fussing over him. But try to understand why I was cautious – we'd been building up some base-line normality, and anything that caused that line to wobble was a concern. I was happy he was happy, and I would rather he was happy than the alternative, but excuse me if, after working so hard to find some level of sadness we could all live with, I wasn't thrilled to find that hard work in jeopardy.

"I'm ▮▮▮▮▮!" he said, and that made no sense to me whatsoever, I thought for a second he had lost his mind –

"I've been cast as ██████████ in the school play!" "Oh," I said, "that's nice, is this something for class?" "No, Dad, I just told you, it's the school play, it's the big school play, and all the school will be watching, and all the parents too, and I'm ██████████!" "Tell me what this is about," I said, and Mum said, "He's trying to tell you," and Dad said, "Why not let him tell you?" and they looked as thrilled as he was, and I thought, it's all right for you, he isn't your son, is he? Philip said, "Just before Christmas the school put on the school play and everyone auditions and I auditioned and not everyone can get a part, but I did get a part, and it's the best one!" I said, "Well, let's think about this for a second," and Mum said, "Isn't it wonderful? My grandson the actor!" and I said, "Let's just think for a second. Philip," I said, "Philip, are you sure about this? With everyone staring at you, is that what you want?" "Yes!" he said. "And you'll have to wear something silly, ██████████ wears something silly, right, like lavender green?" "That's Robin Hood," said Dad, and Philip said, "Yes! Yes!" "And all those lines? You're going to learn all those lines, and what if you forget them, and what if you stammer?" "Be pleased for him," said Mum – "I'm overjoyed," I said.

██████████ was now the only thing Philip talked about. ██████████ – and Mr Cooper. Mr Cooper was the teacher who had cast him in the part, and was directing the play after school each Monday, Wednesday and Friday. Not only did I have to listen second-hand to Mr Cooper's opinions about every single rehearsal, but also about world news, about Art and Culture, about life in general. "Can we have spaghetti tonight?" Philip asked. "Mr Cooper likes spaghetti!" Or, "No, I don't want to go to the zoo for my birthday, Mr Cooper thinks it's cruel." "What happened to Miss Collins?" I asked. "I thought she was sweet." "Mr Cooper teaches me everything now," said Philip, "and he says I'm going to be great!"

Christmas was still nearly three months away, a long time before the play would open. I honestly thought Philip would change his mind. He'd get bored of ▮▮▮▮▮▮, the way he'd got bored of everything I'd tried to share with him – Lego, or football, or walking with me to the shops. He didn't want to read *Harry Potter* at bedtime any longer. Now he wanted me to read ▮▮▮▮▮▮ with him, night after night, and test him on his lines. I'd have to sit on his bed and act out all the characters. Captain One-Hand and Tiger Lollypop and the Tink Fairy and the Missing Boys, and I'd give the Missing Boys all different voices to make it more exciting. One time he said to me, "You don't do it properly. You never do it properly!" And from that point I was barred from his bedroom, and it was my parents who took him to the NeverPlace, who read with him and laughed with him and tucked him in at night.

"You remember when we went to see ▮▮▮▮▮▮, when you were a little boy?" Mum asked me. It was over breakfast one morning. Philip wasn't speaking to me again; he only raised his head and looked at me when ▮▮▮▮▮▮ was mentioned. I said that I had never seen ▮▮▮▮▮▮. She said, yes, I had, they'd taken me to the theatre as a treat. I *must* remember, surely – "Did Dad like it?" asked Philip, and she assured him that I had. I'd been a bit scared of Captain One-

Hand, but I'd found the tick-tocking crocodile very funny. "I have never been scared of Captain One-Hand, or in the least amused by a crocodile," I said. "I have no memory of that whatsoever. You must have taken some other kid." Philip said, "I think my ███████████ will be better than your ███████████, no one will forget me!"

And I began to read ███████████ for myself.

When the rest of my family were all together in the bedroom, playing at pirates and fairies and what-have-you, I sat in my own bed, and studied the text. I had to buy my own copy, so Philip wouldn't know. I kept it under my pillow.

The first time I read the play clean through I just couldn't see the appeal. I thought that maybe the flying sequences could be interesting to watch – although I did wonder how even the great Mr Cooper would pull off that particular special effect, and did hope he wouldn't endanger too many of the children's lives in the process. But I found ███████████ himself strangely colourless. He seemed to breeze through his own adventures – he didn't care all that much about Wanda or the pirates, he didn't care about the Tink Fairy or the Missing Boys, he didn't even care about his occasional brushes with imminent death. I felt a certain sympathy with him for that. After all, I didn't care about them either. But ███████████ came across like a bored parent watching a school production of his life story – so airily detached from all the overegged attempts at charm and magic that he seemed like the play's own worst critic.

I felt similarly the second time I read it, and the third time, and the fourth time. It was somewhere around the fifth that

I started to think that ▮▮▮▮▮▮'s indifference had a tinge of bitterness to it. When he tells us that death is an awfully big adventure, it's something he secretly longs for. Not for the giddy thrill of it, as the lines suggest – but because it would be some way of escape from his miserable little play. Whether it would turn out to be a big adventure or mere oblivion, death would at least mean he never had to interact with Tiger Lollipop any longer.

And it was then I understood that within that bitterness it was the very repetition of his adventures that was causing him the problem. And that each time I read the play back, I was forcing him to live through them all over again. If I would only put the book away, then I could give him some peace. If Philip in his bedroom next door would stop reciting his stupid speeches then finally, maybe, just maybe, the poor boy could get to sleep – and grow up – and put away childish things – and get on with his life. This was what forever condemned him to be a little boy – a child held fast within his own trivial fantasies and so defined by them that he would never be allowed any other life, not a jot of it – no life, and no death.

I wondered whether, at the beginning, back when Barrie had first written the play, ▮▮▮▮▮▮ had actually been happy.

This was around the time I began reading ▮▮▮▮▮▮ several times a night. If I read it really slowly, I could almost feel ▮▮▮▮▮▮ squirm on the page – and just as soon as I'd reached the finale, just as ▮▮▮▮▮▮ might feel he'd been safely put back within his box, I'd quickly turn back to the beginning of the play and start over. I could sense his desperation as he'd realise once more he'd be forced to claim back his shadow, to fly to the NeverPlace, to build Wanda a house. He'd buzz through the text like an angry wasp trapped beneath a glass.

Yes, I was torturing ███████████. In my defence, I felt no resentment towards the other characters. Because they *would* all move on. That was their point. It was just ███████████ that I hated, the boy so determined to wallow in an ever-constant present – with never a consequence to his actions – never looking to the past except with airy contempt, never contemplating a future where he wouldn't be exactly, sickeningly the same.

Sometimes my bed would seem so empty without Harriet, but at last I could be glad she wasn't there beside me, glad that her body couldn't brush against mine in the night, that there'd be no body warmth, no sound of her sleeping, or sighing, or snoring – glad that I wasn't stuck in a past I missed, a past I'd never realised was going to turn into a *past* because I had complacently believed it was my own ever-constant present, that I'd never be dragged into a future where I was all grown up and alone. I was glad – because it meant that I wouldn't disturb her. I could leave the light on from dusk 'til dawn, and read ███████████.

At work, people complained I spent the day yawning. In my coffee breaks the first thing I would do is pick up ███████████, if I couldn't get any rest, why should he?

I began to realise that ███████████'s lines were changing. Not the words. The words always stayed the same. But the way in which he would say them. New anger. Or new exhaustion. Or sometimes, when he was at his worst, a new special pleading. I'd refuse his pleas, of course. I would read on.

Philip said, "Mr Cooper thinks I'm the best one in the play! That I'm the best ▮▮▮▮▮▮▮▮▮ he has ever seen!" I'd been avoiding Philip for a while. I said, "You don't want to get a big head, though. And what about the other kids at school? Once you stand out from the crowd, they won't like you any more. They'll start to hate you." Philip's eyes shone bright. His stammer was gone. They were ▮▮▮▮▮▮▮'s eyes, it was ▮▮▮▮▮▮▮'s diction. "But everyone *does* like me," he said. "Of course they all like me. I am the Pan-Child."

One night I got careless. I hadn't drunk enough coffee maybe, or perhaps I was just too tired. I suddenly woke up in bed – and the light was on, and the book was open on my lap. I'd fallen asleep reading it. And when I picked it up, I couldn't remember where I had got to – whether I was supposed to be in the Darling house or in Tiger Lollipop's lair, on the mermaid lagoon, or on the pirate ship – I was lost in the NeverPlace – and I scoured the pages, and I realised that it didn't matter which scene I turned to. The adventures and hi-jinks went on, but ▮▮▮▮▮▮▮ wasn't part of them. He was nowhere on the page to be seen. At last he had escaped.

I heard a scratch against the windowpane. And, quick as thought, I switched off the bedside lamp, I plunged the room into darkness.

I sat there, propped up by the pillows. I listened hard.

I knew ▮▮▮▮▮▮▮ hated me as much as I hated him. I knew he would kill me if he could – he'd cut off my hand, he'd poison me, he'd feed me to the crocodiles. And I stayed frozen for several minutes, I think – long enough that I began to think I must have imagined the noise. I could relax – I could ease myself deeper under the bedcovers. (But not turn on the light, not yet, not open the book again, not yet.) And then, there it was, I heard it – what did I hear? It was sharp. A cutlass? ▆▆▆▆▆▆▆'s own fingernails? Scraping against the glass. It couldn't get in. He couldn't get in. But he knew that – the scraping was slow and deliberate, he was teasing me, he was letting me know that he was there. That he was watching me. That he wanted me dead.

It was another half-hour of silence before I dared move. Another long while after that before I got out of bed. Tiptoed my way to the door – never looking round, never looking to the window – for fear I would see ▆▆▆▆▆▆▆? (For fear he wouldn't be there any longer, he had found his way in after all?) And then I was through the door, out of the bedroom, down the stairs, down to safety.

The lights in the kitchen were on. Dad and Philip sat at the table. They were hugging. Mum stood apart, watching. I said, "What's going on? Did he have a bad dream?"

Mum said, "Ssh."

Dad said, "I don't remember my mother. Not really. There's this picture of her in my head, but she's old and sick. That isn't her. That isn't the mother who looked after me and loved me when I was small. She's gone. She's gone. And as the years go by, I know that I have now lived more years without her than the years we got to share. I have spent most of my life as an orphan, and she's really just the smallest part of me, and that makes me sad. But it doesn't matter. We had mothers, you and I, and we lost them, through no fault of our own. And you and I, that's a bond. We're in a special gang."

"Can I join your gang?" asked Mum.

"Of course you can join our gang," said Dad. "Can't she, Philip? She's lost her mother too."

"I want to join your gang," I said. "Let me join your gang. Can I be in your gang?" And they stared at me, and I looked at them, my son, my father, and my mother who wasn't lost and who was still alive and healthy and who was never going to go anywhere.

I went back up to my room. I was pleased to see that ▮▮▮▮▮▮▮▮ was back in his book where he belonged. I checked the window. There were some light scratches on the pane, but I couldn't swear they hadn't been there before.

4

It was only as I approached the pub that I realised I had no idea what Mr Cooper looked like, or how I'd find him. But he certainly seemed to know me – he gave a cheery wave from a small, quiet table away from the bar – and as soon as I saw him, I realised of course I would have known him too, somehow there was no one else he could possibly have been.

"Let me get you a drink," he said. "I'm going to have a beer, what will you have?" I said that a beer sounded fine, and he nodded happily, as if somehow his own choice had been vindicated. There was quite a queue at the bar. It didn't matter. He waved his hand, and he was served instantly.

"There we are," he said, giving me my pint. "Don't worry, it isn't poisoned!"

"I'm sorry?"

"It isn't poisoned. The way Captain Hook poisons Peter's medicine in Act Four. It's a ▮▮▮▮▮▮▮▮ joke."

"Aha," I said, and Mr Cooper beamed. He took a sip from his beer. The foam clung to his wispy beige moustache.

"Before we say anything else," Cooper said, "may I just tell you what an absolutely splendid son you have. He's bright, and funny, and eager – oh, he's so very eager! He's a credit to you, and I'm sure you're very proud."

I said, "I'm sorry about all this, and I know that pulling Philip out of the show at this stage must cause problems, but my mind is made up, and I think it's best." Mr Cooper just sat there smiling. It annoyed me. "You don't seem too bothered."

"Oh, Johnny," he said. "I may call you Johnny, for old times' sake? Johnny, this happens every year. Every year we'll do our ▮▮▮▮▮▮▮▮, and there's a moment when the father gets cold feet. He phones up the school, he writes to the headmaster, he might even write to the local paper! Of course he does. It's an unnerving time, when you see your son begin to Pan. It'd be strange if you *didn't* take fright. I'd think less of you. I really would."

"Thank you," I said.

"But you fathers always come round in the end. And do you know why? Because when a boy is chosen to be ▮▮▮▮▮▮▮▮, it's not only an honour, it's the pivotal moment of his life. Do you know how many of our ▮▮▮▮▮▮▮▮s have gone on to be captains of industry, or to serve in the Cabinet? Do you know at least how many get accepted, sight unseen, to study at Oxford or Cambridge? The father may be scared of losing the child he knows, but at some point he must accept that's the natural order of things – the child must fly the coop, so to speak, quite literally as ████████, flying, ha ha! And the father must put aside his fears, and, if I may say so, however understandable it may be, his complete and arrant selfishness."

He smiled even more widely, and took another sip of his beer. He replenished the layer of foam that was still fizzing and popping upon his upper lip.

"It's not selfishness," I said. "I don't mean to be selfish. But I just think. With all he's been through. With all *we've* been through, with what's happened... we deserve... we have the right to..."

He waited for me to run out of words before he continued. He gave me that much respect.

"I must tell you," he said. "Because it's exciting, and oh, it excites *all* of us, the whole school! It's wrong to have a favourite Pan, I'm sure you know that, with all their different foibles, you learn to love each Pan on his own terms. But between you and me, the rapport he shows with Tinkerbell, the stoicism he displays in the drowning scene, and his courage, and his humour, and his poise, oh, it's the talk of the staff room. It's the talk of the playground itself! He's special. I have seen more Pans than I've had hot dinners, and they all do well, that's the magic of the Pan-Child, isn't it? But I think your son may be the very best. I think he may be..." and he whispered it, "...*definitive*."

I hated that foam on his moustache, it was disgusting, why didn't he wipe it off? I wanted to laugh at him. I wanted to laugh into his stupid foamy face. "Are you saying you do ███████████ every year?"

"Of course, it's a school tradition. Going back the generations, to the time of Barrie and before. We've always had our ████████████."

I wondered why I felt light-headed, was it the beer? "But *Peter Pan* is a bit shit, isn't it?" I said. I dared to say ████████████, I actually dared to say ████████████ out loud! "I mean, I've read it once or twice. Sorry, but it's shit. Sorry, but there it is. And if you're devoting so much of your life to it – well, sorry. And every year, well. I won't say it. But it's sad. You're sad, that's what it is."

I thought at least he'd stop smiling.

"I went to the school when I was a boy," I ploughed on. "And there was no ████████████ in my day, what bollocks."

"Oh, Johnny," he said. "You don't recognise me, do you? I thought you knew, I'm sorry, I honestly did. I recognised you instantly! Really, you've hardly changed."

I stared at him. Tried to see the child behind the tweed jacket. "But you killed yourself," I said. "Didn't you?"

He gave the question genuine consideration. "Oh no," he said. "No, I don't think so. That doesn't sound my kind of thing at all."

"You jumped out of a window. They say you fell, but of course you jumped, we all knew that."

"Let me get you another drink. Shall I get you another drink? I shall get you another drink." And he was up from his chair, he was up to the bar, he was nimble, he was quick. I thought maybe I should go home, I should escape while I had the chance, but my legs felt heavy, I didn't want to move them, and dear God, I was tired, I just felt so *tired*. And then he was back with my new pint. He set it down in front of me. I saw that he hadn't bought himself one.

"How did your wife die?"

"I beg your pardon?"

"I like to understand the history to all my ████████s. The absence of the mother from their narrative is vital, it's absolutely vital. Some years we make do with kids whose parents are divorced, it's a compromise, but what choice do we have? Imagine how delighted we were to find out Philip's mother was genuinely, non-metaphorically, *deceased*. No, imagine it. Really imagine it. Are you imagining it?"

I said that I was imagining it.

"I've asked Philip what happened to his mother, but he won't tell me. Or, not won't. *Can't*. As if he doesn't even know! Do you know, Johnny?"

"It was an accident."

"Oh, I assumed it wasn't deliberate! I always gave you the benefit of that particular doubt."

I didn't say anything else. I refused to say anything else.

Mr Cooper sighed, and for the first time he stopped smiling. He wasn't angry, though; he was sad. "No matter what promises they make to you on stage, the actors who play ████████ do grow up. They grow old, get sick, then die. In a play of so many wonderful truths, that's its most terrible lie. Poor Robin Williams, look what he did to himself, shocking.

Bobby Driscoll, you've heard of him? He's the little boy who voiced ███████████ in the cartoon film. Found dead a few years later, drugged to the nines. And your own son." His face contorted in such a way that it looked quite kindly. "You are aware, I hope, that your son one day is also going to die?"

"Well, of course. Of course I know that."

"Good."

"What are you saying? What the hell are you…?"

"He'll be ██████████, and he'll dazzle the stage, he's such a bright little star. And he'll announce that he'll never grow old. He'll stand there in front of the whole school, in front of everyone, and he'll *promise* you, he'll never grow old, and he'll be a boy forever." And Mr Cooper reached out and touched my hand. I thought I would be sickened, that his skin would be too hot, or too cold, or too in-between even – it was just skin, it was just ordinary skin, that was what was so appalling. "Really," he said, "it shouldn't be allowed."

"It's revenge, isn't it?" I said. "This is some sort of weird revenge."

Mr Cooper's hand, still on mine.

"For what we did. For the way we treated you."

Still on mine.

"I'm sorry," I said. "Forgive me. Forgive me. Forgive me."

And he released me. He raised his arm, and for a moment I thought he was going to strike me, even though his face was as placid and as smug as ever. Instead, he raised it to his mouth. He made to wipe the foam off his moustache. Then he changed his mind. He lowered the arm once more. He opened his mouth. Out came the tongue. He licked it away.

"I feel so bad about what happened at school," said Mr Cooper. "We always find excuses, we say we were just children then, don't we? When really, we're the same people we ever were. But I am sorry. I really am. The way we made your life so hard. We ought to look out for the stragglers, shouldn't we? We ought to take care of them. But we don't. Though, actually, I don't know – is there a sort of honesty to that? Say one thing about children, with all their cruel adventures, they're not hypocrites."

"No," I said. "I was the popular one. I was the one who bullied you."

"Ssh now," said Mr Cooper. "And that day in the playground. Do you remember? You tried to run, but we came at you from all sides, we kicked you to the ground. We held you down. We made you open your mouth. And the things we put inside it! Mud. Leaves. Worms, I think!" He giggled. "Do you remember? Well, of course you do, how could you forget?"

"No," I said.

"And then," he went on. "I'm sorry, but it *is* quite funny! And then I took off my pants. And I got out my cock. And I pissed into your mouth. I mean," he giggled again, "it's outrageous, really! The things boys get up to! I pissed in your mouth, and then some of the others pissed in your mouth, there we all were, just pissing away. Until you gave in. Until you told us that you liked it."

We said nothing for a while.

"Your son is going to make a wonderful ███████████. And you are going to be watching him that night. And you are going to sit in the front row, and applaud him, and feel proud."

"Yes," I said. "Yes, I will."

"Thank you," said Mr Cooper. "No, I mean it. Really, thanks."

You'd imagine that that would have been the end of the evening, and I would have gone home right away. But in fact I went to the bar and bought us one more round, and we changed the subject and chatted about other things quite happily, we didn't so much as mention ███████ again, and it was quite a pleasant evening.

5

It was only a few days later we had the news about Mr Cooper. The headmaster invited us all to a special meeting: the schoolchildren, concerned parents. The headmaster didn't look quite as young or energetic as the last time I had met him. He told us he would try to answer any of our questions. Yes, there had been a horrible accident. Yes, Mr Cooper had fallen to his death from his bedroom window. No, he wouldn't have suffered. In fact, from the expression on Mr Cooper's face he seemed to have quite enjoyed the experience, he had photos if anyone wanted to see? And yes, there had been a note. Mr Cooper had been very particular about leaving a note, it had been retrieved from the clenched hand of Mr Cooper's corpse, and it was addressed to the cast and crew of the forthcoming production of ███████ (tickets already on sale via the school website) – and now the headmaster wanted to read us all that note. He put on his glasses, cleared his throat, smoothed out a piece of paper that had got rather creased in the fall. "The show must go on," he read. "The show must go on. The show must go on. The show must go on. The show must go on." The headmaster folded up the note, and put it back in his pocket. "The show *will* be going on," he said. "Mr Cooper seemed very emphatic about that."

I was worried how Philip would react: another death, and so close to his mother's, and so similar too. He said, "Mr Cooper's job is done. We have no further need of the Pan-Maker." And then he gave a sad lopsided sort of smile, and let the tears flow from his eyes, and I was glad, I didn't want to think my son had become some sort of monster.

As for me, I was doing well. I was sleeping longer, working better, feeling calmer; I had put away the book, and was no longer bothered by any night-time visitations. Things seemed to have improved since I'd had that helpful meeting with Mr Cooper – I felt at the time that it hadn't gone as well as it could have, but somehow he'd managed to put my mind at rest, and that subsequent decision to fling himself to his death had been an added reassurance. I'd almost forgotten that Philip was still rehearsing ▌▌▌▌▌▌ – I didn't see that much of him any more, and we didn't find much to talk about when I did. I was surprised when one day my parents asked me what I was going to wear to the performance that evening. What performance? "It's your son's big night! Don't say you've forgotten!" I said I wasn't sure I was free – I have a busy schedule – I'd have to check my diary. Fortunately, it turned out I had nothing planned for the rest of my life, so

I could fit him in. My mother said I should dress up smart, and my father went through his wardrobe to find me a nice jacket and a tie. I didn't see what the point of that was. We'd be sitting in the audience, we wouldn't be the ones on stage with people wasting time and good money watching *us* – but my parents did insist.

Children of all ages outside the school auditorium, checking tickets, selling programmes and plastic cups of orange squash. All dressed in costume: pirates and Red Indians and orphans and fairies. One Indian squaw sells us our squash – "You're Philip's family, aren't you? Oh, he's so good! Oh, you're going to love him!" A fat boy in fairy clothes shows us to our front row seats. The room is packed full of other children's parents. "But none of them," whispers Mum in my ear, "are parents of the Pan-Child! Aren't you proud?" I wish Mum wouldn't whisper in my ear. It feels so hot and wet, it tickles.

The lights dim. The curtains open. The entertainments begin.

In ▮▮▮▮▮▮▮▮, it takes a little while for the hero to make his entrance. The audience has to be patient. Before we get to the headline act, J. M. Barrie has padded out his play with lots of back-and-forth between Wanda Darling and her tedious family. I watch all the little children fill out the parts. They fail to impress. Most tellingly, Wanda, whose only real narrative function is to act as the audience's viewpoint, is performed by a little girl with an adenoidal voice and not even a smidgen of charm. It is hard to believe her own parents can love her, let alone an elemental figure of chaos like ▮▮▮▮▮▮▮▮. But I think to myself that maybe the casting is deliberate – they're building up to something – the actors are deliberately shit to make my son look good in contrast. I expect that when he finally bounds onto the stage with all of his mercurial energy fizzing he will look all the more impressive.

Enter ███████████. Through a window, in search of his missing shadow. And also, of course – enter Philip, my little boy. He's dressed all in green. Green tunic, green leggings, and a silly little green cap. I wish I could say I take some pride in him – I try to dredge some up, I swear it. But in truth I think he looks like a tosser. I'm genuinely surprised the audience isn't laughing at him. I'm surprised that his fellow cast members aren't laughing too, and jeering, and calling him names – that they aren't now holding him down on the hard stage boards and forcing open his mouth and making him swallow mud and worms and piss.

He mumbles his way through the opening lines. I strain to hear the dialogue.

And I'm not expecting good special effects. But when his shadow is stitched onto him, they just dump a brown rug over his shoulders. Not even a *black* rug; it's brown. And when ███████████ encourages the children to take to the air and fly – I mean, I know they can't pull off *real* flight, I know they're not suddenly going to transcend the laws of physics. But I still hope for a little more effort than seeing a bunch of kids flap their arms by their sides and jump around making whoosh noises.

So, come on – what *am* I expecting? A revelation of some sort? I think so, yes. I think I've earned that. I have been

awaiting the arrival of the Pan-Child for months now.
Some power from my waking nightmares, some magical
force that'll justify all I've been through, that'll change the
shape of the world – or, at least, change the shape of my *son*.
Just change him – that's not too much to ask for, surely?
A transformation, perhaps, yes, that I wouldn't just see
Philip, that awkward stammering kid who still cries for his
mother most nights (because I hear him through the walls,
oh yes, and he's been doing this for *ages* now, for Christ's
sake, how long is this going to drag on for, does he think his
grief is greater than mine, why is that, why does my son *feel*
so much more than me?) I didn't want to see Philip come
through the window, I was sick and tired of Philip, I wanted
to see ███████████. And I *dreaded* his arrival, I know he
hates me, I know he wants me dead, I know he'd rather I'd
been the one and not his mother (but, ha ha, I wanted the
same thing! I would rather he'd died and I'd got to keep his
mother, no hesitation, what do you think about *that*?) – I was
terrified that ████████████ would suddenly appear on the
school stage right before me, that spirit of evil mischief that
has plagued me for so long. But there would have been a *relief*
to it too, wouldn't there? To have seen the Pan-Child at last,
even full of murderous rage. My enemy before me, even if I
were at his mercy, even if he were the last thing I would ever
see. To see my son become someone more powerful than his
poor lonely shitty father could ever dream to be.

I tell you what I'd expected. I thought that I would lose
my son to ████████████. That he'd put on his stupid fucking
green tunic and his stupid fucking green cap and that he'd

become unrecognisable. And I would never get him back, not truly. That we'd go home tonight and we'd take off his costume but there would always be some part of him that was ███████████ still, that he would forever be mysterious and magical and unknowable. That I would have lost the mother, and now I could lose the son. And it hadn't happened – it *hasn't* happened – it's just my son pratting about on stage, no better than the dreadful Wanda or the dreadful Tink Fairy or the dreadful Captain One-Hand.

At the end of the first half ███████████ finds himself in dire straits. He is trapped on a rock in the middle of a lagoon, and the sea is rising, and he will surely drown. Before the act ends the script says he will fashion a boat from a bird's nest, and escape triumphantly into the interval. But first he must stand all alone, suddenly aware of his mortality and the real possibility of death, and address the audience.

Philip looks out at us. "To die," he says, "will be."

And then he stops.

…*An awfully big adventure*, I want to call out. That is the line. That is the famous line. It is the best line in the play.

"To die," he says again. "To die."

He flaps his arms at his side, as if he's trying to fly again. I don't think he even knows he is doing it. Is he stammering? I don't think he is stammering. There's no anxiety to it, the frustration he feels when he can't get his mouth to form the right shape, the anger, the way his eyes will goggle with embarrassment. He just stares at us all. He stares at *me*.

And this is how the story could have gone. I could get up from my seat now. Climb onto the stage, break the fourth wall – I could rescue him from this. Not just the rising tide, but the shame and the confusion. I could wrap him in my arms in front of the world and tell him I love him and that I'm here for him and that I can do better, and things will be hard for a while, but they will, one day, be better. You don't need ████████ any more. You have me. I could tell him that, and you can pretend that's what I did, let's pretend that. It makes for a better ending.

He stares at me. It's the most powerful I have ever seen him. I'd say that at last he has found his ████████, but it isn't true. It isn't that. At last ████████ has deserted him. This is my son, as strong as he can ever be.

"To die," he says, one final time. Then he sits down upon the rock. And the curtain falls.

During the interval I expect to hear other parents talk about how dreadful my son is, and how awkward the ending to Act One had been, and how they'd be demanding their money back. Instead they seem happy chatting about the limited talents of their own children. "I'll get you an orange squash," I say to my parents, "see you back in the theatre." The queue is long and slow, and by the time I have my drinks people are resuming their seats and the lights are dimming. I make to pass the orange squash to my mum and dad but they aren't there.

Act Two opens with Wanda playing mother to the Missing Boys. At some point ████████ will make his entrance and all the children call him Father. I have always hated this scene, the way even ▇▇▇▇▇▇ manages to be a better dad than I am, even though he doesn't want the job, and can't understand the responsibility involved. I know the exact moment Pan is supposed to appear – I have read this, of course, so many times. I wait for him. I wait.

The scene continues without him.

I know something must have gone wrong. But there is no hint of panic on the stage, no one is vamping to cover a scared little boy who has missed his entrance. No one in the audience seems concerned either – and some of them must know the play, some of them must have been testing their kids on lines too, surely? Everyone, fictional and real, seems happy with the story that unfolds.

Wanda and the Missing Boys defeat Captain One-Hand all by themselves. The Tink Fairy never drinks the poison to save the Pan-Child's life, because he has no life to be saved. The NeverPlace muddles along quite cheerfully without him. No single mention of him is made again.

And I want to get out of my seat, but I can't quite manage it. And I want to call out for Philip, but I don't want to make a fuss. I look for my parents either side of me, but the seats are now occupied by strangers who will never call me son. I have three orange squashes to drink; they are syrupy, has someone forgotten to dilute the cordial? I can feel it thick on my upper lip as it starts to foam.

The play ends at last. Not with ▇▇▇▇▇▇, and his avowal to stay a child forever, but with Wanda back in her mother's care, and with all the Missing Boys adopted. And it's such a lie – and where's my mother? Where's my dad? Why have they abandoned me? (Are they in the NeverPlace?) And what's the bloody point of having parents at all if they're just going to disappear? The curtains fall, then rise again to show the entire cast in two long lines, waiting to bow to our applause.

And I know Philip won't be there. That he's been erased, as surely as ████████████ has been from his own narrative. But I'm wrong – he is there, I can see him – and the relief of it makes me cry. I still have my son, my parents are gone and my wife is gone but my son is there before me. He's in the second row, behind some nondescript fairy. He's still wearing his green tunic and he still looks like a prick.

I want to rush up and hug him, but let's face it, the moment has passed.

I try the hug when he comes offstage. "Don't, Dad, not in front of everyone." I can see how I embarrass him. I look around one last time for my parents. He sees me searching. "It's just you and me, Dad," he says. "Let's go home."

It's been a long day. And when we get indoors, I am so tired.

"Come on, Dad," says Philip. "You know the drill. I'll help you up to bed." He takes my arm, and I lean into him gratefully.

As we go up the stairs, I tell him, "You were really good tonight."

"Thanks."

"No, I mean it. I was really proud of you. Your mum would have been proud too."

"It's okay."

"And your grandparents. They would have been so proud too."

"Dad, it's okay, it's okay."

We are in the bedroom. He sits me down on the mattress. "I'll give you a hand with your trousers," he says.

"There's no need! I can manage!"

"I know you can. But, look! And there we go."

"Thank you. You were so good tonight."

"And I'll hang them up here, do you see? Now, is there anything else you need?"

"What will you do now?" I ask Philip. "Now that ██████████'s over. Poor Philip, with ██████████ gone. No more ██████████ any more!" And I'm crying again, I can't help it, I don't know why.

Philip says, "I'll just get on with something else, won't I? There's plenty else out there."

"Yes," I say. "Yes. I suppose so."

"There's plenty else. So there's no need to be upset, is there? It's just silly, isn't it? Let's just cut that out." And I look at my son, and there's no ██████████ in him, but I think I might catch a bit of Harriet. Yes, there she is, there's my baby.

"Straight to sleep now, Dad," he says. "Anything else you need before I go? A glass of water? How about I open a window?"

"No," I say. "I'm fine. I'm fine. I'm fine."

"I'll open the window," he says. "Get you some fresh air." He kisses me gently on the forehead, and I press my head up against his lips, hard, I don't want him to go. He turns out the light. "See you tomorrow. Pleasant dreams."

"I'm fine," I say. But he has already left, he's shut the door behind him and now the room is dark and full of mystery. And the only light is the moon, streaming in through the open window, and I can hear something scratching against the pane, like a tree branch, or a bird.

And On 'til Morning

LAURA MAURO

A little soul woke in a strange field that was not home.

Summer-pale grass, frayed by the heat; the unending blue of a sky which seemed as though it had never known clouds (though of course this was impossible; there must have been clouds somewhere in the world, and there is, after all, only one sky). It might have been home, except for the fact that it smelled nothing like a home ought to. It smelled of nothing at all. No sweet hay-scent, hard-baked earth, dusty underfoot; no wild flowers blooming in distant meadows. And the little soul realised then just how silent it was, too; birdsong and soft wind and the merry percussion of crickets, all gone, now, in the throat of some great and empty thing, some silent beast, whose mouth was the colour of July.

And the little soul said, where am I?

But of course nobody answered, for there was nobody to answer, and so the little soul shook itself, got to its feet, and off it went. And as it walked, it seemed that there were things stranger still about this place, which was not home. The field itself seemed to go on for eternity; no matter how far the little soul walked, there was only more grass, sungold and dry and swaying gently in a breeze the little soul could not feel. And though the little soul's skin was lit bright by sunlight, it felt no warmth; nor did it need to shield its eyes from the light, though it was noon, had been noon the whole time the little soul was walking, the distance of which, it realised, it could not quantify.

The little soul was perturbed. It turned to face the direction it had come from, and saw nothing there but the same empty fields, the same violently blue skies. And the little soul thought, it's no good retracing my steps when I cannot remember where I was before, so it resolved to continue onwards.

Had there been a before? Surely there must have been, if the little soul was possessed of notions of home, and the certainty that this was not there. And what, in any case, was a home? Somewhere where the air smelled like dry grass and sunflowers, the little soul supposed. Somewhere where voices called one's name. Somewhere where one had a name. It seemed a shoddy definition, but the little soul did not have much else to work with.

It would be nice, the little soul thought, wistfully, to have a name.

On the little soul walked. Such hot earth ought to have burnt its bare soles, but it felt no discomfort. It wondered at the clothes it had woken in. Pastel nightgown, wash-faded and worn. Somewhere in the recesses of its memory – or perhaps imagination – the little soul thought that it was passing strange to be outside in bedclothes, without so much as a pair of socks. But these were lesser mysteries, and so it kept walking, and in minutes or hours or days the distant sky began to grow dark, and curdled with blue-grey clouds, and the grass grew wild and tall until it became trees, gnarled and old and so very many. A forest, the little soul realised; there was a forest on the edge of these fields.

The little soul did not want to continue on towards the forest, but what more could it do? It could scarcely stay in the fields all its life, even if the sun there was kind, and the sky as blue as an eye. The little soul was not afraid – or at least, it did not know it was afraid, for it did not know the name of fear, and so it thought that to shiver so was only the proper response to the majesty of such a sight. The light would find it there, it thought, as it started toward the long grass; the light would always find it, for it always had.

There was a girl, once, and she was loved.

There was a girl once, and she dreamed she was loved.

There was a girl, and she built a world where love should be, upon the absence of love; it was a small world, barely enough to fit inside, but somehow she did, and whenever the night seemed too long, whenever her lonely bones shivered inside of her, and the song of her hunger kept her from sleep, she would wrap that world around herself, and the hurting seemed so small, the hurting seemed so far away.

The forest was very dark, and very quiet. The sun's warmth filtered through the trees, becoming scant as it reached the ground far below. The damp, loamy scent of undisturbed soil, of leaf-rot and mulch. These, the little soul knew, were life-smells, and they brought it comfort as it walked deeper into the silent trees. Its footsteps were so light that when it looked down, it realised it hadn't made so much as an imprint in the soil. It seemed strange to the little soul; it knew it existed, but it seemed as though the world did not. As though the sun and earth and breeze were unaware of its presence.

A deep green shadow descended with each half-mile, like low-hanging fog. Soon, the little soul struggled to see the path ahead. The trees above were bowed, embracing one another with thick, heavy foliage; it might have been day, or night, but the little soul could no longer see the sky, and there was no birdsong, no chitter of animals, no sign at all that anything but the little soul existed here. The little soul wrapped its arms around itself – seeking comfort in its own solidity, its own realness – and it called out: Hello? Can anyone hear me?

The words echoed between the trees and into the unseen distance, as words are wont to do. The little soul held still for a long moment. Perhaps there were other little souls in the forest, all lost and wandering; perhaps their voices were too quiet, the forest too vast. Oh, thought the little soul, sitting despondent on a gnarled knot of mossy tree root, knees drawn tight to its chest, I've made such a terrible mistake. It ought to have stayed in the light. It ought to have lain down beneath the golden sun, and closed its eyes, and slept there, like it had when—

The little soul paused. A sound, thin and trembling, like the wet wings of a butterfly. It turned its head, chasing the source. Somewhere, something was crowing. Slowly, the little soul uncurled. It wasn't a lost kind of sound. It was a joyful sound, a summer sound, like the lakeshore, crystalline at the height of noon. The little soul wasn't certain it had a heart, but something inside of it leapt with relief. It straightened its shoulders; turned east, and ran laughing towards the sound.

A hunger that persists beyond one's natural limit ceases to be hunger. It becomes background noise, a low hum in the soundscape, and pain creeps in, gradual as disease, until you forget what it's like to ever have been hungry. You send it away from you. Buoyed off on pieces of yourself, trussed up and drifting towards an inexorable horizon beyond which only the night lives, unending, like the edge of the world. And all that remains then is the core of you, as small and lovely as a marble in the shell of a palm.

The little soul let laughter carry it. Dancing through the forest, light of foot, and it did not matter that it could hardly see what lay before it, for only beautiful things made summer sounds. It flew, and such was its joy that it did not notice the way the breeze failed to comb fingers through its hair, or how its laughter did not bounce from tree to tree. On towards that bright and lovely sound, the night closing in around it like the fingers of an enormous hand closing one by one by one.

Hello, the little soul cried out. Hello, hello, can you hear me? Oh, won't you come to me? You must be so alone out here, in the shadows. You must be so cold and afraid.

And a voice replied: I am no such thing.

The little soul stood very still. A smile was etched on its face, pinning the corners of its mouth to its ears; it turned circles in the dark, listening to the soft sound of movement in the trees above. It must be a bird, the little soul thought. A clever bird, which knew how to talk. It remembered seeing something like that in a book, once, though it wasn't sure what a book was. There were birds that talked, and their feathers were the colour of sunset, of cornflowers, of the moon on the water.

Well, said the little soul. If you are not afraid, why don't you come down from there?

Aren't *you* afraid? the voice replied, a little tersely.

The little voice was troubled by this. What should I be afraid of? it asked, staring up into the high branches, where the shadows were depthless. It could not tell where the sky ended, nor where the trees began.

There came laughter, dry, like wind in the leaves. Of this, the voice elucidated. The dark. The end. The world beyond the hill. Doesn't it scare you?

The end…? said the little soul, frowning deeply now. The end of what?

Why, life of course, the voice said, and high up in the trees a pair of eyes flashed into being, as cold and strange as stars.

There was a boy once, who wanted so very much to stay a boy forever.

There was a boy once, who was half a bird, and half a heart; who spoke the fae-tongue and sang their mischief, and they loved him for it.

There was a boy, who was once a girl, and he stood at the apex of the world, where the waking stretched out in one direction, and the sleeping in the other; the living and the dying, the light and the dark. He built himself a home in the middle, in the dreaming, the life-in-death, and he sang songs to the faraway stars so for the first time in centuries they might no longer feel alone.

The little soul felt confusion heavy on its shoulders, like a caul it could not shed. There was no hill, it said, gazing up at the eyes high above. There was just a field. I walked and walked until the forest appeared, and then I walked some more.

Oh my, the voice said, hushed now. You've forgotten, haven't you…?

The little soul became quite cross. Listen now, it said. You talk in riddles, and I won't have it! Why, you're not even bold enough to speak to me face to face. Hiding all cowardly up in that tree! Well, I shan't pay you any mind. I must find my way out of this forest. And off the little soul stomped, all puffed-up and huffing, and it thought itself very brave indeed for having spoken its mind.

The eyes followed alongside, dancing merrily through the trees. Well! the voice replied. I only came to help you, but since you've been so rude, I don't see why I should.

I don't want your help, the little soul said, lifting its chin high. Go on. Away with you.

Well! the voice said again. Its eyes spun around in one quick motion; the little soul imagined they must be floating upside-down. What a funny child you are. I rather like you.

The little soul snorted. I don't care, it said, and saw fit to stomp even faster, but something stopped it in its tracks. Wait, it said. Staring up into the trees for a long, breathless moment, and the eyes stared back, unblinking, the chill glimmer of diamond. You called me a child.

Yes, the voice replied. Because that's what you are.

But I'm a little soul. Aren't I? The little soul glanced down at itself, and registered, for the first time, the thin shape of its legs, its scraped-up knees peering out from beneath the nightdress, which it remembered waking in back in the field. Turning its hands slowly, palm-first, then around; quick-bitten fingernails, scuffed knuckles, a dusting of freckles like constellations. Was this what a child looked like, it wondered? Such an awkward, knobbly little thing it was, so skinny and oddly formed.

Tell me, the voice said, with something a little like kindness. Do you truly not remember coming up the hill?

No, the little soul replied, and frustration welled inside of it, like blood from a wound. I told you. I woke up in the field. I thought it was home. But I don't remember what home is, and I certainly don't remember a hill, and now here you are, teasing me so. Don't you think that's cruel?

The eyes flickered shut. The little soul thought, for a terrible moment, that it had finally chased the voice away; that it had offended them awfully, and now it would be all alone here, in this dark forest, at the end of life. But there came the rustle of branches, and a flash of silver, and something tumbled from the trees with the grace of water.

Home? said the voice, which belonged now to a shimmering white bird; a boy's face, nestled proud among the feathers, and those eyes, starbright and beautiful. Oh, little one. Where you're going is so much better.

Home is a name spoken fondly, by familiar voices, who love you.

Home is the thing with walls, with windows, through which the light shines, illuminating love; the warmth in the pit of one's stomach, the pleasant shiver of recognition upon waking from a long sleep. It is the people who keep you safe.

Home is the island at the end of the forest where the lost ones live.

It is the only home they have ever known.

You see, said the bird-boy. Sometimes, children get lost on their way to the end. Well, it's not so surprising. The forest is very deep, and without love to light the way one tree looks rather like another.

What a strange bird you are, the little soul said. You say such odd things.

I'm not a bird, the bird-boy said, preening his silvery feathers, which the little soul thought seemed a rather bird-like activity. But that's not important. You are lost, and I'm here to guide you. Isn't that a wonderful thing?

The little soul considered this. Yes, it said, I suppose it is. But you still haven't explained where I'm supposed to be going. You said it's better than home. The little soul gazed at its own feet, dirt-scuffed and ragged. I think I should rather like to have a home, it said, on a sigh.

I'm bored of talking, the bird-boy said, with sudden impatience. Here. Climb on my back. You're only a little soul, so you'll weigh nothing at all. Come on, come on, hurry up. You're not the only lost one I need to guide tonight.

The bird-boy's feathers were pillow soft, and warm as a sunbeam. The little soul clambered carefully up until it sat astride the bird-boy's shoulders, and although it seemed a precarious balance, it knew with certainty that it could not fall. The bird-boy would not allow it. I'm ready, it said, and when the bird-boy crowed, announcing its departure, the little soul felt the sound reverberating, joyful, like a plucked string deep in its heart.

Up they flew. The trees parted, bowing their great green heads respectfully, and deep blue night poured into the forest, spilling into the shadows. The little soul imagined a breeze in its hair as they rose above the canopy, skimming the topmost branches for sport. The forest seemed to go on forever; it could no longer see the summer fields in the far distance, nor the end the bird-boy had spoken of, and the little soul wondered how long it would have kept walking in circles down there, in the dark. Perhaps forever.

Isn't this much better? the bird-boy whooped. Everyone should learn how to fly, it's terribly convenient, and so very fun.

Could I learn? the little soul asked. It *was* fun, after all; the laughter that had hidden away inside of it bloomed once more, and as the music of joy spilled from the little soul's lips, the sky grew lighter and lighter, as though dawn were fast on its way. And it seemed to the little soul that its heart was the sun, that it always had been.

Oh, no, said the bird-boy. Lost little souls like you had your wings clipped a long time ago. But that's all right. I'll only ever be a whistle away, should you want to fly. It's my favourite thing, you see. Well, apart from dancing, and singing, and fighting pirates.

Fighting *what*? But the bird-boy veered sharply upwards then, and the little soul shrieked, but in happiness, for it still did not know the name of fear, had left it behind in the before-place, which it supposed had been home, for a time. They burst through the clouds in a puff of vapour, spinning higher and higher, candy-pink clouds and beating wings and burning-heart sun, all the way up here, where there was no such thing as hurting. And when the bird-boy crowed, the little soul understood that this too was laughter.

Will there be dancing, where we're going? the little soul asked.

Oh yes, said the bird-boy. Dancing and feasting and singing, and all the other lost ones will be so happy to see you. It's a special place, you see. Most people end up in the Silence After. The ones who've lived full and well, who've been loved all their lives. All they want to do at the end is sleep. But you, little one. You get to *live*. For you, the end is an adventure. Isn't that just wonderful?

The little soul lay its cheek against the bird-boy's soft feathers. Felt the hum of his pulse, and pretended it was its own. Yes, it said, softly. I suppose it is.

The Other Side of Never

EDWARD COX

They say the monster was once a beautiful boy, forever young and innocent, but then it fell in love with a girl who grew up...

The air reeks of hot metal, shimmering with heat. Rusty ash snows from an ulcerated sky. Smoke ghosts up from an island of black rock that rises from molten seas to form a mighty hill. Atop the hill a palace serves as a crown of mist and shadow. With the orange light of a furnace glowing dully through its darkness, the palace is a fitting sanctum in which the monster slumbers, festers in its hatred, and dreams of destruction. But the monster isn't all they say it is.

"Now," a voice begs. "Do it *now!*"

Funny; I'd almost forgotten Darlene was with me. I pay her no mind, eyes fixed on the monster's palace. Surrounding it is a forest of crucifixes. So many of them, hundreds, ornamenting the hill right down to the base. To each cross, a winged fairy is nailed. Fabled creatures, long lost and forgotten, once magical and bright. Seeing them now as statues cocooned in shells of hardened ash, it's difficult to believe they were once called Guardians of Imagination. This grisly display represents a final battle, the fairies' last stand against the monster.

"*Please*," Darlene whispers. "Open it."

She's talking about a small wooden case in my hands. It's cylindrical and slim, about the size of a fat cigar. Unscrewing one end, I tap out a thin roll of yellowed parchment, brittle with age. Unrolling it and seeing what's on it brings a smile to my lips. Mr Jungen had said that I'd know what to do when the time was right. He and Darlene and Dr Verloren – they said I didn't know who I was. But I do now.

Darlene says, "Please, it's time."

On her knees just behind me, her Stetson has collected a layer of ash-snow, and her shirt is wet from a bullet wound. Despair covers her face. Perhaps Darlene considers herself a revolutionary. Perhaps we both do. If she wasn't already dying, I'd kill her myself. Strange; there are blank spots in my memory and I can't remember exactly when the tables turned, how much time has passed – hours? Days? – but she is no longer the one in control as she had been since the moment she stole my life.

I first met Darlene on a coach. I didn't notice she was on board until it was too late.

It was shortly after the draft and I was packed in with around thirty other convicts, travelling the desert road beneath a brilliant sun. All across Never, coaches and trains and airbuses full of criminals were heading to the centre of the island like a war-fleet. This happened every generation; the monster would wake again, the Rift would open at the Lagoon, and the Haken Ministry would empty out its prisons. Thousands of convicts repaying their debt to society by forming a vanguard, the first wave of fighters sent to stop the monster leaving its lair in Always to cross the Rift into Never. Most of us were too happy to be out in the sunshine again to consider that we were Haken's cannon fodder.

It felt like freedom. No shackles, only one guard sitting up front next to the driver behind a cage wall. Someone cranked up music and a few bottles of firewater were passed around – quality stuff, much better than prison hooch. I must have drunk too much and passed out, because when I woke up the coach had stopped, and my forehead was pressed against the cold window. The desert plains were silver beneath moonlight. In the distance, the multicoloured aura of the City hung in the sky. Weird; the City was a long way from the Lagoon.

My fellow convicts were sleeping in their seats, heads bowed, dead to the world. The single guard was in the same state. My throat felt swollen, a numbness in my tongue. It was then I noticed the driver making her way down the coach. She didn't bother checking on any of her other passengers and headed straight for me. Her gait was fluid, sure and predatory.

"Hi," she said. "They call me Darlene."

It's a mystery how I didn't notice her when I first boarded. Such a distinctive look: a black Stetson and matching shirt, denims tucked into well-worn cowboy boots, and sunglasses reflecting moonbeams, as bright in the night as the teeth she revealed with a grin.

"If I told you that we could heal Never, just the two of us, would you believe me?"

Maybe she had mixed something in with the firewater. My voice, my thoughts, they just wouldn't work, and it didn't seem important to question what the hell this stranger thought she was doing; it seemed somehow impolite to stop her unzipping my prison jumpsuit to expose my chest and stomach. Darlene peered close and took a keen interest in my birthmark: a pinky-brown oddity that would have resembled a hook if my belly button didn't turn it into a question mark.

"You're not a nice man," she said with another grin. "Dangerous, and you can't be trusted. But I've got something that should curb your enthusiasm."

She dipped a hand into a satchel hanging from her shoulder and pulled out what looked to be a wooden cigar case. She unscrewed one end and slid free a small roll of parchment.

"This is old, written in crocodile blood, and we'd both better pray that it works." Darlene opened the parchment, took a breath, and then read aloud. *"While time chases us all, the stars look on forever..."*

These words... I knew them, like they rattled a cell door in a distant dungeon of an old dream, and their effect was immediate. My will drained away, the night grew darker, and from that moment on it never occurred to me to question anything Darlene said.

I don't recall how we got to the City. Or what became of a coach full of convicts. The next thing, my hair and beard had been shaved to bristle, my prison jumpsuit swapped for civilian clothes, and Darlene was pulling me by the hand through dirty streets and crowds of people.

A menagerie of lights and music and growling traffic assaulted us. You could smell the vice, the money, the temptation, the corruption – the stench of one giant empty promise where it was easy to fade into background noise. A voice called out from a darkened doorway, offering some seedy show that involved a genuine live fairy, captured near the Lagoon. Darlene growled like the traffic and dragged me away as if fearing I was gullible enough to be tempted by such an obvious lie. Besides, my predilections sailed in a different direction. The City had once feared my presence. Until they caught me.

Pushing through the crowd, Darlene said, "This place used to be a forest," like I didn't already know. "Can you imagine that?" She sounded like her brain had an itch she couldn't scratch. "All those trees, all that wildlife, and the first thing we did was build the City on them."

The first thing we did. She was talking about the Haken Ministry's doctrine, an event they called the Exile, when we had to flee Always and make Never our home... generations ago.

Darlene stopped at a street vendor and bought a small bottle of firewater.

"People forget that *we* allowed this to happen," she said, scowling at her environment. "Never is founded on imagination. Infinite possibilities. But all we could imagine was the world we'd lost, so we rebuilt it here without ever considering what else we might achieve. Because that's what Haken wanted us to do." She took a long pull from the bottle. "The Ministry couldn't have dug a deeper grave for imagination if they'd tried, and *we* let them do it. That's how *we* repaid the fairies' sacrifice."

The fairies. Once friends to the monster, but when it got busy ripping our world apart, they evacuated as many of us as they could to Never before giving their lives to trap the monster in Always and keep us safe. Not that the monster ever stopped trying to get to us, whenever it woke, whenever it hungered for destruction.

Another pull of firewater and Darlene coughed. "Imagination didn't die with the fairies, you know. It's still there, down deep in Never's foundations, where nobody bothers to look anymore." She finished the bottle and took my hand again. "A few of us know where to find it, but not enough. If the fairies were here, they'd *release* it, back into the wild, where it belongs. Haken wouldn't like that at all."

It should have dawned on me then exactly who Darlene was. An *imagus*. Fables, myths, campfire stories – the imagi were as legendary as the fairies themselves. It was said they could tap into the ancient rites of Never, the ways of an age long gone, and create whatever they willed from their imaginations. It should have dawned on me then, but it didn't until later.

Another blank spot and I was in darkness. Darlene was speaking. Spewing Haken doctrine again. It sounded like she was telling herself a comforting bedtime story, an official story that I'd heard more times than I could count.

It went: When the monster was a young and beautiful boy, he met a girl from Always and spirited her away to Never, where they imagined adventures of the wildest kind. They were happy together, a friendship beyond compare, their days filled with laughter and danger, every dream coming true, and they fell in love. For a while. Because the girl's feelings didn't stand the test of time.

The boy knew something was wrong when the girl refused to stay young like he did. She grew older and older, until the day came when she confessed a desire to return home to Always. The boy, confused and dismayed, didn't understand. He begged and pleaded for her to stay in Never; after all, she loved him as much as he loved her, didn't she? But the girl was resolute. It was time to be a grown-up, she said. And she left.

Heartbroken and alone, the boy wept for days or weeks or months or years – it was hard to be sure, for he had no concept of time, as time had little meaning in Never. His love for the girl did not wane; it flourished and burned bright until he could stand her absence no longer. The boy returned to Always to win her back, so they might relive their heady days of wild dreams and laughter. And love.

But when the boy found the girl, he discovered that time had run out for her. She was an old and brittle woman, lying in her deathbed. She had lived a long life, had loved and married another. She had birthed children who had birthed children... Worst of all, on the day she died, the girl could not remember the boy – not him or Never or their adventures together. And so the boy's love rotted to monstrous hate.

"...and that hate was directed at grown-ups," Darlene said. "The savages who ruined everything in their path, most especially love and imagination. The monster lost control of its own imagination and... well, I'm sure you of all people can empathise with what it did next."

It occurred to me then that she was talking to me, so I opened my eyes.

Dirty streets had been swapped for a shabby hotel room. The bruised glow of neon lights shone in through a window. Threadbare carpet and water stains splotching the ceiling. I was standing at the foot of a bed, naked from the waist up. Darlene sat on the floor beneath the window, an open laptop balanced on her knees, sunglasses alive with the light from the screen.

She said, "Here's the truth. If I hadn't kidnapped you, Haken would have put a bullet in your head the moment you arrived at the Lagoon, and this whole cycle with the monster would have continued, generation after generation."

Even then, whatever spell I was under prevented me asking what I was to her. Why me? But I did have the presence of mind to note her uncertainty when she raised the idea of the

Haken Ministry having me executed. It was an uncertainty I shared.

"We're going to break the cycle – Haken's and the monster's," Darlene said. "You see, I frighten the Ministry because... because I know what they don't want anyone to know, and it might change Never beyond their control..."

She trailed off as her laptop gave a hiss and her sunglasses reflected a change of image, the face of a man.

"Mr Jungen," she said with a respectful nod. "The extraction was successful."

A pause. Then: "I need to see it." The words were spoken with authority but came dry and wheezing like dusty breath from lungs close to giving out. "Show me."

Darlene got up and turned the laptop around. I saw my image on screen, grainy, half-naked, face docile. A box in the corner of the screen showed an old, old man lying in bed with a tube in his nose. Hairless and pale, his skin was as thin as paper, lined with blue veins. I knew death when I saw it, and death was visiting this man.

Darlene focused the camera on my birthmark, giving Mr Jungen a close-up of my navel turning a hook into a question mark.

Mr Jungen made a contemplative sound, but said no more and the silence stretched on. He closed his eyes and looked to have fallen asleep. Or died.

"Mr Jungen?" Darlene said.

He came alert and fell into a short coughing fit that clearly pained him. "We're close to the end, Darlene," he wheezed. "But now more than ever we have to be alert to Haken's traps."

"There're no traps." Darlene kept focus on my birthmark. "He's from the right family. His bloodline checks out."

"Of course he's the right person. That's not what I meant."

"I doubt Haken even realises he's missing yet."

A dry, angry sound came from the laptop. "I've known people who underestimated the Haken Ministry before. None of them are alive now. Do you know why this man was imprisoned?"

"Yes." Darlene looked at me and I could see the unspoken word in her eyes: murderer, a killer, many times over – and I make no excuses. "The rite you gave me is keeping his urges in check."

"Listen to me, Darlene," Mr Jungen said. "All these years Haken held this man in a cell, and you believe no one ever noticed his birthmark without understanding its significance? That no one is monitoring his movements to get to *us*?"

Again, uncertainty crossed Darlene's face. I'd often wondered why the Ministry locked me up when my crimes against the City should have carried the penalty of death.

Mr Jungen said, "You must keep moving, Darlene. No stopping now until the end."

A shadow fell across the window. A muffled hum, low and heavy like a bumblebee. Darlene placed the laptop on the bed, and while Mr Jungen scowled at me from the screen, she opened the window and let in the unfiltered chaos of the City – that familiar and comforting wash of dangerous, squalid life that I'd missed for the last ten years but remembered while dreaming in a cell. Just outside the window, a drone hovered on four rotary blades. A package hung from its undercarriage. Darlene unclipped it and the drone flew away.

She held a wooden case, small and cylindrical like the one on the coach. "Another rite?"

"But not for you," Mr Jungen warned. "He'll know what to do with it when the time comes. Understand?"

"Got it."

"Under no circumstances is that case to be opened while it is in Never. Take him and it to Dr Verloren. It's time she unlocked the back door out of Never."

"We'll get going."

"Good. And Darlene..."

On screen, Mr Jungen, already slumped and decrepit in his bed, somehow sank further into his pillows. From outside there came a spitting sound followed by a chiming impact and the crash of something shattering on the ground.

"The Ministry has found us." Mr Jungen's dry, ancient voice was full of resignation. "They've taken out my drone." He chuckled bitterly as Darlene rushed to the window. "They're inside my house, Darlene. They're bringing a bigger adventure for me—"

The old man's dry voice choked off and there was a flurry of blurred movement on the laptop, juddering, broken moments before the screen froze on the image of a silvered face, someone wearing a mirror-mask.

Darlene snatched the laptop off the bed, took one look at it, and hissed, "Pirates!"

She closed the laptop and stuffed it into her satchel. That was the moment I finally realised she was an imagus.

With her hand still in the satchel, Darlene closed her eyes, whispering something too fast to catch. When she removed her hand, the laptop had changed to a silver pistol – a long, gleaming six-shooter like those from old tales of the Wild West. Darlene looped the satchel over her shoulder, cocked the pistol, and said, "Keep close."

Which, of course, I had no choice but to do. I was almost amused by her panic. Pirates – City slang for Haken's secret police. Merciless bastards allowed to act with impunity. They were always in the background, watching, listening, waiting, and I knew them intimately. Ten years ago, the Pirates had hunted me down and put a stop to my work.

The escape from the hotel only comes to me in snippets, but I do know that it was around about here that Darlene got shot. I remember the hallway outside our room, the sound of Pirates thundering up the hotel stairs to our floor, and Darlene kicking open the door to the room opposite. A drug deal or some such was taking place there. One of the dealers jumped to his feet and aimed a gun at us. Darlene's pistol took off the back of his head, and then we were climbing through a bathroom window onto a fire escape. Shots rang out behind us, but I don't think they were aimed at us. The Pirates must have got into a gunfight with the dealers, and maybe that held them up enough to allow us escape time.

Down on the alley floor, there were more Pirates waiting. Darlene's pistol blazed and roared as she backed us out of the alley, and it seemed that she couldn't run out of bullets. Or miss. The power of an imagus' imagination, I suppose. Mirror-masks shattered with sprays of bloodied shards as we made it onto a busy main street where the gunfight panicked the citizens, frightened them into stampeding and covering our tracks.

Darlene must've taken the bullet in that alley, because the next thing, she was leaning on me, bleeding heavily, and we were in a rusty elevator, heading down and down, far beneath a city of stone that had once been a forest, to the underground house of Dr Verloren…

Pirates wore mirror-masks not only to preserve their anonymity but also to reflect the face of the one they hunted. In those reflections, criminals saw their sins and their own fear at having become prey.

Years ago, I considered myself less a revolutionary and more a man with a calling. I'd spent years in the City searching for the right kind of weeds with roots that needed poisoning. Oh, I never believed I could change the world, but I did serve a greater good.

Suppliers were my targets, those whose deaths had a knock-on effect for dealers and buyers, creating brief bursts of light between… whatever darkness Haken would allow to rise next in the City. I never hid the bodies. Quite the opposite, in fact. Mangled and displayed, they were easily found. Haken tried to write it off as gang wars, but they and the criminals knew what kind of animal was on their streets. And those brief bursts of light I created – they made everything seem better, just for a while. That was my mission, my calling. That was my work.

I'd been tracking this woman. For the life of me, I can't recall her name. She organised a Red Room in a secluded warehouse buried deep in the City – a real torture, blood, death, whatever-the-viewer-was-paying-for kind of affair. My plan was to take out the organiser's hoods then give her a starring role in a Red Room special all of her own. But at the warehouse, twenty or more Pirates were waiting for me, their masks reflecting my sins. It was flattering, really. My arrest was the end result of a huge sting, and I was thrown in an isolated cell for ten years. But I never suspected that my capture might have been the first move in a long game that Haken was playing…

Down and down in a rusty elevator. Down and down to a cave-like tunnel, haunted by echoes and the chill dampness. Cameras tracked our progress, watching with intensity from the walls. Darlene leaned on me, shuffling and grunting in pain, bleeding profusely from a bullet wound in her shoulder. The tunnel ended at a circular door, big and metal, all locks and combinations like the vault of a major casino. With a supreme amount of effort, Darlene whispered words of imagination. And then, after another blank spot, I was on the other side, in a house beneath the City.

A ragtag room, chipped wooden cases stuffed with books, cracked leather chairs. I stood alone before a bank of monitors. Many screens displayed security footage from the tunnel cameras, but the centre one aired a live feed from the Lagoon. There, a smoky, fiery rip in the air caused the

Lagoon's emerald water to darken and bubble, threatening to wrench wide into a gaping hole. The Rift. The doorway between Always and Never.

But there was also a back door, Mr Jungen had said.

I could hear a clock. But the sound was somehow *off*, like it was all *ticks* and no *tocks*.

Darlene was out of sight, but I could hear her voice. She didn't sound as though she was in pain anymore. She was talking to Dr Verloren. They were discussing Mr Jungen. Darlene was certain he was dead, and Dr Verloren agreed. "After all this time hunting him, the Haken Ministry would not have let him live." Her voice was aged yet musical. Darlene was upset about the loss; Dr Verloren not so much.

They talked more, and I understood there was a long standing feud that never healed. The doctor said she would never wish harm upon Mr Jungen, but if the old fool hadn't been so precautious and meticulous in every little thing he did, they would have dealt with the monster within their own generation.

"Still," she added, "he did acknowledge that time was not on our side in the end. And he at least retained some belief in me. Enough to trust you, Darlene, even if it came at a high price."

Darlene moved in front of the monitors. She still wore her Stetson but not her sunglasses. Her eyes were brown. Her jacket and shirt lay crumpled on a chair to one side and she stood in a sports bra. Blood stained her skin, but the bullet wound had been dressed and she was moving freely. The dressing looked to be gauze of some kind, like honeycomb but pearlescent, reflecting spectrum colours. Another trick of the imagi.

Darlene said, "Mr Jungen was convinced that Haken found us by tracking their prisoner. He said it was time to show me the way into Always."

"Yes, the end is here," Dr Verloren replied. "It's a miracle you managed to keep us half a step ahead, Darlene."

"So, we go now?"

"A moment first. *He* deserves to know."

When referring to me, the doctor's voice held disgust. On the monitor behind Darlene, a molten mass leaked from the Rift in one big drip to splash steaming into the Lagoon.

Dr Verloren came into view. Small, as old and grey as Mr Jungen, but in much better health, she took the jacket and shirt from the chair and threw them to Darlene before sitting. She glared at me through thick spectacle lenses with an expression like she had personally witnessed every murder I'd ever committed. The clock continued to *tick* but not *tock* and I noticed an oil painting on the wall to my right, between two bookcases, stretching floor to ceiling. As wide as a door, it depicted a tower clock with a body made from myriad cogs. The hands on its cracked face were stuck at one minute to midnight.

"The Haken Ministry is the only government Never has ever known," Dr Verloren said to me. "Their seat of power is built upon fear of the monster. Just the threat of it keeps people in line, stops them questioning, because we came to believe that Haken is our only protection against the monster's madness. A madness you share."

Darlene buttoned up her shirt, staring at me silently while the doctor spoke.

"Haken tells us the monster has a murderous vendetta against those who lose youth and innocence, those who *grow up* generation after generation. This is the doctrine each of us is born into. But what if I told you that we imagi know the doctrine is a lie?"

On the monitor, the Rift had stretched noticeably wider over the Lagoon. The image panned out and showed ranks of soldiers lining up before it. Oddly, I wondered if any of the convicts I began this journey with were among them.

"How many murders do you think Haken has committed? How many lives have they wasted to perpetuate this endless fight against the monster? I should imagine your body count pales in comparison. You believe you have a calling, and you are right to do so, but your vile mission in life was misguided."

The doctor sat forward, eyes bright behind thick lenses. "The girl from the story? The one who had children who had children who had children – she married a man named Haken, did you know that part? Her grandson founded the Haken Ministry. He was responsible for rebuilding our lives after the Exile, for reimaging Always in Never. Oh, he claimed it was for the good of all survivors, that *imagination* had brought us to the brink of extinction, but in truth he coerced and manipulated because he desperately needed to keep the monster away from his family. The girl's family. Because in every generation, one of her descendants is born with a peculiarly shaped birthmark that represents all that was lost."

Darlene stopped inspecting the bullet hole in her shirt and joined in: "The monster didn't lose control of its imagination because of *grown-ups*. It never let go. The boy is still searching for the girl."

Tick, tick, tick…

"Peace is what the monster truly wants," Dr Verloren said. "An end to its search, its frustration and loneliness. And if we're very lucky, that *peace* will free imagination, send it back into the wild."

"Once we have that," said Darlene, "all we'd need would be the right kind of guardians who could let imagination flourish and release Never from Haken's chokehold."

"Which is where you come in." Dr Verloren studied me. "Do you have any idea how many of your relatives the Ministry *removed* because of that birthmark? Any one of them could have set the monster free. And now, *you* will."

Sacrifice was the only word that came to mind. It brought my calling into sharp relief.

The conversation ended with the orange pulses of a warning light accompanying the inexorable *ticks*. The monitors surrounding the image of the Rift picked up movement in the tunnel outside. Pirates were making their way towards this room, a host of guns and mirror-masks.

"Fuck," Darlene said.

Dr Verloren stood before the screens. A second passed, then she said, "Mr Jungen's rite. Give it to me now."

Darlene fished the little wooden case from her satchel. Dr Verloren transferred it to my hand, then ordered me to lay my free hand on the painting between the bookcases.

As soon as skin touched oil on canvas, the clock sprang to life. Cogs and intricate workings turned and rattled. The minute hand trembled, its *ticks* strained; and then, as though it had been ready and eager for generations, it finally *tocked* onto midnight.

The painting swung inwards, revealing a smoky darkness that reeked of hot metal.

"Go," Dr Verloren said, staring at the monitors. "I'll hold them off."

"Come with us—" Darlene froze at the sound of Pirates at the door. One of the screens was filled with fiery sparks from a metal cutter.

"All the world is made of imagination." Dr Verloren switched off the monitors and looked at me. "*Anything* can be yours if you sacrifice *everything*. Now *go!*"

And then Darlene was pulling me by the hand into smoky ruin.

Dr Verloren's doorway disappears the moment we step into Always, as do the tricks of the imagi. Whatever power of imagination was healing Darlene's wounds stops working. Whatever control she had placed on me vanishes. Then we are alone, in the here and now, facing the monster's palace of mist and shadow.

On her knees, bleeding and in pain, Darlene says, "Please…"

Up on the hill, surrounded by crucified fairies, the monster awakes with a sob that trembles the ground.

In my hands, the rite crumbles in the hot wind. Fragile parchment swirls away as dust and flakes into the ash falling from the sky.

"No," Darlene groans.

If she believes an opportunity is wasted, she's wrong. The rite, written in the fading red ink of crocodile blood, was already in my memory. Like it knew me. Like it knew where I came from, *who* I came from.

Up ahead, between us and the monster's palace, the Rift appears, high and wide, ripping the very air open. I catch a glimpse of the Lagoon, but then soldiers come pouring through. Darlene whispers something, trying to heal herself or summon another weapon, but she fails and falls unconscious while staying upright on her knees.

Some soldiers are Pirates, mirror-masks alive with the putrid colours of Always. Most are regular infantry, a first wave of convicts sent to fight for their freedom. Too many to count. They form lines and aim their rifles at us. An order is barked and they open fire.

Bullets buzz around my head like a swarm of angry bees. None of them hit me. The volley rips through Darlene, however, bullet after bullet, tearing flesh and shattering bone, until she is reduced to an unrecognisable mass of red. Somehow, her Stetson survives. I pick it up, consider a single bullet-hole, then put it on as a fresh volley fails to hit me, as if Always itself is shielding me.

The rite burns clear in my mind as if waking from a dream. *Words* hadn't graced the ancient parchment; it had been music. Music of a kind that followed not a melody but a rhythm, beats – the beats of two hearts. Imagination for my hands.

The monster weeps and Always shakes.

Another barrage of bullets, another failure, and the soldiers change tactics. The order goes up to fix bayonets and charge. As they come for me, I raise my hands, pausing for a second before clapping them together with a sound like thunder. I draw them apart and clap again, again and again, following the music of heartbeats coded inside me. It is a short piece, loud and steady concussions interspersed with fluttering butterfly wings, and I perform it over and over. With each repetition, echoes well up and radiate from my hands like shockwaves that race away, through the soldiers, up the hill, and to the monster's palace.

The charge falters. I continue clapping. Soldiers turn as the sharp cracks of breaking stone come from the hill. On hundreds of crucifixes, the hearts of fairies are hot-wired into beating again. They break free from their cocoons, shedding stone, tearing hands from nails, and they rise together in a swirling murmuration, massing as a black cloud. The soldiers open fire at them, and they retaliate.

Only when the fairies attack do I stop clapping. Like speeding angels of death, they fly into the army. Some soldiers try to run, back through the Rift to the safety of Never, but it's too late for that now. With teeth and claws, the fairies wreak havoc and carnage among the ranks, too fast to stop, killing without mercy.

The slaughter takes but a moment, every soldier dead, but the fairies don't let up. They escape Always through the

Rift, flying away to the land they once called home. There, they might survey what has become of Never and release the old ways buried in the ground. Imagination for a new and better generation, beyond Haken's control. But only when the monster knows peace.

When the last fairy escapes, the Rift closes, perhaps forever, and the monster sobs and calls.

I walk through the field of corpses to the hill. By the time I reach the first crucifix, the monster leaves its palace, coming to meet me as a mist of smoke and shadows. It envelops me. My birthmark itches and burns. From out of the murk, a figure emerges – small like a child, I think.

A voice, timeless and innocent and lost, says, "Absence makes the heart grow fonder."

It's like a warm embrace, and I reply, "Or it can make us forget."

The Lost Boys Monologues

KIRSTY LOGAN

JOJO (THE JOKER)

I'm the baby boy of the band. You know? I do pranks. Grin
a bunch. Do finger-guns or peace signs in photos. Tongue
out, bunny ears behind the other guys' heads. Twisting my
face in dumbass ways. Always moving. Never myself.

And you know what? I realised I hate pranks. I always
have. I hate that the only person laughing is the one doing
the prank. A joke is meant to be a shared thing. A gift, even.
You already know the end of the joke, so it's not funny to
you, it's not a surprise. You share it for the joy of the other
person's surprise. But the role says pranks. The role says little
brother. So I do it. The thing is, I also am a little brother. *Was*
a little brother.

My big brother, Jack. He was everything, you know? That
sounds cheap. It sounds easy. It's like something a ghostwriter

would put in our autobiography. And I don't want it to be easy. None of this is easy.

You have to understand what it was like, growing up where we did. It was the kind of town with one stoplight. You could drive there at three a.m., shut off your engine, and just listen. It was that quiet. You felt like you could hear the moon. If you held your breath, you could hear the stoplight buzzing. It wasn't like you had to stop at the light. There was never anyone else there. If you wanted, you could roll your car right to the centre of the intersection and just sit there. You could get out of the car and lay down in the road. Just you and that waiting. And that glowing red light, that devil eye, watching you.

Then *clunk* and the light would change. Like heavy gates being unlocked. Like getting let out of prison. Or being put in. *Clunk*. Bet you never knew stoplights had a sound.

I know this because Jack used to take us on night drives. We'd go up to the hills so we could look for UFOs. He had this Thermos of coffee, something in it, whisky I guess. It burned your throat as it went down. Made everything fuzzy. He only let me have a bit.

There were ten years between me and Jack. He was nineteen, ready to leave. I was nine years old. I still had a teddy bear. I'd shoved it to the back of my closet, and I'd die before telling any of the guys in school. But I wouldn't let my mom throw it away. I don't know why Jack took me with him up to the hills. Company's company, I guess. That age difference put us on different planets, I see that now.

Up in the hills, my chest glowing hot from the coffee, Jack and I would lay on the hood of his car and stare up at the sky. Sometimes a star would move and I'd think it was a shooting star, but Jack said it was an airplane. An airplane was even better than a shooting star, because they were only good for wishes, and an airplane was real. An airplane could really, really take you somewhere.

Aliens! Hello! Jack would shout up at the sky, and I'd repeat it like his echo: *Hellohellohello!*

Then he'd laugh, so deep it vibrated through the hood of the car, and I'd feel his laugh right through my ribs, through my lungs, like it was coming from me.

We lay there like that for hours. Just watching. Just waiting. I know I fell asleep sometimes. I was just a kid, and I had school in a few hours. But I'd never say no when Jack woke me to drive to the hills, and I'd never ask him to take me home. We'd call to the aliens, tell them they were welcome. Tell them we'd take them to our leader. I don't even know all we said. Stuff we'd heard on TV. Stuff we'd read in comics.

One night Jack had emptied the Thermos right to the dregs, and things were getting kind of sloppy. His legs were spidering on the hood, his blinks got real slow like his eyelids were hard to lift. I thought he'd fallen asleep and was mumbling, dreaming something, but then suddenly he yelled out, eyes still closed, yelled right up at the empty black sky: *Take me away from here, alien friends!* He took a breath and then he yelled again, so loud I could hear it scrape in his throat, it must have hurt: *Take me! Take me!*

His voice caught at the end and he made a joke of it. But

none of it was a joke. It never was. He drove us back home again and went to bed without saying anything.

Then one morning, Jack just wasn't there.

His car was in the drive. His wallet and keys were on his dresser. But his bed was empty.

My mom reported it, but no one cared. Why would they? He was a nineteen-year-old boy in a nothing town. All he'd said for years was that he wanted to leave. I knew he'd never leave my mom to handle it all alone. To handle me, I guess I mean. I think my mom knew it too, though after a year of no Jack she was less sad and more mad. *He never even called*, she'd say. *How could he not call?*

And the thing is, he would have called. He never would have left us, but if he had, he would have called. Maybe the aliens did come for him. I don't know. I'd like to think so. I wish they'd come for me too. But they didn't. Boss did instead.

JUDD (THE BAD BOY)

So I'll tell you about this one night, and it's my birthday, you know, a big one, my twenty-first, but I feel about a hundred and fuckin five, I'm still skinny and my dick can still get hard but the shadows under my eyes, Jesus fuck, the pocks in my cheeks, I look like shit and I know it. I can't stop cracking my knuckles, popping them every five minutes, and I'm in that house on the hills, Boss's house, the one all glass and the only lights real far away so you can only see yourself in the window, you know, your own fuckin self staring back at you all the time. Boss loves it, made me parade up and down about a thousand times while he took pictures, I don't know what happened to those pictures, do you think he put them someplace, did he sell them? Are there people right now looking at my face, owning it, like did he—

Okay. Okay. The house. I don't want to be here but I am, I don't have anywhere else to go, and it's not so bad because Boss isn't there, he's on some scouting trip to bumfuck nowhere to find some new boys with soft throats and big goo-goo eyes the girls will like, high butts and little plastic pecs, the type you want to rip their clothes off but you also want them to say please and thank you to your mom, you know. We're getting past our prime, even I can see that, even little baby Jojo is getting long in the tooth for this business, he's nearly twenty now, ancient in boyband land. Even pretty boy Jakob is starting to look more like someone's uncle than their big brother, he's only twenty-fuckin-five but this work, this business, it kills you, it sucks and sucks from you and it never stops, and I think about those boys, those new boys that Boss has gone to snatch out of the football field or the mall or right out of their own fuckin bedrooms for all I know, and I think about what will happen to them, what Boss will—

But I guess I won't worry about that until Boss is back because Jun is staying there with me, he said it was going to be a quiet one, just me and him. He's gone out to get a cake or some shit and I'm just waiting and it's not long after the hospital and the 911 call and I still think no one knows about it, stupid right, I'm a stupid fuck, why would I ever fuckin think—

So it's just me and Jun, and I hear the door open so I figure it's Jun coming back.

He tells me to close my eyes cos it's a surprise.

I lift my hands.

I put them over my eyes.

Not because I want a surprise.

Because I can't stand looking at my own fuckin face in those endless windows anymore. I think I'm gonna puke because I know right away it's not just Jun, I can hear feet and feet and feet coming through the door. Boots and rubber sneakers and so many clackety high heels, so many people I can't even count, and I keep my hands over my eyes because I actually think for a second I'm going to cry like a fuckin pussy and I want to be able to shove the tears back in with my hands before anyone sees. I feel the lights in the house go out around me, and I hear the sound of a match strike, and whispers and shushing and giggles. I know there's a cake, I know they're lighting candles, and I wanted it to be me and Jun, that's all I wanted, I'm only twenty-one and I shouldn't have made it that far, I shouldn't have made it past that night, that's when I should have died, lying there in that shitty stinking hotel room, everyone else long gone, not a friend in the world, having to be found by my dealer, my belly full of pills and a needle still stuck—

The house, the house, the fuckin house, okay! Fuck, I'm losing track. They're all singing "Happy Birthday" and I want to keep my hands over my eyes but I don't want to look stupid, I know they're all looking at me, so I drop my hands and it's a huge pink cake, the frosting already starting to drip from the heat of the fuckin inferno of candles, and the burning cake looms towards me and all around it crowd a hundred of my closest friends, and I don't know a single one of them, every one of them is gonna leave me to die on a puke-stained hotel carpet, and they're all wearing masks of my face, paper masks printed with my face, a hundred fuckin Judd Lees and I guess they're all a happy fuckin twenty-one, one of the Judds even has the little red sale sticker still on it, my face costs 50 cents, did you ever wonder how much your face was worth, because I never did but I know the answer anyhow, and I look at my hundred identical faces in the flickering light and I take a breath so fast and so deep I suck in all the heat from the candles and I think I'm gonna choke and puke all over the huge pink cake but I don't, I blow out the candles all at once, and a hush falls, and a dark, and in the rustling nothingness before anyone puts on the lights I feel a hundred of me, there, waiting.

JAKOB (THE HEARTTHROB)

I used to have this – I guess, dream. I want to say it's a dream. It's about a hotel. We stayed in a bunch of hotels after "Save You With Love" came out. All types: fancy-ass five-star ones with lobbies you could park an airplane in, boutique ones where everyone used fake names and there had definitely been a hushed-up murder, motels with dingy paintings of deer and pools that hadn't been cleaned in forever. We were on tour for years, it felt like. Wherever we went, they wanted more. However many cities we visited, it was never enough.

Sometimes we slept on tour buses, but we never liked to if we had a choice. The girls, they – I'm not saying they scared me. That would be stupid. A bunch of teen girls – pre-teen, some of them, there with their moms, and if we were going to be scared of anyone it would be the moms, they screamed for us just as hard, and they'd do anything, *anything*. The things they said to me, you wouldn't believe. Just sidle up at a signing or a meet 'n' greet and whisper this *filth* in my ear. Sometimes I didn't mind it, the MILF sort, you know, telling me exactly how they wanted to suck me, which parts they wanted me to fuck and how hard and for how long. But there were hundreds – *thousands* of them. Their perfume and their lip-gloss and their tits pushed right up, over and over. And it wasn't just me, though I was the heartthrob, the main target. The things they said to Judd, the absolute shit they said to him, you couldn't make it up. Fuck me till I bleed. Call me slut, call me bitch. Choke me, kill me, I want your face to be the last thing I see. They wanted me to fuck them, but they wanted Judd to fuck them *up*. It's not that we were scared. It's not that *I* was scared. Don't think I was scared.

But like – you don't *know*. You can't know. Once they found the bus and they knew we were on it, I don't know how, teen girl ESP, some *Carrie* shit, and they wanted to get inside. *Needed* to get inside. They tried opening the door and of course it was locked, and they tried picking the lock, and they tried knocking on the door and the windows and the sides of the bus, and we were all just inside staying quiet, and it was funny, we were like laughing and shit, trying to muffle it, daring each other to open the window and grab a handful of tit – the moms', not the girls', shit, I'm not like *that*. But they were getting mad. They started like shaking the bus, working together, all pushing at once. I don't know if they were trying to push it over. I don't know what they planned to do if they managed to. We always had security, big guys, *massive* guys, but they must have been on their lunch break or some shit. They finally figured out what was happening and pushed their way through, all beef and brawn, and like dispersed the crowd. We got back to playing games and ragging on each other and doing push-ups and whatever, and it was all fine. Not like we were scared. But like – also we never spoke about it again.

This dream. Or I think it's a dream. It's hard to remember that time, and I don't like to think about it if I have a choice. I'm in a hotel at night. Something wakes me. I don't know what. I think, to myself, I could go to the mini-bar and see if there's anything left – I could call, even, get something sent to the room. But instead I just lie there. I think about rubbing one out to help me sleep. I think about Jenson's girlfriend to start me off, and then I replace her with Jojo's girlfriend, not that we're meant to have girlfriends but obviously we do, but I keep getting distracted by the noise from the hall.

It's not a loud noise, but it's insistent. Footsteps, slowly walking up and down the hall. Every few minutes, a gentle *tap-tap* on a door. But the weird thing is, it's not the same door over and over. It's someone walking, *tap-tap*, a pause, *tap-tap*, then walking to a different door, then *tap-tap* again. As if they're not looking for a room, but for any room. Anyone.

No one answers. And like – is there no one on this floor? Is there no one in this hotel? I can hear my own breathing.

I can hear my heartbeat. I can hear the hum of the mini-fridge and the click in my throat as I swallow. Step, step. *Tap-tap.*

I want to go to the peephole and look, to see why this weirdo is shuffling up and down a hotel hall at 4.30 a.m., but – I'm not scared. Don't think I'm scared.

And then the steps come to my door. I hold my breath, waiting for the *tap-tap*. But it doesn't come.

I can see the twin shadows at my door. Someone is standing there. If I looked out of the peephole, I'd be eye-to-eye with them. I can hear them breathing. Is it just my breathing? Is that my heartbeat or theirs? Did I just hear them swallow?

They don't knock on the door. They don't walk away. And I don't look out of the peephole. Because if I don't look, maybe they won't go away. Maybe I'm not the only one here.

JUN (THE SENSITIVE ONE)

If you'd asked me at any point over the past decade, I would have refused to talk about this. Not that you would have asked me; you wouldn't have known to ask; just like I don't know how to answer.

I guess you want to know if I loved him. If I love him. If any of it was real.

The songs weren't real; we didn't write them, no matter what it said in the teen magazines at the time, no matter what Jenson might tell you now.

The fans weren't real; they forgot about us as soon as the

next batch of boys appeared on the horizon; and I don't blame them for that, it's the way the machine works.

The roles we took on weren't real; I was the nice boy, the sensitive one, while Judd was the bad boy. He was good at playing it; he got the tattoos, he got the drug problem, he learned to use the word *fuck* as punctuation. I think I was good at playing it too; basically did the opposite of everything Judd did. Perhaps that's where it all started; because I was watching him so closely, figuring out my role as the reversed mirror image of him.

After a show one night, back on the tour bus; Judd high off something which at the time I figured was the fans and after that realised was the drugs and later after that hoped was me; Jojo's head spinning with the newness of it all, the bigness of it, the way the lights caught in your eyes. Jenson was organising things and making sure we had all we needed, being the big brother as usual; and right then Jakob said, *Man, they love us, they really love us.* I get it was a reference to some speech, some kind of jokey thing. Jakob always was the joker; though it wasn't his role so he only did it for us. It was clear it was a joke because he clasped his fists in front of his face and raised his eyes heavenwards.

Judd said something then; I think I was the only one who heard him: *They just love what we do.*

Even then; even then. He knew something the rest of us still had to figure out. I know it took me a while to figure it out. Over a decade, if you want the truth; that's why I can only talk about this now.

But—

That's not how it happened. It merges; it shifts. The night when Judd said that, we were in a hotel room; red light in the room; a low throbbing heart. The way his bare skin looked in that red light; the dark pits of his eyes. *They just love what we do*, he said, *not like you*. I remember I didn't say anything back to him; I was afraid that it wasn't true; that I didn't love him for him; that I didn't even love him for what he represented; that I didn't love him at all. More than that, I was afraid that he didn't love me; if I could tell myself that I didn't love him then it didn't matter if he loved me; it didn't matter if it wasn't real for him as long as it wasn't real for me either.

But—

It's moving again; it's changing; I can't get a handle on it. I think that was from a fan-fiction; we used to read them aloud to one another; act them out as a joke, though I think we both knew it wasn't a joke. "The Red Room", the story was called; it was about me and Judd confessing our love for one another; ridiculous, the sort of thing you get in fan-fiction, as if just because millions of girls and possibly millions of boys loved us, we'd love each other too; that we'd see one another's lovableness and be unable to resist. That red light, that confession; only a story, not really me and Judd; though did we read it in the story and then act it out and then it wasn't acting, it was true?

But—

It won't stay put; the memory won't lie still. Judd didn't say that to me, did he? It's a lyric from the song. "Save You With Love". *They just love what we do, not like you, not like you, your love is true, ooh ooh ooh.* A message to a million strangers that they're different, they're not like the others, each girl is the one girl who can save us. The truth is I was alone in the hotel room; I'd gone to the bathroom, still half-asleep, heels dragging dreams after me like a blanket; I got back and someone was in my bed; Judd was in my bed. My heart burst bright red, low throbbing. *Judd*, it said, *Judd Judd Judd*. I got closer to the bed; he was lying oddly, covers pulled up over his shoulders, on his side with his back to me, facing the wall. He held the sheet up over himself, clasped in his fists in front of his face; he was hiding. From me. With me. I reached out and the room was lit red and full of shadows; like the inside of a mouth; like the deepest part of a kiss; I reached out and gently pulled the sheet down from Judd's face.

It wasn't Judd; it was nothing; it was my sheets bunched up and twisted where I'd thrown them aside; accidentally faked into the shape of a person.

I think this happened; I don't know if this happened; I don't know if I read it or imagined it; if it did happen, I'll never know, because I was the only one there.

Did I love him? Was any of it real?

JENSON (THE OLDER BROTHER)

I didn't go into this foolishly. I wasn't like the other guys. They were plucked out of their lives – Judd got spotted in the mosh pit at a show, Jun was in his high school's glee club, Jojo was sitting outside an honest-to-God Dairy Queen in this little town where he grew up, and Jakob, I forget, I think he was a model in an underwear catalogue and got the gig like that.

But me, I applied. I wanted it. It was an advert in the paper, if you can believe that.

Travel! Riches! Girls! Fame!

The advert can't have said that. But that's what I remember it saying. Or at least, that's how I read it. You had to send in a photo – face smiling, face serious, profile, shirtless, full body – and a tape of you singing. In retrospect, I don't think they listened to the tape. Lost Boys, the band was called, and in calling it that Boss knew exactly what he was looking for. He could have made a band of any boys, but he needed particular ones. Ones with nothing to lose. Ones who were already lost.

I was meant to be in college on a football scholarship. But I tackled bad and then fell bad and busted my knee. One second, one snap, and that was it. It didn't feel like a second. It felt like forever. That collision, that sudden meeting of bodies. A slow, endless breaking. It still hurts, that knee injury. All those dance routines damn near killed me, but I never complained. After all, I asked for this.

I never regretted the band. The others, I think they did. But it was different for me. Boss saw me as a colleague, I think. Not an equal, more of a subordinate, but still a worker. Not a tear-out poster that could move. Not a character he made up in his head. Not meat.

There was another way I was different. I knew what it was to have something, and then lose it. Perhaps that's why I coped better when Lost Boys, the next big thing, ended up nothing more than a one-hit wonder. It helped that I'd been smart enough to get myself a songwriting credit on "Save You With Love". I always knew that was going to be the hit. I didn't know it would be the only one, but hell. Can't have everything.

There are sacrifices to be made, I know that. In love, in fame, in football, in everything. My sacrifice was for – I don't want to tell you her name. It's irrelevant. I could call her anything and the story would be the same. The same long, slow collision. I don't even know how to talk about her. I could tell you all about who she was, where she came from, what mattered to her. But I don't want to, because the truth is that what mattered to her wasn't me. Not the way I wanted to matter.

I think that's what drew me to the band. Drew me to Boss, even though I knew he was a bastard. I didn't know what he was doing with the other guys – doing *to them*, I guess, as it was hardly a two-way thing. Or maybe it was? I never asked for details. I don't think I wanted to know. And at the time, I assure you, I didn't know. Even now I don't know if it was just Judd, or Jun too. They were always his favourites, even though Jakob was meant to be the pretty one and Jojo the cute one. You'd think a guy like Boss would want them pretty or cute. But who the hell knows what a guy like that wants? I don't even want to think about it.

The thing about ignorance is that it's selfish. Not everyone gets to put their hands over their ears. But I did. I do. I learned that it's better not to ask questions, because it's guaranteed you won't want to hear the answer.

I would have quit it all for her. Even at the height of the success of "Save You With Love", those brief shooting-star months when we were the hottest-burning things on the planet, I'd have left it all in a second for her. I'd have shacked up in some mom-and-pop town, raised kids, worked in a tyre store, sold real estate, fixed toilets, scooped cones at that damn Dairy Queen where Boss spotted Jojo. I'd have found some other way to get to college and fought to get into whatever fancy place she was accepted, followed her like a puppy across a dozen state lines. But I didn't, because she didn't want me to. It can kill you, being a knight to a harsh mistress.

Did I mention I was the big brother? The sensitive one? The overthinking one who read big books and was allowed to have (some, carefully selected, specifically worded) opinions? Boss knew how to give us the right roles. I'll give him that. He knew how to pick them.

That injury I got, the one that changed it all – it still hurts me. Does that make it better? Does that count as atonement? Sometimes it feels like my leg is caught in a trap. I can feel the teeth digging into me, rusted but still sharp. I don't even twist to try to escape from it. I just lie there. Even in winter, even though it makes my busted knee ache, I sleep with the window open. Just in case someone comes for me.

A School for Peters

CLAIRE NORTH

Wendy Spoon was six when she was taken to the School for Peters. She didn't remember much about the time before, only that the men who took her said that she was "fresh" which she thought was something that you said about fish, and that her pigtails were absolutely perfect. She thought she remembered her mummy braiding her hair, using her fingers as a comb, but Mrs Sweet told her she was imagining it, that her mummy hadn't been a real mummy at all, and that was why she'd gone away.

Even then, Wendy Spoon had known Mrs Sweet was lying. Her mummy hadn't gone away. She'd been right there when her mummy died despite her many months of trying to imagine the best, most glorious feast for her daughter, the most extraordinary and incredible spread of food – can you picture it? she'd asked – roast swan stuffed with roast goose stuffed with roast chicken stuffed with roast duck all served on a golden platter surrounded by caramel apples? Tell me you can picture it, dear.

Even though her mummy had imagined really, really well, and really, really hard, just like the government said she should, she had still secretly made Wendy Spoon eat what few crumbs she'd managed to scavenge from Mr Patel the bus driver at number 17, and Mrs Kavenaugh the housing lady at 53. Maybe that was why Mummy had died. Maybe by giving Wendy Spoon real food, actual stale bread and a few yellowing peas, she hadn't believed enough, hadn't been able to imagine they weren't hungry hard enough, and that was why she'd laid down to sleep on the mattress in the corner of the room, and never woken up.

On her first night in the school, Wendy Spoon tried to cut off her pigtails with a blunt pair of craft scissors. The older Wendys caught her and called Mrs Sweet, who screamed that Wendy Spoon was an ungrateful little wretch and locked her in the naughty hole. The next morning she was taken over to the boys' wing where the Peters lived, and they all lined up in an orderly queue to call her names and throw eggs. (Real eggs, not imaginary eggs. Wendy Spoon was too dull and stupid a child to appreciate the power of the imaginary egg yet, though she would learn.) Their teacher, Mr Strong, graded each Peter on how well he belittled, how viciously he threw, and gave notes after, awarding the smallest and weakest of the Peters a D- for, he said, deliberately aiming at Wendy Spoon's feet, instead of her face, and the bravest of the Peters an A+ for leaning in and whispering in Wendy's ear, "Your mummy never loved you," while slowly, carefully, grinding the sharp shell of the egg into Wendy Spoon's cheek.

Wendy Spoon did not attempt to cut her pigtails again.

For the first few years, the Wendys didn't have much contact with the Peters, except twice a month at all-school assembly when they would perform lovely little songs for the assembled boys, who would practise either booing the stupid little babies or applauding politely a sweet female ditty, according to a system that the Wendys never understood. When they were nine years old, that changed. Each Wendy was assigned a Peter to look after, usually a boy of eleven, and would be expected to turn down the covers of his bed, clean his shoes, wash his socks, bring him breakfast and repair his PE kit.

Wendy Spoon was assigned a boy called Peter Blue.

As assignments went, he could have been worse. His father was a Peter like him, and was a famous owner of expensive things, like private jets, football clubs, newspapers etc... What little Wendy understood from her few whispered words with Peter Blue, his father didn't actually do anything other than own things, and that was ideal. Doing things was for boring grown-ups. Peters were more imaginative than that.

Twice, Peter Blue thanked Wendy Spoon for her work by giving her an imaginary pile of sugared candies, which she politely and meekly accepted, sucking on them thoughtfully and taking her time to really savour the taste – a tingling mint – while he looked on. Once, for reasons she didn't fully understand, Peter Blue bounced on the bed she'd just made, his muddy shoes coating the white, crisp linen with smears of brown and black, and screamed at Wendy Spoon: *"She needs to take her medicine!"*

Wendy Spoon wasn't sure what had provoked Peter Blue that day – it wasn't her place to know – but she felt reasonably confident it wasn't anything she had done. Nevertheless, all the other Peters gathered round and held her by the hair and the throat, pinched her nose and pried her jaw apart as Peter Blue tipped the noxious, burning medicine into her mouth in a great, lung-bursting, gagging gasp of stomach-heaving flame. The Peters were not graded on how well they did this – they were already old enough to be well-versed in the high arts of medicine – but when Mrs Sweet found Wendy Spoon heaving and sobbing in the toilet after, she just tutted and said: "You must imagine yourself being better."

Imagination, her teachers explained, was the greatest gift. It was what made Peters and Wendys the most special of all the children in all the world.

The Wendys weren't encouraged to have friends.

Friends were distractions, and created dramas and needless, unhelpful imaginings.

Playmates, however, were essential. Through play the Wendys could imagine themselves making and serving tea, engaging in polite conversation, cleaning their future homes, raising their future children.

Wendy Spoon's favourite playmate was Wendy Pepperpot.

Wendy Pepperpot had come to the school a little older than many of the others, but had such a gentle demeanour, such a meek and malleable form, that the teachers had felt sure they could make her into something wonderful. For a while she had indeed been the star pupil, with deft needlework skills, thoughtful yet minimal conversation, a good head for household finances and all the qualities that would make a truly supportive Wendy for a dynamic, powerful Peter. But when Wendy Pepperpot was assigned to Peter Yellow, it all started to go wrong. Peter Yellow was an extremely promising Peter. His father was a senior government man – Minister for Treasure, no less – and Peter Yellow could often be heard pronouncing on the kind of imaginings his father was so famous for.

"There is only so much treasure in the world," he would explain, "and Peters, being the strongest, the smartest, the best at everything, are therefore the best people to have most of it!"

This was an idea that Wendy Spoon had secretly sometimes heard referred to by another name: *economics*. Wendy Dust, who knew a lot of secret grown-up things that she wasn't supposed to, said that was what all the boring Johns and Michaels of the world called it. There were even some people who thought that Johns and Michaels should be in charge, or worse – maybe the wicked Tigerlilys or the great unnamed Lost Children of society, the ones too boring and stupid to have the big ideas that the Peters did – but the Peters always killed them, gunning them down along the picket lines and hanging their bodies along the lampposts as a warning to all. There was, after all, only so much treasure to go around, and the Peters were always willing to imagine the best possible solution for what had to be done.

Peter Yellow was a very imaginative boy. When the Peters went pirate-hunting, heading out in their big yellow bus to chase miscreants and vagrants, with Mr Swash the PE teacher blowing his bright orange whistle to fire, Peter Yellow always killed the most in the most exciting of ways. He was so good at it that by the time he was fourteen, he was given the highest honour in his age group – that of Pan, set for golden things. People whispered and swooned and said how lucky Wendy Pepperpot was to be Wendy to a Pan, and Wendy Pepperpot simpered and smiled and said she just wanted to see the boys were tucked in bed at night and didn't miss their supper – a good, well-graded answer.

However, one night when they were both thirteen, Wendy Spoon was woken by the sound of gentle sobbing from beneath the sheets of a neighbouring bed. Naturally she knew she should ignore it – Wendys weren't allowed to cry, and were meant to report it, but everyone knew that so long as you cried with your sheet over your head it could be allowed to pass. So, Wendy Spoon rolled over and tried to imagine that it wasn't happening, just like she'd been taught. But the crying did not stop no matter how hard she imagined it, and eventually Wendy Spoon rolled out of bed and tiptoed over to the tent of sheet and blanket that was Wendy Pepperpot's bed.

"Pepperpot," she whispered. "Pepperpot, what's wrong?"

The sniffling paused, but the sheet did not part. Wendy Spoon wormed her way under the edge a finger at a time, until she had crawled into the hollow made by their bodies on the lumpy mattress. It was almost perfectly black inside, the faint moonlight through the high windows of the dorm diluted by the sheet, but Wendy Spoon had never feared the dark. "Pepperpot," she whispered again. "Stop crying, please, or you'll be sent to the naughty hole."

A sniffling, a sound like snot being rubbed on the long white sleeve of a nightie, another shuddering breath. Wendy Spoon fumbled in the black until her fingers brushed a modestly clad knee, then tangled with a damp, cold hand. "What's wrong, Pepperpot?" she breathed. "What's the matter?"

"It's... the kiss," whispered Pepperpot "Peter says he can see my kiss."

Wendy Spoon caught her breath, a little too loud, a little too late. She felt Pepperpot shudder again, the tears welling up, and squeezed the girl's hand harder. "Maybe he's wrong," she breathed. "Maybe he just saw... another thing. It doesn't have to be your kiss. Not yet."

"But he's Pan! He's never wrong. What if he tells the grown-ups? What if they say they can see it too?"

"It won't happen," declared Wendy Spoon firmly. "You're not grown up yet. It's too soon. You'll see."

Wendy Pepperpot said she believed Wendy Spoon, and she was sorry that she had been crying and wouldn't do it again, and both knew that she was lying.

Four days later, Wendy Pepperpot came into the dormitory with the mark of the kiss upon her lips. The other girls gasped, staring in speechless knots. The red lipstick was a modest blush across her mouth, there for all to see. Wendy Pepperpot gathered her small suitcase of clothes and a neatly folded sheet, and moved into a room away from the other Wendys without saying goodbye. None of the others knew exactly what happened when it was decided that there was a kiss lingering in the corner of your mouth. But no Wendy who had been seen with it upon their features ever returned to the dormitory of the girls, nor wore big white collars and flower-pink skirts, nor had their hair down nor talked of silly things ever again. Instead, they would wear stiff black dresses and call the other Wendys "lovely children", even if they were still the same age, and learn to laugh in a short, low way, as if wryly amused at some passing prattle, rather than in shrieks of innocent delight. And one day a Wendy would give her kiss to a Peter, and be his forever, to support him in all his brilliant ideas and genius notions as he went out into the world to imagine a better future for all the Lost Children of the land.

No Wendy who had ever had the kiss upon her lips had ever tried to run from the school. But one night, when the autumn wind was howling from the west and Wendy Spoon thought she could hear the wild drumming of the wicked Tigerlilys beating over the high school walls, Wendy Pepperpot fled.

She never made it over the wall.

Wendys were not taught how to run, or climb, or fight. These were skills that the Peters would have, in order to keep Wendys safe. There was no denying what she was trying to do, though. She'd cast off her uniform for a pair of stolen rubber boots and a big brown overcoat, pulled her hair into a ragged ponytail and stolen food from the kitchen, piling bread into her pockets and even a few meagre coins of treasure pilfered from a teacher's desk. The whole school was dragged out of bed at one a.m. to stand, shivering in their nighties on the long lawn before the big house, as the rain howled in sporadic sheets of cold and the crows muttered disturbed annoyance from the swaying hawthorn tree.

Wendy Pepperpot was stripped naked, like the naughty girl she was. In the flashing torchlight held by the younger Peters upon her body, Wendy Spoon could see bruises, some old, some new, across the girl's goosebumped grey flesh. Then Peter Yellow – the Pan of the school – was given a graduate's sword and with great dignity and sombre aplomb, as befitted his station, stood behind the kneeling Pepperpot, and with three strong blows, cut off her head.

Later, in the dark, Wendy Spoon tried to imagine that Wendy Pepperpot was alive.

She imagined it with all her heart, squeezed her eyes shut to try and black out the image of the girl's severed head.

Imagining it did not make it so and, in a way, that made things even worse.

Wendy Spoon was one of the last in her year to come into her kiss.

Wendy Dust, who knew about these sorts of things, told Wendy Spoon to giggle at everything that Peter Blue said, and to play with her pigtails, and often be seen skipping and playing tic-tac-toe in the playground. These were the kinds of things that could keep the kiss from emerging. Hidden under their tented sheets, Wendy Spoon asked how Wendy Dust knew so much, but Wendy Dust shook her head and whispered it was best she didn't know yet, lest the knowing also bring on her kiss too soon.

Wendy Spoon thought Wendy Dust was probably right, and took extra efforts to giggle and smile and make silly little mistakes that would earn her prickings by needles upon her thumb from Mrs Sweet. But even with all these contrivances, it couldn't last forever. One day, when planting pretty little flowers that would grow beautiful and yellow in the summer sun, Wendy Spoon's mind wandered and she forgot to sing a happy little song. In that moment of lapsed attention, she became aware of eyes upon her, and looking up saw Peter Red – one of her least favourite of all the Peters – watching her, mouth hanging open and extended finger quivering in her general direction. In a moment of horror she realised what she'd done, but too late.

"The kiss! The kiss!" howled Peter Red. "She's got the kiss!"

All the other Peters gathered round to see it, and though some weren't sure, the collective consensus soon grew that yes, why yes, Wendy Spoon indeed had a kiss in the corner of her mouth, and all the boys crowed and howled and called for teacher, who examined Wendy Spoon's face with great seriousness, tugging and pulling at the flesh of her cheeks, turning her head this way and that, then with a firm grasp about her jaw finally nodded once and said: "Wendy Spoon, gather your things."

Wendy Spoon did not cry as she cast off her little pink dress, or when Mrs Sweet pressed the waxy lipstick into her mouth.

Once you had the kiss upon you, you could not even cry under the sheets.

She moved into a room of her own – which she quite liked – and was given charge over a group of younger Wendys, instructed to teach them how to look after all the new Peters coming to the school. She did this without question, and studied hard at the new lessons she must learn. For the first time she had a male teacher – Mr Slightly – who spoke to the blackboard in front of him instead of the girls at his back, in the tone of one puzzling out a new and complicated problem rather than a lecture he had given a thousand times before.

"Boys cannot grow up," he explained. "Some think they can, some even think they have. In schools for Johns and Michaels, they teach the fallacy that boys can ever be anything but boys. Here we have no such illusions. No matter the age of the body, boys are incapable of emotional growth and must therefore be tempered and served by girls, who are more prone to aging. This is your duty."

Wendy Spoon was astonished to find her hand in the air, and when Mr Slightly did not turn to see it, she was even more amazed to hear her own voice, slow and modulated, speak. "Mr Slightly? Did you ever grow up?"

The chalk froze on the board, the breath turned to ice in the throats of the other Wendys. Then slowly, like a glacier cracking, Mr Slightly revolved to behold the class, and seemed almost surprised to discover students in it. His eyes settled, blinking, upon Wendy Spoon, and after the longest pause he replied: "Alas, I did grow up. And I am worthless now."

Though Wendy had come into her kiss, she was still expected to look after Peter Blue.

Despite this, Peter Blue did not pay Wendy Spoon much attention. In a way, Wendy Spoon was grateful for this. She had been taught some of the things that were meant to happen now – the presentation of the thimble, the discussion of how many children she'd have when she was a mother, and so on – but Peter Blue didn't seem in a hurry to do anything but play rugby and take pot-shots at rogue Tigerlilys from the walls.

"He'd better do something soon," muttered Wendy Tea, as they stood in line waiting their turn to perform light airs upon the piano for the entertainment of guests. "If Peter Blue won't give you a thimble, there's nothing to stop another Peter doing it instead."

This worried Wendy Spoon. On the one hand, she wasn't sure she wanted any Peter to give her a thimble at all. But then if it had to be someone, she could do a lot worse than Peter Blue, who at least seemed affably uninterested.

She tried to imagine the kind of Peter she'd want to give her a thimble.

She found it hard. No matter what boy she shaped or pressed into some sort of mould, some ideal Peter who'd always protect her and keep her safe, they seemed to pop straight back out of her imaginings into their truer, real-life forms. This was not, she knew, how imagination was supposed to work.

As a Wendy with a kiss upon her lips, she spent more time amongst the boys now, padding down the wood-panelled halls between their classrooms as the sounds of their lessons drifted through the air.

"Did you steal the cake?" boomed the teacher's voice.

"I did not, sir!"

"But I saw you do it!"

"Respectfully, I don't think you saw what you think you saw, sir."

"Don't lie to me boy, I know what I saw!"

"If you think you saw me steal the cake, then I cannot help that. But I know that I did not steal the cake, and if there was icing on my fingers it was because I thought any cake that I did eat was meant for me anyway. Even if I did eat the cake, all the other Peters do it too, so I think it's very unfair that you are accusing me of lying and that you are a wicked person for doing this to me. You're clearly just jealous that I have cake, a jealous and resentful sort who doesn't want anyone at all to have any cake ever."

"...not bad, boy. Not bad..."

And still Peter Blue did not give Wendy Spoon his thimble.

Everyone was waiting for him to do it. The other boys crowed, cackled and stamped their feet when he passed by, but he just bowed his head and ignored them. It was disgraceful, the other Wendys said. It was the kind of behaviour you'd expect from a John or a Michael, not a leader! Not a Peter! He was letting the whole school down.

In the end, Wendy Spoon took a risk. She imagined herself doing it many times before she managed to do it for real, waiting in his room after the bell had rung, his shoes all laid out neatly at the end of the bed and a hot water bottle under the duvet just the way he liked it, and hands on hips barked as he came through the door: "Why haven't you given me a thimble?"

To her surprise, Peter Blue burst into tears.

He sat on the end of the bed, his head in his hands, and wept. Wendy Spoon had no idea what to do with this, so she patted his shoulder and said, "There there," as he bawled like some sort of lost boy.

"I'm going to be like Father," he gasped between snuffles. "I'm going to have all sorts of brilliant ideas about what to do about Lost Children and barbarian Indians and wicked pirates. Mr Swash says that's what makes us Peters special – our imaginations. I'm imagining all sorts of things I'm going to do to them. All sorts of things. All sorts of things."

She stayed with him until he stopped crying, his head nestled against her chest, arms around her middle – but still he did not give her a thimble.

"I'm sorry," he whispered, as she finally let herself out of his room. "I'm sorry."

"Read this," whispered Wendy Dust, one day as she and Wendy Spoon were practising making darling little cakes for the darling little children they'd have. A crinkled pamphlet, pressed into a square the size of the palm of her hand, slipped from Dust's to Spoon's hand.

Wendy Spoon showed no sign of having received it, said not a word, and later that night devoured it by torchlight under her sheets. She couldn't imagine how Wendy Dust had got it into the school, but there it was, in black and white.

A Cry to Freedom – by the Tigerlilys!

My brothers and sisters, it read, *we can build a new world. A world where girls become women and boys become men...*

It spoke of ideas that Wendy Spoon had only loosely grasped – of poverty and hunger, hardship and the realities of the world beyond the school walls. Some words seemed faintly familiar from a past long ago: housing estates and corruption, social welfare and the freedom of the press. These were ideas that were not meant for Peters, let alone Wendys. They were boring adult things droned on about by boring adult people; hardly relevant topics for the future leaders of the world who needed to imagine better things.

As well as the grown-up boring words, there was an image on the back, drawn in scarlet ink. Wendy stared at it in fascination, this strange picture of a Tigerlily. Her body was ostensibly female, but there was no pinched waist, no delicate features, no stick arms modestly clad. Instead, with rich dark skin and deep dark eyes she blazed defiantly from the page, one hand holding her war spear high, the other resting on the drum that beat for freedom.

She burned the pamphlet in the furnace at the bottom of the school, but not even fire could burn this new, wicked imagining from her mind.

It was Peter Russet who gave Wendy Spoon his thimble.

This astonished everyone. Everyone had assumed that Peter Russet would give his thimble to Wendy Wash, who had loyally served him since he was twelve. But on a whim, because he felt like it, he walked up to Wendy Spoon in front of the whole hall, grabbed her by the wrist, and jammed his thimble in her palm.

The Peters crowed and danced upon the tabletops as Wendy Spoon stared down at the little glittering object in her hand, then back up into the flushed, beaming face of the boy who'd given it to her.

"Thank you," she heard herself say. "I will cherish it."

Wendy Wash openly wept and Peter Blue didn't meet her eyes, as she slowly and calmly put the thimble on a chain about her neck.

In the night, Peter Russet came to her room.

"I'm going to take your kiss now," he said, pulling her nightgown clear.

"Of course, Peter," she replied. "How lovely."

When Peter Russet graduated, Wendy Spoon went with him.

His father had already purchased him a flat in Kensington, overlooking the park, so Peter and Wendy didn't have to worry about boring things like money that would get in the way of their big ideas. Nevertheless, because he was ultimately a leader who needed to lead, Peter joined a bank in the City.

He had no qualifications, no training, but that didn't matter. He was a Peter, one of the elite, the imaginative, great leaders of this world. "I've had an idea for a start-up!" he would exclaim to the other Peters gathered for poker night, who would crow and spill their whiskey on the soft white furnishings. Wendy would sigh with an amused tilt to the corner of her lips as though to say, "boys will be boys" – and top up their glasses and turn on the TV, where more Peters would explain how pathetic it was that Lost Children were jealous of all the good things the Peters had, and how treasure didn't grow on trees you know and if you didn't have any treasure it's because you hadn't imagined having it hard enough.

Sometimes, very rarely, a John or a Michael would come over from the office.

Wendy always found them baffling creatures. Dressed in grey three-piece suits with scuffed brown shoes, they'd wait in the hall as if embarrassed to sully the living room with their somewhat grubby appearance, and stare slack-jawed at the golden fittings and glass chandeliers with an uncultivated envy that all Peters knew well. Then Peter would remember they were there, and grudgingly call them into his office, and Wendy would hear words like "fiscal responsibility" and "realistic plan" muttered through the door, before at last Peter would scream over their dull and droning negativity: "*Why can't you just get it done?*"

Through all of this, Wendy did not get pregnant.

This was a source of much confusion to both of them, and particularly to Peter's father, who wondered out loud if their Wendy was broken.

At night, when he was sober, Peter would take Wendy's kiss, and during the day Wendy would imagine having children as hard as she could, but none of it seemed to make a difference. At last a Michael whispered that maybe she should go see a doctor, and with tears in her eyes Wendy went to a dreadful place where a dreadful boring grown-up with tired baggy eyes and creases in her trousers droned dreadful boring grown-up things and finally said: "We really need to do a sperm count for your husband."

At this, Wendy stormed from the room, and for the first time in a long time allowed herself to sit under a sheet shaking – not crying, mind, not now – until she heard the door close and Peter come home.

She didn't tell him what the doctor said, of course. The very notion was unthinkable. Instead, she tried to imagine even harder, and when he took her kiss she told herself how lucky she was, how very, very lucky, and what a brave Peter he was, even when he fell asleep on top of her halfway through, the alcohol rolling off his breath.

And in the night, she heard the Tigerlilys' distant drum.

"*Girls become women! Boys become men! Girls become women! Boys become men!*"

Peter grabbed his sword and rifle, as did all the other Peters in the apartment block, and they went out into the street to have a roaring good adventure. Wendy locked the door and made lasagne for when he came back. Cold water was the trick for getting blood out of clothes, but even so, Peter had marched off in his best pyjamas, and flannel was almost impossible to clean.

And still, Wendy didn't have any children.

"Peter," she said, one night after he'd, with some boredom, taken her kiss. "I spoke to a… a doctor. And she said… she said maybe you should have an appointment too… that maybe the sperm…"

That was the first time he made her take her medicine. He bent her backwards over the edge of the bed and poured it down her throat, squeezed her mouth shut until she swallowed, then dragged it open and made her drink some more.

After, when he was done and she lay retching and gasping on the bedroom floor, he turned his back to her and said, "Wendys should make Peters take their medicine. Not the other way round," and went to sleep on the sofa, because it wasn't right that Wendys – even bad Wendys – should sleep anywhere other than in the comfort of their beds.

The week after, some Tigerlilys stormed into Peter's office. They managed to start a fire in Forex Trading before the Peters were able to drive them off. Wendy did her best with Peter's jacket, but the blood just wasn't shifting, and again – more angry at the Tigerlilys, she felt, than at her – he made her take her medicine, his body pinning her against the kitchen fridge until she had gulped every burning drop down.

And one night, when the Peters were playing poker and laughing at the pirates they'd slain, Wendy played soft piano in a corner and found herself imagining something… different. Something old. Something new.

It was dangerous – so, so dangerous – every Wendy knew how deadly it could be to imagine anything other than the prescribed fantasies. But there it was, despite herself, slipping into her mind.

She imagined…

…a house without a Peter.

No crib rocking in a corner.

No loving nursery rhymes.

No kisses in the corner of her mouth.

No pressed collars, no ironed shirts.

No singing a little happy song as she prepared the supper.

No boys.

No girls.

Just… her.

And in her imagination, she held her war spear high and drummed the drum of freedom, and she was not Wendy at all, but Tigerlily, painted in scarlet, taller than the apartments even of Kensington that she crushed beneath her bare, calloused feet.

And still she did not get pregnant.

Sometimes Peter made her take her medicine – but this was just something he did, when he'd had a bad day and the Michaels had been too boring for words, or the Lost Children had barricaded Waterloo Bridge again with their ridiculous demands for boring things. The Tigerlilys said no one could imagine food or heat or medicine, and the Peters had scoffed and said they weren't trying hard enough. Wendy had scoffed too, as was her duty, and said they were all such naughty little children, but Peter barely looked at her now, whatever she said out loud.

And now, secretly, when he forced the medicine down her throat, Wendy didn't imagine her belly growing big, or the laughter of her children, but instead she closed her eyes to see the Tigerlily, striding like a giant across the earth; glorious, blazing, free.

"Where are my pants?" demanded Peter.

"Here they are, my lovely," she replied, and he struck her, thoughtlessly, across the mouth for having been so lax a Wendy as to let him get out of bed without his normal pants in their normal place. It was not a hard blow, and she did not fall, but swaying, tasted the iron of it on the inside of her cheeks. He was already gone, the thing already forgotten – if he remembered it, he would deny it in the evening. I don't remember hitting you, he'd say. It's outrageous that you'd make such a thing up in order to hurt me. You're a cruel, horrid Wendy.

"They say that I'm treating the Johns poorly," scowled Peter in the evening. "And the Lost Children are whining all the time. It's so *unfair.*"

Unfairness was a common topic of conversation amongst the Peters when they came over on a Sunday night for cards and whiskey. All the things people wanted of them, all the demands they constantly made – it was exhausting! Draining. Didn't people understand how difficult they were being?

"We really do need to see your husband," sighed the doctor at the hospital, and now it seemed to Wendy that this woman, with her greying hair and bending spine, had something of the divine in her. Something that didn't care for the eyes of boys or girls alike, something that could say phrases like "unprotected sexual intercourse" and "less than thirty-nine million sperm per ejaculation" like she was talking about doing the dishes. Wendy found that fascinating; enthralling. Wondered what kind of lost creature this woman was to have come to such a place. Wondered if the doctor envied Wendy as much as Wendy envied her.

"People just don't understand me," whined Peter, as Wendy painted over the bruise upon her cheek. "Everyone just wants everything from me all the time!"

"She's broken," exclaimed Peter's mother, an old Wendy who always smelt of lavender and never removed her white cotton gloves. "You've given your thimble to a broken Wendy. We should send her back!"

"Does she take her medicine?" demanded Peter's father,

scrutinising Wendy's swollen face. "Good girls must take their medicine!"

And the one evening – one not particularly special evening: "What's this?" demanded Peter, throwing the plate onto the floor. "You know on Friday we have chicken! Why don't you ever listen to me? Don't you understand how hard it is being Peter? Are you stupid? Are you a child?!"

Wendy made her usual apologies as she knelt amongst the fossilising remnants of cream sauce and fishy flakes, carefully separating out the largest shards of broken ceramic from amongst the cooling meal seeping into the carpet. "I thought you'd like something else tonight, but there's chicken in the freezer, I can have it defrosted by—"

"That'll take forever!" exclaimed Peter. "That'll take a thousand years! Fuck! I'm going to call for a pizza. Can't you do anything right?"

Slowly, nodding, Wendy rose, scoops of dripping dinner slithering down the dustpan she held in one hand.

On the TV there was a show about the wonderful houses of the best Peters, those who were Pan, those who were free to play games and live their lives without boring things and were truly the most wonderful of all.

Outside, the war drums of the Lost Children beat, louder every night now, bright as the orange fires glistening in the suburbs of the city.

"What do you mean you don't have pineapple?" drifted Peter's voice from the telephone in the hall. "You've got to have pineapple!"

With fish still clinging to her fingers, Wendy walked

sedately to the kitchen, scooped the remnants of the meal into the bin, washed down the pan, set it on its hook behind the door, dried her fingers, and opened the kitchen drawer.

It was very bad housekeeping to keep the kitchen knives in a drawer rather than on a magnetic strip on the wall, but Wendy had never been taught how to go about attaching such things and felt too embarrassed to ask a John or a Michael for help. So from the drawer she pulled the largest, sharpest knife she had, and holding it calmly in her right hand, proceeded from the kitchen to the hall.

Peter was still on the phone. "Well how long will it take? I don't care, I want it *now...*"

"Peter," she said softly, but he didn't look up.

"...well tell them to do it faster! I don't care how, just use your imagination!"

There was a bowl of potpourri by the door, and a wooden shoe rack that Peter never put his shoes into – he just dropped them wherever he felt like it, when he remembered to take his shoes off at all. The carpet was thick, soft beneath her bare feet.

"Peter," she repeated softly, and again, a little louder: "Peter."

"What?" he barked, not raising his eyes from the furrowed frown he had fixed upon the pizza menu in his hand, as if by will alone he could make the options before him somehow better.

"Grow up."

It would have been nice, Wendy thought, for Peter to see the knife as she drove it into his neck.

Then again, imagination was a wonderful thing.

Chasing Shadows

CAVAN SCOTT

1.

The kid's shadow looked wrong. Troy didn't know why. There was just something off about it, like it didn't fit. The kid, a couple of years older than them, with messy sandy hair and a slack mouth, was big. Not fat but solid, a real bruiser. Troy spotted the lad standing beneath a streetlamp while he was playing air hockey with Bryan Newton. The guy hadn't been there when they first arrived at the bowling alley for Matt Colman's birthday; Troy would've noticed that. Troy always noticed stuff others didn't spot. "Our own little Sherlock Holmes," his dad always said, and there was no way the Great Detective would miss a kid that size hanging around outside the Drakeford bowlplex, wearing a *Back to the Future* T-shirt two sizes too small for him.

Just like his shadow. That was far too small, as well.

Slack Mouth was still there when they piled out into the street after the party, almost bouncing off the wall thanks to the sugar in the countless fizzy drinks Matt's brother Dan had bought them before impressing the pretty girl in the next lane by hitting strike after strike after strike. The bruiser just stood, watching from beneath hooded lids as Billy Wilson, always the class clown, snatched a bendy Batman from Bryan's hand. Bry had won the rubber superhero on the grabber, the gang of friends now laughing and snorting as Bryan jumped up and down, desperately trying to pluck the figure from the air as it sailed repeatedly over his head, tossed from one set of hands to the next.

"Cut it out, guys," he wailed, his fingers almost – but not quite – reaching the flying toy. "Guys!"

Bryan didn't stand a chance. He'd always been the shortest of the group, a fact the others – especially Billy – never let him forget. Finally, he got lucky when Matt fumbled a catch and Batman overshot. Bryan may have been short, but he was fast. He saw his shot and took it, darting past the birthday boy to scoop the caped crusader from the floor.

"Matty!" Billy groaned, rolling his eyes. "Why do you have to be such a butterfingers?"

"Why did you have to throw it so hard?"

Bryan just brushed dirt off Batman's rubber cowl and thrust the toy towards Matt.

"Here, you take it. Happy birthday."

"You sure?" Matt asked, accepting the toy.

"Yeah. I prefer the Hulk anyway."

"Thanks, Bry."

"No problem."

"Aww, sweet," Billy teased, clinically incapable of dealing with any show of affection, even between friends. "You two want to have a kiss and a cuddle, too?"

Matt threw Batman at Bill's head and Bryan laughed.

And all the time, Slack Mouth kept watching. He watched as Dan pulled out a Polaroid camera and took a picture of the group, Billy grabbing Bryan in a headlock, and watched the cars arriving to pick everyone up.

Mr Wilson arrived first for Billy, the rest of the parents following close behind. No one was there for Bryan. This wasn't unusual. His mum worked late most nights, and he only lived ten minutes away. Yeah, he'd have to ride his battered old bike down the darkest of dark lanes behind the bowlplex, but it was a journey he'd made plenty of times. That didn't stop Troy from calling out when his dad pulled up in their Ford estate. "Do you want a lift? You can put your bike in the boot?"

"Nah," Bryan called back, throwing his leg over the Chopper that had already been second-hand when his mum bought it for him two Christmases ago. "I'll be okay."

"Okay," Troy echoed, slipping into a seat covered in dog hairs from Trigg, his family's cocker spaniel, named after his dad's favourite character in *Only Fools and Horses*. "See you at school tomorrow."

"Not if I see you first!"

Troy slammed the door and they drove off, Queen's greatest hits playing as usual in the Escort's tape deck. Troy glanced over his shoulder as Freddie informed them that another one had bitten the dust, Matt waving from beneath the bowlplex's neon sign, the rubber Batman still in his hand.

There was no one else there, not even under the street light. Slack Mouth had gone.

2.

Bryan wasn't at school the next day. Troy and Billy cycled round to his place on the way home, expecting to find him propped up on the sofa watching *Rentaghost* or something, but Mrs Newton answered the door. That alone should've told them something was wrong. She was usually at work by now.

Bryan was in bed, lying on his back. He looked sick, really sick, his face chalk-white, his messy brown hair slicked across his scalp with sweat. He still hadn't reached home when his mum returned from work the previous night, and she'd started to call around, checking to see if he'd gone back with anyone else after the party. She'd tried Billy's place first – the two of them having been inseparable since primary school, despite Bill's constant teasing – but there'd been no answer. Billy told her they'd visited his grandparents on the way home from the bowling alley, stopping for a cup of tea, which was too much information, but Billy never knew when to shut up, even at the best of times.

It turned out Mrs Newton stopped her call-around soon after that anyway. There was a knock on the door, and she'd found Jim – the Newtons' elderly neighbour – holding an unconscious Bryan in his arms. He'd been walking his dog with his wife, Beryl, and had found Bryan slumped in the lane behind the bowlplex, completely sparked out, his bike next to him. Jim had carried him home, Beryl wheeling the bike while their dog yapped and pulled against its leash. Bryan eventually came round as Jim laid him on the sofa, murmuring all kinds of nonsense about Batman and Matt and something about a lightsaber, of all things. Bryan didn't even like *Star Wars;* he was a Trekkie through and through.

His mum called the doctor, but they couldn't find anything wrong with him, saying it was probably a virus. Doctors *always* said it was a virus when they didn't know what was wrong. They'd prescribed paracetamol and told Mrs Newton to phone back if Bryan's condition didn't improve within a few days.

"I should phone back now," she said as they stood in Bryan's bedroom, a dog-eared *Octopussy* poster above his bed, Roger Moore's eyebrow cocked as if 007 also distrusted the old quack's opinion. "He's barely said a word."

She sighed, shoving her hands into the tabard she wore for the cleaning job she performed when she wasn't working at the Raglan Arms, the pub where she had first met Bryan's dad and where she'd heard he'd done a runner years later.

Neither Troy nor Billy knew what to say, but she spared their embarrassment by flashing a sad smile before offering them a glass of squash. "See if you can get any sense from him," she said as she left the room. "I'll see if we've got any biscuits. Think there's some Jammie Dodgers in the tin."

"Bry?" Troy asked, stepping closer to the bed. "Bryan, you okay?"

"'Course, he's not okay, you idiot," Billy hissed, genuine worry written over his face. "Look at him."

"Look at yourself, Zitface," Bryan whispered back without opening his eyes. "Just try not to break the mirror, yeah?"

"Oi," Billy said, breaking into a grin and dropping down onto the bed. "You're supposed to be sick."

"Only sick of you." He tried to laugh, but the laugh turned into a cough, dry and harsh. Bryan's mum appeared at the door as if summoned, holding a tray with three glasses of Ribena and a plate of biscuits.

"I told you to sit up," she said, plonking the tray on Bryan's bedside cabinet, almost knocking his Snoopy lamp over the edge. Bryan loved that lamp, the last present his dad gave him before disappearing from his life. Billy teased him for still having it beside his bed, but Bryan didn't care, even though the paint on Snoopy's bulbous nose was peeling off and Woodstock was missing an eye.

"Here," Mrs Newton said, Bill jumping up from the bed as she fussed with Bryan's pillows, propping her son up. "There, that's better. Have a drink."

She leant over, picked up a glass of squash from the tray and put it to his lips.

"Mum," he moaned, grabbing hold of the glass himself with shaking hands. "I can do it. I'm not a baby."

"You're *my* baby," she reminded him, brushing damp hair out of his eyes. "And always will be, whether you like it or not."

She straightened, looking down at her son with concerned eyes, and turned, absently switching on the Snoopy light to illuminate the biscuits. "Sorry, there's only Rich Tea. His lordship must have scoffed all the Jammie Dodgers when I wasn't looking."

"I didn't!"

"Well, it wasn't me."

"Rich Tea are great," Troy lied, but there was no need to be rude. "Thank you, Mrs Newton."

"Yeah," Bill echoed. "Thank you."

"My pleasure," she replied, her hands back in her housecoat as she left the door. "Just don't keep him chatting all evening, okay? He needs to sleep."

"We won't, Mrs Newton," they called in unison before their heads snapped back to their ill friend.

"Jesus Christ, Bryan," Billy exclaimed as soon as she was gone. "What happened?"

Bryan shrugged, taking another sip from his squash. "Dunno."

"You don't know?" Troy said. "You were found lying on the ground."

"And you look like shit," Billy added.

"Bill!"

"Well, he does."

"I can't remember," Bryan said, twisting to put his glass back on the tray.

Billy jumped to take it from him, placing it next to the untouched biscuits. "Nothing at all?"

Bryan shook his head. "No. One minute I was riding home, and then…"

"Then what?" Troy prompted.

Bryan rubbed his head. "I really don't feel very well."

Billy plopped back down on the bed beside him. "Then what, Bry?"

"Then I was on the sofa, Mum fussing over me."

"What about the lightsabers?"

Bryan looked at Bill as if he'd gone ga-ga. "Lightsabers?"

"Your mum says you were talking about them when you came round."

"Why would I be talking about lightsabers?"

"Because you're a nerd."

"*You're* a nerd!"

"Will you two knock it off?" Troy said, turning his back on them and walking over to Bryan's desk, which – as usual – was covered with their friend's drawings of his favourite superheroes copied from a pile of old comics. "This is important."

"Not as important as Bryan's boyfriend," Bill said.

Troy sighed, picking up a ragged copy of *Transformers* and flicking through the pages as they bickered.

"I haven't got a boyfriend!"

"But you want one," Bill teased. "Why else would you call for him in your sleep?"

"Who?"

"Matt. Your mum said you were moaning his name when they brought you home. 'Oh, Matt, Matty, Maaatt.'"

There was a whoomph as Bryan chucked his pillow at Bill, not that it shut him up. Nothing shut Billy up.

"That's probably what happened."

"What?"

"You were dreaming about your first date on the way home and came off your bike, knocking yourself out."

"Shut up."

Bill sniggered, repeating Matt's name over and over, but Troy wasn't listening. He was staring at a page in the comic, an advert in the middle of the Machine Man story near the back. He'd seen the same poster the previous night on a T-shirt that was far too small for its wearer.

"What if that's not what Bryan was saying," he asked, still staring at the picture of Michael J. Fox.

"Huh?"

Troy turned back to them, holding up the page. "What if he was saying 'Marty'?"

Bill frowned, obviously thinking Troy had gone nuts. "Why would he?"

Troy took a step closer to them, still clutching the comic. "There was a kid outside the bowlplex last night, watching us in the arcade. Watching us leave."

"Wearing a *Back to the Future* T-shirt," Bryan said quietly, his eyes slipping out of focus.

"So?" Bill asked.

"He grabbed me," Bryan said, his voice wavering as he started to remember. "In the lane. It really hurt."

"When he grabbed you?"

Bryan swallowed, shaking his head. "No. When they..." His voice trailed off, the colour fading from already pale features. "They..."

"There was more than one of them?" Bill asked, picking up on the word.

Bryan nodded. "The boy..."

"In the T-shirt?"

"And a woman. She was holding something bright... really bright."

Now there was no teasing. Bill leaned in closer, concerned for a friend he cared for more than he'd ever admit. "What did they do to you, Bryan? Did they hurt you?"

Tears filled Bryan's eyes. "I don't know," he said, sniffing. "I can't remember."

"Hey, it's all right," Billy said, clasping Bryan's hand. "We'll work it out, won't we, Troy?"

He looked up when there was no response. "Troy."

Troy still didn't answer. He was just staring at them both. No, that wasn't it. He wasn't staring at *them*, but the wall *behind* them, the wall beside Bryan's bed.

"What?" Bill asked, glancing over his shoulder. "What is it?"

"Your shadow," Troy said quietly.

"What about it?"

"Bryan hasn't got one."

"What?" Bill yelped, leaping up from the bed as if scolded.

"But I've got to have a shadow," Bryan said, waving a hand at the wall, only there was nothing there. Billy's shadow was where it should be, as was Troy's when he stepped into the light to test his theory, but Bryan's had vanished completely.

3.

"He's a vampire," Billy squeaked.

"I'm not a vampire," Bryan insisted, but Billy was already counting a list on his fingers.

"You're as white as a sheet, look like Eddie Munster, and probably have fangs. Go on, show us your teeth. I bet my entire Hammer collection you have fangs."

"Will you keep your voice down," Troy hissed. "His mum will hear."

"Good. Someone has to do something before Nosferatu over there drains our blood!"

"Shut up, prat-face," Troy said, picking up Snoopy and waving the light in front of Bryan. It gave the same result, whatever the angle. No shadow. No shadow at all.

"Why's it doing that?" Bryan sobbed. "What's happened to me?"

Troy shot a look at Billy, almost challenging him to double down on the Dracula bullshit. When no more nonsense issued from Bill's mouth – miracles *did* happen, after all – Troy told them about Slack Mouth and the shadow that didn't fit. It sounded bonkers, but nowhere near as crazy as Bryan inexplicably losing his shadow, or the thought that occurred to Troy as he spoke. People got mugged all the time in the lane behind the bowlplex, their wallets and Walkmen stolen. What if the same happened to Bryan, but instead of a few five-pound notes wrapped in faux leather or a portable tape player, it had been his *shadow* that had been stolen?

4.

Maybe they should've gone to Bryan's mum. That would've been the smart choice for many, many reasons, but there was no way she would've let Bryan go with them.

Instead, they waited until it was time for her to head off for her job at the Raglan Arms, making the boys promise her they'd stay with Bryan and call if his condition got any worse.

It certainly didn't get any better, especially when he pulled on a sweater and struggled to get his antique bike out of the shed. In the end, Billy was forced to help him when it became blindingly obvious that Bryan could barely open the door, let alone lift the cheap frame over the tools and black sacks that littered the floor. Cycling to Matt's house was even worse, Bryan weaving across the pavement as if drunk, slowing their convoy down to a crawl. Troy told him to go home, but he wouldn't, not until they worked out what was wrong with him. Bryan had guts, that was for sure, but Troy couldn't help but feel a shiver every time they rode under a streetlamp and the yellow beam picked out the shadow of Bryan's bike, but never its rider.

5.

Matt thought they were joking when they explained what had happened, but couldn't argue that something was very wrong when they made Bryan stand under the light in his bedroom. He was still shooting glances at Bryan's lack of a shadow when Troy asked to see the picture Matt's brother had taken the previous night.

"The Polaroid?"

"Just show me, will you?"

And there he was, Slack Mouth, all the way in the background, his face bleached out in the spotlight from above, although there was no way of checking whether his shadow looked dodgy, not at the angle the photo was taken.

"Do you know who it is?" Matt asked, but Troy shook his head. Bryan said nothing, looking ready to drop, but Billy thought he recognised him.

"From school?"

"Yeah. But not in our year. Older than us."

"Older like my brother?" Matt asked.

They got lucky with Dan, who was working on his motorbike in the garage. Yeah, he recognised him all right, the freakazoid. Slack Mouth's real name turned out to be Eric Cropp, a real loner, according to Matt's brother. The kid never had any friends, which wasn't surprising as he smelled as bad as he looked, and he looked as sick as hell.

"Missed loads of school as far as I can remember," Dan said, glancing up at Bryan, who was leaning against a worktable covered in tools. "You're not looking too clever yourself, kiddo. Should you even be out?"

"Do you know where he lives?" Troy asked, ignoring Dan's question, even though Bryan was in no condition to answer himself.

Dan scratched his chin, stubble rasping under oily fingers. "Sure. At least, I did. I doubt they've moved. But I warn you, if you think Eric's a freak, wait until you meet his mum."

6.

Dan was right; the Cropps hadn't moved, although, given

the state of the place they called home, none of them could work out why.

Troy, Billy, Bryan *and* Matt had biked across Fairfield Common to get to their estate, although Bryan soon had to resort to pushing his mount rather than riding it. By the time they reached Shepton Street, he could barely breathe and was forced to sit on the side of the kerb, gasping for air like a fish floundering out of water.

"Should we call his mum?" Matt asked.

"Do *you* want to explain to her what he's doing here?" Billy replied. "I don't know about you, but I like my knackers where they are!"

"I'll be fine," Bryan wheezed, his voice barely louder than a whisper. "You go. I'll be right behind you."

"It's all right for him," Billy complained as they left their bikes with the rapidly fading Bryan and crept deeper into the rundown estate. "But what are we looking for, anyway? Do any of us know what we're doing?"

"No," Troy said plainly, "but I don't think any of this is all right for Bryan. He looks like death."

To be honest, Eric Cropp's house didn't look much better. In fact, even calling it a house seemed like a kindness. The place was little more than a shack, a prefab bungalow built after the war, just one of the hundreds that still dotted Drakeford despite only being a temporary measure to the housing crisis of three decades before. Most had been pulled down, and the vast majority of those that lingered here on Teal Estate were well cared for, if a little twee. What was it with prefab owners and garden gnomes? It was like an epidemic of the bloody things, all red cheeks and pointy hats.

But there weren't any gnomes in the Cropps' garden. Actually, there wasn't much of a garden at all, just an impressive collection of dandelions and nettles. The prefab itself wasn't much better. Its flat roof sagged in the middle and what was left of its once cheerful paintwork was now chipped and weathered. It was like something out of the horror films Billy pretended to watch – covering up the fact that he was scared of just about everything, especially that Bryan might one day realise just how much he liked him – but maybe the comparison had less to do with the décor and more with the blood-curdling screams that rattled the grimy windowpanes from the inside.

"Maybe I'll go check on Bryan," Billy said as the first yell rang out.

"You're coming with us," Troy commanded, grabbing Billy's arm and dragging him towards a window that looked into a gloomy living room. The threadbare curtains were drawn, but there was enough of a crack that they could peer in, although what they saw made no sense at all.

Eric Cropp was slumped on a rickety settee, his feet resting on a flocked pouffe missing its tassels. At least, they were *supposed* to be resting. The kid Troy still thought of as Slack Mouth was squirming in his seat, kicking at the stool with one foot, the other clamped tight by a woman who was taking a sewing needle to her boy's heel.

She was sewing something to Slack Mouth's bare foot, something that had no place being in her hands.

"Is that…" Billy breathed, before repeating the query one more time for good measure: "Is that…"

"Bryan's shadow," Troy confirmed.

"But it can't be! That's insane. That's… that's…"

Words failed Billy for the first time in his life, but no one could blame him. The shadow, dark in the stark glow of the prefab's fluorescent lighting, writhed and pulled, desperate to break free of Mrs Cropp's grip. Bizarre though the sight was, there was no doubt they were looking at Bryan's missing silhouette, a shade that was as scared as their friend was sick.

"Hold still," they heard the woman croak as she continued to jab the needle into Slack Mouth's foot, sewing the stolen shadow into place with a thread the colour of the night sky. She was as thin as her son was chunky, arms gaunt but stronger than they looked. There was no way either Slack Mouth or the shadow were breaking her clutches.

"I don't want to do this anymore," the older boy wailed, his voice muffled by the window. "It hurts too much."

"And it'll hurt all the more if we don't get this thing attached before it fades away altogether. You know how sick you'll get."

"But I don't want it. I don't want it. It's not fair."

"Quit your complaining. I'm doing this for you."

"No, you're not," the boy howled, digging his fingers into the settee's arm as the needle looped through his bloodied skin, fixing the shadow in place. "If it wasn't for you, I'd still have *my* shadow. I wouldn't need another one and they wouldn't keep fading away. It hurts, Mum. It really, really hurts."

"Stop being so ungrateful. I made the deal for both of us, remember. Think what we got in return. We'll never go hungry again and no one can ever touch us, not with his protection. It's for you, my love. All of it."

And still, she sewed, the needle going in, the needle coming out, Bryan's shadow unable to escape despite clawing at the air with transparent fingers.

The boys jumped at the sound of a voice behind them, the shadow's previous owner hauling himself past the gate they'd left open. "What is it? What do you see?"

"Jesus, Bryan!" Billy shouted out. "Don't *do* that."

Troy shushed him, but it was too late. On the other side of the window, Mrs Cropp's head snapped around, revealing a haggard face that twisted into a snarl.

"What's that?" she hissed. "Who's there?"

Bryan swore under his breath, and all hell broke loose.

7.

It was almost as if the shadow heard Bryan's voice, weak though it was. The dislocated shade jolted in the direction of the window, pulling Eric heel-first from the settee. His not inconsiderable backside made contact with the filthy carpet, his knee cracking into his mother's chin as he was dragged past the old crone. She cried out, dropping the needle and thread as the shadow shot forwards like a greyhound that had caught whiff of a rabbit. Eric squealed as he was dragged across the small space, while, on the other side of the window, Troy and the others leapt back in the nick of time, Billy grabbing Bryan as the shadow swept through the window like a ghost slipping through a wall. Slack Mouth followed a second later, but the lump of a boy didn't glide effortlessly through the glass pane. Instead, he smashed through the glass, screaming as razor-sharp shards flew everywhere at once. He landed in the middle of a particularly impressive crop of stinging nettles, turning the air blue as he thrashed around in pain. The shadow, suddenly anchored in place by the flailing brute, reached for Bryan, who, scared out of his wits, scuttled back like a spider, Billy right beside him.

Troy couldn't tell who was screaming more, his friends or poor stung Eric. Or maybe it was the shadow which, with one last titanic effort, hurled itself at Bryan. Eric yowled as the stitching broke, blood squirting from his punctured skin. The shadow flew forward as if launched from a cannon. It barrelled into Bryan, knocking him from Billy, who cried Bryan's name in terror as his unrequited crush tumbled away, a rolling mass of arms and legs, some solid, some see-through.

But when they came to rest in the light from the shattered window, Bryan's shadow was where it should have always been, perfectly mirroring Bryan's shake of his head as he tried to clear his terrified thoughts.

Troy wished he had a clear head himself. It was all too much. Eric was rolling around in the vicious nettles, clutching his bleeding foot and surrounded by the detritus he'd brought through the window with him: the contents of a table that had, until a few minutes ago, rested beneath the windowsill. Anyone else would have perched a lamp on the table, or maybe a cheap vase from Woolworths, but not the Cropps.

No, they had a statue of a creature that looked like it would be more at home gracing the cover of a Heavy Metal album.

The figure had the head and legs of a goat but the body of a man, bat-like wings spread out wide from its broad back, one still connected, the other now snapped off and lying beside a pair of thankfully extinguished black candles.

Strange though this all was, it did nothing to prepare them for the frankly pant-wetting sight of Eric's emaciated mother charging around the side of the crumbling prefab, screaming bloody murder with a knife held above her head. The weapon's blade was burning bright, gleaming like a torch as the woman brought it slashing down towards Bryan's feet. Billy didn't even hesitate. With a cry of defiance, he threw himself forward, slamming into the woman, their bodies connecting with a dry crunch. Mrs Cropp toppled back, the knife, still shining, skittering from her hand.

"No!" she screeched, kicking Billy aside with more force than any of them would've thought possible. Billy flew across the garden, slamming into a partly demolished fence. Mrs Cropp didn't even look up. She scrabbled towards the blade on all fours, cursing as a young hand scooped it up.

"Troy!" Matt shouted, tossing the weapon over the woman's head as they had played piggie-in-the-middle with Bryan the previous night. Troy reached up without thinking, snatching the knife's handle as if the blade was made of rubber rather than shining metal sharp enough to remove fingers.

Eric's mother whirled around and lunged at Troy, but he had already twisted, throwing the blade at Billy.

"What the hell!" Bill exclaimed, his former bravery forgotten, but wise enough not to catch a spinning knife, especially one glowing like starlight. The tip of the blade thudded to the ground and, barking in triumph, the old woman dropped upon it, clutching for the handle.

She never found it. Instead, a set of much younger fingers closed around the knife, fingers that until recently had been trembling and clammy. Bryan pulled the blade clear before she could grab it and, for a moment, Troy thought he was going to bring the knife slamming down into the woman's hunched back. That's what would've happened in a film, the gutsy hero dispatching the bad guy in the final act, but Bryan was a fourteen-year-old kid from Drakeford, and none of his favourite superheroes ever took a life. Not that there was time to be righteous as Mother Cropp – that's what they would take to calling her in years to come – launched herself at Bryan, knocking him onto his back.

"Give it to me," the old crone hissed, scratching at Bryan as he struggled to wriggle free. "Give it to me, right this minute."

Troy and Matty grabbed the woman at the same time, trying to pull her back, although she remained powerful despite resembling Skeletor after a crash diet. Billy yanked at Bryan's sweater, doing his best to drag him from beneath the witch, because that's what she had to be, right?

"Where's the knife?" Troy yelled.

"I don't know!" Bryan called back, grabbing hold of the old woman's wrists to stop her from clawing the eyes from his head.

The answer came with the song of the luminous blade slicing through the air, a sound that registered seconds before Mother Cropp howled in pain.

She rolled onto her back, looking up at her son, who loomed over them, the knife in his hand.

"What have you done?" she wailed. "What have you done?" Eric ignored her as he stamped down as if crushing a spider.

But it wasn't a spider that wriggled and pulled under his heel; it was his mother's freshly severed shadow.

The old woman wailed in agony as Eric reached down, grabbing the squirming shadow by its scrawny diaphanous neck and dragging it up from the ground in a thick fist.

"Eric," she pleaded, trying to grab hold of his legs to haul herself back to her shadowless feet. "Don't do this. Please."

He stepped back, taking her shadow with him, and she crumpled to the ground, any strength she'd once had instantly deserting her.

"I don't know, Mum," Eric said, peering at the writhing shade as if it was a goldfish he'd won at the fair. "Maybe this one will stick. Maybe this one will grow on me."

His slack mouth turned up for the first time since Troy had seen him skulking around the bowlplex. It wasn't a pleasant sight, but the relief in his eyes was evident.

Eric sniffed, looking down at his mum, who had passed out, the pain she'd inflicted on so many finally overwhelming her as it had Bryan the evening before.

"Sorry about yesterday," the older lad said, looking directly at Bry. "Really, I am. She'll never make me do anything else, I promise. Not ever."

The boys had formed a ring around the woman, who was lying unmoving in the scruff, eyes fluttering beneath paper-thin lids.

"So what now?" Billy asked, too shaken to realise that everyone could see him holding Bryan's hand.

Troy didn't know, for once, although the boy he'd dubbed Slack Mouth had one final favour to ask – which was a bit of a cheek when you considered everything that had happened in the last twenty-four hours.

Still, Eric Cropp held up his mother's wriggling shadow and asked it all the same:

"Don't suppose any of you kids know how to sew, do you?"

Saturday Morning

THE BEARDED MAN WHO DOESN'T KNOW ANY STORY TO TELL HIS CHILDREN WAS ONCE JOHN.

ANNA SMITH SPARK

The man says: It is my fault, of course. I say to her, "It is my fault, of course." She says, "Your fault, yes."

I have the empty beds. And I remember from her noise now, the grunting noise she made and I made at their conceiving – I remember. sweat, and her eyes fixed closed, and I thought I'd never manage, and the smell that came afterwards that was a dirt smell I thought would not be the same. Her white nightdress, good white lace tangled up around her waist. I have not lost my passion: I never had passion in cold or heat. Whores, yes – once or twice – or more – I'm a normal man, knowing, and my friends at varsity have had whores, and my friends whom I knew from their parents since we were children – but I do not think of being children – I do not think of my children. My friends, after a long evening, come up here, over here, in here with us like every man does, and I was willing, or, yes, I went alone often, after they took me for the first time or the third time, I am not an unnatural man, you understand, I know what to do with a woman, long hair on a pillow, crooked white arms, legs spread beneath a worn sheet. But with her – and she didn't know what she was doing, I expected her to know, somehow, because she was a woman, and I, without the help of those women – I thought it would not be the same. Trembling, thus, doubting, in their conception. She made them, I did little in their making.

She has not cried like this before, at least I haven't heard her except once on the other side of a closed door when she said it was nothing and I didn't speak of it. We have a good marriage. I am a good husband. She is a good wife. So I — but I don't see — what else — an absurdity, I said to her, a man has control, does he not, over his house, and his family, and his dog, and his servants? Come out, I shouted. Come out! Or it's the slipper! This is you being naughty children, you're upsetting your mother, she's upset with me. Come out, this isn't what my children do. There was silence, in the silence I heard my wife weeping, I heard the coal waggon, I heard the dustmen in the street. Come out, I shouted. Or it's the slipper for you. I am a good man, a kind man, a kind father, and a man has to have authority in his own house, you see? Come out, I thought it was funny, I have only tried to make you laugh with me…

It wasn't funny, I knew it, but look, I was – like the way you children play…

And now I have nothing left against my ruins, and my ruins are all that there is of me.

She wore a white dress that night, and a white dress when we married, and a white nightdress of good lace those nights they were conceived. I shall grow old now without seeing her truly. Like a white frightened bird, she retreats away.

"I knew," she says, "what might happen," and I knew. But I didn't ever say. She caught a shadow in the window: I did believe it – but: my young daughter! Every man knows what that shadow is. Feels it breathe behind him. The shadow has to be pretended away.

Not my daughter. Not my daughter. No one shall have her but I. She will remain here, dry house, cold dry sorrows, dull hands dull head.

But if it came to it – even for her – I would not fight him.

We went out that night; she wore a white dress, white as milk, white as teeth, white as snow. My medicine was white. White sauce on the fish, with parsley; white wine in clear glasses. White wine is yellow, not white. White snow on the ground. White stars overhead. The dog had peed in the yard where I chained it. Dog piss on the snow is the colour white wine is. A happy evening: myself, friends from the city, their wives, one I learn later is pregnant with her first child. She is the only one of the women wearing a white dress. Then the women go into the drawing room, we men talking over the port. Mine host, genial, port in a crystal decanter heavier than the one we have at home, better port, too. But his tie is not so well tied as mine. After all that. Our host had a brother who was in the Royal Sussex. His portrait is in the dining room and the decanter is kept under it. My glass is slightly smudgy in one place. Badly dried. Poorly trained servants here. We talk about the proper things.

We go home later than I had intended. I had intended to leave earlier, come back to unchain the dog, peep in at the children. It had been only gentle snow, I was hoping it would snow further, for in the morning if it was deeper the children could all three and the dog go out in it. I was happiest myself as a child when it snowed. One street to run home, the snow has stopped, she tried to be laughing when we went out, because of the snow, but I think all the time she might be angry with me. "It will be a good dinner," I said when we walked there. She said, "Yes." Running home, the snow is all gone from the streets.

Her lips are white like the medicine and like the milk and like her dress.

But it was meant as a joke and a game. I love my children. I am a good father and I play funny games with my children. Come out, I shout around the house when we come home. Come out or it's the slipper for you if you don't come out now. Can't you see your mother is crying. You've made her cry, you beasts.

I confess it, I was afraid.

Around the children, of the children – I have always been very afraid.

When we were first courting.

I hurried to ask her, before the others, the same childhood friends. There was no time to wonder. I beat them all to ask her. Those same friends with the sharing of downy-haired fine white arms, yes, shameless, yes, all of us. But it's not until you see a woman that you realise what a wife should be. I made haste to beat them all, she was there in the parlour, tea and toast after. I prepared my face at the door; when I had asked it, dared to ask it, she prepared her face also to give her reply, there was time for that, her reply, from her prepared face. Thus we must be courting then. I remember one time in our courtship – we walked in Kensington Gardens – why Kensington Gardens? – I heard a baby crying behind a shrub pitilessly, its nurse trying to shush it then its nurse ignored it, that also I confess frightened me and frightened her more, we hurried away, her skirt I remember caught up a branch all laced with dead leaves. After we had walked a long time we went into a tearoom because I was cold in my hands, we had walked too long in silence till the silence tired her out. "Let's stop for a cup of tea and something to eat," she said to me. The streets were suddenly made narrow and empty, nothing, how foolish not to be able to take a woman to a tearoom! And when we found one at last, she found it, it was tattered and going out of fashion even then, very ornamental in the way of overdoing over-rotting things, "Oh, very Beardsley," she said and I confess I did not know what she meant. The window was full of plants with thick green leaves. We sat in a crowded corner with the windowpane running with damp from our breath, all the crowds seated there breathing damp breath, they all seemed to be watching me and her prepared face and my prepared face. I ordered tea and cakes for us, the tea came in a pot with a Chinese scene painted in blue but the lid was chipped, but her cup made a lovely sound, like a bell, when she replaced it in her saucer. She didn't eat much, but she crumbled two cakes one after the other into dry sandy crumbs on her yellow plate. Crumbs of pink icing on her red lips, on her white hands, on her yellow plate.

I have pretended many years that I will one day win her. I admit, to myself – I will never win her. I was not made to win her.

Then those nights in her lace nightgown, caught up around her waist, in the dark, that woman smell after that I think should not be here in this room with us.

A girl first. A girl. Oh! I was delighted: her bunched-up red face, she did look like a cauliflower as my wife said, her red tiny fists. She looked angry. "Baby girls do look angry," my wife said. They put her in white too. I had been pacing long in the hall trying to make of it all nothing of importance. The servant girl Liza hid somewhere below. She was a child herself. The fog was yellow around the windows, I felt as though I was not there but somewhere very far away. I remembered that day when I tried to court her. The other men who were slower than I had been. For weeks after she was hanging in such a way that she might vanish at any moment. And that, I fear, was in some way my fault also.

I am a married man with wife and child, respectable; I have a house off Bloomsbury Square. The man at the next desk to me in my office has a wife and his brother is in the Royal Sussex. If my daughter dies of mumps or measles or any of those other commonplace drownings – it will be my fault, of course.

I am a man. I know the shadow that will come in through the window one day.

A daughter.
Milk and water.
Oh she oughter.

I court her.
I caught her.

We return to Kensington Gardens for a walk: it is summer now. A woman runs past us, her face and her eyes are very red. "Good grief, this place is a madhouse," I say loudly to my wife, who must be frightened, "they need to start keeping a policeman at the gates. These women shouldn't be allowed in these respectable places." "We should go home," my wife says, she sounds frightened, yes, "let us go home now." We are by the Long Water, we have to go fast fast slow up towards Hyde Park Place. "Shall we stop at that tearoom we found?" I ask her, for I am trying to reassure her all is well. She looks blank; she does not remember. She says, "No, let us go home." By the gate into the Bayswater Road a bird sings.

A boy. A son. An heir. She suspected, she says, when we walked in Kensington Gardens, she saw a boy's face, she says, like a cabbage, in the Long Water that day. She says a boy is different to a girl and I say – "Well, yes, it is, you know," I say, but she, she looks at me. A son and a daughter. And a son is yet more fragile than a daughter, it seems.

I write with extra care in my ledgers at my desk in my office. I wipe my pen nib with extra care, I am careful with the blotting paper, I accept a second glass of port to discuss the proper things. I call the serving girl Liza "the servants" when I am out discussing the proper things. I visit a woman with long hair on the pillow, brown downy hair on her thin arms. I read the stocks and shares every day.

Thus, if I do these things properly, my son will live. A man's son lives.

Then another. Two boys. I am blessed in my life and there is great happiness, such joy in my house those evenings. Yet still, after they have survived and are old enough, they will survive long enough to become my children: I am ashamed and afraid of them. The man at the next desk to mine – the bigger desk, better light, better shade on his lamp there, I swear the leather cover on his ledger is a better shade of red – he had a brother in the Royal Sussex but he – he does not have sons.

I am growing old, to have three children, two sons. I have done what I could and should.

The man at the next desk to mine had a brother in the Royal Sussex. When I was a child there was a beggar who would sit in the street, he had one leg and one arm and one eye and he had been a soldier. One day the police arrested him. I saw a man beat his son in the street once. The man was drunk. The boy was drunk, though he was a boy. He lay in the street with his head cut open. I thought then, how can a man do such a thing? I thought, but a man must have authority. I was too timid to raise a hand to my sons, and now my sons have flown away. Come out, I shouted. Or it's the slipper! Come out now! Even the dog, when I chained it up: I sat in the hall and bit my own fist.

I am not an unnatural man. But I think, I think… I have

never dared to pursue my wife, I have never presumed myself anything more than I am. Before her, I must pretend. Before my children, especially my sons. And oh they do love me, do respect me, as she does. Though she is not won. She married me in her white dress, and in her white nightgown with white lace at her breast and her wrists and her waist, and she must respect me then. I was the first, I hurried to ask her before the others, she set her face, I set my face, I watched her hands move in just the way they moved later crumbling pink-iced cakes upon a yellow plate, in just the way now they crumple upon a counterpane on a child's bed – she could have rejected me, if she was not won by me. She could have said nothing when I spoke.

I could have turned back. Let another man on foot get there before me. And I could go now with my life unchanged, and fuss only about smudges on a glass in another man's dining room. I could have turned away, unset my face. I too need not have spoken. I was not made to be in the Royal Sussex or to lose a limb in foreign dust, I was not made to sit even at the larger lighter desk. I was not made, then, to be a father to three children, to two sons.

I was not afraid when she told me that they were gone. There. It is said. She told me they were gone; I knew, as she knew, where they had gone. We have both been children, and we know. And I was not afraid. I was not grieved. Though I told her I was grieved. Though it is my fault they have gone.

I sit at my desk, with my ledgers and my pens. Frowning in the evening at a smudge on a port glass, with my tie uncomfortable that I fiddle with and make worse when I go out to piss.

I grew old even as I was a child: they will never endure to grow old.

Excitement! Derring-do! Fighting! Heave a cutlass! Ready! George Darling in an adventure with pirates and Indians and crocodiles and wild beasts and flamingos!

And let us add also dinosaurs; ancient Egyptians; dragons; wizards; tigers; long-beard dwarfish heroes, elf-mocked, axe-aged; cats that dance and sing...

I, George Darling, I shall be the hero, I shall dress in scarlet, I shall take the centre of the stage and strut there, I shall stand upon a rock above deep caves where the sea in secret chambers echoes, I shall crown myself a king with garlands of brown seaweed, I shall hear the mermaids distant sing.

And I was too frightened for adventure. I should only drown if a mermaid ever sang to me. I was not born a hero, I was not meant nor taught such things.

But my sons...

They shall dare to do, to be, to speak entire. They shall presume everything. Their lives will be measured in sword thrusts, in glories, in battles won, mouths kissed. They will not be – they were not – afraid.

They will not through force or through desire—

they will not become mere men.

Thus: I am proud of my sons.

And my daughter. Yes, I confess, sometimes I... she takes, compared to my wife, my sons, she takes...

If she had come later, second or third, after a son. Then, I think, it would have been different. All of it, would have been different.

But: my daughter, then. She will never grunt and groan as my wife has been forced to. She will never lie with her hair loose on a pillow, a nightgown tangled around her waist. She has been caught and won the whole of her, she is a mother and yet – she is untouched by hands such as mine and will remain untouched; she will never stoop to such as me. She will have her prince, her children, without enduring such as me.

Thus: I am proud, yes. Beneath the grief and shame that I wear outwardly, I am filled with pride for my children. Look, I would cry to the crowds that flow over the London bridges, look, behold: what I have done. See what I have done.

They will not grow old, they will not become hollowed out or empty. I wear a disguise of grief and penitence, but in my heart I wear rejoicing.

So bright, so bright, the stars that night – for them!

Newborn stars that night – for them!

You who flow over the London bridges, you great crowd there, so many – you must regret, as I regret, all your grief, like my grief – that you could you did not dare not be – as them.

My sons: who will not suffer the disappointment of becoming men.

I will sleep in the dog's kennel.

I will sit all day in the dog's kennel.

In the dog's kennel I will talk and eat and shit.

Not in her bed with the white sheets and her loose hair. In the dog's kennel I will sit to crawl my penmanship in blue ink black ink blank ink in red leather ledgers the smell in the leather of the shambles yard the smell of dinners talking of the proper things the smell of women's parted thighs on white sheets, I will write those columns of long numbers summed to nothing one two skip a few ninety-nine one hundred I will clean copy draft clean copy at my desk which is gloomy with the lamp that is not as bright as my friend's lamp because he had a brother in the Royal Sussex even though I have sired children.

My disguise. "Keep the Dog far hence, that's friend to children!"

I will be a man ruined. Act: the man ruined. Disguise myself as such a hollow thing. I, too, will not be a man as others are made men. She will sit in her chair, she will brush her hair, she will fasten a bracelet, sing. I hear her music from the room beyond my kennel: I shut my eyes, will not hear her music. Let the children in the crowd follow me, cheer, be understanding: if she turns her face to mine, I, the Dog, I will avert my gaze. "My sons," I will say only, "my sons, who will not grow old, who were not ever the wretchedness of men!"

My fault, of course. I own it.

That is the end.

And yet.

But yet.

Life is very long, life is a shadow merely. My life is long and dull.

I would want that. My children, my sons my daughter, I would want their lives to be long and grey and hollow and dull.

I would want them to go on, peaceful, bored, boring, questioning. Long, long, I would want them to go on.

I do not want the universe to shift and turn for them. I do not want the stars to be born and die. I do not want magic, glory, wonders, oh, I am sure such wonders of death and glory are wonderful things but for myself, the quiet, the crowd faceless eyeless that sweeps across the bridge. The man, old, balding, greying, unexcited, withered dugs, withered, flaccid manhood, and the regret. The quiet dull world of dare not and doubt and stale pink-iced cakes on yellow china, oh very Beardsley! Tea in a cracked cup, the smudge – so careless – of a maid's finger on the crystal of a glass, her cup when she replaced it rang on the saucer like a temple bell.

A whimper in dry silence. Nothing. Merely. Grow old, live long long into the shadows. Father sons yourselves in passionless embrace. I have never seen my own wife naked. Myself, naked, my female parts my male parts hanging flaccid, I have not seen myself naked these thirty years I think. Live on like that, long, long, long and dull with the dull repetitious nature a dog takes. Better than glorie and cannon is the ledger on the desk with gloomy lighting. Not the brilliance and the scarlet: blue ink, black ink, blank ink. Śūnyatā. Māyā. Honi soit qui mal y pense.

I lower myself to silence, creep upon the stage a few humble scenes. Be humble men. I do not regret nothing, no. But I have managed all without harm to much but me. There is no great tale of my life's thread, mere fragments, disconnected, fading voice of desk clerk, husband, father, son. I was not in a war, I was not burned, I have scuttled safe, self-doubting, always doubting, paced in gloom through empty streets. I have, I will – be safe. Though I will be tired, o'erlooked, forgotten, laughed at – I will stretch on. I grow old. I will grow old. I will feel and know and be these many fragmented things.

Some little peace. No little peace. Self-doubt, self-fear, meekness, self-loathing. I never dared. Thus – another's heart – I never dared to touch with bitterness or pain or grief. The Dog, that cur, mange-ridden, toothless, pissing, that's loyal old friend to greater men.

The man at the next desk to me had a brother in the Royal Sussex. He would be tall now and handsome almost I think as you. Come out! Come back! Or it's the slipper! Come back, grow up, grow old, dull, weary, tired, withered, inward outward dead. Do not strut upon the stage a hero. Play a few scenes that make some nameless faceless person laugh then swift forget. Tithonus without his handsome curl, grasshopper dried, old poor sybil-man, never kissed by woman's silvered love-dropped lips. A bearded man without a story for his children. A little, shrunken, failed and failing man, a cypher merely, straw and shadow, hollow, wordless—

who has not meant harm to anything.

The Land Between Her Eyelashes

RIO YOUERS

The recent rains had roused the back garden into verdant, tumbling chaos, with everything overgrown and overly colorful, the blooms so replete with hydration that they drooped heavily. Marcy believed she could curl one hand around their stems and feel the life pulsing through them. The trees, too, with their rich, dark trunks and abundant branches. They offered a great lacework of shade, while catching beats of sunlight on their many fabulous leaves.

"Isn't it beautiful?" Astrid asked. Her smile was another source of light, as engaging now as it had always been. Some things, Marcy reflected, were not so quickly diminished.

"It really is." Marcy brushed her hand through a cluster of foxgloves, as high as her shoulder. They swayed and dripped. A couple of bees circled indifferently. "And the smells. Everything... it's all so alive."

Astrid nodded, one arm looped through Marcy's, needing the younger woman's support as they walked through the garden. It was only a distance of fifty feet – give or take – between the back door and the little guest house, but it took almost three minutes to traverse it, due in part to Astrid's illness, but also to their meandering route around the overgrown foliage.

"It had all been so lackluster only weeks ago," Astrid noted, as they avoided the willow's spread, its vinelike branches brushing the ground. "The grass was yellow. Do you remember?"

"I do. That heatwave drained the life out of everything."

"It all came back, though."

They arrived at the small building, although it was actually quite large, Marcy noted – she'd only ever seen it from the main house before, tucked among the trees and shrubs. Astrid reached into the pocket of her dressing gown and took out a large set of keys, which she handed to Marcy.

"Three locks on this door. I honestly can't remember which keys open which locks. It'll be a matter of trial and error, I'm afraid." There was a hint of mischief in Astrid's eyes, although this was not unusual. She often wore the expression of a youth with a lifetime of impish adventure ahead of them, which was both heartbreaking and wonderful, as if her eyes, like her smile, hadn't received the same dreadful news as the rest of her body. "Have at her, Marcy. I'm in no hurry."

There were at least twenty keys on the three interlocked rings. Marcy regarded them with some bewilderment, then started with the first key in the first lock, working her way through them until she got a match. Astrid had dropped into a lawn chair positioned outside the guest house, content to survey her garden while Marcy worked. "The birds are so loud today," she remarked, cocking her head from side to side. At one point – Marcy had progressed to the third lock – she plucked a caterpillar from a nearby leaf and giggled as it crawled over and between her fingers, captivated by even the smallest of things.

After several minutes of trial and error, Marcy had all three locks unlatched. She wiped a mist of sweat from her forehead, then turned to help Astrid, who was rising with some difficulty out of the lawn chair.

"Thank you, Marcy," Astrid said, and a slight frown touched her brow. "Oh, I seem to have said that a lot to you over the years."

Marcy smiled. Being Astrid's primary caregiver paid the bills, but being her friend – and they'd become quite close in their time together – had given her so much more. Astrid had a way of making everything better. Maybe it was that she listened and cared. Or maybe it had something to do with that twinkle in her eye, an unquenchable enthusiasm for life that elevated everything around her.

"All these locks," Marcy said, gesturing at the guest house door. "What *do* you keep in here?"

"You'll see."

Marcy opened the door and both women stepped inside, one supporting the other. With no idea what to expect, Marcy was neither surprised nor disappointed to find nothing out of the ordinary. It was a functional, if slightly old-fashioned, guest room, the most modern thing being a digital alarm clock (unplugged) on the bedside table.

"This is… nice," Marcy said.

Astrid nodded, sat on the edge of the bed, and gestured at a door off to one side, in itself unremarkable except for the two locks that secured it.

"Be a dear," she said.

"More locks?"

"The last two." Astrid nodded at the jumble of keys still in Marcy's hand. "The padlock is a Yale, I believe. It should be stamped on the head of the key."

"That'll save me some time," Marcy said, and it did. She unclasped the padlock with the first Yale-stamped key she found, and had the second lock opened only a couple of minutes later.

"I'm getting good at this."

"Your reward awaits." Astrid stood up from the bed and crossed to the door, passing through a band of sunlight beaming in at the window, so fiercely bright that it rendered her, frail as she was, near invisible for a moment.

A room of wonders, although this was not obvious to begin with. There were a number of boxes placed on wall-to-wall shelves, in different shapes and sizes. A few were elegantly crafted wooden boxes, most were of the plain cardboard variety. Marcy looked at them, a bubble of curiosity rising inside her.

"My collection," Astrid said. She turned a slow circle with

her hands spread. "Knick-knacks, really, most of them useless, of value only to people who are willing to spend money on them. But they've brought me some pleasure over the years, and value is not only tied to money, as I'm sure you know."

"Yes," Marcy said. She noted that there were no windows in this room, only a bare bulb hanging from a cord in the middle of the ceiling. An air filtration system kept everything fresh and dry. "Well, you certainly have me intrigued, Astrid. Five locks... how could I not be?"

Astrid uttered a dry chuckle, one hand pressed to her chest to keep it from developing into a long, cackling cough. She steadied herself and crossed the room, selecting a long, thin box from the shelf.

"What's this?" Marcy asked, taking the box, although it wasn't heavy.

"Winston Churchill's cane," Astrid replied.

Marcy frowned, then lifted the lid off the box. Sure enough, there was a wooden cane inside, sitting on a bed of velvet. It had an ornate, varnished knop and a slightly worn tip.

"His actual cane? Or a replica?"

"His. One of many he owned." Astrid reached into the box, took out the cane, and gave it a gentlemanly twirl. "He gave some of them away, you know. This one was gifted to my Uncle Hartley, who lost his leg in World War Two."

Marcy smiled, taking the cane as Astrid handed it to her (and unable to resist giving it a gentlemanly twirl of her own). She shook her head, suitably impressed, and returned the cane to the box.

"Delightful," she said.

"Isn't it?" Astrid placed the box back on the shelf and walked over to another, this larger and too heavy to lift. She signaled Marcy closer, then lifted the flaps of the box. Both women peered inside.

"My brother's having this," Astrid said. "It belonged to a serial killer named Emory Grist, who was killed in a house fire in 1910, and who many people believe was Jack the Ripper."

It was a vintage typewriter in olive green, with bone-colored keys and U-shaped typebars that resembled a small ribcage. Marcy shuddered at the sight of it. She couldn't imagine even touching the machine, let alone using it to write with.

"It's a horrible thing," Marcy commented, stepping away so that she couldn't see it. "I apologize for being so frank."

"Not at all. I quite agree with you," Astrid said, closing the box. "My brother is welcome to it. He's always been an intolerable turd."

Marcy giggled, covering her mouth with one hand, and this got Astrid giggling, too. They were, for just a beat, like two girls sharing a naughty secret.

The moment passed – brief seconds, but altogether precious – then Marcy swiveled her head from side to side, regarding the stacked shelves. Her eyes shone, perhaps drawing on some of the wonder in this hidden, locked away room.

"Winston Churchill's cane, Jack the Ripper's typewriter. This is a veritable trove of curiosities." She looked at Astrid, one eyebrow raised. "What else do you have in here?"

Quite a lot, as it turned out. The two women spent the next forty minutes looking through the various boxes, uncovering rare items, from the enchanting (Benny Goodman's clarinet), to the lovely (Mae West's earrings), to the chilling (a lock of Ted Bundy's hair), to the comically absurd (Huggy Bear's sunglasses). Astrid was all out of breath before they got even halfway through, and had to retreat to the guest room and sit on the bed to recuperate.

"Do you need to go back to the house?" Marcy asked, sitting beside her. "Get all comfortable in your favorite chair? I'll fetch you a cold glass of lemonade and put *Bridgerton* on."

Astrid flushed and fanned at her collar. "Tempting, dear, but no. I have something in there for you."

"I really don't need anything."

"No, you don't, but you're getting something, just the same." Astrid smiled weakly and flapped a hand. "My whole family has been clamoring for this and that, putting their requests in. Jonathan wants the cane. Dolores wants Elvis's belt buckle. Honestly, they're like dogs, all of them, waiting to be fed."

Marcy wrinkled her nose and rubbed Astrid's shoulder tenderly.

"There's nothing like having your bones picked clean while you're still alive."

"I'm sure they just..." Marcy trailed off. She'd hoped to say something encouraging, but the only words she found sounded false, even to her. "They just want something to remember you by."

"Ted Bundy's hair?"

"Well, maybe not *that*."

"You're being kind." Astrid lowered her chin, looking down her nose at Marcy in a way that was both schoolmarmish and motherly. "They want the things they can sell. That's all they're interested in. Money."

"Well, I don't know about—"

"Ghouls, all of them. Bah!" Astrid flapped her hand again, then looked Marcy deep in the eye. All her emotions were present – her own room of wonders. "But not you, Marcy. You've been a good friend, and you've looked after me these past three years, when it's been… difficult, to say the least. What's more, you never asked for anything in return."

Marcy's mouth trembled. She managed a smile, a mostly sad twitch of the lips that fell away too quickly.

"I lost my mother when I was twenty years old. I was backpacking across East Asia at the time, concerned with my own worldly experience." Marcy's voice cracked just a bit. She cleared her throat and inhaled through her nose. "I should've been there for her, and that's a guilt I've carried for fifteen years. I wasn't about to repeat that with you."

They said nothing for a brief moment, brimming with sweetness and sadness, then the miscellany of emotions dropped from Astrid's eyes, with one exception: that invigorating light of impishness.

"Come on," she said.

The box was carved yellowheart, detailed with palm trees and stars and cresting waves. It was the size of a shoebox, its lid fixed with brass hinges and a hook-shaped clasp. Astrid lifted it off the shelf with little effort.

"For you," she said.

Marcy took the box. The peppery redolence of the oils worked into the wood made her nostrils tingle in a pleasant way.

"Thank you," she said. She had no idea what to expect (there were some *curious* curios in Astrid's collection), but the box itself was rather beautiful, and she was sure she'd find some use for it.

"Open it up." The impish light in Astrid's eyes hadn't faded at all.

Marcy placed the box on a table-high shelf, then swiveled the clasp and lifted the lid. Although she had no expectations, she was still surprised (*dumbfounded* might be a better word), and perhaps a little disappointed, to see what was inside.

"A hook," she said, trying to keep the bafflement from both her tone and her expression.

The old typewriter was horrible, the lock of Ted Bundy's hair was chilling, the shoes that John Denver had been wearing when his plane went down were macabre, but the hook was an unsettling combination of the three. It was large enough to hang a barracuda on, but this was not used for big-game fishing. It was a prosthetic hook, made of dull, unblemished iron, with a dramatic bend and a sharp point. Its socket was deep black, embossed with a skull and crossbones. The skull had glimmering rubies for eyes.

"A hook," Marcy said again. She would have preferred Mae West's earrings.

"Yes," Astrid said, staring at it fondly. "It's not so much *what* it is, but rather whom it belonged to. And yet more crucially, where it came from."

"It looks like a pirate's hook."

"Bingo!"

"Blackbeard," Marcy guessed, her brow furrowed. "Was he a real pirate?"

"He was. His name was Edward Teach." Astrid shook her head. "But he didn't have a hook."

"Davy Jones?"

"The Monkee?"

"The pirate," Marcy said, with a little smile edging onto her face. "As in Davy Jones's locker."

"Oh, I believe that's just folklore. A sailor's ghost story."

"Really?"

"I think so." Astrid shrugged, then flapped a hand. "But it doesn't matter. No, not Davy Jones."

Marcy tapped the center of her forehead, as if this would help her think. A cast of pirates – all of them fictional – sailed through her mind. She looked at Astrid with a blank expression.

"Pirates are not my strong suit," she said.

"So I see." Astrid brushed one finger over the embossed socket. Her eyelids fluttered and she removed her hand quickly. "This wonderful, magical artifact once belonged to James Hook, the pirate captain of the Jolly Roger."

"Okay," Marcy said. She smirked. "Well… *okay*."

"You don't believe me?"

"It's just…" Marcy looked around the room, at the boxes on the shelves, suddenly questioning the credibility of everything here. Huggy Bear's sunglasses, Mick Jagger's comb, Salvador Dali's paintbrush. *Really?* "Captain Hook is a fictional pirate. I mean… Peter and Wendy, Neverland, Tinker Bell… none of it's real."

"Says who?" Astrid regarded Marcy in that schoolmarmish way again. "Doesn't all fiction contain a breath of reality, or more?"

"I suppose it does, but…" Marcy looked at the hook, staring into the skull's ruby eyes. "This is a prop, right? From a movie, or perhaps from the original play?"

Astrid blinked and pushed her lips together. She looked a little disappointed, or maybe that was just the tiredness. Either way, Marcy resolved to play along. What harm would it do?

"I've had this since I was eight years old," Astrid said, turning her gaze back to the hook. "It was a gift from an anonymous benefactor, along with a note that simply read, 'To live would be an awfully big adventure.' Unseemly though it may be, it's my most valued possession… and it's most certainly *not* some worthless prop."

"I'm sorry," Marcy said. She gave Astrid's hand a gentle squeeze. "I didn't mean to—"

"There's a sunshiny, shadowy place between reality and make-believe," Astrid interjected, but not rudely; she spoke the words as they occurred to her, and before they slipped from her mind, which they'd been wont to do since her illness progressed. "It's true enough to step upon, and formed always with a pinch of magic. Dr Alexander Knott knew this. He made it his life's study, and wrote several essays on the subject."

"Dr Knott?" Marcy shook her head. "I'm not familiar with him."

"He was Hook's old chum from Eton."

"Hook was an Etonian?"

"He was indeed. And that *is* well documented."

Marcy, while believing not a word, appeared suitably impressed.

"Anyway, Knott went looking for Hook after he disappeared – assumed lost at sea – and he returned many years later with a single memento: this hook." Astrid touched the embossed socket again – and again removed her finger quickly. "He published a paper and lectured at Balliol College about what he'd discovered – the 'land between your eyelashes,' he called it. But the Balliol fellows have always been a stiff, proper bunch, and they had no patience for Knott's fanciful tales."

I'm hardly surprised, Marcy thought, but she kept her mouth closed.

"As I understand it, Knott tried for years to get an audience. An academic, credible audience, of course – he wasn't one to stand on a soapbox in Speakers' Corner and rant." Astrid paused for a moment, her eyes glazed, a slight rasp in her breath. "Eventually, he moved to Edinburgh, where he became a raging alcoholic, and drunkenly regaled his stories in pubs across the city."

"A different kind of soapbox."

"Quite. I'm sure it was a case of 'any port in a storm' at that point."

Marcy cleared her throat and nodded politely. The skull's ruby eyes glimmered in the overhead light. They looked reproachful, as if they sensed her disbelief.

Maybe Astrid did, too, but she continued, nonetheless: "Dr Knott was quite the attraction, apparently, and his stories about the 'land between your eyelashes' became well known. So I ask you now, Marcy, is it possible that a certain young Scottish writer – a student at the University of Edinburgh, no less – was influenced by these stories, handed down, as I'm sure they were, over the years?"

"J. M. Barrie," Marcy said. "Yes, I suppose that is possible."

Astrid nodded, satisfied. She closed the lid of the box with a punctuative snap, and swiveled the hook-shaped clasp into position.

"It's yours now, Marcy."

"Thank you." Marcy smiled. "I'll keep it safe."

"I'm sure you will," Astrid said. She gestured at the door. "We should head back to the house, but I'll end our conversation with this: not everything is as it seems. Is it a hook, or is it something more?"

Marcy frowned. She opened her mouth to question this, but Astrid was already shuffling toward the door.

"You've proved yourself quite adept at unlocking doors," she said, throwing another mischievous glance over her shoulder. "Come on, there's still time for *Bridgerton* before my nap."

Many weeks can pass in a person's life without anything of consequence happening – many months or years, even. Then there are times when everything happens at once, and life is bottlenecked with incident. This was certainly the case for Marcy, edging out of that summer and into the crisp, brown days of autumn. To begin with, she discovered that her partner of seven years had been cheating on her. Geoffrey had his faults (he made a boar-like snorting sound when he ate, and used a kitchen knife to scrape the dirt from beneath his toenails), but Marcy had always believed him a faithful man – and would've continued to believe it had he not left his phone in the car when he went to pay for petrol, and a string of messages from his lover flowed in. Two days later, and perhaps because she was still reeling from this revelation, Marcy fell down the stairs of her apartment building. Sixteen cement steps, from top to bottom. She broke her arm and fractured her spine, with doctors telling her she should consider herself lucky. On her third day in hospital, Astrid passed away.

Of all these incidents, Astrid's passing affected her most deeply. Marcy had been denied the opportunity to say a final goodbye, and – bed-bound and corseted as she was – she would also miss Astrid's celebration of life.

"Sneak me out in a wheelchair," she said to Finlay, her brother, visiting her at the hospital. "I'll say my goodbyes and come back. The nurses won't know I'm gone. They sometimes go hours without checking on me."

"Not happening," Finlay said, arranging the flowers he'd brought, then helping himself to one of her Black Magic chocolates. "Bedrest is essential. Doctor's orders. Any small movement could cause a deformity of the spine. Do you want to walk with a stoop for the rest of your life?"

"Of course not."

"Give it two or three months and you'll be breezing around like normal." He offered a small, sympathetic smile. "Just be grateful you're thirty-five, not seventy-five, otherwise you'd get that wheelchair, whether you wanted it or not."

Finlay was right, although it pained her on a level deeper than the compression in her spine. By way of compromise, Marcy decided to have her own special moment for Astrid. She would recall precious memories, and listen to Astrid's favorite music (Wings, Pink Floyd, Suzi Quatro), from right there in her hospital bed. It would be sweet.

She asked Finlay to bring her the hook.

"It's a silly thing," she said, "but it was important to Astrid. It's on the mantelpiece in my living room."

"What kind of hook?" Finlay asked, raising his eyebrows in a cartoonish way.

"An ornamental pirate's hook," Marcy said, straight-faced, as if she were requesting a paperback novel or a more comfortable set of headphones. "Just grab the box and bring it here. It's wooden, carved with palm trees."

Finlay, much to her relief, asked no further questions, and brought the hook the following morning, before heading off to his home in Winchester.

"Take care of yourself, sis," he said, and Marcy mumbled something in reply. She was groggy, dosed up on painkillers… but by five o'clock that evening, she was up and out of bed, moving freely and without pain.

She had seen the land between her eyelashes.

She'd been lost in memories of Astrid, propped against her pillows, idly caressing the hook in her lap. Pink Floyd played through the speaker on her phone at a volume that wouldn't disturb the other patients in her ward. She felt the embossed skull and crossbones and the two rubies beneath her fingertips. Her eyes fluttered. Everything faded for a half-second and she saw a flash of something that looked like ocean, blue-green and moving coolly. Marcy gasped and opened her eyes fully, but continued caressing the hook.

Not everything is as it seems, Astrid said in her mind. The hospital ward wavered. Marcy sank deeper into her pillows. Her eyes closed slowly.

Is it a hook, or is it something more?

There was a burst of light, a falling, *slipping* sensation, then the world Marcy knew – and everything in it, including her physical form – was somewhere else.

She had become a fizzing, flickering light whooshing over a surreal landscape. She saw crystal lagoons and mountains and high, cascading waterfalls. Vividly colored birds flew beneath her. Animals called from the treetops.

A dream, she thought. Yes, of course. She was in her hospital bed, dosed up on painkillers, and had simply fallen asleep. Except Marcy, at thirty-five years old, had fallen asleep *thousands* of times, and she knew this was no dream. She was hyper-aware, for one thing, and in complete control, able to adjust her speed and altitude, and to call out with a voice that sounded like tiny chimes in a breeze.

It was exhilarating, but terrifying, too. She had vacated her body. Only the light of her soul remained. If this wasn't death, it was close to it.

"Let go!" Marcy said suddenly. She envisioned her hands – her right wrapped to the fingers in a solid white cast – releasing the hook, and a split-second later she was back in her hospital bed. Her ears popped with the suddenness of it. She caught a vague aroma of the ocean, then it was gone. The sounds of the ward buzzed around her: peoples' voices, telephones ringing, machines pinging, curtains being drawn on their U-shaped rails. Her heart galloped. The same Pink Floyd song played on her phone. She'd been gone only seconds.

"Okay," she said, and breathed slowly, composing herself. The hook was in her lap, looking, once again, like nothing more than a movie prop. That was when Marcy noticed that the fingers of her right hand – extending from the cast – were not as dark and swollen as they had been. She wiggled them in a way she hadn't been able to since before her tumble down the stairs. She made a fist and felt no pain, only a dull throb in her forearm, at the point of the break.

Astrid spoke up in her mind again, her voice so clear she might have been sitting in the chair next to her bed: *There's a sunshiny, shadowy place between reality and make-believe. It's true enough to step upon, and formed always—*

"With a pinch of magic," Marcy finished, breathing easier, although her heart still thumped too fast. She ran her fingers over the embossed skull and crossbones, looking into those ruby eyes.

Is it a hook, or is it something more?

"A key," Marcy whispered, and smiled. The song on her "Astrid Playlist" changed from Pink Floyd to Wings.

Her eyes began to flutter. She felt the land between her eyelashes tugging at her, like a child taking her by the hand, wanting to show her something.

"Okay," she said, and wrapped her left hand around the hook's bend. The hospital ward flickered. She inhaled and smelled the ocean. "Let's fly."

This time she was gone for longer.

Marcy swooped over a sublime shoreline – clear water and bone-white sand. From above, the coral was beautifully shaped and changed color as she watched, cycling through lilacs and greens and yellows. Bioluminescent sea life darted and billowed, the strangest creatures she had ever seen. Marcy trilled at the sight of them, then turned inland. Within seconds, she was weaving through the jungle understory, beneath hanging vines, through vibrant foliage. A howler monkey ran along beside her for several wonderful moments, leaping from one branch to the next, matching her speed, until she soared upward, through the canopy and into the clean, open air. The island – Neverland, Marcy told herself, this was *Neverland* – was mapped out beneath her, as colorful and varied as a quilt.

"Oh my," she said, and laughed. "It's real… it's all *real*!"

She accessed her memories of Barrie's story, and uncovered more magical places: the Neverwood, Marooner's Rock, the Home Under the Ground. They were all down there, *somewhere*. As was the adventure and mischief and passion for life.

"Thank you, Astrid," Marcy said. Her light shimmered delightedly. She took a moment to just *be*, then considered her corporeal form, positioned in a hospital bed with a fractured spine and a broken arm. Even *imagining* this caused her light to dim, and she heard the clang and clash of that other world – the thrum of machinery and the great whine of time. The idea of going back there sent misery through her bones.

"No," she said. "Not yet."

Marcy descended at breathtaking speed. She fizzed and crackled over the treetops, then stopped to rest at the edge of a lagoon, where she watched the mermaids swim.

By eight p.m., Marcy had discharged herself and was heading home in the back of an Uber, leaving three very confused doctors studying various X-rays, all of which showed the impossible: that her right arm and spine had (mostly) healed. "A medical marvel," Doctor Number One declared. "As close to a miracle as I've ever seen," said Doctor Number Two. Only Doctor Number Three dismissed the results, shamelessly blaming the "incompetent buffoon" who'd taken the original X-rays.

Marcy – who knew the truth, as illogical as it was – left them to their debate. She sat in the back of the Uber with a ridiculous smile on her face and the hook, in its box, in her lap, and she didn't let go of either the entire way home.

Her joy was short-lived. She returned to her empty apartment, and a note from her landlord reminding her – in austere, no-nonsense uppercase – that her rent was overdue. THREE WEEKS OVERDUE, in fact. Of course, losing Astrid meant that Marcy hadn't only lost a friend, but also a source of income.

No money. No friends (not *quite* true, but the few friends she had were married and swamped with children). No partner (goddamn Geoffrey, that cheating son of a bitch). Marcy had healed her fractured bones, but her life would require more attention.

She grabbed the carved wooden box from the coffee table, flipped the clasp, and opened the lid. The hook's bend caught the overhead light, making it appear more silver than iron.

She could start by selling the hook, she supposed – perhaps use it to solve her financial problems. Or maybe…

"I can use it to disappear."

Marcy imagined flying over the Neverwood, not just a soul-like light, but a full-bodied, flesh-and-bone person, with Peter holding one hand, and Wendy the other. She would laugh with them until she was exhausted, then alight in the treetops and sleep on a frond large enough to support her weight.

Her swift departure from hospital meant that she hadn't missed Astrid's celebration of life, which, in light of everything, brought Marcy a welcome measure of joy. To be able to pay her respects, and say goodbye, might be just the closure she needed for another door to open.

It took place at Astrid's house – her sister's house now, who'd already looked into putting it on the market – with people dropping in and out throughout the day. The house was more or less as Astrid had left it. The vultures hadn't swooped in yet, but they were circling. Marcy watched with interest while members of Astrid's family walked around assessing the various goods on offer. *Ghouls, all of them*, Astrid had remarked. Marcy wondered if the various curios in the locked room of the guest house had already been claimed.

Most of the guests were gathered in the back garden, where a small table of food and drinks had been set up, and classical music played through a Bluetooth speaker at a volume barely loud enough to hear. (Marcy briefly considered pairing her phone with the device, and blasting out "Devil Gate Drive" by Suzi Quatro – Astrid's favorite song.) The afternoon sun lanced through the branches of a sprawling oak, and the breeze carried an autumnal chill. The garden had been tidied up, Marcy noted. Many of the trees and bushes had been trimmed, and the fallen leaves raked into a tall pile that Marcy was tempted to leap into. She was obviously in an impish mood today.

It was not particularly well attended, at least not in the hour or so that Marcy was there. Astrid, like Marcy, had few dependable people in her life, a common bond that had brought them closer. She'd never had children, although she'd been married (and divorced) twice. There were a few of her colleagues from her teaching days milling around, and several family members. Marcy recognized Astrid's brother – the man who'd claimed Jack the Ripper's typewriter – and offered her condolences.

"Thank you," he said, except he'd sneered it, looking at her as if she didn't belong. Then he sloped away to talk with someone else. Marcy recalled Astrid saying that her brother was an intolerable turd, and smiled to herself. Astrid was rarely wrong about anything.

Marcy had a more pleasant conversation with Dolores, Astrid's older sister.

"Oh, Astrid talked about you often," Dolores said, shaking her hand. She had soft, wrinkled skin, as white as the sand in Neverland, and long red fingernails. "She thought the world of you, my dear."

"She was special to me," Marcy said, a slight tremor in her voice. "I started out as her caregiver, but we soon became friends."

"Yes, yes, I know, she told me." A big smile from Dolores. She had the same nose as Astrid, a similar bone structure, but there was no mischief in her eyes. "You made her final years very comfortable. Thank you for that."

Marcy pulled a Kleenex from her handbag and dabbed at the crescents beneath her eyes. "I already miss her terribly. She had such an infectious *joie de vivre*."

"And such a generous spirit. So giving."

Marcy nodded, thinking about the hook and everything it had given her. She'd used it early that morning, while it was still dark, landing on the beach in the moons' light (there were three moons in Neverland, each impossibly large and full of silver). Marcy had fluttered for a moment in her soul-light form, watching a sea turtle shuffle across the sand, toward the water. Its shell shimmered like stained glass, its eyes were blue jewels, and although she buzzed around it like a bumblebee around a flower, it paid her no mind. It lumbered into the water, and was soon submerged by waves and carried away. Marcy flared happily, looking at the scuff-like tracks the turtle had left in the sand. She decided that she wanted to leave tracks of her own, and focused on her physical form, sitting in the darkness of her empty home with the hook in her hands. Marcy concentrated, attempting to draw herself more fully into Neverland... and after many minutes – perhaps as long as an hour – she experienced a subtle change. Her light dimmed, but expanded. It adopted a new, longer shape. She saw a swish of dark hair, the ghost of one arm.

"I'm doing it," she said. Her voice was more her own, less chime-like. "It's possible." And Marcy knew, without doubt, that as she was materializing in this world, she was disappearing from the other.

She "walked" along the beach, gaining substance with each step. Within a hundred yards, give or take, she started to feel the sand beneath her feet, pushing up between her toes. Marcy looked behind her and saw a dozen vague footprints, as if left by somebody only a whisper or two heavier than air.

I'm here, she thought. But she was still there, too.

A fairy boy and girl emerged from the treeline and flew along the beach toward her, leaving thin silvery trails that didn't fade for several seconds. They whizzed around her, this way and that, as fast as hummingbirds. Marcy giggled and offered her palm. The boy fairy hovered for a moment, then touched down on it. He weighed as much as a bottlecap.

"Are you a goose?" he asked.

"He means a ghost," the girl fairy said. Her smile was ten times smaller than any other smile Marcy had seen, but twenty times more beautiful.

"I'm not a ghost," Marcy replied, still giggling. "*Or* a goose. I'm a human being, from… the other place."

"You're not, though," the boy fairy retorted. "You're both and neither. You've got one boot left and one shoe sideways."

"An inbetweeny," the girl fairy added. "If you're not here *nor* there, then you're nowhere."

"And that's no way to be," the boy fairy said.

"Yes," Marcy said, and all the mirth plummeted from her expression. "I suppose you're right."

"I'm sorry?" Dolores asked. The creases along her brow deepened.

Marcy blinked and shook her head, snapping back to the here and now. "You're right," she said, swallowing hard. "Astrid. She had such a generous spirit."

Dolores smiled, but also appeared a little more uncertain about Marcy. She took a small step backward and glanced toward the snack table.

"A fighting spirit, too," Marcy said awkwardly, if only to say *something*. "I understand Astrid was sick for several years. She kept fighting, though. That's—"

"Several years?" Dolores cut in, giving Marcy an odd look. "I see. So she never told you?"

"Told me…?" Marcy shrugged.

"Astrid was diagnosed with leukemia when she was eight years old. It was quite aggressive – had already spread to her liver and spleen, if I remember correctly." Dolores gave her head a little shake. "Some of the details are fuzzy, I'm afraid. It *was* a long time ago. What I do remember is that the doctors gave her six months to live."

"Oh," Astrid said, a tiny gasp of a word. She recalled what Astrid had told her in the locked-away room – that the hook had been gifted to her when she was eight years old, accompanied by a note that read, "To live would be an awfully big adventure." How many trips to Neverland had she made over the years? How often had she dipped her toes in its healing waters?

"Astrid lived with her cancer for sixty-one years," Dolores continued. She spoke with a little more tenderness, perhaps registering the surprise in Marcy's expression. "It never went away. Not completely. But it became less aggressive, and stopped spreading. At least until a few years ago."

When Astrid decided that she'd had enough adventure, Marcy thought, and had locked the hook away.

"She truly was a marvel," Dolores said.

"She was," Marcy agreed. Her mouth trembled. She wanted to add something, but had nothing more to say. Dolores spared her, politely excusing herself from their conversation. Marcy drifted around the garden for a worn, dazed stretch of time, entirely disjointed, not talking to anyone. Nobody approached her. Nobody really even noticed her. It was as if she had mostly faded away.

A goose, she thought, with a small, secret smile. An inbetweeny.

She drove home, listening to the news on the radio. More bombings in Ukraine. An increase in COVID-related deaths across the UK. Another school shooting in the US. Tears spilled suddenly from Marcy's eyes and she had to pull over until they had passed. In Neverland, there was a place where the fairies went to sing, and the vibration of their voices formed a kind of sonic rainbow. There were lagoons filled with breathable water, and fruits that brightened the soul.

J. M. Barrie wrote, "To live would be an awfully big adventure," a sentiment that eight-year-old Astrid had embraced. Pan's take had been similar, yet altogether different. He'd said to Wendy, "To die would be an awfully big adventure." And after sixty-one years, Astrid had embraced this, too.

The sun was halfway over the horizon by the time Astrid got home, painting her west-facing windows in a golden-red light. She made herself a cup of tea, then sat, very alone, in her favorite armchair. The hook was in her lap, its familiar weight and shape altogether comforting.

"Adventure," she whispered, understanding that she had a choice. She could be an inbetweeny, and perhaps live for many years, or she could reinvent herself in the land between her eyelashes, and leave deeper footprints in the sand. *Real* footprints. But to do so would mean fading away from this world, blinking out of existence for good.

Marcy, ever so lightly, ran one finger over the magical artifact. She felt the pull immediately – the bright snag of the hook.

The skull's ruby eyes stared up at her.

Boy

GUY ADAMS

They fucking love it. And who can blame them? Look at me. I'm the answer to all your questions. I'm the be all and end all. I'm the full stop. I'm the cock of the walk. The chancer, the dancer, the rip-roaring, oven-basted beauty that's going to break your heart.

(And anything else that gets in my way.)

I'm the captain of the bruise cruise. I'm the clenched knuckle. I'm the pop and bang. The firework. Bullet right between the eyes.

I'm a laugh. The joker in the pack. Bantz. Bantz. Bantz. Ho. Ho. Ho.

My ribs are eight cylinders. Roar straight out of first. Purr. Growl. Guzzle.

I'm the reason God folded his first fanny.

Slippery Jack. The lad. The guy. The boy who never grew up.

Look at me! Propping up the bar, pints for the boys. Wet the whistle, pints of wife-beater and keep 'em coming. Belgian foam moustache. Nothing finer for the top lip. Except maybe whatever this lovely has on the melt. Tell by the way she's standing. Can't get enough of it. Summer days are the best. Thin cotton, nothing waiting to be peeled. Quality Street quim, unwrapped and popped in the mouth, soft centre sugar.

She's been giving me the eye all evening. Trying not to. Trying to hide it. But I know. I can tell. I know what women are thinking. 'Course I do. They all want the same thing and they're welcome to it.

The toilets are no damn good, no room to move. So it's out the back and a recycle bin rendezvous, hers hoisted up, mine tugged down. She can have the lot. Shots on the house. Down in one.

Back to the lads and barely a breath has passed. Air is full of fruity vape steam, sweat-stirred Lynx and the hoppy mad huff of sloshed Stella. Have it! Have it! Have it! Lost boys on the lash. My bin bang has vanished, or if she hasn't, I can't see her anymore. I'm looking ahead. I'm looking at tomorrow, but I bet it never comes. It doesn't have to for people like me. 'Cos I'm never going to stop, never going to uncurl. I'm the flex, I'm flying and I never want to come down. None of us do.

Toots has been living up to his name I see, bloodshot eyes and sugar-crusted nostrils. If that naughty boy lays another line he'll bounce to the stars.

His Nibs, tie-knot like a silk apple, splashing the cash, notes folded round the fingers like gymnast tape, a bunce buffer to pull himself painlessly through life. He wafts a few pfennigs at the lass behind the bar, and her attention is won, drinks all round.

What there is of Slightly is draped over the shining upholstery, spreadeagled, like some bird has strung her tights out to dry. Christ but the boy's thin. Skewers for bones. You could use him to pop a balloon.

Curly's whirling on the dance floor, a dandelion pogoing to pop's cracked-open graveyard. You'll never get it wet like that, Curly old son, sensible skirt's gonna run a mile from those moves.

"We need to go!" I shout, always one to see the way the planet's curved. This place is drained. Squeezed out. Desiccated and desecrated.

Outside and the heat's brought all the best sights: skirts that give up early, thighs for sighs and necklines that can't be bothered to stop, bouncy-castle breasts, a jiggle to tickle the prick. God love a whoregust night.

"Look at that smelly cunt," says Curly, twitching tufts towards a bit of pavement furniture. Tramp's wearing yesterday's stomach contents, a bile-yellow bib laid across greasy Kappa jacket. Gut gravy turning navy to a colour without name. The sort of shade schooldays billy-no-mates would wear, dreckwear marine, cheap games kit. Mummy shops at Asda.

"Spare change?" it asks. It doesn't know who it's talking to, this crumbling pile of mouldy bones. These farts in stained cotton. God's Great Mistake. It holds up its arm and would you fucking believe it, it's a hand down. One short. Gone.

Lopped off. Lost. Waved goodbye. A metal hook scratches at its greasy head, furrowing its greasy scalp. Filthy fucker. Makes me want to kick wicked. This cunt's getting the only thing I've always got spare.

"Couple of quid for a sweet sip?" I ask it, all charm, all smile. Look at these teeth, fucker, watch them bite.

"Trying to get enough for the shelter," it says.

"Boooollsheeet!!" cackles Toots, fresh out of benefit of the doubt.

"Cunt's thirsty," mutters Slightly. Christ, I wish he'd cough up a few extra decibels, thin and quiet, the boy's a fucking ghost, an abstract fucking notion, barely fucking there.

His Nibs is hanging back, like this smear, this skid mark, might stain His Lordship if he strays within six feet. "Fuck him," he says, tugging at his tie, purple silk tongue draped across his belly, trying to get a lick of his rich, rich balls. "Let's get to another bar."

But I'm feeling tense. You'd think I'd be a darling right now, wouldn't you? Cumshot and beer soaked. You'd think I'd be treacle. You'd think I'd be a song in the wind. But I'm tense. Yes. I'm itchy. I'm coiled. I've got sweat trickling down my back, a salty slug trail dripping arsewards. I've got an ache in the heart. I'm of a mind to fucking dance.

"Tell you what," I say to it, always a reasonable man. "I'm not going to give you money. Fuck that. Money has to be earned. I earn it. These cunts all earn it. You can earn it too. I'll buy something off you. How would that be?"

It looks confused. An animal that can smell the adrenaline in the air. It knows something's sour.

"I'll buy that hook off you," I tell it. "That pathetic prosthetic. I'm going to use it as a back scratcher. Unstrap that. Strip back to stump and I'll bung you twenty quid. What do you say? We got a deal?"

"I can't do that," it says and there's a shake to its voice, it wants to tell me to fuck off, I can see it, it wants to tell me to fuck right off. But it's not stupid. Not completely. There are five of us and only one of it. Basic self-preservation. Keep it calm, turd, keep it fucking civil. The wind can change ever so quickly.

"You can," I tell it. "And you'd better. I've got an itch, you see."

"But…" And it doesn't know how to finish that sentence. All it's got in its head is fresh air. And my foot as I foxtrot that fucker's forehead. Stomp and squeal, stomp and squeal, I swear that slimy shit's hip pops out as I hoof it. It thunks. Crunches. Moans.

By the time I get that plastic fucking arm off it the thing's sticky, but it's a point of principle, hook's coming with me.

"Jesus, Pete!" Toots hoots as we run like the veritable fuck. "You're a mean cunt, you know that?"

Yes, Toots, yes I do. Self-awareness is not something I lack. Always been the same. Since God was a boy. Bounced around homes, anger to burn, nobody wanted to take me on. Wild horse, frothing at the mouth. Tame that? No chance. Young offender, university of life, school of hard knock knock who's there? Me, that's fucking who, deal with it.

Another club and it's lit to the tits with neon and promise. Prosthetic down the pants to get past Chubby McFuck, the door boy. Black puffa jacket, a bloated ball, bounce you off the walls my son. A blackcurrant ready for the squeeze. He can't quite look me in the eyes as I give him a purr, growl at the back of the throat, can't help it, wild dog ways, it was either that or I pissed on his shoes.

In we go and it's as dark as I like it. Dark as a cellar. Dark as a bodily cavity. Dark as my fucking heart.

The music's in your meat, low bass buzz, thump, thump, thump, I can feel it working on my bones, setting my pelvis all a-fizzy.

Head to the bar and we've got some HGV Harriet underfoot, blocking the public right of way.

"Shift yourself, Milardy, thirsty boys coming through."

Look at her with her mad red hair, her crocodile skin jacket lit up by lasers, a sci-fi bollock painted purple. She turns round, slow like an oil tanker, and gives me a stare. I'll take you on, I think, go a few rounds. Bet we'd have a bit of fun. I hint as much in a wink.

"Buy you one for your trouble?" I suggest.

"Fuck off," is her answer.

And, you know what? That's fine. That's good. Because I wouldn't touch her with yours, face like a visit from the council, eyes like a stomach upset.

I give her my best grin. I'm feeling warm, you see. I've done my daily exercises. Look, you can tell, there's the ill-gotten gains, jean-stuffed. A lopped off lob on. Hook cupping the fellas, giving them a little chrome-tickle. Maybe I'll use it to go fishing later, reel myself in a little salty dream of the ocean. But not here. No, this isn't for me. No way. Bet she bats for the other team anyway, look at her, side of beef rolled through the sale aisle at H&M.

She's got a tattoo on the tit, dainty little fairy, leg cocked and surrounded by sparkle as she prepares for a strafe run on the boob chasm.

"You alright, Tink?" shouts the woman behind the bar.

"Yeah," says the woman, looking me up and down, John O'Groats to Land's End and all the way back again. "Just some mouthy prick."

"Tink?" I ask, because I'm still at home to easy-going. "What sort of fucking name's Tink?"

"None of your business, arsehole," she says, leaning on the bar in a manner I can only describe as extremely fucking brave. I mean, Jesus, she acts like it doesn't matter that I'm here.

I look down at her arms, even more tattoos, cunt's like a scribbled Stilton. "DARLING WENDY" says her forearm.

"The wife, is it?" I ask. Knew she munched.

She sticks up her middle finger.

"Save it for the missus," I suggest, "give her enough of a wet wiggle and she might ignore how fucking ugly you are."

She stares at me for a minute, necks her drink – sparkles of ice, like swallowing a constellation – then leans forward. "Wendy was my daughter, arsehole," she says, "died when she was just a kid. Some poor bastards don't have the choice to grow up."

Then she gives me the knee and Oh Christ but that's not good, is it? A solid thrust, a tree-trunk of a leg slammed scrotewards. She gives it all the welly, all the hoof. I can hear her grunt of effort over the music. A shot-putter's sigh. It would be apocalyptic even if it weren't for my smuggled booty. I sink down to a floor carpeted in a greasy grade-one buzz cut. I think I've bitten off a flabby crescent of lower lip. That tramp's hook has just been hammered into my groin and I can feel the hot piss of blood, pints of it, thick wife-beater, foaming and fresh, showering my thighs.

I look up at the muscled fuck who's brought on this calamity and can't believe the cunt's smiling. Look at her! She fucking loves it! Cunt.

She walks off and I can't seem to do anything but slump forward. Lost all my drive, old son, that's the truth of it. Lost my steam. Lost my mojo. Face hits floor, head propped up on my wrist. The sound of my watch tick, tick, ticks and you can't help but envy it. It'll fucking outlive me. Where are my boys when I need 'em? Where are the lads? Jesus. Can't help but wonder what's the fucking point of 'em?

Someone's turning the music down. Or is it just me? Hard to say. I'm going. All but gone. Away with the fairies. Down in one. Jacked in lad. Last orders.

The boy never did grow up.

Never Was Born His Equal

PREMEE MOHAMED

In this place nothing is elegant, everything is chaotic and broken and mismatched, because the inside of a complicated toy is always more interesting than the toy as a whole. In this place trees of laughable height and serenity spring up overnight, their leaves as big as bedsheets, all watery greens and blues like the illustrations of a children's book. In this place every strange night-time sound is a delicious puzzle for the dawn.

And so it is this morning: the boys tumble from bed at Peter's shrill summons, and arrange themselves like ants around the dawn's disaster. A footprint in the earth! Not just any footprint! A dozen smudgy toes, a deep shocked oval: O! If it were full of water, they could all swim in it.

"What was it, Peter?" one of the boys squeaks, a fair-haired little thing; Peter cannot remember his name. He has had bad dreams this week and seems to be forgetting things at an alarming clip.

Peter puts his hands on his hips and frowns into the muddy abyss. "I declare," he says ominously, "that it is one of those *thunder lizards* we have sometimes seen prowling the Islands of Red Clouds."

They gasp and dance and unsheathe their tiny daggers. Around them the jungle breathes its heavy fumes: intoxicating, stealing away the last vestiges of childish sense, filling their brains with mist. "Avast, avast ye!" Peter soars into the canopy, brandishing his own knife. "We must hunt the beast! Lest it return to our camp and trample our new mother!"

"Yes! We must protect Wendy!"

"No beast shall come near her!"

Wendy. He's forgotten her name overnight too. Well, what's in a name? He remembers that she has dark hair, and blue eyes, and she has been here for a little while, and maybe she will be here a little longer. But the boys are calling for blood, and he does not (in truth) like the look of these footprints, and he floats ahead as they run below, their faces still plump with baby-fat, killers all.

As they hunt, trampling excitedly through the undergrowth or swinging on vines, passing fairies can tell them nothing; their tinkling voices are faint with terror. The lagoon is empty of mermaids, even though the day is sunny and hot. Peter lands on a favourite basking rock and calls for them, but none emerge. They have retreated to the deep blue places, far deeper than even the most adventurous boy can dive.

"I suppose it eats mermaids," observes another boy – Dash,

his name might be. Or his nickname, for Peter cannot remember his real name either. "Horrible beast."

"Horrible." Peter plays his pipes, the boys hushed and licking sea-salt from their lips. But the mermaids do not rise even for their favourite song. Dark clouds, flat-topped and dense as anvils, close in swift silence; a trickle of smoke blows and is gone.

"Monster," someone says.

"Mermaid-catin' monster."

"We'll put its head up in the drawing room," Peter decides.

The boys whoop their approval, and they romp into the forest again, and no one points out that the clubhouse does not have a drawing room; it is all too much fun. Only Peter feels that he is flying through his own cloud of darkness, invisible to the others. Only his vision seems clouded.

Soon they reach a strange region, a land of several imaginings, of slaty stone, snow thick upon it, strange thin trees like hair. The air smells of pine and burning. Tigers and bears pass them by, knowing they are not today's quarry; and great snakes with nearly human faces; then a pair of noodling chimaera; and just once an enormous bird who (though Peter does not know it) has been created by a little boy whose nurse has been reading him *One Thousand And One Nights* passes near Peter so closely that its silvery, silken wings brush his face. These are not the usual beasts of their land.

The great footsteps in the snow eventually lead to a cave, and Peter lands, beckoning to his hearty crew to brace for battle. "We are many," he murmurs, and they snarl and nod; they love this best, his faith in them. "When I say now... *now!*"

Into the cave they rush, hearing the breath and rumble of the thing, the *thing*, clearly a monster, and it emerges from a thrilling cloud of sepia fug: a head, yes, ragged fangs black with the flesh of its unlucky victims, glittering red eyes. A shambling hulk, slow to reveal to itself in full—

Peter freezes. Like a rabbit spotting the circling dot of a hawk, his eyes widen, his body stiffens. The ringing in his ears drowns out the cries of the boys around him, darting at the thing, hurling their daggers at it; he can barely see them. His hands are ice. He neither feels nor hears his pipes falling to the snow. And then he is running, still half-frozen, sluggish, unable to soar, stumbling back to familiar places.

His every instinct is to hide, to find somewhere dark and small. He forces himself onto his accustomed throne, worn smooth with the passage of countless years, and stares into the firelight. The boys mutter mutinously. The big ginger-haired boy, Doc, and his ferretlike sidekick Bullseye – they are taking turns shooting looks at Peter all too simple to decipher. A boy is an open book. They cannot dissemble for long. Peter forgets and remembers and forgets and remembers, but he never forgets this.

"Enough!" he bellows, loudly enough that birds rocket from the treetops, and Wendy darts from the house, startled, drying her hands on her dress. "You all forget yourselves! I hear you say it! I am your leader, and you shall have no other! Do you not recall who I am? I am *Peter Pan*. I ran away the very day I was *born*. The fairies in Kensington Garden taught me to fly and to fight and to drink black rum like a pirate king! To sharpen my sword on the bones of dragons! You call me a coward? You would never dare fly with the souls of dead children!"

"Maybe you're not afraid of souls," Doc says, squatting beside the fire; his green eyes glitter like a cat's. "Well, so what? You're afraid of the monster in the cave! You said we would catch it – chop off its head – and then you ran!"

The other boys murmur and glare. *Lily-liver. Yellow-belly.*

"That's called strategy!" Peter snaps, rising from his throne. The movement is abrupt, and combined with his high, shrill voice, the boys back away in surprise as well as fear. It's enough for now. He continues, flatly, "And if you're not sharp enough to know what I'm about – then you're not sharp enough to lead! Now everyone go to bed! This minute!"

When he stirs again from his throne, the moon is up. He watches it for a long time, thinking. It is a typical moon of this place, an aggregate of all the most amazing moons children have ever seen: full and golden, filling the clearing with light as bright and thick as cream. He knows he should sleep but he fears it. And it's strange, so strange: he thought he no longer felt fear. He cannot remember the last time he felt really afraid of anything. Something must be done.

He slides easily from the polished wood and pads off into the cool of the trees, watching for the places where his own kingdom becomes another – where a pilfered Karl May book has resulted in a cactus-studded desert next to an Indian jungle, where a visit to the museum has created titanic lizards now torpid and snoring in their dens.

As he crosses from trees to scrub, he realizes he is being followed, and his dagger flashes into his hand: but it is only Wendy, ambling across the turf in her slippers in eerie silence.

Peter puts up his blade, rolling his eyes. "I order you to go back," he says. "It's dangerous out here for a girl."

"It's just as dangerous for a boy as it is for a girl," she says. "And you can't order me around, either! The others are fast asleep... what are you doing here, Peter?"

"I'm..." What *is* he doing? He remembers a moment of terror, of looming, of red eyes and filthy smoke. Their campfire in the clearing burns as clear and clean as moonlight. There is no smoke here, as there is no smoke in dreams. He shivers, though the night is warm. "I'm going to go kill a monster!"

"What sort of a monster?"

"A *strange* one. So you can't come."

"I'm still coming." She walks on his left side, her pale dress shining in the dappled darkness. "I was telling the boys a story..."

He is interested despite himself. "What about? Will you tell it to me?"

"It's about a man called Trusty John," she replies quietly. "It's about being true to your king when you're sworn to his service."

"Wendy, you are very wise," Peter says after a long time; but he cannot bring himself to say more. Has she calmed the growing mutiny? A terrific trick! But the boys love a story, and they hang on her every word; and if she says they must be loyal to Peter, then loyal they shall be. What power she has, this repository of new stories.

The land around them has shifted again, or subsided, or intertwined (as it sometimes does) or slid apart (as it sometimes does), and when he finds his pipes again they are not in the snow, but on fine blue sand. He cups the retrieved bits in both hands. "You know, the Great God Pan himself gave these to me. I suppose he'd be upset that I broke them…"

"You didn't break them," Wendy tries to soothe him. "They fell. You could tell him that…"

"Oh no; I don't expect I'll see him again. He said I would be the last being he ever spoke to…" Peter shakes his head, and puts the pieces in his pocket, where they rattle mournfully with his conkers, pebbles, bits of chalk, slingshot, and arrowheads.

The cave is gone entirely, but the thing has left its footprints on the sand, and he and Wendy track these easily until the warm familiar land is left behind and the sky overhead burns with winking stars. It is strange to be out here with this quiet-moving girl, instead of the shrieking pack of boys. Sometimes he looks down and sees their shadows conversing in silence on the sand, then swiftly re-positioning themselves when spotted.

"Oh!" Wendy covers her nose with the back of her hand. "*What* is that awful smell? There's nothing out here!"

They instinctively move back-to-back; Peter's dagger shines in the moonlight. This time, *this* time, he won't—

The thing rises from the sand a stone's throw away, bigger than before (he's quite sure), far bigger, like a mountain, a faceless thing belching terrible smoke, a thing of darkness and fire, and, incongruously, a filthy, greasy top hat as big as a house. The twin spotlights of its scarlet eyes scurry across the sand like glowing mice: here and there at first, and then right to Peter's feet, where they remain, erasing his shadow. His knees turn to jelly.

"Oh, run!" he croaks before he can stop himself. "Run, run!"

The creature gives chase, lumbering after them with terrifying speed. All around them the world tilts and shifts, so that they slide down a sand dune and fetch up in a grassy pasture, then before they can race across it have slid knee-deep into a slippery tidepool, all starfish and slimy seaweeds. Peter wants to fly, but in his panic can no more launch himself into the air than a stone; and he won't leave Wendy behind, who runs with such stalwart silence at his side.

What now? cries the monster, and its voice is terrible, earth-shattering; the clouds ripple and flee ahead of it. *Eh? Wretched whelp? Raise your voice to me again?*

"I do, I do!" Peter gasps as he runs, but the defiance is flimsy and thin. "I'll have at you, I'll cut you to ribbons!"

Oho! I'll flay you to dogmeat, you worm! I'll hang your skin on the post of my bed!

Wendy runs into the web first, and cries out in surprise, waving her hands before her face; Peter is moving too fast to avoid whatever it is she's hit, but under their combined weight the clinging stuff tears and leaves them scrambling on hands and knees, not on the soft needles of the pine forest they have just left but something hard, both familiar and unfamiliar: cobblestones.

"What a strange part of my kingdom," Peter whispers breathlessly. "Whatever is it?"

"It's... I believe it's a city."

This place boasts no close and looming moon, only a faint white sliver far overhead, and no stars at all. He nearly swallows his tongue when Wendy unexpectedly slips her cold hand into his, but he holds her tightly. They will lose each other in this darkness if they don't stay close.

Behind them, the ground trembles as with thunder. The thing is catching up. They don't dare run across the rain-slicked, uneven cobbles, but walk as quickly as they dare, coughing in the thick, sooty air. "Oh," Wendy whispers suddenly, pointing. "Look up there..."

Peter stares, impatient to be moving again; there are buildings around them, there must be somewhere to hide from the terrible thing. "I don't see anything!"

"Next to the window – can't you read the sign?"

"No!"

"It's Myrdle Street... Peter, we're not in your kingdom at all. We're in London!"

"What's London?"

"England, Peter!" She tugs him forward, and they hurry towards the dim golden squares of lit windows, some covered with nothing more than torn oil-paper, most open to the smoky night. "Where I'm from – where *you're* from, for Heaven's sake! How did we come here? And why aren't there any gas-lamps?"

Get back up there! Wretch! Filthy whelp! If ye eat the food from my plate, ye'll do as I tell ye!

The monster follows them no matter how they jink and dodge through the filthy streets, which are empty but for oddly insubstantial forms – no thicker than a shadow, vanishing moments before a collision, like fog. The red bricks are coated in a patina of soot as thick as paint, dirtying the children's outstretched hands. When they pause to catch their breath under another dimly lit window, Peter stares at his palms as if he can read their language: the empty creases across the soot. Memory itches the back of his neck, incomplete. Something about this writing… this, just like this, white on black…

The door at his back begins to creak open under his weight. "Quick! We can hide in here!"

It's a tight squeeze even for them; surely the monster is too big to follow them inside. In fact, it is the entrance to a coal chute, and they slip down the metal ducting on a layer of fine dust, bumping and whimpering, to a splintery wooden floor.

It is not quite as dark in here as outside; a single candle burns low in a dented tin holder. Wendy lifts it cautiously and looks for more candles, finding none – only sticks of broken furniture, torn clothing, shattered crockery, canvas bags of tools. Everything is covered in black dust.

The thing roars and thunders above them, shaking the walls. Peter stares at the filthy fireplace as if hypnotized. "Can he come through there? No, I think not," he mumbles. "No, he never could…"

Wendy watches him, confused. Even when she brings the candle close to his pallid face, his pupils are as big as pennies. "Peter?"

"I… never had a mother. I never had a father. I had…"

His voice trails off; the house shakes again, and with a crack like a gunshot the table behind them collapses, throwing a pile of clothing to the floor. Wendy stoops and picks up a tiny jacket, black with soot and grease.

The candle-flame gutters as the great pulpy fist batters the window. And then the light is gone, and it is two children in a dark house, and Peter's kingdom has never seemed so far away.

"I had," Peter whispers again. "And he smoked… a foul… pipe…"

"Peter." Wendy fumbles for his hand and cannot find it. She throws the jacket to the ground and sets the candle down, wincing as hot tallow splashes the back of her hand. "Peter, when you came to my house… when you found me, do you remember?"

"No. I don't remember anything, I…"

"You told me a story. You told me to believe you… to believe or we would never fly. You must tell one now, Peter, you must. And you must tell a story only you know. For *him*."

He cannot hear everything she is saying, only her thin frightened voice; perhaps she is crying. He tries to summon up the old flame inside him, the ever-burning coal, saying, *This is me, this is who I am, hear me!* but there is nothing. He cannot remember how to do it. He cannot remember anything. But this *smell* and this *voice*…

No. Yes. No.

Yes.

"Once upon a time," he begins, moving cautiously in the darkness, his hands out. "Is that how you start it? Once upon a time, I didn't have a father. I didn't have a mother. Nothing at all. I lived in a strange place with lots of other children and I…"

He finds something warm and slippery – Wendy's tallow-covered hand. They clutch one another, gasping in only the briefest moment of relief. The ceiling creaks and shudders, and great lumps of soot and broken brick tumble from the cracking chimney. In a moment, Peter is sure, the whole place will come down on them – this is not like the treehouses of his home, which will never harm a child.

"A man found me. Oh, it was so long ago… he must have become an old man and died, I'm sure of it."

"But you didn't grow old," Wendy whispers. "And you didn't die."

"Once upon a time," Peter tries again, backing them away from the rattling hearth, "an awful old man bought a little boy from an orphanage, and he said, *Ho ho, ugly wretch; I could break your neck like a chicken, I could drown you like a cat…* He sent the boy out to work and bring back coins. He sent him up chimneys and into coalbins and down into the pipes of the world… and one day… one day…"

The bricks of the fireplace crumble into sand, and the chimney follows a moment later, with a terrific crash like a ship running into the reef of the lagoon; and a moment later the roof is torn away, and the sickening smell of cheap, wet tobacco fills the room. Peter and Wendy fling themselves behind the broken table.

"Peter, finish!" she cries.

"I can't remember… I can't…"

"Yes, you can!" She shakes him by his collar, sending the leaves and feathers of his shirt spinning in the wind of the monster's breath. "You know what happened – even if it's terrible, you must say it—"

"What good will it do?" Peter protests, freeing his shirt from her fist.

"You both need to hear it!" she shouts. "You both do! It is why he hunts you, Peter – it is why he follows you! You must say it!"

Peter shuts his eyes as the shapeless fist, covered with scars and hairs and boasting an inhuman number of fingers, reaches for them both. Broken brick, shattered glass, splinters of wood rain down. The terrible day dances behind his shut eyes like shadow-puppets before a fire. It is all there, perfect in every detail, down to the final shapes of bone and blood.

"And one night, the man became angry," he says rapidly. "And he took the poker from the fire, and he went to the boy and he…"

"And he killed him," Wendy whispers into Peter's ear, for the pause is growing too long, and the creature outside is becoming angrier and angrier. "Didn't he. The man in the top hat, with the pipe, who beat the little boy to make him go up chimneys, he killed him. And it wasn't like in my land…"

"No. It took a long time, and it…"

"…wasn't clean or easy like in a story. And then, when the little boy was dead…"

"He went to a dark place," Peter says, and something flares up under his chest: not the past but the present, bright as the feathers of a cockerel. He gulps at the cleaner air, raising his voice. "But in the dark place, he was *flying*. For he was a soul going to Heaven, as innocents do… and Peter Pan took his hand, and said, *I will come with you, I will show you the way*, and he said – the dead boy said – *I* said – *No, don't take me there, take me somewhere else and I will do anything you say*, and Peter Pan said, *You have spent one lifetime already doing whatever you were told – will you spend another?* And we went to his kingdom, and one day Peter Pan came to me—"

Peter is shouting now, kicking the table away, leaping to his feet, cutting his hands on the edges of brick. His voice rings in the empty street like a struck bell, drowning out the wind, the snarling creature, the roar of its flaming eyes. "And I said, *Yes!* I said, *Yes, I will be the next Peter Pan! I will be him!* And I flew into the air like – an eagle all made of sun and cloud! And I said, *Ker-keri-keriiiii!*"

With a tremendous crack and bang of light, the monster vanishes; Peter flies backwards into the rubble, and it takes him and Wendy a long time to disentangle themselves and climb out of the ruins. All around them Whitechapel has become smudgy and indistinct – like a charcoal drawing. Even the sliver of moon is gone.

They trudge back the few blocks to where they had come in, and crawl carefully through the rip back into their own land, where the palest blue dawn is just beginning to climb over the hills. "We shall both have to have a very long bath," Wendy says.

"I shall set the boys to heating water for you the *moment* we return," Peter says solemnly. "You shall have an enormous bath, Wendy, and you shall sit in it as long as you like."

Wendy takes her velvet sewing-bag from her waist and carefully stitches up the rip between places, sighing over the sooty marks her fingers leave behind. Above them, birds watch and sing. The sun is well up by the time she declares the job done and that they can return to the treehouse.

"How did you know how to kill that thing?" Peter finally asks, just before the familiar treetops come into sight.

"I don't know," Wendy admits. "But I did think... well, I suppose I thought that it wasn't really a monster but a memory of a monster. Or a nightmare."

"Perhaps it got through a tear in my dream," Peter says thoughtfully. "Like the one we went through. And so when I remembered..."

"Then it became just a memory instead of a real monster," Wendy says. "This place makes people forget, I think. You forgot that memory, but it didn't forget you."

They step into the clearing, and study the boys who dozed off around the fire, and listen to the faint snores of the ones asleep within the protection of the ancient trunks; and Peter remembers something else now, remembers that first glimpse of the glittering golden boy who led him through the empty air into a scene just like this: small sleeping forms, thumbs slipped into half-open mouths, the promise of a childhood like the one he had never had.

Peter smiles, and gestures for Wendy to cover her ears. Then he cups his hands around his mouth and looses his loudest, wildest crow. "Everyone up! Everyone up, my fine crew! We've slain the monster – and we've such a story to tell you!"

The Shadow Stitcher

A. K. BENEDICT

She followed me for months before I saw her. All through winter, I heard her footsteps behind me, but every time I turned round, nobody was there. In spring, I felt her breath, cold as last words, on my cheek and still I couldn't spot her. It got to the point where I couldn't step onto the cherry blossom strewn street without checking over my shoulder.

"What's wrong, love?" Ed, my husband, asked, when I stopped in the middle of Sainsbury's, two tins of beans in my hands, looking both ways down the aisle.

"I've got that feeling again," I replied, shivering. I was as cold as if I'd been popped into one of the freezers.

Ed pulled me to him. "Sian, love. There's nothing, and no one, there, I promise you. You're imagining it because..." He tailed off.

I stepped away from him, folding my arms. "Go on. Don't stop."

"It doesn't matter, I—"

"No, what were you going to say?"

Ed looked down to the trolley-scuffed floor. "Isn't it possible that your brain is suspecting things because of what happened to..." Again he left his sentence incomplete, as if all that had taken place in the last year had finished already.

"Can't you say his name anymore?"

Ed turned to the shelves, twisting tins until their labels were all pointing in the same direction. "Of course I can. But talking about him endlessly doesn't help. Why put ourselves through even more pain?"

"Say it then." I knew I shouldn't be pushing him away like this, but I couldn't stop. "Say his name."

"Please, Sian. Don't."

"Then I will." My voice came out louder than I had intended, climbing into the industrial vaulted ceiling and getting lost in the pipes. "Our son's name is Murphy and he's been missing now for one year, seven months, eighteen days and two hours. He would now be seven."

An elderly couple stopped and stared at me. A man walked quickly past us, glancing our way as he placed a kiss on the head of the child in his papoose.

I felt a cold wetness on the back of my neck as if it were an ice lolly, slowly licked. "You're nearly ready," the cold voice of a woman said in my ear.

I spun round, trying to grab her. Stumbling into the shelves,

I sent chickpea cans clattering onto the floor, but my arms were empty.

When summer arrived, it came with a sunny spell that conjured away the clouds. A heatwave scorched London's rare lawns and blistered my skin. Our house was full of unsaid words and fruit flies that settled on the surfaces like escapee punctuation marks. We sat in front of the fan and let it stuff the silence with white noise.

On our anniversary, Ed took me to the place of our first date – the digital cinema in Wandsworth. Back then we watched *La La Land,* now it was the latest Wes Anderson. Seeing the world through Anderson's trademark yellows, blues and pinks gave me as much of a boost as the sugar-crusted popcorn. I felt myself smiling, face muscles aching from previous disuse.

After, in the bar, Ed brought over a ramekin of pistachios and a bottle of Prosecco. He poured us each a glass and raised his. "To us."

We clinked and drank, clicked open pistachios and fed them to each other. My heart felt as if it was being reinflated. Just slightly. But enough to feel like maybe it could be halfway full again.

"I've been thinking," Ed said, taking my hand and twisting my wedding band round and round on my ring finger. "How about we book a holiday before you go back for the next term? My big project ends in a week. We could go somewhere new."

I pictured us on sun loungers beneath a bluer sky in a less humid climate, eating olives and tzatziki by the sea and drinking pine-tinged wine. But there would still be the shadow of Murphy between us.

"We can't leave," I said. "What if he's been kidnapped but is still in London? What if he's trying to find us, and we're not—?"

"You know how unlikely that is, love," Ed interrupted. He'd heard all that many times before.

Even though I knew Ed was right, I had to stay. "I couldn't be happy away from here."

"But you're not happy when you *are* here."

"When Murphy comes home, I'll be happy again," I said.

The woman's voice whispered in my ear, "You're on."

I drained my glass, knowing I'd have heartburn later.

Next day, in the afternoon, I was shopping in Bluewater when once again I felt her following me. I turned around and saw a tall and extraordinarily beautiful woman stood in front of me. I couldn't stop looking at her. Her cheekbones were sharp and carved, her skin shone, her leonine eyes almost yellow in the artificial light. Even though she was willow-slender, her huge shadow swept across the tiled floor like a dark bridal train. Without even looking down, shoppers went out of their way to not step on the shadow. She held out a hand that seemed for a moment to be made of twigs and then I refocused on her elegant fingers. Without thinking, I shook it. Her hand was ice-smooth but colder.

"You can see me at last, Sian," she said. It was the voice that had been speaking to me all this time.

"It's you. You're the one who's been stalking me."

As she nodded, it was as if a sweet, tiny bell tinkled. "I have been behind you, rooting for you."

It occurred to me that I should feel afraid, but I didn't feel anything at all. "The right time for what?"

"You have something I want, and I have something you want."

"I don't want anything."

"That's not true, is it, Sian?" She placed her thin fingers under my chin and lifted it till I was staring straight up at her. She seemed as tall as the ceiling yet no one else was looking. We were both invisible. "There's someone you want back very much indeed."

I felt like air had been sucked from my lungs. "Murphy," I said. "You have him?" My voice sounded as parched as my heart.

"I know where all the lost boys and girls are."

"Take me to him." I grabbed at her long coat but it twitched and hissed in my hands. Her shadow seemed to grow even larger.

"I will," she said, "but first you must let me do something."

"Anything. I don't care what you do, just show me my child." All I could think of was Murphy running into my arms, and holding him so tight he'd laugh and tell me to let go. Of the joy that would flood back into me and all the happy times we would have as a family again.

"Good. I was hoping you'd say that." She then reached into her handbag and pulled out a long black needle. She held it up to the light and, very delicately, mimed poking thread through before grabbing hold of my neck. "This will hurt."

The needle dug into my skin and the pain burned through me like grief. My screams reached up to the balcony yet no one turned our way.

The woman twisted the needle out, then back in again, pulling taut invisible thread. She tutted like a disgruntled governess. "Hold still and this will soon be over."

"What the fuck are you doing?"

"I am stitching your shadow to you, of course." She said this as if it was obvious, her candle-flame eyes focused on the needle.

"But why?" My voice was small. All I wanted to do now was curl up on the mall floor and cry.

"Never mind that for now. You'll get what you want and, once a year, I'll collect my dues."

"And now I can see Murphy?"

The woman nodded again. This time, though, her neck made a noise like branches snapping. She gestured to a sign saying "Lost Property". Underneath, a door formed in the wall, and opened. Murphy appeared, holding Raffi, his giraffe plushie. He was wearing the same pyjamas as the night he disappeared.

He rubbed his eyes and looked around, then saw me. "Mummy!" he shouted.

"Thank you!" I said as Murphy ran towards my open arms. I realised then that I didn't know who the woman was. "What's your name?"

"Darling. Wendy." The woman looked down at me and

Murphy and a look of her own pain crossed her face. Then her shadow swept over her and she disappeared, but it didn't matter, I had my lost boy back.

I rocked Murphy backwards and forwards and felt my heart fill up to the three-quarter mark. "Let's go home."

"We don't need to know," I said over a chippy dinner as Ed asked Murphy where he had been and who had taken him and other questions. I stroked my son's soft golden hair. "None of it matters, apart from that he's back."

Murphy grinned. His teeth were exactly the same, the same milk teeth in place. "Can we have chips every night?"

"No!" Ed and I said at the same time with the biggest of smiles, not meaning it at all. If he wanted chips every day, he could have them.

Murphy then climbed into my lap and I felt his familiar weight and warmth. I tried not to think about how he hadn't changed at all in the time he'd been lost.

"We'll go to the police in the morning," Ed said, as we all settled into a cuddle on the sofa. "Make a statement. Then we can look into getting you back to school and seeing your friends."

Murphy nodded, and rested his head against me. "I didn't like it, where I was, Mummy. I didn't like the shadows."

Ed looked over at me, his forehead creased and questioning.

I nuzzled my forehead into Murphy's hair. It smelled of honey and dirt. "No more shadows, sweetheart, only light. From now on we concentrate on being happy."

Autumn came early, and with it a flurry of leaves and a new school year for both Murphy and me. There were some struggles – my new cohort was a bit of a handful and Murphy found it difficult to settle back into life with his friends. His nightmares were also a worry, as were his screams that ripped through the house every night. The psychologist said that Murphy's lost memories were resurfacing in his sleep but were forgotten again by morning, when he would fly out of his bed and onto mine and Ed's. The police couldn't find a Wendy Darling that fitted her description, at least not one alive. They had given up trying to find out where Murphy had been and were instead focusing on the many other missing children of London.

Overall, though, things were improving. Ed's project led to a promotion and we took that long-awaited break over Christmas, a winter holiday in sun-soaked Australia.

I lay on a lounger by the pool, watching Ed teach Murphy the back stroke. I loved them both with all of my semi-rehydrated heart, and there I was, in an idyllic setting, with my family, and palm trees, a book and a choice of cocktails in Wes Anderson colours, yet I wasn't happy. It was as if I didn't know how to be happy anymore. I shifted to get more comfortable, and my shadow followed, closely, behind.

Winter melted into spring, which petalled into summer. One afternoon in August, Murphy ran across our patch of brown lawn, shrieking with laughter as Ed sprayed him with the garden hose. I watched them from the kitchen window as I boiled the kettle. I knew at a distance that I was glad to see their smiles.

Suddenly, my neck felt wet, and cold.

"Your shadow tastes delicious," Wendy said, stepping out from behind me. She seemed thinner, and her mouth appeared bigger. "I've come to collect."

"What do you want now?" I asked. I heard the tiredness in my own voice.

"I stitched your sadness to you and you've been growing it for me. Now it's Lughnassadh, and I have come to collect my dues." Wendy's voice sounded like leaves being crunched.

"What do you mean?" I said, instinctively standing between her and Murphy. If she had taken him once, she could do it again.

"You may know today as Lammas, the grain harvest. But I am here to harvest what you have been growing for me."

She took out a box of matches and a pair of black scissors, as shiny as beetles' backs, from her bag. Opening the scissors, she snipped a piece from my shadow.

Pain flowed and sadness swept over me and I felt everything I'd been through along with my shadow child. My keening echoed through the house. "Why are you doing this? Why can't you leave me alone?"

Wendy watched her own shadow swirl about her, as if impatient to move on. In that summer light, I could see the skeleton under her skin, like a dry leaf held up to the sun. Her tear-filled eyes fixed on me, then, gold coins in water.

"You made a bargain with me for what you wanted, just as I made a deal with someone else, a long time ago."

"What did you ask for?"

"The love of a boy called Peter. I was told, by someone very much like me, that he would fall for me, but, in exchange, from that moment on, I could eat nothing but shadows and sadness. I agreed, desperate for his touch and adoration. And it worked – he loved me, and, for a while, I flew. Then he discovered what I had become to win him, and he was lost to me forever. Just as I will forever be hungry, so shall you."

Wendy lit a match and held it to where my shadow met my skin. The flame seared shut the tear in the shadow. Numbness settled on me again like a black swan on an empty nest. "Will I ever be happy?" I asked Wendy.

Wendy didn't answer. She was too busy groaning with pleasure as she filled her stretched mouth with fresh slices of my shadow.

This is not a story sitting comfortably in the past. There is no happy ending here. Only a warning. If you see her, run. She can smell the sadness in your shadow and will stitch it to you forever. Run as you have never run before. Her eyes are Wes Anderson yellow.

She says she's a Darling, but she's really a devil.

A House the Size of Me

ALISON LITTLEWOOD

Tony stands on the doorstep with his hand raised, as if frozen in time, and perhaps he is. He's picturing Maimie, his sister, as he saw her years ago: a green satin dress that kept no secrets, her waved hair gleaming like glass, the indecent smear of her lipstick. He doesn't wish to see her now, not at all, but still he left his posting on the Continent the moment he received her telegram, racing towards London on the next steamer. There never was any question of refusing to come. Somehow he always did exactly what Maimie wanted him to do, even without accounting for the circumstances, which were so very pressing – nay, terrible. *Frightful.*

Of course, Maimie had always frightened him a little too.

He has to force himself to knock on the door. He must knock, because this isn't his house any longer; it is Maimie's.

The clatter of thundery feet that arises makes him realise his journey has been in vain – mercifully, *gladly* in vain, because here must be Polly after all. He spreads an uncle's exuberant grin across his features, one that doesn't entirely fit, but the door opens and it isn't Polly; of course it isn't, he can see at once from Maimie's face that the child is still missing. What did he think – that Maimie would have found her under the nearest gooseberry bush?

His niece has been gone for days. And she is only four years old, the exact same age that Maimie had been when she decided to stay out all night alone in Kensington Gardens.

Now his sister's skin is dry. She has tiny creases about the lips and eyes, and her hair, while still shiny, looks lank. She manages a wry smile.

"A bowler, brother?"

Tony crushes the brim of the old-fashioned hat in his fingers. Of course, Maimie would prefer a fedora or a homburg, but then Maimie would be thinking of Clark Gable or gangsters, not a man in a government office, doing government work, *adult* work. "It has a certain dignity."

"Of course it does," she murmurs.

He tries to ignore the disappointment in her voice as she ushers him inside, but most of all, he tries to forget the dreams he suffered on the steamer: the sense of being followed, the stench of musk and animal; the breath of a great beast warm against his neck, mingling with the sound of the boilers and of Maimie's voice, whispering and whispering in his ear.

They must wait for dusk, Maimie says, before they go to the Gardens. That is when the fairy house appears. Polly will be inside it. The problem is, the house could be anywhere within the gates. It appears wherever it chooses and can be whatever size it wishes; the house, and therefore Polly, might be no larger than a reel of thread.

Tony watches her mouth move and wonders for his sister's sanity. Has she, in her fears for her child, become four years old again herself? That was when she'd sneaked away from their ayah to stay in the Gardens and look for fairies. The ground had been covered in snow then. Maimie had slipped into it as if it were an eiderdown in which to sleep and the cold had likewise slipped into her, and in whatever delirium that followed, she imagined that fairies had built a house around her to keep her warm. Ever since then, she said, Peter Pan wanders the pathways, and whenever he finds a lost child, he puts them in the house. Unless he's too late; then, he digs their graves. He places stones over them marked with their initials, always in pairs, since that looks less lonely than just one.

Tony shakes his head. Maimie most likely doesn't *want* to grow up. She probably thinks that not doing so is the very best thing of all, that four years old is the finest age for anyone to be. But his sister is over thirty. She's a *mother*. She has – blessedly, and for a time at least – been married. Blessedly because of that night, of course; the one where she'd slipped away during a large dinner party, had reappeared with the shameful marks of sweat on her dress and that red smear at her mouth. Tony still remembers what she told him when he'd asked, coldly and very, very calmly, what she imagined she'd been doing.

"*Thimbling*," she'd said, and she'd had the temerity to smirk at him, Tony, in his new smart dinner jacket and bow tie. That word: for years afterwards, it put images in his head he did not like. It made him feel queasy; he found himself taking leave of his own fiancée, permanently and without ceremony or fuss, the very next day.

Now Maimie stands there like a queen and tells him what they must do: find a house that does not exist. He imagines peering down through tiny little windows to see a tiny little girl looking back at him, holding out her tiny little hands. It would be his niece, of course – though Tony has seen the child precisely once and, truth be told, doubts his ability to recognise her. In his mind, she has shrunk to the size of an illustration in one of Maimie's books. Is that what this is about – Maimie's imagination, running away with her at last?

Maimie glares down at him. It's as if she sees all the thoughts in his head. She says, "You were the one who was meant to go."

Tony squirms. She's right, he was. He'd boasted of staying up all night in the Gardens, not Maimie. When it came right down to it, though, he'd been afraid. He had chosen comfort and security and a warm bed over adventure, and it was Maimie who had taken his place. She came back cold and exhilarated, and with her head full of stories. She also returned half wild, of course, but then, he never was sure which came first; perhaps adventure happened to Maimie because she was more than a little wild already. The wild was inside her; Tony had always sensed it there, something that wasn't kind and wasn't safe.

While Maimie waits for darkness to fall, Tony slips away to his father's study. He vaguely remembers a very tall, shadowy shape of a man sitting in the studded leather chair, though he has barely been inside the room before. It is his sister's study, now. Her books are lined up on a shelf: *The Stillness of the Gardens. A Midnight Adventure. A House the Size of Me.* And on the desk is her work in progress, illustrations and sketches scattered haphazardly beside her paints and pen.

He scowls down at the things she has conjured from the depths of her mind. While Tony turned to adult business, Maimie always remained in this children's world; it was what she was good at.

Her next book appears to be full of birds. They are fantastical; impossible. They do not look safe and they don't look kind. In fact, they look malevolent. Rapacious. They have feathers of every hue and sharp eyes and beaks like swords. Among them stands a little girl in a trimmed pelisse, not blonde like Polly, but dark, like Maimie. Next to her, jotted in Maimie's hand, are the words:

They shan't have my fur.

And beneath that, she had written:

But they did.

With a start, Tony remembers one of the stories that Maimie brought back from her adventure in Kensington Gardens. She had claimed that Peter Pan was in love with her. She'd said he made her promise to stay with him, but that she had gone back on her word. If she'd stayed, she told him, the birds would have wanted her clothes; they'd have taken them from her to make their nests.

They shan't have my fur. The phrase makes him uncomfortable in ways that Tony doesn't want to think about. It gives him the same queasy feeling as *thimbling*.

He lets the pages fall, a catalogue of madness, no more. Why has his sister been lauded for her work and not sectioned? But children seem to love her books, while Tony finds them disturbing in ways children do not. He is considering that perhaps there is something very wrong with the whole damned lot of them, when he hears his sister's voice calling his name up the stairs.

It is time to go back to Kensington Gardens.

Maimie is wearing a day dress with a coat trimmed with fox and her demeanour is locked up tight as they walk, without a word, towards the park gates. Tony can see the Gardens as if they are before him already: the seven Spanish chestnuts, the Wiggly Path, the Hump, the Baby Walk. In his mind, everything is peaceful and bright and ordinary, just as he has always known it, but this evening the sky is purple, gouged with orange slashes, and the breeze carries a chill on its breath.

When they are about to slip in at the gate, Maimie pauses. She turns and gestures towards the grand houses lining Bayswater Road, and the swallows swooping about their eaves. In a murmur, she says, "Peter Pan loves those best of all the birds. He thinks they're innocent, because they're really the spirits of little children who died. They build their nests in the roofs of the houses where they once lived. Sometimes they try to go back; they fly in through the nursery windows, but the mothers weeping there never recognise them."

Tony does not reply, but quietly he is horrified. This is the worst thing of all; it is worse even than the grasping greedy beaks of the monsters she has created with her pen, the ones who like to make nests out of little girl's fur-trimmed pelisses. Worse even than the *other*...

No: not so terrible as that.

Still, when Maimie reaches for his hand, as if he were a child, a *little* child, he takes it. He walks with her into the Gardens. They wander pathways that seem so much smaller than they used to and Tony waits while Maimie peers under bushes and fallen leaves, as if, by pure wishing, she could find her daughter peeping back.

But there is no magic. There are no roads made of red ribbon to lead the fairies to their revels, no glow-worms to light their way, no Peter Pan to make strange, mystical music on his pipes. The world is just as Tony believes it to be and he is comforted, despite all his sister's darting about and under and through. Still, he imagines Peter Pan, hiding behind that bush or this tree, always just out of sight, grinning and insouciant as he walks the gardens, stalks the gardens, hunts for lost children. Or perhaps he is busy burying them, the ones he failed to save – because he came too late, or because he decided to keep them for ever and ever?

"He isn't here now," says Maimie.

Tony realises she is watching him, a mysterious smile twitching the corner of her lip. She stoops to examine the ground under a holly bush, straightens and sucks a droplet of blood from her finger where a leaf has pricked her.

"He only lives in the Gardens sometimes. Mostly, he lives in his own world. You can see it, most likely at the hour when it isn't quite dark and isn't quite light, and if the stars allow it. You won't always realise what you're seeing, though. You'll just catch a glimpse of it, floating upside down in the Round Pond. There are trees. Jungles, even. His land is an island, and it's close, but also very far away.

"I've created another beast, Tony. This one will be able to follow him. It'll go into that other land, and if Peter doesn't give Polly back, I shall make it eat him."

Tony stares at his sister, who is shaking with the intensity of her rage. He isn't really seeing Maimie, though. What he's seeing is the first beast: the one she created when she was four years old and Tony was six. She made it from imagination and words, and she sent it after Tony, night after night. *It's outside the door. It's under the bed. See? That's the gleam of its eyes, reflected in the window.*

Maimie had always seemed a perfectly ordinary, if irritating and somewhat disobedient child, so long as daylight lasted. At night, though, Tony had been a little bit afraid of her. And he was afraid of the beast as he felt it creeping closer, breathing down his neck, sending its stink across the room. He would lie awake, imagining what it looked like, while Maimie simply closed her eyes and fell asleep, her hair spread across the pillow, and smiled sweetly at her dreams.

Eventually, she took mercy on her brother. She explained

to him that the creature was a huge and rather wicked goat, and she had sent it away to live with Peter Pan.

Now he looks at Maimie as she stands there, her eyes full of gleam.

"This one's worse than the other," she says, and Tony flinches, as if he's been pinched.

"Of course, I *mean* to make it eat Peter. I shall try, if it comes to that. It's just… this one keeps getting away from me."

She turns and keeps on down the path, which is full of shadows. Leaves rustle. Breezes whisper.

This one keeps getting away from me.

Of course it does, Tony thinks. Because madness is like that, isn't it? Seeing fantastical things that aren't there. It's just that Maimie has been doing it for so very long, it's all begun to seem perfectly ordinary to her. And he, Tony, always knew it would go wrong. He never should have left. When Father died, he should have put his foot down, made her take responsibility. Made her grow up. Well, look where it has got her. *Just look.*

He does look, his gaze probing the twisting roots and branches around him, and he sees a little house nestled beneath them.

Lights shine in its windows. Smoke rises from the chimney. Such a sweet little house, perfect in every detail. So very dear. So very near.

He reaches down and peers in at the windows, but they are too small, and then he hears a sound behind him. It is Maimie; she lets out a cry, kneels at his side and snatches the house from the ground. She holds it up to her eyes, peering in, twisting it this way and that so if Polly really were inside, if she could be so small, she would surely be tossed from wall to ceiling to floor.

But Maimie's expression fades. She opens her mouth and speaks in a croak.

"Empty."

Tony catches the house as it drops from her hand. The roof and walls are made of wood, he realises. The bricks and tiles are crudely painted on and the little curtains are nothing but scraps of gingham. There never could have been any chimney smoke; there was no light beaming from the windows.

He tosses it aside, nothing more than a child's discarded toy, and he turns and runs after Maimie. She doesn't stop when he calls after her, doesn't stop until she's doubled over by the gate, hands on her knees. Her face is red. Her hair is awry.

"He must have sent her home," she says, and then she runs on again, and there is nothing for Tony to do but follow.

The next morning, Tony awakes in a house as empty as a child's toy. Of course, it always was; Polly hasn't come home. The police haven't called. She might have vanished into the air – as has Maimie, he realises when he dresses and goes downstairs. His sister hasn't gone far, though. He spies her through the window, standing in the front yard, her head tilted back. Tears are running down her face.

Tony pulls on his shoes and hat, steps over the threshold and goes to her. The neighbours might see. He wants to take her arm and pull her inside. He wants to wipe away her tears with his thumb, but of course he does nothing of the kind.

His sister is staring up at a solitary house sparrow, fluttering about the eaves.

"She's dead," Maimie says, and Tony has that odd feeling again that his sister is reading him, that this is something he knew all along, that somehow he has always known. Still, he opens his mouth to say that sometimes a bird is just a bird, then words spill from her in a rush, and something inside him recoils.

"This is Peter's revenge," she says. "He's taken her, because I said I'd stay, but I didn't. Because I chose to grow up. Become a mother. Peter doesn't like mothers. He thinks they're inconstant. Faithless. Perhaps I am. I did love him, once. I meant to be with him. I flew into his arms – that's a kind of wedding, where he comes from."

She swivels her head towards the Gardens, so very near yet so far away; another world, almost. And she starts to walk, striding out like a man, her face set like a man's, and Tony wants to seize her, shake it out of her, but he already knows he cannot stop her. And so, once more, he trails at her heels.

As they enter the Gardens, he realises that Maimie is speaking, though whether to him or someone else or just to herself, he isn't certain.

"Peter doesn't like people to see him," she says, "because he's not quite human. He never was quite a child. He pretends to play like a child, but he never truly can. I don't think he's ever been a child, not really. He's old, to begin with. Much, much older than he looks.

"Beware his pipes; they are so very lovely. They can sound like silver sleigh bells or falling snow. Like the sound of your name on a lover's lips – like the way they look at you when night falls and the world retreats."

Things he doesn't want to think about wriggle and squirm in Tony's mind. *She's mad*, he tells himself. *Quite, quite mad.* He must get her home. Call a doctor to come and examine her. To depress her tongue and make her say *argh* and write on a piece of paper that yes, madness, that's it; that is all it can be.

But Maimie is leading him back to the leafy path of yesterday, so ordinary now, the leaves shifting in the breeze, the sunlight shining cheerily from the green. She stoops beneath a bush and whirls to face him, her eyes wide. She holds out two small stones. Letters are carved into them; each is marked with a P.

Initials – for Peter Pan? No: they are her daughter's initials. Polly, followed by Pattison, the name of Maimie's husband before all of that was swallowed up in the shame of separation and divorce.

Shame that has been too much for her, he can see that now.

But Maimie doesn't look ashamed, only unutterably sad, and he realises what she thinks: that Pan has failed, or decided not to save her daughter. That he has buried her here and set these stones above her for gravestones. But they don't look like gravestones. They're nothing but pebbles, tiny things of yellowish sandstone, so crumbly and soft that Maimie might have carved into them herself.

"I'm going to kill him back," she says.

She pushes past Tony and runs down another path, one that he knows leads to the Round Pond, and perhaps to that strange, elusive world where she claims Peter Pan lives. He reaches for her and the fur trim on her coat slips through his fingers. He lets out a cry of frustration. He's the eldest, isn't he? He's the one who ought to lead the way, who must show her what to do, how to behave. Instead, he's been left to follow again – but in the next moment, he stops dead.

He can hear breathing, coming from the bushes to his right. Breathing that is surely not a rabbit or a fox. And then comes a rustling – close, and too loud; much louder than the breeze turning the leaves, much louder than Maimie's footsteps, which are moving away from him, leaving him there all alone.

The air is too warm on his face. Slowly, inevitably, a meat-stink steals over him. Carrion breath. It grows hotter still. Gusts of it. Entirely animal and so very, very here.

Tony takes a shaky step. Peers into the bushes. Reaches out and pushes aside a handful of leaves.

And he sees the thing that Maimie has created. He does not see all of it, though; it is too big. His mind cannot encompass it. He sees it in pieces.

It is made of scales and muscle and slither.

Of claws and teeth and gleam.

It is slime and stink and snap.

All snick and snack.

It is made of Maimie's imagination, which in so many ways is still that of a child, and that, as anyone knows, is the very worst thing of all. Tony can see at a glance that, as a child would, Maimie has forgotten to give this thing a heart. There is no pity in its eyes; no possibility that it might let anyone off or change its mind. This creature's teeth drip blood. Its eyes beam death.

It is an entirely beastly kind of beast, and Tony throws himself to the ground, pulling leaves over his body. He hopes and waits for Death to pass over him, and after an age that is also not very long at all, somehow, it does. He pushes himself up and he runs.

He finds Maimie's fox-trimmed coat by the pool. Under it are her day dress and her stockings and her shoes. There are no gloves, nor a hat; she had neglected to put those on. Her clothes are not as they should be. They look as if they have been squabbled over. Ripped, rent, ruined.

Ripples are still settling on the Pond. Tony does not think the beast found his sister, though, nor that his sister found the beast. He cannot imagine she waited long enough for that. Her blood was up, after all. She had wanted to find Peter Pan.

And perhaps she did. Little would stand in Maimie's way, once she had that gleam in her eyes. Not Tony, not Pan; no one.

Tony gazes at the strange, drowned world that is suspended in the pool. There are trees growing there. A jungle even, so dense the foliage appears almost black. For a moment, he glimpses curious birds riding the thermals of its skies. They have colours he cannot describe. Their eyes are not just sharp, but gimlet. Their beaks are huge and deadly razors. Maimie's pictures did not go nearly far enough.

Rapacious. Yes.

Back at the house, Tony calls the police. They come and ask questions he cannot altogether answer to their satisfaction and then they go and drag the Pond, but it is large and deep and they do not find her.

Tony goes to his sister's study and riffles through her final work. He reads what she had written there, hearing the echo of her voice.

They shan't have my fur.

But they did.

Tony sits in the empty house, which seems far too large without Maimie in it. Maimie is missing. It has been in the newspapers, much to Tony's mortification, but it is gratifying to see how much she was loved. Who would have imagined that? The way she must have frightened little children, and yet they only wished for more.

For the first time since he came back, he walks slowly up the stairs, and then up the next set of stairs, which are narrower and plainer. He moves along the old corridor after that, until he reaches the little nursery under the eaves.

The room is cold. He realises at once that the window has been left open – for who knows how long? It's a wonder he hasn't felt the draught. But he is only staring at that so hard because he doesn't want to look at his niece's things; his niece whom he met only once.

There is an abandoned school desk, crayons scattered across

its surface. Books piled haphazardly on a shelf. Teddy bears and dolls and more dolls, some with real hair and silken eyelashes, staring back at him. And there, in the centre of the room, is a doll's house.

This one is larger than the discarded toy in the Gardens. It is also lovely. Just right, in every detail. Tony has never seen it before. He supposes that Maimie must have chosen it, paying for it with the proceeds from her book of horrors. *A House the Size of Me.* And it is; the house is just a teeny bit larger than a child; a child the size of Maimie, in fact, when she was four years old. The perfect size. The perfect age to be, for ever and ever.

He moves towards it, and with a start, realises that everything isn't as it should be after all. A bird must have found its way into the room – and as he thinks this, it appears: a swallow swoops in at the window and flits to the eaves of the little house. There, it has been building its nest. A tiny cup made of grass and mud bulges from its clean straight lines. He can smell it, he realises. Something not quite right.

He walks towards the house. The bird flits away again, sits on the windowsill, watches him.

Tony bends and puts his face up close to the windows. He peers into the house. He stays there for a very long time.

Tony is getting dressed. Preparing himself. He is wearing his shirt and his suit trousers, mainly because he doesn't have anything else, but the bottoms of his trousers are rolled and his collar is open. He has thrown his coat to the floor.

Who needs a coat on adventures? With a jaunty flick of his wrist, he bowls his hat into the corner. He has set aside his watch-chain and waistcoat, his collar studs and cufflinks and necktie. On reflection, though, perhaps he will need that; he picks it up, runs the silky fabric through his fingers. After another moment, he ties it around his head.

Maimie was right. She was always right. He was the one who was meant to go. He should have been the one to face the Gardens, at night when the stillness fell. He had been a boy who boasted and preened, but he had only ever been there by day, when the place was almost civilised. By night, other things walked its paths. Things *not*-civilised. The trees and grasses hummed with strange music that stirred the blood, made the heart beat faster.

That is when the beasts roam. That is when Peter Pan walks abroad, looking for lost children.

Tony goes downstairs. He picks a kitchen knife from Maimie's supply. Chooses a wooden chopping board, a hole conveniently drilled for his fingers at one end, for a shield.

He wishes he could talk to his sister. He wishes he could go back. When he'd heard of her divorce, he had been so very cold to her. He wishes now that he could tell her it surely wasn't so terrible as that. Even their king had given up his throne for the sake of a divorcée, no matter how she was stained by it.

At least Maimie *had* married. She'd had the adventure; she'd had the stories.

And what had Tony done?

He had grown up.

Yet now he wonders if he ever really had. Even while he dressed in a grown-up's clothes and sat at a grown-up's desk and made decisions a grown-up should make, he had failed to recognise that there are terrifying beasts in the grown-up world too. There are beasts made of chances lost, of things left too late. There are beasts of words unsaid, of a hand not taken; lips not kissed, a ring returned. Of vows never uttered. Children never born.

At least Maimie had known the truth. And she had been right: not all children grow up.

He whispers a promise to his sister. If she has not killed Peter Pan, then Tony will. A kitchen knife, believed to be a sword, becomes a sword. Tony will wield it. He'll summon Maimie's creature and herd it before him until it strikes Pan down. Who better than Tony to set against the boy? Pan had always belonged to the wild, while Tony belonged to all that was ordinary and plain and decent. They were natural enemies.

Tony walks towards the park. He ignores the raised eyebrows and muttered imprecations, the nurses that pull their charges a little closer, the mothers who wheel their perambulators a little quicker. As he heads into the green, choosing his path without hesitation, he feels younger with every step.

Then he hears it: a sound that is as near to him as breathing. A smell. A feeling. A beast; all the more frightening because he does not know what kind of beast it is. But he knows enough. He raises his sword and readies his shield.

The monster comes. And here, against it, stands Tony. He is aware that he has never cut a very prepossessing figure. He is all snack and no snick. All meat and no muscle. All slither and no teeth. He thinks he might have gleam, though; just a little. The beginnings of it, anyway. Gleaming, after all, is not something he is accustomed to. But he thinks that maybe he can learn. He thinks that maybe it will be enough.

He throws back his head, the tails of his necktie swinging about his ears, and lets out a war cry.

Not so very far from here, he can see the Pond. It looks grey under the grey sky, but Tony knows there is a world held within it, just on the other side of its veiled surface. That is where he will take Maimie's beast. She created it for this, after all. It will do his bidding, will slip into the depths with nary a splash, and Tony will follow. He will swim deep and somewhere, somewhen, he will find himself falling through the air. He wonders if he will ever land, or perhaps if he will never land at all.

Perhaps he might even fly.

Silver Hook

GAMA RAY MARTINEZ

The *Walrus* glided through the water without making a sound. Even her oars dipping beneath the waves didn't so much as ripple the surface. The fog hung thick in the air, and there was no wind at all. That had always seemed to be an ominous sign to John.

He strode across the deck, his wooden leg thunking on the planks. Wisps of mist swirled around him. Though not the captain of this particular vessel, the crew went silent as he made his way to the forward rail. No one wanted to attract his attention. He stared into the fog for several minutes before anyone spoke.

"Captain on deck!"

Tom Morgan bellowed the cry that he always gave when Captain Flint came out of his cabin, but the crew had long ago stopped responding, and most of them returned to their work. Flint wandered toward the bow, stopping beside John and leaning on the rail.

"Any sign of it?"

"No, Captain." The air felt heavy, and John Silver shivered, a thing he hadn't done in decades. "I don't think we're going to find it."

The captain stood up straight. "Oh, and why not?"

John shuddered. "Can't you feel it? He doesn't want to be found."

Captain Flint smiled and shook his head. John peered through the man's ghostly form to see that many of the crew had stopped to listen to their conversation.

"Land ho!"

Ben Gunn's voice was like thunder, and the crew rushed toward the rail as fast as they could walk or float. They stared ahead as the island came into view like a gleaming emerald in the mist. Flint laughed.

"I do not care about other men's wants."

John nodded and took a small step forward, as much as the rail would allow. His wooden leg, which was so much a part of what he had once been in life that it had followed him into death, made a loud *crack* against the plank. He scanned the island that had served as a sanctuary to the only member of the *Walrus*'s crew to have escaped their fate. As the captain of a cursed ship, Flint was empowered to find the spirits of any who had ever served on his crew, whether they were alive or dead, whether they had served a week before their death or two hundred years. Even an island as strange as this, with magic that had allowed their quarry to evade death for centuries, wouldn't prevent them from claiming the spirit of James Hook.

The ship sailed into the bay. A cool breeze licked ocean spray across the faces of the crew, and whispers of fear and awe rippled through them. Some had been dead for near two centuries. John himself had walked the ghostly deck of the *Walrus* for almost a hundred and fifty years. In that time, he had never felt the ocean spray… until now. There was power in this place. And magic.

"There," David Pew's gravelly voice said as he pointed to an empty spot in the water. The rest of the crew fell silent. Even dead, Pew was feared more than any pirate, save John himself. "It's there, at the bottom of the bay."

Flint nodded. Pew had been blind in life, and fearsome in spite of that. Now, there were sunken pits where the rest of them had eyes. And although John couldn't see anything beneath the waves, he didn't doubt that Pew knew the exact location of the item they sought. The old seaman had shed more blood than any two others, and he often bragged that he remembered the location of every drop spilled. Flint gave John a curt gesture and pointed at the water.

"Get it."

John gritted his teeth. In life, Flint had feared him, but they had all committed unspeakable crimes while they were alive. For his wickedness, Flint had been cursed by some forgotten sea god to be the captain of this damned ship, and a spirit could no more disobey his captain than a living man could stop his blood from flowing.

John stepped over the railing and drifted to the water's surface. It felt odd as he sank in, as if his body was trying to remember what being wet felt like. The sapphire water barely obscured his vision, and it had to be at least a hundred feet before his sight faded into unending blueness. Fish of every shape and color swam around him. All the sea creatures darted away when he neared. An eel snapped at his hand before swimming away. As he sank lower, a chill washed over him, and he half-expected to see ice chips floating in the water. Pew was right. The curved object practically glowed in front of his eyes, and he went straight to it.

Touching physical objects normally required great effort, but his hand lifted the cold metal easily. It felt like it would freeze to his skin. He suppressed a shiver and rose through the water far faster than he had descended. As soon as he was back on the deck, he tossed it down. The rusty hook that had once graced the arm of the captain of the *Jolly Roger* clattered on the ghostly wooden planks just as a raven's caw drifted from the island. If the stories were to be believed, this hook was as much a part of its former owner as John's leg was of him.

Flint ran his finger along the metal. After lying in the bay for who knew how long, it should have been dull, but as soon as he touched the tip, a drop of ethereal blood, maggot-white and with a faint glow, welled up. They gaped at it. Blood was a thing of the living. For the dead to have it…

"I summon you, James," Captain Flint intoned. His voice carried power, the power of a captain to summon a hand to the deck. "I call you to service."

As his last word faded from the air, the sea calmed and the ship went as still as if it were beached. Power hung in the air.

John hadn't felt anything like it before, but the looks on the faces of his crewmates told him this was exactly what they had expected. The deck shuddered, and the sails billowed out as if catching a strong wind, yet the *Walrus* didn't move.

"No!"

The scream came from nowhere. If John still had blood, that cry would have turned it to ice. The deck planks cracked and split apart. An elaborate hat with a long feather was the first thing to emerge from the opening. The man wearing it had a face twisted in agony. His hair brushed his shoulders, and his greatcoat would have been considered fine in the court of any king in the world. Where his left hand should be, there was a hook that almost seemed to gleam with its own inner light. When a ghost returned, he looked the way he envisioned himself, and the hook on this man's hand had been so much a part of his identity, that even in death a version of it remained at the end of his arm, looking just as sharp, if not sharper than its physical counterpart.

"Welcome to your fate, James," Flint said with a sneer.

"No," Hook cried out. "No, I won't go with you!"

He ran to the rail, but Flint's voice rang out.

"Stop!"

James hesitated. For a moment, John thought he caught a glimpse of another ship, almost as large as the *Walrus*, flying the skull-and-crossbones flag. Then James leaped from the deck, shrieking, and the ship and the pirate both vanished into the mist. The crew stared in stunned silence. No one had ever been able to disobey a cursed captain's call.

"Strange magic in these waters," Ben Gunn said. "Maybe we should leave it be, sir."

Flint glared at him, and John was sure that if he'd been able, he would have erased Ben from existence. The deckhand backed up so fast he tripped over his own feet. While some of the spirits floated through the air with ease, Ben Gunn had never mastered that skill, and he tumbled heavily to the deck. Flint sneered and turned the hook over in his hands.

"He won't get far." Then he turned to the four men standing with him on the bridge. Black Dog, a huge man with only three fingers on his right hand, hovered just off the ground. Billy Bones, his weathered face looking more like parchment than skin, stood alongside the bearded Israel Hands. Nearby, David Pew paced back and forth. The four waited for Flint, having realized what John had not. The hook would draw them to their quarry.

"This hook. It misses its owner," Flint mused.

He held the object out to John, who hesitated for only a moment before taking it. It thrummed in his hands, pulling him toward the spot where Hook had vanished moments ago.

"Follow it. Take him prisoner. He belongs to the *Walrus* now."

Black Dog popped his remaining knuckles, and Pew's mouth split into a hungry grin. Bones and Hands looked apprehensive.

Flint clapped a hand on John's shoulder. "I've waited many years for Hook to die. Do not fail me now."

John nodded to the others, and they dove into the water. Once again, they were greeted by that almost-splash as they dipped beneath the surface. The water felt colder than the air, and though the others said nothing, they kept close to John as they plunged into the depths. The water carried clicks and hums. Billy cried out as a red fish appeared seemingly out of nowhere and swam through his face.

Without warning, a haunting song washed over them. John had heard whales calling before, and this might have been what they sounded like underwater. Their tune slowed, and he found himself yearning to hear more. Black Dog's snarl brought him back to himself. He blinked. A school of fish, each bright yellow like the noonday sun, swam nearby, scattering as soon as the spirits started moving again.

"Mermaid," Billy Bones said.

"Mermaids are just stories," Black Dog said.

John could hear the laughter in the old pirate's voice, but they all looked to where Billy pointed. A woman with skin like new fallen snow and eyes like twin obsidians glided through the water with more grace than any spirit had ever managed in the air. John had sailed the seas for almost half a century as a man, but he had never seen anything like this beauty. Almost without meaning to, he floated toward her, but before he had gotten close, she turned in his direction. Her eyes widened and she darted deeper into the sea.

John wanted to go after her, but the hook in his hand quivered and forced him aside. He grunted and motioned to the others, and they headed deeper into the bay. John wasn't sure what he was really seeing at first, but before long, there could be no doubt. It was upside down, and holes had rotted through the wood in various places, but it was definitely a ship. Almost as long as the *Walrus*, barnacles covered the hull.

The Jolly Roger. A ship was the core of a captain's power, and a dead captain, if he knew how, could use that power to summon his crew.

"Faster, lads!" John cried out. "If Hook reaches that ship, Flint will make you wish he never called you from the grave!"

But Hook was already there.

A singsong voice cried out, rippling through the water with a sonic boom.

"Smee, Starkey, Teynte, Cecco, Mullins! All of you, to me!"

The ship rumbled and took on a pale glow. The planks rattled against each other, and fish scrambled from the holes in the hull even as streams of bubbles rose from every opening. The water itself hummed with power. For a moment, John felt the weight of the ocean pressing down on him. When the sensation passed, ghostly figures were rising from the hull: a dozen of them, from one so short he might have been a child if not for his beard, to another who would tower over even Black Dog.

Hook turned his sharp eyes to John and his men. In John's hands, the newly recovered hook bucked and strained. James Hook raised an arm, and without even a word, his pirates attacked.

The crew of the *Walrus* were quickly surrounded. A tall ghost lunged at Black Dog, but he batted the sword aside like it was a switch held by a child, and his other fist connected with the new ghost's stomach. The force of the blow sent him down a dozen feet. Had he been more experienced, he would have been able to prevent himself from falling, but he was too new. He slammed into the sea floor so hard he sent ripples through the sand. That was something young ghosts often didn't understand. The world was only as real as you allowed it to be.

A pair of ghosts rushed at John, but he sidestepped one and shoved his knife into the neck of the other as it passed. It screamed and exploded into motes of blue light. John didn't stop there. No sooner had the other ghost tried to turn around than John threw his knife at him, hitting the pirate in the chest.

The crew of the *Walrus* had been outnumbered nearly three to one, but a ghost gained power as time went by, and those that had existed for mere seconds could not stand against those who had roamed the sea for longer than a human lifetime. The fight was over in minutes. Israel Hands had a slash across his left arm, and motes of light bled out, but other than that, none were wounded.

"Where's James?" Pew asked, his own sword dripping with ghostly blood.

They all looked at the remnants of the ghosts around them, but saw no sign of James. John held up the hook and concentrated. It gave a faint tug toward the surface. Too faint.

"He was toying with us," John said through clenched teeth. "Trying to distract us!"

A laugh rang out, and before John knew what was happening, James himself was flying past him. John turned just as James's spectral hook sliced across Billy Bones's stomach. The pirate just had time to look shocked before dissolving into motes of blue light. Black Dog managed to bring up his sword just in time to deflect the ghostly hook. James's other hand held a knife which he used to slash. The blade sliced into Black Dog's stomach, but an instant later, Pew slammed into James, sending him flying before any more than the tip of his knife had sunk in. James tried to strike at his new attacker, but Pew pulled away a heartbeat later. The two pirates stared at each other, James with his eyes full of rage and Pew with empty sockets that could have swallowed whole worlds.

James surged forward, spectral hook and knife flashing. Pew didn't move as his foe approached. There was an exchange too fast for John to follow. Then, James was past Pew. Neither moved for several seconds. Pew's hand went to his gut as he bled pale blue light. He grimaced, and the wound closed. James, for his part, seemed completely uninjured. John's breath would have caught in his throat if he'd still had any. They had made a mistake, and a bad one. They had assumed that because James was a new ghost, he would be weak. And he was, in a way. Weak compared to what he would one day become, but Captain James Hook had been one of the most fearsome men to ever exist. Even a weak version of his ghost appeared to be a match for the spirit of David Pew.

"He can't beat us all!"

John had covered the distance between them before he was finished speaking. Black Dog came at James from above while Israel Hands came from below. Pew slashed, but James spun, knocking the blade aside with a knife that should have been too short and driving the spectral version of his hook into

John's arm. With a sharp tug, he sent John down, crashing into Israel. James moved like a snake, dodging around Black Dog's sword, scooping up the real hook that John had let slip from his fingers and jamming it onto his arm.

James flew past, rushing for the surface. Splashes of blue light scattered everywhere, and before anyone could react, James had burst free.

"After him," John shouted, grabbing a fallen sword as he went.

By the time the pirates had regrouped above the surface of the water, they could barely make James out as he disappeared into a wooded cove at the island's shore. A few other spirits, Gunn and Morgan among them, joined the group and they flew into the forest.

As they neared the edge of the woods, the island emitted a low, dangerous energy that blew through the pirates' ethereal bodies like fingers trailing through water. The others all bunched up behind John. He grumbled at them to move forward, but though they might fear him, they apparently feared James more. Even Pew refused to move first.

"Together then, or Flint will have your hide after I'm done with you."

Invoking the name of their captain spurred them to action. The canopy obscured all but the occasional dim ray of sunlight. Birdsong went silent as soon as the ghosts entered the trees. Spiders scurried across the ground, and John could just make out a snake slithering through the fallen leaves.

Ben Gunn shivered. "This be an evil place, John."

"Only because we're here."

Then John raised his fingers to his lips, sensing a barely perceptible shift in the air around them. He didn't think. He just swung his sword in the direction of a wide tree. Ghostly steel clanked against ghostly steel, and James stepped out of the tree, having caught John's sword on his hook.

"You can't cheat fate, James," John said through gritted teeth. "You were crew aboard the *Walrus* before you had your own ship, and we are all cursed. You're coming with us."

"Not today."

James pushed him back and the fight began. Black Dog, who had been following from above, hovered in the air for a second before diving at Hook. Pew rushed at him from behind while John himself met James head on.

Living or dead, John had never seen anyone move like James. He flowed around the attacks, slashing and stabbing like death given form. He sliced open Tom Morgan's neck, destroying him just as he jabbed his spectral hook into Black Dog's eye, half-blinding him. John gained half a dozen shallow cuts, and it was all Pew could do to keep James from skewering him. They outnumbered him and had the man surrounded, but still, James was winning.

The sound was so soft that, at first, John wasn't sure he was really hearing it. A faint ticking came from the shadows, slowly growing closer, and James froze. John hadn't realized it was possible for a ghost to go pale, but James did. His eyes focused on something behind John, who hesitated. He took a step back and looked over his shoulder.

A crocodile, as large as any John had ever seen, stared at them through the trees. Its eyes focused on James, who shrieked. It was just an animal, though, and although they could see them no animal could harm a ghost. It was only when John saw the look in James's eyes that he understood. All spirits had an instinctive fear of the thing that killed them. John motioned to the other pirates, and they surrounded James, each putting their blade to his neck.

John approached the frozen pirate, now paralyzed by fear. Without a word, he took the real silver hook from James's arm, leaving his ghostly one exposed.

"Flint fancies this for his personal collection. Perhaps you'll have a chance to earn it back under his service."

James's mouth opened and closed. John thought that he might be about to try something, but then James's gaze flickered upward, and his eyes went wide.

A rooster crow as loud as thunder came from above. John looked up and gaped. A boy, no older than twelve with a bright green shirt, was diving through the air, coming to a stop no more than a dozen feet above them. He wasn't a ghost, so clearly he was as magical as this place. The boy carried a curved sword, and rather than being afraid, like most children would be, he seemed amused by the sight of them.

"There you are, Hook. We've been looking all over for you." He gestured to the crocodile, who gnashed his teeth greedily.

Pew snorted. "Get out of here, boy, this is men's business."

Laughter echoed through the woods. "A boy? Oh, I'm much more than a boy. This is *my* island, and Hook is *my* enemy. He might be dead, but he doesn't leave until *I* say so."

The boy dove at him. Pew had always been a cruel man, and even in life, hurting children had never bothered him. He lunged. But the boy darted around Pew's strike, flew behind him, and drove his own weapon into the eyeless pirate's back. Pew barely had time to look surprised before the crocodile's powerful jaws closed around his legs, and he came apart. Benn Gunn tried to raise his weapon, but he didn't have a chance before the boy skewered him. Injured and half-blind as he was, Black Dog growled and lunged at him. Though only a third of his size, the boy knocked away Black Dog's attack with a casual ease. He stabbed the ghost twice in his right arm and once in the leg, laughing all the while. Black Dog screamed with rage and lashed out, but the child moved through the air as if he had been born to it. He got in front of Black Dog and held his blade forward, impaling the pirate with his own momentum. Then the boy threw his head back and crowed. It should have been silly, but that sound was just as unnerving as any raven's call.

The crocodile, finished with Pew, slowly turned towards James and John.

James uttered a single word. "Run."

John obeyed.

As he emerged from the woods, the ghostly form of the *Walrus* came into view. Flint would be furious. John and the others were crew aboard a ship of the dead. Being destroyed was more painful than anything mortal man had ever experienced, but finding peace was not so easy as that. The first of those James had seemingly destroyed would have already reformed aboard the ship. They would no doubt laugh when they heard of the child, but that would stop once Pew and Black Dog reappeared. That a boy... *a thing* – for it could be no mere boy – should so easily defeat them was no laughing matter, and Flint was no fool. This place – Neverland, as James had called it – was under that thing's protection.

John looked at the hook in his hand, the one that was even now tugging him toward the island. James was safe for now, but if he ever left the island… Well, there was nowhere he'd be able to hide.

The Reeds Remember

JULIET MARILLIER

Twigs crack under my bare feet. Leaves tremble with my passing. A bird calls, troubled. *Go! Go!* The rasp of my breathing is another presence in the woodland, another clue to the hunter. This is the third day of running, the third day of hiding. The third day of listening for his footsteps, his voice calling to me, honey and poison: *Syrinx, I love you! Do not fear me!* Lies. Such bare-faced, shameful lies. He is a god. He is a leader. And for all his strong adult body, he is a wilful child.

After it happened, on that first day, I ran back to my oak, my heart, my haven. I hid in her high branches, pressing my body against her trunk, taking comfort from her strength. Much later, as darkness fell, I crept into her hollow, where squirrels had kept me warm through the long winter. My oak was my safe place; I was her nymph; she was my home. Here, not even Pan could touch me. I fell asleep to the soft calls of owls. At daybreak I woke to feel a shivering through the great tree, though the air was still. In the upper branches crows perched, exchanging cries of doom. *Flee! Flee while you can!* I wept as I climbed down; I touched my brow to my heart-tree's bark and whispered words of love. My tree was trembling deep within. I thought the crows had unsettled her. I followed their warning and moved away, seeking another hiding place. Pan would weary of the chase eventually. Then I could return home. So I told myself, trying to believe it.

I found shelter in a rocky cleft high above the valley floor, screened from view by a solitary fir. I had not been there long when I heard the sounds: voices from down the hill, by my heart-tree, and the hungry rasp of a saw. And then I felt it: terror, pain, the knowledge of approaching death as the teeth gripped and the wound grew deeper and deeper, cutting off the sap that was her lifeblood. I made myself bear witness, moving out to stand beneath the fir. I saw my heart-tree shake and shiver and fall. The many seasons of her growth, the years she weathered, the creatures she sheltered and nurtured and loved, the thousand stories she held within her… gone. All gone. I stood transfixed, numb with shock. Pan had done this. Not for the wood my tree might have provided for the building of useful things. Not for the hearth fires her boughs might have fed to keep folk alive through a harsh winter. No; only because of me. I understood, then, that he would stop at nothing to get his way.

I must have uttered some sound, some anguished cry that carried above the voices of Pan's followers, busy with their act of destruction. He turned his head, seeking as a wolf or bear might. I shrank back behind the fir, and he did not see me.

Now it is the third day, and he is on my track again. I am a thing of cold sweat and terror. His pursuit is relentless. Sometimes, when he draws near, he calls out to me: *Syrinx, sweet nymph! Let me be kind to you! I will show you delights beyond your imagining!* Can he not understand what I have shown him, over and over: that his advances fill me with disgust?

My head is dizzy; I must rest. For now, I can hear neither his voice nor his footsteps. I am in woodland not far from the valley floor, and here is a young oak, her foliage fresh green, her limbs still learning to stretch for sunlight and rain. All oaks are friends to my kind. I sink down beside her, my whole body aching. I close my eyes; I imagine this is my own oak, my once-upon-a-time tree. Long ago she was young like this, and full of hope. I breathe, one, two, slow, slower. I listen. Perhaps he is truly gone. Perhaps he has lost the scent. Oh, let it be so.

The sounds of the forest: a breeze through the canopy, the conversation of birds, a furtive rustling that might be marten or badger or fox. Somewhere more distant, the sweet song of moving water. Streams follow their winding courses through this woodland. Still pools reflect a tracery of high branches, and above them, patches of sky. Sunlight, cloudscape, midnight stars: each lovely in its own way. My heart steadies. I hear no sounds of pursuit. Time to draw breath, time to make a plan. But where can I go? What hiding place is safe from a god with all his thoughts bent on conquest? It seems I have outrun him this time, but he will return. He will not leave me alone until he gets his way.

"My tree is gone," I whisper, touching gentle fingers to the young oak. "He killed her, and I am broken. Artemis could have stopped him. But she will no longer protect me. Did I deserve such dire punishment? Was my offence so great?"

I hear it then – the tender, silent voice of the tree. *Tell me the story.*

"We were on the hunt." It hurts to tell it, to relive it, so soon after the loss of my oak. "Artemis was in the lead, bow at the ready, tall and strong in her doeskin tunic and leggings, her hair in a crown of braids. The rest of us fanned out under the trees, treading silently as we advanced in pursuit of deer. When the goddess reached the stream, she lifted her hand to signal a halt. The woods were quiet. If this watercourse was home to naiads, they had chosen not to show themselves.

"Artemis went suddenly still, her gaze fixed on the water. I was one step behind. I looked down, wondering what had caught her attention so, and saw something moving in the shadowy depths, something white and silver and gold, a graceful ripple through the pond weeds. Oh, it was magical! It was lovely! A salamander, but far bigger than any I had seen before, a glowing, majestic creature, surely a queen of her own kind. I opened my mouth to speak, but Artemis signalled silence, a finger to her lips, and I swallowed my words. Then Artemis handed me her bow and gestured to Nephele, who was acting as her spear-carrier. Nephele passed over the weapon.

"Artemis narrowed her eyes and readied the spear. My heart clenched tight. Surely the goddess wouldn't – but it seemed she would. I willed the creature to swim away, to dive deep, to save itself. The salamander looked at the goddess, gazed up toward its certain death unblinking. It was beautiful. It was trustful. It was innocent. As Artemis drew a deep breath, as her body tightened for the throw, I dropped the bow and flung myself at the goddess, knocking her sideways. We both went down. The spear slammed into the earth and stood there, quivering. I scrambled to my feet. My heart was racing. I risked a glance toward the water. The salamander was gone.

"I put out a hand to help Artemis up, but she rose in one fluid movement, not touching me. Her face was a mask of cold fury. We were her chosen few, loyal and obedient. I had laid rough hands on her; I had impeded the hunt. I had broken the laws of the goddess.

"There was so much I wanted to say: how it is one thing to hunt for food, and another to chase and kill for the sheer thrill of it. How remarkable that creature was, how full of deep magic. For in the moment when I saw it, I recognised that every animal, from the smallest shrew to the black bear, from the shrimp to the great whale, was part of the earth's magic, a wonder of its own particular kind. But I knew Artemis would be deaf to my words. That was plain in the way she looked at me, then ripped the spear from the earth.

"'Begone, Syrinx.' Her voice was glacial. 'Quit my sight.

This reckless act has lost you your right to my protection. Do not think to seek out your sisters; they will not help you.'

"A shiver ran through me, chilling me to the bone. It was not only a doom for me, but also an order for the others: they must shun me as Artemis wished or risk losing their own places among her chosen followers. Did she mean I was banished forever? I could not ask.

"I turned my back and walked away. I made no apology. In my heart, I knew I would not hunt again. And now I am here in the woods," I tell the little tree. "On my own, running, hiding, running again. Not from her. From Pan. With a hundred willing women to choose from, he has fixed on one he cannot have, should not have. He would have pursued me season after season, if it were not for the protection Artemis gave me. While she was my goddess, while I was her nymph, he could not touch me against my will, though he tried to lure me many times. Now she no longer protects me, and he is hunting me. My binding vow of chastity means nothing to him. He cut down my tree, all because of that. I am afraid."

The oak sapling trembles, echoing my sorrow. High above us a bird shrieks a warning: *Move! Move!* Pan is coming, with his proud horns and stamping hooves and his mind fixed on his own satisfaction. He speaks of love. Such honeyed words have captured many, both mortals and my own kind. He excites them; they open to him as flowers to the sun. But he loves neither woman nor man. He craves the chase, the pursuit, the wildness, the smell of flesh and sweat and seed. It is as if he lives in his own strange world, whose rules

only he understands. I think perhaps he loves only himself.
As for his followers, they are loyal as much from fear as from
admiration. Some find his wild moods thrilling, yes. But
some have nowhere else to go. Some live in terror of what may
happen if they leave him. Lost souls, all of them.

Quick, quick! A flutter of tiny finches sounds a fresh alarm.
I gather my failing strength. I cannot outpace him forever.
There is a stand of ancient oaks on the far side of this valley.
If I can cross the stream safely, if the naiads do not take it into
their heads to toy with me, perhaps I can find a hiding place
among those trees. "Farewell, sweet friend," I whisper to the
little tree. Then I run. Down the slope, weaving a perilous
way, for moss-coated rocks rise from the undergrowth as if
determined to send me sprawling. I dodge, I skip, I jump,
arms outstretched for balance on the treacherous ground.
I leap, and my foot comes down hard to lodge itself in a stony
cleft. Pain spears through my ankle. I fall to one knee, clumsy
as a human woman.

I cannot get up. My foot is on fire. How can I wrench it
free? Hot tears wash my cheeks; I clench my jaw tight. I must
not make a sound. *Breathe, Syrinx. Breathe, then free yourself.
Save yourself. Are you not sworn to purity?* I will not call to
Artemis. I will not give her the satisfaction of punishing me
further with her silence. Somewhere within me, grief turns
toward anger.

I count to three and haul my foot out. The pain is terrible;
a sob escapes my lips. I clench my teeth and stagger-hop
on down the hillside. From somewhere behind me comes a
triumphant burst of laughter, then the clatter of his hooved

feet on the stony ground, closer, closer. I blunder on, tears blinding me. *I am a huntress*, I tell myself. *Fleet of foot, stealthy and strong. Quick-witted. I will not give in. I will die rather than let that creature lay his hands on me…*

"Don't be foolish, Syrinx! You're hurt! Let me help you!"

Gods be merciful! He is gaining ground with every halting step I take. And he has boxed me in. We are almost at the stream. Here it pools between banks rich with tangling water plants, ferns, cresses, mosses. Each step is torture. Try to clamber around that way and I will not last to the count of ten. I can smell him; he is just behind me. I teeter on the bank, high above the pool. I never learned to swim.

"Syrinx, no! Wait, let me—"

I jump. The water envelops me, a chill shock, and then it is in my eyes and nose and mouth and I can't breathe. My chest hurts. Air, air, I need air… but he will see me…

Something coils around me, drawing me sideways under the surface. Not Pan; something strong and smooth and gentle. *Be calm*, a watery voice says in my mind. *Be still*. As I struggle not to breathe, not to drown, it swims me into a place of shallows, and now my face is clear of the water. I suck in blessed air. But… something is different. Everything is different. Everything is odd, a confusion of colours and shapes, and the water that scared me so has become a friend, kindly on my skin, but my body feels strange, wrong, ungainly. My foot no longer hurts. I can hear Pan shouting, weeping, but his words make no sense. All around me is a rustling green-white curtain that was surely not in this pool before. Reeds. This must be near the edge. He will see me. I struggle against whatever is holding me, and someone – some*thing* – speaks in my mind. It is the same liquid voice as before, calm and measured. *Do not be afraid. He cannot see you here. You are safe. But… it has been necessary to make a change.* A pause. *You can swim now. Over, under, through. But not yet. We will stay here in the reeds until he is gone.*

I speak as this being does, using my mind only. *A change? The reeds, to shield me?*

There is a smile in the voice as it says, *That, yes. And a change to you, to deceive the eyes of those who would harm you. I will release you now. Stay here beside me, still and quiet. He believes you drowned. He is sad, angry, thwarted in his desire. Let us wait and see what he will do.*

The restraining hold loosens. Now I can see both my rescuer and my own body. She is both woman and salamander, a sleek, graceful creature of white and silver and gold, and she smiles as I look at her. I know her. The delicate filaments of her hair spread out on the water, pale as dawn light; her eyes are full of wisdom. She is both sweet and powerful. Her wide salamander mouth curves up in a smile. As for me… I look at my body, wondering if this is all a strange dream, knowing it is not. I have glossy skin of oak hues, mottled green and brown; short limbs with stubby fingers and toes. I have a tail… I do not know how to be in this body. *Is this change forever?* I ask her.

Wait, says the salamander woman, or perhaps she is a goddess. *Be still. Wait until he is gone.*

Cursing and sobbing, Pan makes his way down to the shallows, where he splashes about not far away. I shrink back, trembling. My companion steadies me with a hand on my shoulder.

Wriggle down, she says. *Leave only your eyes above the surface. Yes, that's good. Now you can watch him.*

Through a low gap in the reed bed, all but submerged, we watch. Pan's words sound garbled – in this new body, my perceptions are changed – but the salamander woman translates for me. *What sorcery is this? I saw you fall, I saw you drown, yet there is no body to be found! Some foul magic has reduced you to this bed of reeds, your life, your life, your beauty, all gone! Oh, wilful nymph, what have you done to bring down this fell curse?* He takes a long knife from his belt and begins to slash away at the stems, wading in further to do so, muttering all the time. My companion tells me he speaks of foolish nymphs and his broken heart and what he will do with this strange harvest. He talks of music. Of making a set of pipes whose tunes will express a sorrow more bitter than any experienced since the beginning of time. His hacking, stabbing knife makes a furious percussion. I think he is more angry than sad.

With a goodly bunch of reeds under his arm and the weapon back in his belt, Pan stands on the high bank. He looks out over the pond and speaks in ringing tones, as if to address every last newt and dragonfly dwelling here. Or perhaps this is meant for the salamander woman, if he knows of her, or for the unseen naiads – who can say? I still cannot make sense of the words. My companion's voice sounds in my mind again, translating. *I will return and play my mourning song. From that day on, this will be a place of shadows and sorrow, a place where no man can feel joy.* Pan turns and walks away.

A chill creeps into my bones. My actions have brought a curse to this lovely place, this gentle saviour. *I'm sorry,* I tell her. *You rescued me, and now...*

A slow smile creeps over the salamander woman's face. Her eyes are bright; is that a look of mischief? *And you rescued me,* she says. *A place of shadows and sorrow? Those are empty words. Pan has no authority here – his curse is meaningless. As for his vows of love, if he believed you transformed into reeds, and his response was to hack those reeds to pieces, the fellow has a peculiar notion of what love is.* She flicks her tail dismissively, sending a trail of dancing droplets into the air. *Wait and see, Syrinx. Only wait. And while you are waiting, try out this life: part nymph, part salamander. Move between earth and water, as you will.*

Oh. This leaves me breathless. *You mean I can be either nymph or salamander as the wish takes me? I can choose? I can change to protect myself, to shield others, to keep my home safe?*

I will teach you the art of it.

And she does, for as long as it takes for Pan to return home; to wait until his reeds are fully dried; to measure and cut them; to bind them together with cunningly knotted twine. She shows me the mysteries of the ponds and streams, the places where a salamander can travel secretly, the other creatures who dwell in the watery depths of the forest pools. The naiads do not play tricks on me. Instead they welcome me, almost as if I were one of their own kind. They are full of life. They ask for the story of what brought me to this pool, the tale of Pan and Syrinx. I tell it over and over, and always they want more: *What did Pan say then? And what did you say? I would have slapped him!* They start to tell the tale themselves, changing it a little each time, making it anew. I wonder if folk will still be telling tales of Pan in a hundred years, a thousand, even more. What would such tales be like? Perhaps they would make him into a hero.

As a salamander, I swim and dive and twist and turn in a freedom near-magical. I learn the patterns of water on my new body, the rushing falls, the flowing stream, the deep, enveloping pool. I learn to rest during the heat of the day, under a rock or a sheltering log. When night falls, I catch insects with my long tongue. I learn the crunch and flavour of them. I learn which fish to avoid, and which I can swim alongside. I learn my companion's name. It is Selene – apt for a creature of moonlight and rippling water. She teaches me the slow, strange magic of turning from salamander to nymph and back again. The naiads watch and laugh and applaud my success. I welcome their friendship. But it scares me to be back in my old form; my fear of Pan is not so easily banished. In some ways he is like a child, yes. But this is a child without self-restraint. A child attuned only to his own wants. A child with the power to draw others into his strange games.

The day comes at last. Pan returns to the pool with his reed pipes in hand. He settles on the bank above us. A crow has forewarned us of his coming. Selene and I are waiting in the reeds, hidden from his sight. The naiads also watch; everyone knows the story now. On the banks and in the water, voles and martens, fish and turtles lift their heads in expectation. Dragonflies hover; beetles pause in their tracks to hear how the tale ends.

He lifts the pipes to his lips and begins to play.

The reeds remember. Their plaintive tune rings out across the water for five notes, six, before Pan drops the instrument and hunches over, both hands clutching his groin. A cry of agony bursts from his lips. Blood trickles between his fingers.

A terrible magic, Selene says with perfect calm. *Each stem slashed, each stem that sounded its note of sorrow, is a cut to his own proud reed.*

A confusion of feelings washes through me. *Your doing?* I ask her. *It seems... quite cruel.* It also seems rather appropriate, but I do not say that.

Rough justice, observes Selene. *But justice, nonetheless. His curse has turned back on him. This dark magic is not of my making, Syrinx. As for Pan, he is a wayward child. But he is also a god. He will heal soon enough.*

As Pan kicks the reed pipes into the water, then staggers away, I hear the naiads laughing.

Pan never returns to the pool. We see nothing of him, and I am glad of it. But Artemis comes, not long after the day when he played his cursed pipes. She stands by the water's edge, with Nephele on guard not far away, and looks out toward the small island where I sit in the company of wood-ducks. I keep the form she is accustomed to. As a salamander, I might well find myself speared, stuffed with herbs, and served up on a platter. Artemis does not speak, and neither do I.

She watches me awhile, then gives a grave nod. It is no apology; a goddess does not say sorry. But I take it as a message of respect and acceptance, and I return it in the same spirit. She does not invite me to rejoin her followers, sparing me the need to refuse the offer.

I am no demi-god, but I am more than mortal, and my kind are long-lived. I stay with Selene and the naiads over many seasons, while the young oak grows tall and strong, spreading her branches wide, building her canopy. When she is ready, she offers to be my heart-tree; my tears of joy are all the answer she needs. Pan may have recovered quickly. For me, the healing has been slow. But now, at last, I am whole again.

No Such Place

PAUL FINCH

I mopped grimy sweat from my brow. "What do you think?"

Denny seemed vague. "Gonna be a lot of fatherless boys when we get home."

I followed his gaze through the glassless north window and across the meadow, where at least twenty bodies were scattered like butchered meat all the way back to the farm gate. They neatly outlined the path we'd taken in our flight from the sunken lane where the 20mm cannon had first picked us out.

"I'm hurt," came a hoarse voice. "Corp..."

Private Harcourt lay curled amid loose bricks and burned woodwork. His face was ash-grey; fingers clawed at the crimson froth seeping from the rent in his belly.

"Keep your head down," I muttered. I turned back to Collins. "Well?"

"Well what?"

"Christ's sake, Denny, snap out of it!"

A rifle round screamed off an internal pillar. We ducked instinctively. All of us. Except Denny Collins. He shook his head.

"*Panzergrenadiers*, mate. They can march over anything. They'll march over us."

"They can bloody try." I rounded on the others crouching in the dust and debris. "Benson... set up the Bren on the top floor. Find yourself a good position. Put fire on the north and east approaches alternately. Harris, east window."

"I've no rounds left," Barney Harris complained.

I scuttled over to Harcourt, who still twitched feebly, and threw his carbine to Harris, then unsnapped the casualty's ammo pouch from his webbing, and tossed that over too.

"Corp?" The lad brushed my hand with his bloodstained paw. His eyes were holes melted in tallow. "I can't..."

"You've got to stow it for ten, okay?" I whispered, knowing he wouldn't make five. "They're going to come at us with everything. I'll get you to a medic after that." I sidled up alongside Harris. "Take this." I offered him the Webley as I peeked through the shattered window.

"Lieutenant Brownlow's, wasn't it?"

"Not going to need it now, is he?"

"Not for me, Corp."

"Movement north-east!" Benson shouted down.

I switched position, spotting a row of helmeted, khaki-clad figures running stooped along a meadow-side ditch, cutting out of sight behind a hedgerow.

"Denny, get your arse over here," I hissed.

Collins muttered as he stared at the fallen relics of our platoon, then asked, "You and Joy got kids, Ron?"

Another bullet flew through the interior, ricocheting from an exposed girder. I backed to the pillar as dust plumed down, clicking a fresh magazine into my Sten. "You know we haven't."

"Me and Marcie have. Twin boys."

I glanced east, spying significant movement behind the meshed leaves of the hedgerow. "What's your fucking point?"

"Two years old last Christmas." His dust-browned features cracked into a manic, clownlike grin. "Thank Christ for that, eh? Thank Christ for small mercies…"

With a *PTCHUNG*, another round hit the girder, powdered dust exploding. "Denny, get into position now!" I shouted "Or I swear, you'll never see them again!"

"Wouldn't put a bet on that, Ronald, old mate." He lumbered to the east window, hefting his Lewis, laying its barrel on the ledge. "Sincerely, I wouldn't."

Over on our left, the hedgerow sagged brutally downward, crackling into nothingness as a steel leviathan rumbled out: a Panzer Mark IV, brutally battle-scarred, sun-dried earth shaking as it juddered forward. More Panzer troops kept low as they loped behind it, though we had a good angle on them.

Denny whooped as he opened fire. The Bren overhead thundered. We all of us shot and shot, their infantry going down like skittles, though the Mark IV kept coming, dust erupting from its caterpillar treads, the 75mm barrel swivelling in our direction…

"Not going to the hanging?" Terry Butler asked me.

I'd only just arrived at my desk. Hadn't lit a Woodbine yet. "Why would I?"

He looked surprised. "*You* arrested him."

I got the smokes out. "Seen enough men die."

He snorted. "Not getting a conscience, I hope?"

"I'm not getting a conscience about doing my job, Sarge." I hung my coat on the rack. "But I've seen enough men die."

He glanced at the clock as he got on with his typing. "Be over in twenty mins, anyway."

I nodded, grunting. I wouldn't have been able to make it to Pentonville if I'd tried.

My eyes averted from the clock, which read eight-forty, to the suspect gallery on the far side of the Squad Room. Someone had already obliterated Lazenby's rodent-like mug by using a felt tip to etch a blood-red cross over it. It was a bit previous in this case, but with only twenty minutes left, did it really matter?

I certainly wasn't getting a conscience about Roy Lazenby. The seedy, snivelling bastard had pimped his own wife out so much she'd looked sixty when she died, even though she was only forty. In the end, he'd decided he needed a new, fresher model. So he'd cut her throat and dumped her on a rubbish heap. Tried to make out a punter had done it. It hadn't been difficult breaking him down in the interrogation room. None of these blokes on the margins of the underworld are ever as tough as they like to make out.

DI Wilberforce slouched in, raincoat buttoned only at the top, as usual, briefcase, also as usual, tucked under his arm rather than carried by the handle. He was a big, solid block of a man of about fifty, but his hair and moustache were already snow white and he looked permanently harassed. He stopped and stared at me.

"What're *you* doing here?"

"Rumour has it, guv, I work here."

"Why're you not at the prison?"

"Taking Sally-Anne to the pictures tonight. Didn't think a hanging was the right mental preparation for seeing my daughter."

"Never miss mine," he said glumly. "Always feel it's best to see the job through to the end. Please yourself."

He took his hat off as he lurched into his office, slamming the door behind him.

A phone rang. I ignored it, glancing dispiritedly at the pile of folders on my desk.

"Murder Squad Central?" It was Malcolm Mulgrave, the youngest guy in the office.

He listened intently for several minutes, interrupting now and then but only to ask for more details. After he hung up, he sat pondering, before getting up and knocking on the DI's door.

"Better be good because I'm busy as hell!" Wilberforce yelled.

Mulgrave went in warily. Across the room, Terry Butler's smoke hung from the side of his mouth. His eyes were fixed on his typewriter as he bashed keys, but I could tell he was earwigging. Truth was, it was a red-letter day when Mulgrave took a call and didn't then come straight to one of us to ask for direction. Usually, he went nowhere near the brass. Whatever conversation he was now engaged in, though, it didn't last long.

The door swung open again.

"DC McKane!" Wilberforce remained seated but leaned sideways so that he could spear me with his beady little eyes. "Your desk's currently clear, isn't it?"

I shrugged. "I've got some paper I need to—"

"Haven't we all! Go with sonny-boy here. Pop down the Elephant. See if there's anything in this 'lost boys' business."

"Lost boys?" I asked as we drove across Westminster Bridge.

Mulgrave looked surprised that I didn't know, though, to be fair, surprise was his regular expression. He was so new to the job he didn't have his own police driving certificate yet, but as the Commissioner's nephew, he'd made CID in two and the Murder Squad in three, which had to be a record. I swear, his fair hair was more like baby fluff.

"You not been reading force bulletins?" he asked.

"Humour me."

"Well, there're a few bad lads down Elephant and Castle."

"Get away."

"Seems they've been dropping off the chart."

"Come again?"

"Disappearing."

I *had* heard about this actually, but hadn't paid much attention to it. They were toerags for the most part. Burglars, pickpockets, rent boys. Typical types who are never destined to live long. They'd die overdosing on pills or crashing stolen cars or knifing each other for pocket change or something else equally ridiculous. All these who'd gone missing would be found eventually, down drains or in abandoned properties. I couldn't see the mystery in it, myself.

"They're all fatherless," Mulgrave said.

"What's that?" I asked.

He glanced at his pocket-book. "Every one of them lost his dad during the war. Plus, there're other similarities apparently. There's a DS Bailey, LIO Southwark... reckons we should take a look at it."

I drove on. I knew Les Bailey. He wasn't the sort to raise the alarm for nothing.

"Thinning on top, Bernie?"

He stood in the open doorway, hands in his trouser pockets, braces worn over his vest, eyeing me with cautious disdain. "I'm not rising to it, Ron."

"You'll be wearing a toupee next."

"Hurry up, Joy, will you?" he shouted over his shoulder.

"Doesn't sound like she's listening," I said. "She was always her own woman."

"Better than being yours, eh?" He smirked.

"How's the tax and insurance situation down your depot?" I wondered.

"Look... Ron, I know you can make my life a misery. I don't care, so long as you're not doing it to Joy's anymore." He shrugged. "Come down the yard first thing tomorrow. You might find something, I don't know. And like I say, I don't care."

Joy appeared with Sally-Anne, who looked as cute as a button in a tartan coat, tartan scarf and tartan beret. We weren't Scottish, but Joy had always shown good taste when it came to dressing our daughter in fetching ensembles. It was a pity she didn't extend the same level of discernment to the men in her life.

My ex pushed a strand of copper hair from her face as she handed our daughter over. She was still beautiful, even if she did tend to look tired and sad these days.

"You're bringing her back tonight, you said?" she asked.

I nodded. "No point her staying over. I've got work tomorrow."

"Don't leave it too long after the picture, yeah? She can't be up till all hours."

I picked Sally-Anne up and she put her arms around me. "Doesn't need much beauty sleep, this one," I said. "Me, on the other hand... that speaks for itself. We won't be late." I glanced at Bernie. "Not that I imagine His Lordship here ever needs very long."

Joy reddened. "For God's sake, Ronnie!"

On the newsreel at the Empire that evening, they were still talking about Joe Stalin's death despite it having happened a month earlier. The general sentiment, even in the Soviet Union, seemed to be that no one would miss him. Which made me think again about those lost lads down the Elephant. And then the main feature commenced, and the colourful title sequence trailed across the big screen. It would be another flight of fancy, of course. Another sumptuous cartoon from the kingdom of cartoons. Sally-Anne was already entranced, though it probably wouldn't be much different from the one with Alice and the white rabbit that I'd taken her to a couple of years ago. Personally, I didn't know how I was going to get through it. But then I looked again at the credits, and it suddenly hit home what we were watching... and it was like the hand of fate plucking at me.

The book had sat at the back of my locker for so long I'd forgotten it was there. It was still inside the brown paper packaging with the Broadmoor stamp in the corner, a single rip at one end from when I'd first opened it.

It was a hardback, a 1911 imprint of *Peter and Wendy*, so badly charred on the outside that whatever illustration had once adorned its cover was no longer visible. Even inside, the pages were blackened and flaking round the edges. Just sniffing at it all these years later, you still got a whiff of burn. If this had been the only thing I'd received from Denny Collins after his incarceration, it would have been too confusing to make sense of, but a letter had accompanied it, written in blotchy pen. I sat at my desk and read it again:

Where do you think Neverland is, Ronald, old mate? In this book, Peter Pan gives Wendy a load of gobbledegook about how you get there. Directions that don't mean anything. Something about it being up near the Milky Way. But really,

I think it's a kind of fantasy land that's always out of reach for people like us. A perfect place where childhood never ends, and anyone lucky enough to be taken there has a rare old time with none of the pressures that turn our lives to mud when we get the raw deal of adulthood.

You were my closest mate, Ron. I know we only got to know each other under fire, but what kind of bond does that create? Especially when you serve in so many theatres. North Africa, Italy, Normandy. We were the only two originals left when it ended. So, if I can't talk to you about this in the earnest hope you won't consider me as much a nutter as everyone else does, who can I talk to?

Do you remember that I mentioned this book once before? June 1944, in the Bocage? When we lost so many lads in one day?

It stayed with me, that did, I can tell you.

But when they're dead, they're dead, you know. It's over for them.

Nastier for me was thinking about the youngsters they'd left behind. The desolation those young boys faced, wandering the streets, suddenly knowing in no uncertain terms that this bloke who'd taught you everything, who'd played cricket with you, who'd showed you how to knot your tie properly on your first morning of school, who'd given you the belt when you were up to no good and a shilling later for taking it like a man, that he wasn't just absent from your life now because he was overseas, but... well, now you didn't know where he was, though you knew he wasn't coming back. And that you didn't have the first clue what

*had happened to him because they'd spared you that detail
and even got vexed when you asked about it.*

*Wandering, Ron, aimless. Feeling conned, cheated, picked
on by everyone, even God.*

Lost.

*I knew that feeling intimately, though I was too young to
understand when my mum got the letter in 1916. But I grew
up into that empty world, a bit more gradually than others,
I suppose. More gradually than all those poor little mites
left behind after the Bocage. That's why I fought so hard to
get through. I wasn't doing it for me, Ron. It was for Tommy
and Billy. I could never stand the thought of them joining
that lost troop...*

And then look what happens? Eh?

The Lord works in mysterious and vindictive ways.

*Which is why I must always believe in a place where lost boys
of every ilk can go on playing cowboys and Indians to their
hearts' content, building rope-swings and treehouses, where the
sun never goes down, where no one calls time on anything...*

I went and knocked on Wilberforce's door.

"Yello?" he boomed.

I entered to find him leaning with chin on elbow,
Detective Superintendent Ivor Edwards, gaffer of Murder
Squad Central, standing to one side, holding a stained
mug to his bulldog mouth. The several pages of report I'd
produced yesterday after my trip down to Elephant and
Castle were spread on the work surface between them,

alongside various documents and photos that I'd brought back from Southwark LIO.

Edwards eyed me with interest. Wilberforce looked despondent. The fact we were all in on a Saturday was a clear signal that DS Bailey's theory had struck home.

"Morning, sir?" I said to the super. He nodded and sipped tea. I looked at Wilberforce. "Sorry, guv. Missed something important off my report."

Wilberforce frowned. "Such as?"

"The name of the demented hoodlum responsible for all this."

That got me the audience I'd been hoping for. Edwards scraped a spare chair across, and sat down as I elaborated. Every so often, Wilberforce interrupted. "*This* book?" He nodded at the burnt chunk of paper I'd placed on his desk along with Denny Collins's letter.

"That's right," I said. "It was the only thing of value he was able to recover."

"Value?"

"It was valuable to him, sir," I replied. "It was a story he'd loved since he was a kid. Think it had been bought for him with his mother's war widow pension. He came to associate it with the dad he never knew. Loved it, cherished it. Used to read it to his own little boys whenever he was home on leave."

"And he was home on leave on this occasion?" Edwards asked.

I nodded. "He was wounded shortly after D-Day, sir. It wasn't serious, but we'd seen a lot of combat, so they gave him some R&R. Private Collins had been home one day when his house took a direct hit. Doodlebug. One of the first they sent over."

"He obviously wasn't at home himself," Wilberforce said.

"Down the Crown & Anchor at the end of the road with his missus."

"This girl he half-strangled," Edwards put in, "the one that got him sent down…?"

"Babysitter," I explained. "Mary Turner. Local girl, fifteen or sixteen. She survived the blast because she was out back with a boy she'd been seeing. She couldn't possibly have saved the two children even if she'd been in the house. There was no siren. When Denny – sorry, Private Collins and his wife came back… well, it was pretty horrific. The girl was digging in the bricks herself. Private Collins only grabbed her later when he found out she'd left the kids on their own. By then there were other people around, neighbours, some sailors from the docks – they'd come with shovels and spades and what-not, and they were able to pull him off before he finished the job." I paused. "They must've been team-handed, sir. I knew Dennis Collins. Pound for pound, he was the best soldier I ever served with. The thing is, though, up till the doodlebug, he'd always been on the right side of civilisation. If that makes sense. Then, of course, he tried to hang himself. Used his own braces while he was up the Glasshouse in Colchester. Jumped off the top bunk. This is what led to him being sectioned."

Wilberforce knew my record well enough not to let it show that he thought the links I'd made were somewhat tenuous. "When did he send you the book?"

"Not long after they locked him in the asylum, sir."

Edwards looked thoughtful. "And you think Dennis Collins should be a viable suspect in these lost boy disappearances because of that?"

"That's partly the reason, sir. But also, I've now learned that he was discharged from Broadmoor about six months ago. Which is roughly the time these disappearances started. There's something else, too."

"Go on."

"In all five cases that DS Bailey thinks are likely connected, the victims were fatherless due to the war. On top of that, all of them were thirteen years old."

"That's relevant?" Wilberforce asked.

"As far as I can gather, sir, James Barrie, who was the original author of the Peter Pan stories, lost his brother, David, when he was thirteen. I've read a little on the subject, and several scholars are of the view that this is the origin of the whole thing. As Barrie grew older, he could only ever picture his brother as a never-ageing child. It planted the seed of an idea that... *somewhere*, there was this wonderful fantasy land where every boy who gets lost finishes up and where they can carry on being thirteen forever."

"The Collins twins weren't thirteen," Edwards said.

"No, sir, that's true," I agreed. "It doesn't all align. But..."

"But you want to go and make some hay down Elephant and Castle? See if anyone's seen him recently?"

"Might be an idea, sir. Especially as that's Collins's home neighbourhood."

Edwards sipped more tea. "Keep it low key. At present, there's no such thing as the Lost Boys."

Recently in London we'd had a lot of what you might call deviant behaviour.

Four years prior to this, a resident of Kensington called John Haigh had been hanged for clubbing and allegedly vampirising nine men and women, whose corpses he'd afterwards melted in a drum of acid and spread like corrosive goo on some wasteland down Crawley way. On that occasion, the maniac wasn't known about while he was at large, but that couldn't be said of Gordon Cummins, the so-called Blackout Ripper, who, six years earlier, had attacked at least four women during bombing raids, cutting them up gruesomely with a variety of blades, including a can-opener. Despite restrictions on news reporting, that one caused a minor panic in the West End. And it was this case, I think, that Ivor Edwards had half an eye on. He'd been a DCI at the time, and he'd helped see Cummins get his rope necklace. But when he'd first joined the job, forty years before, there'd still been some old sweats who remembered the original Ripper, and the chaos on the Whitechapel streets as Scotland Yard's finest proved themselves incapable of stopping him. Edwards probably got a flavour of this during the "Blackout" carnage, though at least that had only lasted six days, so things hadn't got too much out of hand. He probably dreaded something similar happening now.

The Murder Squad was a respectable operation these days. We got results, were well spoken-of. The super dreaded losing all that, so we had to keep the Lost Boys enquiry under our hats, though as I've intimated, I couldn't see the fuss myself. The names of these lads might have seemed everyday enough: Graham Colgate, John Cornish, Steven Ratcliff, Toby Jenkins, William Reeves. But, for whatever reason, they'd all lost their way badly. And to my mind, *that* would concern the average Londoner most.

A bunch of tealeaves taken off the street.

Was it really a problem?

"They must have some family who'll miss them," Mulgrave said, scanning pictures as we drove. "I'm surprised the word hasn't already travelled."

"In the neighbourhoods *we'll* be visiting, Malcolm, they go missing all the time. Often 'cause they're on the run or in the clink. Their families aren't keen to put that about."

"I thought you believed there was something in this case?"

"I do, but it'd be easier for us if they'd been found chopped up in sackcloth bags."

"Jesus." He paled. "I hope not."

I didn't answer. It made no difference what we hoped.

"How you doing, Tonker?" I asked.

Philbert Tonks had just departed The Rat's Nest, Newington, by its back door and looked startled to find me and Mulgrave waiting.

"Mr McKane?" he said. "Don't often see you south of the river."

"More's the pity, eh?" I led him out of the yard by his green chequered lapel. "Looks like easy pickings to me."

I steered him down an alley and pushed him against the wall. Steam poured over the top as a locomotive chugged past on the other side. Mulgrave kept a wary watch at the alley's entrance, one ear cocked to Southwark on a raucous Saturday night. It was cold and damp, but the cosh boys and spivs were out and about everywhere. Noisy drinkers moved between the boozers. Tonker smelled of booze himself. He'd spilled some down his Slim Jim tie, but he wasn't a threat: thin, weaselly, his eyes wide and scared.

"What's this?" he asked. "You're Murder Squad, aren't you? I've not topped no one."

"I wonder," I said.

"Come on, Mr McKane… you know I don't do anything heavy."

"So what's this for?" I'd already reached into his left jacket pocket, as that was the one sagging down, and pulled out his sap: it was a thick woollen sock, tied at one end and containing what felt like a snooker ball.

His forehead gleamed with sweat. "Protection."

I held it up for my oppo's inspection. "Does the average law-abiding Londoner go armed these days? What do you think, Mr Mulgrave?"

"Erm…"

"The answer's 'no', by the way."

"No," he said.

I pocketed the weapon and cracked Tonker across the face. It was no more than a slap, but it was loud.

He grunted in pain, then glared at me reproachfully as he fingered the red mark.

"So, what's happening, Tonker? What're you up to?"

"I've already said I've not murdered no one."

"That's why I'm content to give you the flat hand rather than a knuckle sandwich. It's also why I might be persuaded not to search any more of your pockets, even though I know what I'd find in there."

The crack had turned him sullen. "You can't do that."

I took him by the tie-knot. "Tonker, you know perfectly well I can do anything I want."

He scowled.

"So, what's it to be? Do I search you properly, and locate the handful of stolen ration books you weren't able to sell in the pub bogs – and knock your teeth out in the fucking process, by the way? Or do you have a word in my ear and we all go home happy?"

He knew when he was beaten. "What do you want to know?"

"Who's selling boys?"

His eyes widened. He shook his head. "No one does that round here."

"Really? 'Cause I've heard it's you."

"*What!*" This time he looked genuinely shocked.

I shrugged. "Only what I've been told. But how would it play in the cells at Southwark? Let alone if you end up doing ten somewhere like Parkhurst. I mean, I couldn't keep my gob shut about something as serious as that."

Tonker's eyes bugged. "You sodding liar!"

I leaned into his face. "What's that?"

He looked away, so wet with sweat the Brilliantine leaked down his cheeks. "You sodding liar, *Mr McKane*."

"That's better." I fixed his tie for him. "Truth is, it wouldn't matter whether I was lying or not, would it? Something nasty always sticks."

His eyes averted downward. "It's the Slug."

"Old Kent Road? Landlord of The Coach House?"

Tonker glanced worriedly along the alley. "Them's the premises he does it from." His voice dropped to a whisper. "There's a couple of rooms upstairs. He sells boys *and* girls."

I nodded. "How does it work?"

"Piss easy. Punters roll up at the back door, give a coded knock. In they go, take their pick."

"Does the action occur on the premises?"

He shook his head. "They pay first, then take the merchandise anywhere they want, do whatever they want with it."

Mulgrave had come down the alley towards us. "Merchandise?" he said.

"You know what I mean."

"And then what?" I asked.

Tonker shrugged again. "Kids have to eat. They come back so they can get paid."

"And what happens if some of them don't come back?" I wondered.

"Their loss, isn't it? Slug doesn't mind. Lots more chickens in the yard." At which point he took note of the looks on our faces. "This is only what I've *heard*. I don't actually *know*."

"Who's he got on his payroll who's handy?" I asked.

"Well… Tommy Flynn's one of them."

"Tommy Flynn, eh?" I knew Tommy of old. He'd walked out of Arnhem wearing nothing but his underpants. "You'd better tell us everything, Tonker. The more you share, the less chance there is I parade you down the street, shouting about how helpful you've been."

Ex-Guardsmen always make effective beat bobbies. Something to do with them being an average height of six foot five. Add a helmet on top and you've got King Kong in uniform. For some reason, there was an inordinate number of these in the boroughs south of the river. It pleased me no end at half-eleven that night to find eight of them waiting around the corner from The Coach House Inn.

They were under the command of local duty officer, Inspector Lucius Trelawny, a mad-eyed Cornishman with thick bushes of red hair on his cheeks and upper lip. He'd agreed when I'd phoned that we needed to move sharpish on this, and so wouldn't have enough time to fully reconnoitre and then go through the motions of presenting our findings to the brass. Instead, we'd just storm the place under pretence of hunting after-hours drinkers. By all accounts that had been going on here since the blackout. The Slug, a.k.a. Oswald Bowkiss, routinely cocked something of a snook at the local plod, not just treating his regulars to illegal beer, but using his premises as a base to fence stolen goods and make illicit loans. If he was living off immoral earnings too, it'd be an even better collar.

The Coach House stood alone on the edge of a sea of rubble where bomb-damaged buildings had been cleared. Supposedly it had stood here since the eighteenth century, when it had been an actual coaching inn and wasn't even in London. Now it was a drab brick edifice. There wasn't even an arch leading to a yard anymore. Most of the windows on its upper three floors were boarded.

The Slug's official business happened purely on the ground floor, which curious eyes couldn't penetrate due to heavy curtains having been drawn. But now, even though it was getting on for midnight, you only needed to press an ear to one of the frosted-glass panes and you could hear belly-laughs and chinking glasses.

Trelawney could barely contain himself. "Lord help me, I've been waiting for this. You know what you're doing, boys. Everyone take your positions."

Mulgrave and I went to the door at the back. The inspector had allocated us only two of his bruisers because he'd assumed, probably correctly, that if we made an entry through the rear, the customers in the bar would panic and go out through the front. The bruisers and I stood aside, while Mulgrave, who looked the least policelike of us all, knocked on the door in the pattern Tonks had described.

A slat opened, and an ugly mug peered out.

"What do you want?" Mulgrave was asked.

"Love me a bit of chicken," he replied, again as instructed by Tonks.

The slat slammed home, bolts were withdrawn, and the door opened.

I went in past Mulgrave, though the two ex-Guardsmen went in past me, bellowing, already swinging their batons. Tommy Flynn, who'd opened the door, caught one on his cranium and went down like a sack of spuds. The ex-Guards trampled him in their eagerness to get through a dingy curtain into the main body of the pub, where shouting could also now be heard. Flynn was a typical former-Airborne tough nut. Blood spattered his face from where his scalp had split like an orange, but he was already trying to get to his feet. I planted a foot in his chest, forcing him back down, and raised Tonker's sap to my shoulder.

"Easy, Tommy… you want another, just give me a reason." He glared up at me, but lay still. "Malcolm," I said.

Mulgrave dropped to one knee, digging an envelope from under his coat. As he did, I glanced around. We were in a filthy old kitchen, piles of dirty crockery on the worktops, rat droppings scattering the floorboards. I glanced at the curtain. There was a royal hullaballoo on the other side: breaking furniture, more shouting. I could hear the inspector's piratical Cornish tones in the midst of the mayhem.

Mulgrave, meanwhile, was shoving pictures of our Lost Boys under Flynn's nose.

"Recognise anyone, Tom?" I asked. "Give me something good, I cut you loose…"

He glanced up at me, perturbed. Not sure if I was having him on.

I indicated the curtain. "We haven't got much time."

He averted his eyes back to the photos, shaking his head at each one, then suddenly narrowing his gaze. "This one," he grunted.

It was Toby Jenkins.

"You sure?" I asked.

"Took him round there, myself."

"How d'you mean?"

"Geezer who wanted him… can't remember his name, but he's got burns down the left side of his face. Doesn't like going out in public, I suppose. So I took this one there myself. He paid us extra for it."

"Took him where?" I asked

"Merchant Marine Yard, Bermondsey. There's only one building. You can't miss it."

"And did you see the lad again afterwards?"

He shrugged in the negative.

Their loss, isn't it? Tonker had said. Perhaps more truthfully than any of these slimy crooks could ever have imagined. In the background now, multiple pairs of hobnailed boots hammered up a staircase. Trelawney was looking for the chicken.

"Tell us more," Mulgrave said. "How tall was he, how was he built…?"

"No time for that," I interrupted, tossing the sap and hauling Flynn to his feet. I met him eyeball to eyeball. "No lasting damage, yeah?"

At first he looked puzzled. Then he grinned, and headbutted me in the face. I felt my nose break, my eyes fill with salt tears as I tottered back and slumped to the floor. I was vaguely aware of Flynn rounding on Mulgrave, the younger guy retreating across the kitchen, shocked. When Flynn followed him, Mulgrave grasped a dirty knife and shouted: "Back off, ponce!"

Flynn hesitated, and when he heard gruff voices approaching, fled through the open rear door. Mulgrave threw the knife away as I swayed back to my feet. I put a handkerchief to my bloodied nose. "Back off, ponce? To Tommy Flynn? You might fit into this job yet."

Trelawney now marched in. When he saw me, his Cheshire Cat grin faded.

"I was going to say good job, DC McKane. But maybe that would be premature?"

"Sorry, guv. Took my eye off the ball for a second."

He sighed. "Not to worry. We got the rest of them." His eyes rolled to the ceiling. "I hate to think what we're going to find upstairs."

"Time to have a look, eh?"

He nodded and passed back through the curtain. Mulgrave made to follow, but I grabbed his arm. "Not you, *dummkopf*! We've got bigger fish to fry."

The neighbourhood we were looking for was close to the river, mist hanging like grey cloth in its otherwise silent streets. It was a warehouse district, those buildings not fully flattened barricaded off by fences made from doors. Even the intact structures were hulking black outlines, slab-like and soulless in the night.

"Your mate Flynn didn't think it strange, bringing the lad to an address round here?" Mulgrave asked as we prowled.

"My mate Flynn – who isn't my mate – was paid not to care whether it was strange… or weird, or bloody diabolical."

"And *we* let him go."

"Once Trelawny had got his claws on him, he'd have clammed up. That would've been it."

"We sure this fella with the burned face is the same one you knew in the army?"

"Call it an educated guess."

"What's the story there?"

I never saw any value in discussing the events of those terrible years, but Mulgrave, for all that he was an annoying little gnat, had more right to hear them than most.

"June '44, it was," I said. "We were holed up in a French farmhouse when we caught a tank round. We saw it coming and evacuated, but only just. The building was completely destroyed, just vanished in a cloud of fire. Most of us were halfway across the meadow, heading for the nearest cover, so we made it unscathed. But Denny was at the back, pulling a lad behind us who'd been wounded. The casualty fried like bacon in a skillet, I'm afraid…"

"Jesus!"

"But Denny went down in a ball, wrapped himself up tight. Wasn't too badly hurt. Few light burns. Enough to leave marks, but nothing the average veteran would be upset about."

"Sounds like he was a good man."

"War does strange things to people, Malcolm."

He regarded me as I drove. Even in the darkness, he must have seen how tense my jaw was. "If you're nervous, maybe we should get some help?"

"If you can find a call-box round here, I'm all for it."

He pondered this. "Look, it's probably not the same guy.

You say Collins's burns weren't that bad. But Tommy Flynn said he wouldn't be seen in public."

"He didn't say that. He said he *supposed* that was the case. I'm telling you different. I'm also telling you that even a partly burned face would be recognisable to Joe Public."

"So… he wouldn't walk through town with this lad himself because he didn't want to be identified?"

"Correct. Which is why when we arrive at Merchant Marine Yard, I'm going in…" I flipped open the glove-box, "…with *this*."

I laid the Webley revolver on the dashboard.

Mulgrave stared in disbelief. "You're not supposed to have that!"

"I wasn't supposed to have it in the army either, for which reason I managed to smuggle it back home with me. I've only got six rounds, though, so we can't afford to waste them."

Mulgrave looked wearied. "This'll break my career."

"Or make it. You might be a hero by the end of tonight, Malcolm. Though first you'll have to come out of it alive."

Merchant Marine Yard lay at the end of a narrow side-street, which ran straight as an arrow for several hundred yards, more nameless buildings hemming it from either side, the cobbled surface littered with boxes and other rubbish. So cluttered was it that we walked the last fifty yards, at the end passing through an open gate in a row of railings, on the other side of which the yard lay knee-deep in mist, though this wasn't so thick that it concealed the eroded names and epitaphs on the flagstones. In front of us stood another massive structure, though this one had a portico at the front formed by Grecian pillars. Behind those was a jet-black rectangle that I took to be an open doorway.

I indicated the shadow-filled entrance to a side-passage. "Presumably that leads to the rear. Do *you* want to take it?" I glanced at Mulgrave. "Or shall we say 'fuck standard procedure' and go through the front together?"

The look on his face told me all I needed to know.

We entered side-by-side, going along a bare stone passage where the only light, if you could call it that, was a vague dimness about twenty yards ahead. We both carried electric torches, and I was tempted to switch them on, but every instinct forbade it. You don't let the enemy know you're approaching if you can avoid it. A moment later, we stepped through another doorway into what felt like an open nave-like space, and were confronted by a noticeboard standing on wooden legs. A sheet of card was pinned to it, with writing scrawled there. This time I *did* turn my torch on. I had no choice.

It read:

WELCOME TO NEVERLAND

"I hate being right," I murmured.

There was a sudden scuttling from the darkness. I pulled my pistol, and a rat scampered past our feet, tail whipping.

I clicked the torch off, plunging us back into blackness.

"Neverland?" Mulgrave whispered.

"Quiet…" I sidled to the edge of the noticeboard to look further into the nave. The darkness had retreated a little, dull moonlight seeping down through two rows of high, arched windows, one on either side, though most were broken and covered by planks.

It was just enough to reveal the expansive chamber. There was no doubt now that we were inside some kind of antique religious building, though any pews or other furnishings had long been removed. There was an altar of sorts, a slightly raised platform at the far end, with a low wooden railing encircling it. However, as I gazed down there, my vision adjusted further, and I suddenly realised that I was looking at a group of motionless figures.

I grabbed Mulgrave's arm. He froze, also staring.

There were ten or twelve of them, all standing very still, heads turned our way.

A second passed before I levelled the Webley, clicking back its hammer. When I advanced, I pushed Mulgrave sideways, separating us out.

"I say hit the deck, you hit the damn deck," I mumbled. Then I raised my voice. "Armed police officers! Nobody move!"

Nobody did move. At all. Their stillness was somehow terrible as they watched us approach. But a few yards closer, that stillness started to seem odd. I picked up a broken lathe and cautiously threw it. It struck one of them with a *clack*. Stiffly, the figure fell over.

"Shit." I flicked my torch on again.

Lifeless plaster mannequins stared back at us, many of

them cracked and burned, their clothes mostly rags. Clearly, they'd been retrieved from the ruins of bombed shops and storehouses. I didn't feel especially relieved, though; it made a macabre display.

"There too," Mulgrave said, pointing.

I glanced left. Much of the spacious interior was now visible, and about thirty yards off, a stone stairway swept up to what I assumed was an organ gallery. At the foot of it, on the left, stood another pair of immobile forms.

"And up there," he added.

I looked up to the organ gallery itself; this area was deeper in shadow, but I could still distinguish a solo figure behind the carved stone balustrade, apparently looking down at us.

"They been deliberately set up like this?" Mulgrave wondered.

I pivoted, but my torch beam expanded and lessened over distance; it didn't show me anything else I hadn't already seen.

"What I mean is," he said, "people haven't just been dumping them here?"

"*Christ!*" I hissed. He followed my gaze back up to the organ gallery, where the single figure had vanished. I raced towards the foot of the stairs. Mulgrave followed, but as we approached, a curious smell hit us, slowing us to a halt.

It wasn't particularly odious, but I recognised it.

"Formaldehyde?" Mulgrave said.

I turned to the left, where the two other figures stood beside the newel post. This time the torchlight revealed a lot.

The taller of the duo was another department store mannequin, its right hand in the air, what appeared to be a fishing rod in the left, its face bland and cracked again, though its clothing looked new. It had been dressed in flannel trousers and a plaid shirt, with a waterproof coat over the top. But it was the second figure that really struck us. This one also held a fishing rod, but it was shorter and slimmer. It wore a raggedy sweater and short pants rather than trousers, thanks to which we were able to see the wooden struts tied to the backs of its legs with twists of wire. A third piece of timber, a stouter one, an upright pole, stood at the rear, thrust underneath its sweater. It was a tripod, basically.

To hold this second figure upright.

Neither of us spoke as we eyed its yellowed parchment flesh, the blotchy eyes made with paint on the sunken lids, and the garish, red-painted lips, which would probably have looked more natural had the rest of the face not now loosened from the bone.

Mulgrave lurched away, doubled over and retched.

I'd seen more than him, but even I had to swallow back my gorge.

"Which… one is it?" he stammered, when he finally returned.

"It isn't Toby Jenkins," I replied. "This one's dark-haired. Jenkins was a redhead."

"What's wrong with him, this friend of yours?"

"He's no…" I was about to deny our friendship, but it wouldn't have been true. The last time I'd seen Dennis Collins, he *had* been a friend. Instead, I tried to focus on the grisly diorama. "A boy's life… the way it should be. Ever go fishing with your dad, Malcolm?"

He peered at me with confusion and horror.

I lurched up the stone staircase. He staggered in pursuit.

When we reached the organ gallery, there was no organ there. There were no choir stalls either. But there was someone hanging.

That was what I thought. But when we got closer, I realised that this figure, which again was relatively diminutive, was attached to a rope-ladder leading up into dimness, further twists of wire connecting it by the wrists and ankles. When we shone light on it, we saw that it had been dressed in a Boy Scout uniform. We wouldn't have been able to see its features easily because it was several feet up the ladder, but whoever had placed it there had turned its head around. I imagined the exuberant youth it was supposed to represent, the sun shining on a face written with the joy of the great outdoors. Of course, this face registered no such pleasure. Its only saving grace was that it hadn't been here as long as the one downstairs, and thus was more recognisable.

Though this one wasn't Jenkins either. Or any of the others we were seeking

"Awful lot of wayward lads wandering London at present," I said slowly.

"But Sergeant Bailey's list…"

"That only covered the Elephant."

Mulgrave was icy pale in my torchlight. "You don't think…?"

"His catchment area's wider than we thought."

"Ron, we've got to go and report this!"

I was about to reply that these were crime scenes and couldn't be left unguarded, when a narrow door creaked open about twenty yards away. I realise that sounds like something from a Boris Karloff movie, but it was obviously only a breeze sifting through one of the many chinks in this great mausoleum of a building. More interesting to me was the foot of the spiral staircase it exposed.

We had no option but to ascend. We were the police, as I had to remind Mulgrave, not a pair of watchmen from the Abbott and Costello stable.

It took us up to what I imagined would be the top and final floor, an attic of some sort, though the smell up there was particularly terrible, and it wasn't just formaldehyde anymore. It reminded me of Gazala or Alamein, where the intense heat of the North African sun turned even freshly killed men into blackened pulp.

Again, once up there, the light of our torches revealed little at first. It was another immense space, a vast plank floor strewn with rags. However, weak light speared down through a section of the ceiling overhead that was actually a dome, not quite the size of St Paul's but big enough, and seemingly painted black on its inside. Until I realised that actually it was made entirely of glass, but so thick with grime that it was all but opaque. Gradually, this and the spearing beams of our torches revealed more eerie figures standing apart from each other and in small, motionless groups.

We unintentionally diverged as we wandered, agog at what we were witnessing.

In my case, two one-man tents faced each other across a

tiny circle of stones, in the middle of which stood a pyramid of sticks with red foil to represent flames. From the tent on the left emerged a pair of bone-thin shoulders and a head that was more like a turnip with a face etched on it. As I watched, a fat cockroach wriggled free from an eye-socket. The figure on the right stood upright, again courtesy of a subliminal timber framework, though a more complex arrangement had been attempted here, creating the impression that this second corpse was rummaging inside a satchel.

"Ron!" came Mulgrave's urgent voice. "Think it's Toby Jenkins."

I went over to where he shone light on a different pair of figures. One of them was another retail mannequin. It wore cricket whites and pads and stood posed with a bat at the crease, defending a wicket behind which a second figure crouched wearing stumper's gloves. I crouched too, levelled my light, and recognised the aforementioned Jenkins. Not just from his dishevelled mat of red hair, but from the intense green of his eyes, which his abductor had replicated with emerald paint on his closed lids.

I rose back up, dazed.

"How do you think he killed them?" Mulgrave asked.

I shook my head. There was no obvious indication, but that would have been typical of Denny Collins. He was good at killing, though to have inflicted severe or prolonged pain in this situation would surely have defeated the object.

Mulgrave moved away, leaving me with the two cricketers.

I don't know what it was that made me look twice at the batsman. Possibly his face, which had been completely blown away by whatever high explosive had destroyed the shopfront where he'd once been displayed. At least, that was my first impression. But when I looked closer at that jagged jumble of lumps and tears, it occurred to me that I was seeing papier-mâché rather than the usual plaster they make these things out of.

Then it swung its bat.

Striking my pistol hand brutally, sending the Webley hurtling, before swiping up with a backhand, hitting me across the side of the head.

I fell with skull ringing, all senses numbed.

As I lay there, I heard heavy feet clump away, an unintelligible shout, a second smack of willow on bone, and the hollow thud of a body hitting the deck.

I'd been knocked out before. Back in uniform, I got coshed when I walked into a blag down Battersea. In February '44, at Monte Cassino, I was stunned to unconsciousness by a mortar shell. This wasn't quite as bad. I still knew where I was, though I didn't understand why my face was pressed into rugged woodwork. But it only lasted a minute or so, before reality swam back and I was able to lever myself upright, albeit dazed and sick. I tottered first to where Malcolm Mulgrave lay in a crumpled heap, but he was out for the count. Then I heard a clanking of metal, and saw the dark blot of a figure climbing up into the dome by a steel ladder bracketed to the side of a concrete stanchion.

"Denny!" I shouted, though I doubt my voice carried. I was too weak, too groggy.

I headed over there, half-tripping on a discarded cricket bat.

On reaching the foot of the ladder, I tried to focus on the vast domed space overhead. Its apex was forty feet above me, easily. It made me dizzy just looking up, and provided the perfect reason to go and get help. We'd already found the murderer's lair and could account for God knew how many missing persons. On top of that, Mulgrave and I were injured. No one would think it lax of us to have missed out on the actual culprit. But in truth, I was thinking about Denny himself. I didn't know any of the Lost Boys personally; I barely knew Mulgrave. But the best friend I'd had at the worst time in my life was facing death by hanging, and I was going to serve him up to that fate. Unless I could find... well, I didn't know what I might find. I could only hope.

So I climbed, and I climbed, and about twenty feet up, I realised there was a circular gantry not far above me. It was about two feet wide, made from wood, but it circled the base of the dome like a collar. A figure was standing on it, looking down. I assumed it was Denny. I tried to speak to him but there was no reply.

I hauled myself up through a square hatch, and that stink embraced me again.

It was another Lost Boy. Fastened in place with struts and wires. He wore swimming trunks and carried a towel under his left arm. His right hand shaded his eyes as he gazed an infinite distance into the blue haze of whatever adventure he was wrapped in. Well, he would have done if he'd had any eyes. Somehow, I still recognised Graham Colgate.

Behind him, a glass panel was absent. I stepped through it into the London night, which now that it was late, had turned bitter. Frost glistened all along the ribbon-straight footway in front of me. It was about two feet wide, and a perilous prospect, especially as the neatly tiled slopes slanting away on either side also glittered. One misstep, and I'd be carried down to the guttering, and then dropped… what, ninety feet? Beyond that, I saw an endless vista of roofs, chimneys and steeples, many of the latter still broken and leaning.

Then I saw something else.

A figure crouched under a heavy cloak perhaps sixty yards off, at the far end of the footway. I advanced, arms jutted outward. The width of this walk should under normal circumstances be more than adequate, but I was disoriented by the height, by my twirling senses. I was still a good ten yards from the end, when the object of my interest lumbered upright and swung around. I stopped dead. He was shrouded in black to his eyes, which, as I'd already seen, were pits in raddled dough.

"Detective Constable McKane," came a muffled voice. "You see what's become of me?"

I shook my head, flabbergasted. "Denny, what happened? You weren't this badly hurt."

"*Not badly hurt?*" he intoned with bass outrage. "You see this?" His left hand slid from a fold in his cloak; it was a curved steel hook.

Numbed, I tried to remember the man I'd last encountered only a couple of months after the war ended. And then he laughed raucously and threw off his cloak, revealing the cricket whites. I saw that he was two-handed after all; the hook was merely an implement he brandished. A cargo hook, something they'd use on the docks. His mutilated face, he simply removed. I'd been right all along; it was papier-mâché. Beneath it lay familiar features, square-jawed and clean-shaven. Handsome, were it not for the burn marks on the side, though these were mere fingerprints of tautened skin.

"You gullible fool, Ronald, my old mate," he laughed again. "But I imagine you came here *expecting* a monster, no?"

I stood bewildered, teetering, frozen even through my overcoat and suit, while Denny wore a short-sleeved white shirt, with a white sleeveless sweater over the top, and yet looked almost impossibly relaxed.

"What… is this?" I demanded. "Denny, in God's name, what's possessed you?"

"Possessed me?" He arched an eyebrow. "You think the Pan in Peter comes from *that*? An evil spirit? Something demonic? Ronald, you fail to understand…"

"Stop with the bullshit!" I cried. "You fucking murdered these boys!"

He pondered, pursing his lips. "Will it console you to know that I got them drunk first? Did it with a cushion while they slept? They barely felt a thing."

"I sincerely doubt that…"

He shook his head. "You and I know the meaning of a terrible death, Ron. Trust me, it was quick. On top of that, there were other benefits."

I could hardly believe what I was hearing. "Benefits?"

"Now, they'll never grow old and sad…" He smiled, though not at me, as though on the other side of me he was seeing something that pleased him greatly. "Now, they'll always be boys. Enjoying their playtime for the rest of—"

"*You bloody lunatic!*" I snapped. "They didn't ask for this."

"Boys are boys, Ron. They always know what they want… in this case alcohol, drugs, the company of human vermin, so-called adults who if there was any real justice would be strung up on telegraph posts. That's what they *want*. But what they *need* is something else entirely. And now these boys of mine have it."

I was incredulous. "Boys of *yours*?"

"I'm the father they never knew. The firm but caring influence…"

"They had mothers, siblings…"

For the first time, he showed his teeth. "Clearly, that wasn't enough."

"So you killed them?"

"Brought them to Neverland."

"A derelict shell on a bombsite?"

"This place is symbolic, admittedly…"

"*Christ on a bike, Denny!*" I waved my arms at the cityscape. "*This* is real life, okay? *This* is what these youngsters must deal with."

"That's the whole point, Ron."

"You wanted to help them, you could have gone and worked for a charity or… I don't know, even joined us—"

"Joined you?" His face split into a scornful grin. "I know how *you* help them, Ronald, *old mate*. What is it… a clip round the ear, which is never just a clip, is it? Hard time in a borstal or approved school? The system you represent is part of the problem, Ron, not the solution."

"And this isn't? What *you've* been doing?"

He turned thoughtful. "Neverland was always a dream, I admit. You couldn't find it on a map. It wasn't like Fairyland, where you went three times backward round the oak tree and four times forward round the elm, and then up and down the same path twice. Neverland was never so simple. But it's there, isn't it, old mate? So close. You surely see it in your dreams?"

"Denny…" I edged closer. "I grew up in Bethnal Green. You grew up round the Elephant. *We* have no such dreams."

"And that means there's no such place. Because *you* don't believe in it?"

"Enough chit-chat." I moved closer, fixing him with my best "interrogation room" stare. "I'm taking you in. But I can't fight you up here, mate… we'll both end up going."

He pursed his lips again. "Let me ask you a question…"

"There's a chance they'll spare you. You're disturbed, Den. If it's obvious to me, it'll be obvious to a shrink, to a judge…"

"One question, Ron. And if you answer truthfully, I'll come quietly."

I halted, watching him.

He nodded. "Do you *want* to believe?"

"Mate, it's just childish."

"But imagine if it was actually there… *somewhere*." He gestured with the hook, almost overbalancing himself. "A place with no bomb-smashed cities, no crime, no unwashed urchins already on a one-way ticket to jail and rape and mental collapse. And all we have to do is reach out and grab it." He shrugged. "If only we knew where it was, eh?"

"Drop that hook, Denny."

"You see, mate, *I* can't find it either. But it was always too late for us… *don't come any closer, Ron.*"

He raised the hook. It was the first threatening gesture he'd made.

"You said you'd come quietly," I reminded him.

"You need to *try* to believe. I can't be the only one… *don't, Ronnie!*"

I was almost within swiping range. For several seconds we locked eyes, oblivious to the chasm encircling us. He shook his head very gravely, raising the hook higher.

And the gunshot was deafening.

The bullet whipped past my right ear.

Dust puffed where it thudded into Denny's left shoulder. He jerked violently.

But astonishingly, he held his perch.

I glanced back. Mulgrave was advancing, one whole side of his face stained crimson, the Webley shaking, smoke trickling from its muzzle. A loud breath drew my attention back to Denny Collins, who treated me to a curiously triumphant smile. Then toppled backwards.

Lurching forward, I lost my footing. I landed on the walk on hands and knees.

"Ron!" Mulgrave scrabbled up behind, grabbing my collar.

I'd landed so close to the end of the roof that I overlooked it, and couldn't at first make sense of what I was seeing.

About ten feet down, a timber platform, five by five, thrust out. A line was tied to it, a wire or cable, pulled taut as it led away at a gradient, connecting with another building some forty yards off. Then I saw Denny Collins. Hanging one-handed from his hook, travelling the line at speed.

"I shot him!" Mulgrave protested.

"He was always strong," I replied.

But sadly, his rope wasn't. When he was halfway over, it *clunked* loose.

He dropped silently, turning upside down as he fell. The impact was muffled by smog, but still sickeningly loud. Several moments passed before I sensed the pistol next to my face.

"Get rid of that before you shoot someone else!" I snapped. "And get your arse down *there*, for Christ's sake!"

Mulgrave scuttled back. Leaving me squatted on the edge, gazing into nothingness.

When Wilberforce climbed into the Vanguard alongside me, we watched through the windscreen as uniforms, visible by the light of burning braziers, closed off the road.

The DI brushed his white hair flat. "I suppose I should say well done."

I grunted. "Solid coppering, guv. Followed our noses, that's all."

"Bugger of a night. You heard what's happened in Notting Hill?"

I shrugged. I'd been off the grid all day.

"Backstreet shithole called Rillington Place. Total pigsty. New residents move in this evening and the next thing there's murdered women flopping out the cupboards."

For obvious reasons, I struggled to focus.

"We're looking for the former tenant. Bloke called Christie. Who's done a runner." Wilberforce sighed. "Least we don't have that problem here. Though I'd like to know who cut the rope."

"Me too," I replied.

Only on approaching the body had Malcolm Mulgrave learned why the suspect fell. The rope hadn't broken, it had been neatly sliced at its other end. With a clean, sharp blade.

"Former comrade of yours, wasn't he?" Wilberforce said. "Seventh Armoured? Looks like he landed on his head. Doctor says he died instantly."

I nodded.

"Ivor Edwards is coming down. Wants to have a word with you and sonny-boy. Probably bollock the living shit out of you for going it alone, not to mention the unauthorised firearm. Then he'll likely put you forward for commendations." He opened the door and climbed out again. "Must have been off his rocker, that mate of yours. I mean, Jesus, if God had meant us to fly, he'd have given us fucking wings."

I didn't reply. He slammed the door.

I pondered the cut rope, wondering why I hadn't mentioned to Wilberforce what I'd seen. Or to Mulgrave. He'd been heading back down when I'd clocked them. Three nimble figures, lean, agile, fleeing that warehouse next door. Until, right on the edge of my vision, one of them stopped, turned, and issued this warbling, high-pitched war cry.

The sort you heard on cowboy-and-Indian films.

We hadn't been the only ones tracking those missing lads.

Seems the Lost Boys had never been quite as lost as Denny Collins thought.

Far From Home

MURIEL GRAY

On arriving in London, the most surprising thing to Gwendolen was that it was quicker to walk between underground stations than to ride the tube train. Covent Garden to Russell Square, for instance. What a fuss waiting for lifts or climbing 175 spiral stairs. Then the stifling thick air of the platforms and the crush of staring passengers, silent and sullen, sending out signs with their dead eyes and headphones that no question would be answered, no conversation begun, no pleasantries exchanged.

Better by far to walk in the streets. People seemed more alive. So much to look at. So many things happening. She had enjoyed finding the address for the interview by walking. New to this enormous city, then; now, months on, she felt part of it well.

Her employers were a kind, cheerful couple in their forties, though presenting at least a decade younger, and feigning comedy shock and horror if people suggested they were anything but their "showbiz ages". John worked in a television production company that specialised in sensational documentaries about disasters, and Michael was something obscure to do with marketing.

"Oh don't ask," said John. "He has absolutely no idea what he does and neither do they. As long as they keep paying we think it's best left." Gwendolen cherished their constant laughter. Their theatrical glee at her arrival every morning seemed genuine, greeting her each time as if this was her first day at work and they were thrilled she'd turned up. They'd initially quizzed her about Wales, about her life and her family, and then politely left her be when she proved reluctant to share anything but the bare facts.

Her first task of the day was always to take Luath for a walk; their enormous black and white Newfoundland, much too big for the couple's perfect flat but so adored there was no question that the animal took priority above all other concerns.

This was the favourite part of Gwendolen's housekeeper job by far. Luath would pull her like a chariot horse, and their wanderings took them through pretty Bloomsbury streets all the way to Regent's Park, or sometimes along leafy stretches of the canal. Luath was no trouble. Despite her great size she was an amenable and obedient animal, and Gwendolen adored her. Other people with dogs would stop and talk, admiring her, and before long she was greeting the animals and their owners by name.

She would sit on a sunny bench after a long chat with

someone so very different from the people she knew at home and feel as if life really was a big adventure. Here she was now, in the city all her family back in Wales said was too big and dangerous. Where they said she would be lonely, getting ill again and in constant danger. What, they kept asking, was wrong with Newtown anyway? What would happen if she didn't keep taking her medication? If she started seeing things again? What if she walked alone at night in places where girls didn't walk? What if everything that could go wrong went wrong? She had taken it all calmly, then told them with quiet firmness she wanted new things. New places. She wanted to grow up. And she had. Fearless enough to talk to strangers. To make new friends. Making it happen.

John and Michael lived at Number 23 on the street, on the second floor of an elegant brick-built town house, facing south so that the sun poured into their Georgian windows all day long. It ensured the flat was a place of joy, and made dusty corners, of which there were few, easy to find and clean.

Often, when she was polishing the windows, she would look across the street and feel sorry for the people there, in the block that faced north. It was a handsome terrace of the same vintage, but like the side of a dark canyon that never saw the sun. Number 14 was particularly grim. Like a broken tooth in a smile, the entire four-storey-and-basement house looked desolate, presumably a cause of irritation to the occupants of the rest of the terrace, which gleamed with wealth and gentrified metropolitan taste.

She'd asked the boys once who lived there, and they'd wrinkled their noses. Some ill-conceived council housing association project gone wrong. A hostel for homeless minors, but neighbours' complaints about antisocial behaviour and local authority wranglings with greedy developers over ownership of the property had closed it and left it empty.

"A scandal." Michael had tutted. "All that space in a city with so many homeless."

John had nodded, adding in a theatrical low voice he'd heard "bad things" had gone on in there. Michael said John was being ridiculous, and that John liked to think "bad things" went on everywhere.

"He's always wanted to fight bad guys. He just can't find any." Michael received a loving punch, followed by a quick kiss in case it was misconstrued.

"I'll save you from pirates one day," said John with a grin. "You'll thank me."

Ignoring him, Michael continued, "Of course, we thought of trying to buy it. Like every person in London, to be honest. What an investment. But then…" He shuddered.

"Nah."

John shook his head too.

"Eww."

It was an overcast day when Gwendolen opened the drawing-room window to its full extent, as she polished the table beneath. Luath was curled in her giant dog bed, slobbering and twitching as she chased something in her sleep. The still air hung warm and heavy with thunder, and she put down her duster to wipe her forehead, take a sip of her water bottle, and gaze into the street.

A movement caught her eye. The slightest shift of dark behind one of the attic windows at the top of Number 14. She put down her bottle and moved to the windowsill. The dusty windows of the town house across the road were black and empty as usual. Suddenly two paws thumped onto the sill beside her, making her jump. It was Luath, body rigid, teeth bared and a low, quiet growl at the back of her throat, eyes staring fixed and true at the attic window.

"Hey girl. Don't give me frights like that," said Gwendolen softly, bending to rub the dog's shagpile head.

She looked back up again. Behind the near-opaque glass of the arched attic window, a thin figure was standing in the gloom. Gwendolen squinted and leant forward. In response, the figure stepped closer towards the light.

It was impossible to tell who it was. Of slight build, wearing a hoody, so her first instinct was to think it was a teenager. But the harder she peered, the more indistinct it became, though its movement from the shadows to the dirty glass seemed swift and agile.

Without thinking, Gwendolen slowly raised her hand in a greeting. There was no response.

But with that lift of the hand something shifted. The still air around her crackled.

She felt seen. Seen as if all her secrets, all her desires, all her fears had been exposed. Seen in a way that made her afraid.

Luath barked. She bent to shoosh her, and when she looked up again the figure was gone.

Gathering her things that evening as she made to leave, she hesitated and went through to the kitchen where John was cooking, stirring something in time to ear-splitting vintage rock music.

"I think I saw someone across the road today," she shouted.

"Mmm?" said John.

"At Number 14."

John stopped stirring, and implored Alexa to turn down the volume.

AC/DC's music was reduced to a volume that rendered it pointless.

John put his hands on his hips.

"No! Shut the fuck up!! Really?"

"I think so. In the attic window."

John took her hand and led her to the windows overlooking the street.

"Where? I need to see this. Where?"

She pointed. The windows were empty.

John looked then, his gaze moving to the front door. A peeling dark green rectangle with a long steel bar bolted and padlocked across it. Sealed tight.

"How could anyone get in?"

Gwendolen shrugged.

"Maybe there's a window at the back? I don't know."

John made a "hmmmn" noise.

"Squatters?"

She just shrugged again. She was glad John was still

holding her hand. Luath made a noise at the back of her throat.

"I'll call the council."

He kissed her cheek, and in a few minutes Bon Scott was screaming "Rock 'n' Roll Damnation" again as she closed the front door and headed for home.

A small orange juice, a banana and a croissant from Tesco Express was the breakfast of choice for Gwendolen on her way to work. Camden Council was miserly with its public litter bins, so the routine of eating while walking made her finish up before she reached the solitary receptacle on the corner of the street.

She pressed her rubbish into the bin, wiped her mouth, and walked on, fumbling for her keys to the flat. The sound was sickening. A *crack*, like a hollow rock with a liquid interior being hit by a hammer.

The body lay with its head almost folded back under the shoulders, so cleanly had the neck been broken. The limbs were intact but arranged on the concrete pavement as though by the choreographer of an alternative dance troupe. A thick pool of dark blood was starting to creep from under the mess.

Her scream was internal, and in its place there came a small, strangled noise from the back of her throat.

She sprinted towards the horror and fell to her knees, bags spilling on the ground, her hands making helpless patting motions above the body before putting them on the pavement to steady herself. It was a child. Or at least, it had been a child. She wheeled round, searching for help. The street was empty save for a jogger that had turned the corner and was heading towards them, headphones in.

She turned away from the twisted body and this time her scream came with pitch and volume.

"Help! God's sake, help!" She realised the hands she waved were red with blood.

The man took out his headphones and ran to her.

"Whoah. You okay? Have you fallen?"

She stared at him in bafflement, her bloodied hands held out as though begging.

"For fuck's sake. He's dead!"

The jogger frowned. Bent to pick up her bags.

"Can I call someone?"

She turned back to the body. A body that was no longer there.

"No. No, that can't be right."

"It'll be okay," said the jogger, retrieving her fallen phone and keys from the gutter.

"Did you see him?" she croaked.

He patted the last of her spilled items carefully back together.

"No. I didn't see anybody," he said gently, humouring her by looking up and down the street. "Was it someone who was with you?"

Gwendolen touched the pavement where the grotesque figure had lain. Empty. Dry. Clean. As clean as her hands.

"You live nearby?"

She shook her head and looked up. She was kneeling only a few feet away from Number 14, dark and silent, its barred door closed like a cataract. He handed her the reassembled bags and helped her to her feet.

"Just take a minute. You'll be fine."

Keen to leave, the man turned and ran off, reinserting his earphones and checking his watch as though he'd only stopped to tie his shoelaces. This, after all, was London.

She told the boys she'd had a stupid pratfall, to explain her dishevelled state and scuffed knees. There was much cooing and patting and being told to sit down and have some tea. But she wanted to get on.

Luath, pulling like a tug, wanted to turn right today, and Gwendolen's relief that they would not pass by Number 14 was a solid thing in her gut. She didn't look once across the road, and although she knew she would have to do the cleaning faster, they stayed out much longer than usual.

On the way home, they retraced their steps. Luath, normally excited at this point as her bowl would be filled after the walk, stopped at the front steps. As if called by name, the dog turned sharply and fixed its gaze across the street and up at the high attic windows. Once again, the low growl that Gwendolen had heard so rarely rattled deep in the dog's throat.

She pulled the weight of the mighty and reluctant animal inside with effort. The freezer needed defrosting. She focused on that.

It was impaled on the railings this time. The sixth one. And she'd watched it fall. A boy again, she was sure. Arms outstretched as though he had wings and fully expected to fly, instead of falling like a sack to a twitching, writhing death.

Of course, it was her own fault. She had disciplined herself sufficiently and shouldn't have looked out of the window. Passing by the speared heap was the postman, pushing his trolley. Even from up here she could see he was whistling. Her heart turned in her chest for a second as he halted beside the body, and she held her breath. Could he see what she saw? She knew the answer to it even before she watched him casually leaf though some mail wrapped in an elastic band, shuffle the envelopes, and carry on.

She knew the routine. Just look away. Do something else. Anything. Polish the case of John's Native American antique axes collection. Change the light bulb in the portrait light above the painting of the mermaid combing her hair. Put the oven on for the cake. The regular jobs of a good and loyal housekeeper. And then, when she looked back, it would be gone.

Not this time. The body had stopped twitching, but it was most certainly still there. Both arms and one leg hung down, like a holidaymaker asleep on a hammock, the face in its hood turned away from the street. A couple walked by the body holding hands and looking at their phones. The girl showed the boy something on hers and they laughed, continuing their stroll. A uniformed nanny pushing a pram crossed their path going in the opposite direction. The dead boy still hung on the railings, his blood dripping onto the stone below.

The door of Number 14 was open. The metal bar hung loose, the padlock lying on the top step. Its door had swung open to reveal a sliver of the interior, an ink-black hall beyond.

She knew she had to go. Should she take Luath? Gwendolen glanced over at the dog, gnawing at a toy contentedly on the only sofa that was allowed and looking up at her expectantly. She panted as if a walk was to be forthcoming. Gwendolen bent down and put her arms around the living rug that was Luath, and breathed in her smell. She smelt of life, of bramble bushes and muddy puddles, of the wind in the trees and newly mowed grass. No. She had to go alone. It wouldn't be fair.

"You stay safe," she whispered, kissed her on a very wet nose, and got up. Still dressed in her cleaner's weeds of jogging pants, oversized T-shirt and scuffed Crocs, she opened the door and left the flat she loved.

The body had gone but the door was still open. She pushed it further open with effort. The floor was a pyramid of ancient mail. She stepped over it and moved into the gloom.

It smelled of hostel. Damp, peeling linoleum, the stench of over-boiled vegetables that had worked its way for eternity into the building's fabric, the dust that lay thick on every surface.

Gwendolen began to climb the stairs. Cork pinboards lined the walls, papered with long-forgotten instructions on laminated paper. Small patches of graffiti dotted the walls, words written in marker pen, made unintelligible by having been scrubbed at for removal. Every landing was framed by wired-glass fire doors, mostly cracked and hanging open.

Plaster walls had been kicked in. Inside the stairwell an ancient lift towered to the top of the building, its open iron cage stopped midway between floors.

The last landing was long and flat. The top floor. An archway at the end revealed wooden stairs that would take her to the attic. She stopped. There was whispering. She took a step towards the arch and the noise ceased as though a finger had been raised to lips in a hush.

The wooden steps creaked, but the door at the top opened smoothly.

There they were. Six of them. Huddled in the corner of the filthy attic room, the daylight barely penetrating through the murky dormer windows. She knew every face under each of their identical institutional sweatshirt hoodies. Every death had been different. Every one unseen except by her.

There was a moment of stillness, and then the tallest, the one who'd fallen on the car roof without leaving a dent, put his fists in the air.

"She's here! It worked. It worked! She came!"

They cheered, leaping to their feet and making hopping steps, jumping and hugging each other. These long-dead children, a huddled mass of joy.

"Sit."

A cracked but authoritative voice barked from behind the open door and the boys reformed themselves into a huddle like a well-rehearsed team. Gwendolen stepped forward, pushed the door shut behind her, and turned to look at the person giving the command.

It was not so much a person as a creature. The body of a

pre-pubescent child crouched on its haunches, its thin arms round its knees. It wore the uniform hoodie of the boys as a cape, the hood as a hat, the rest of the garment pushed behind its back, leaving it naked and white. The face was the oldest thing Gwendolen had ever seen.

Glittering eyes stared at her from the depths of a blackened mummified face, teeth bared in a lipless mouth.

"They. Are. Thieves."

She slumped to her knees. A boy spoke up, voice trembling.

"We did nuffin'. Straight up. We was just awake when we shouldn't've been, hiding 'cause of the dirty bastard warden, you know? That used to come in the night an' mess with us an' that? We didn't mean to see him."

He pointed to the creature.

"Mistake. That's all. That's all, innit?"

He looked to the others. The dead others.

There was much nodding. The one who had landed on the steps and broken his back said:

"He finks we've got it. We ain't got it."

There was no fear left in Gwendolen. She was numb. Her gaze was glassy and unfocused.

"What have you taken?" Her voice was soft, a gentle scolding but loving mother to a child.

The boys fell silent again.

"My shadow," said the creature.

She regarded them all calmly, stood tall and walked across to the window. The boys watched her in awe. The thin light from the dull north sky was just enough to cast the ghost of a shade in her shape behind her on the floorboards. She looked down at it, then back up at the thing regarding her with its head cocked in mockery.

"You can have mine."

The glittering eyes narrowed. The creature stood; a tiny thing only as tall as an eight-year-old. It moved towards her with the agility of an insect.

Its small white feet with yellow cracked nails stood on the edge of her shadow.

"Make it stick."

She looked across at the huddle of death, the boys lost forever to life and love, then back down to the floor.

"Here. Let me try."

She bent down and pretended to be pulling a needle and thread back and forth in imaginary cloth. It watched her closely, and its stench was making Gwendolen dig deep to keep from retching. She stood straight again.

"There."

It looked down, then back up at her. It stepped back. Gwendolen's shadow stayed where it was.

The creature raised its thin arm and pointed a finger straight at her face.

"Liar!"

It scuttled back behind the door and hunched back into its pose. The boys were pressed closer together now, eyes wide with terror. They were looking behind her.

She turned and peered into the darkness of the rest of the room. Some of the bodies were nearly skeletons, others merely dried husks. Piled like dolls in a corner as though someone had tidied them up like a good housekeeper.

The creature had lost interest and stared into the mid-distance, rocking gently back and forth. A creature that could wait for eternity if needs be. The boys were crying.

She was not the first. All this had happened before and it would all happen again. The door was firmly closed, and she didn't need to try it to know it would never open for her.

She walked to the window and looked down. She could see quite clearly into John and Michael's drawing room from here. Luath was at the window, paws on the sill staring up at her, her silent bark fierce and endless. Her gaze shifted higher and regarded the city stretched before her. Millions of lives. Millions of stories. And now she would become one of them.

She pulled at the latch, which was neither rusty nor sticking, and opened the window with ease. Gwendolen pulled herself up onto the edge.

London really had been a very big adventure.

And now it was time to fly home.

ABOUT THE AUTHORS

Jen Williams is an award-winning author from London. *Her Copper Cat* and *Winnowing Flame* trilogies have been nominated for British Fantasy Awards several times, with *The Ninth Rain* and *The Bitter Twins* each winning the Robert Holdstock Award for Best Fantasy Novel. Her debut crime novel *Dog Rose Dirt* was published in 2021, and her first horror novella, *Seven Dead Sisters*, was published in 2022 by Absinthe Books. Jen has two new novels out in 2023: *Talonsister,* a return to fantasy published by Titan, and *Games for Dead Girls*, a true crime inspired horror novel, published by HarperVoyager. She's also partly responsible for the creation of the Super Relaxed Fantasy Club and is partial to mead, if you're buying. Jen can be found on Twitter @ sennydreadful, on Instagram as sennydreadful19 and her website is sennydreadful.co.uk.

Lavie Tidhar is author of *Osama*, *The Violent Century*, *A Man Lies Dreaming*, *Central Station*, *Unholy Land*, *By Force Alone*, *The Hood* and *The Escapement*. His latest novels are *Maror* and *Neom*. His awards include the World Fantasy and British Fantasy Awards, the John W. Campbell Award, the Neukom Prize and the Jerwood Prize, and he has been shortlisted for the Arthur C. Clarke Award and the Philip K. Dick Award. Find his website at lavietidhar.wordpress. com, or on Twitter as @lavietidhar.

A. C. Wise is the author of the novels *Wendy, Darling* and *Hooked*, and the recent short story collection *The Ghost Sequences*. Her work has won the Sunburst Award for Excellence in Canadian Literature of the Fantastic, and has been a finalist for the Nebula, Stoker, Locus, Sunburst, Aurora, Ignyte, and Lambda Awards. In addition to her fiction, she contributes a regular short fiction review column to *Apex Magazine*. Find her online at acwise.net and on Twitter as @ac_wise.

Robert Shearman has written six short story collections, and between them they have won the World Fantasy Award, the Shirley Jackson Award, the Edge Hill Readers Prize, and four British Fantasy Awards. He is probably best known for his work on *Doctor Who*, bringing back the Daleks for the BAFTA-winning first series in an episode nominated for a Hugo Award. His latest book, *We All Hear Stories in the Dark*, is a strange mix of modern-day *Arabian Nights* and a "choose your own adventure" game, in which the reader has to find their way through a maze of 101 stories. Robert can be found on Twitter as @ShearmanRobert.

Laura Mauro was born and raised in London and now lives in Oxfordshire. Their short story "Looking for Laika" won the British Fantasy Award for Best Short Fiction in 2018, and "Sun Dogs" was shortlisted for the 2017 Shirley Jackson Award in the Novelette category. Their debut collection, *Sing Your Sadness Deep*, won the 2020 British Fantasy Award for Best Collection, and their short story "The Pain-Eater's Daughter" won the 2020 British Fantasy Award for Best Short Fiction. They like Russian space dogs, Japanese toilet ghosts and Finnish folklore. Laura's website is at lauramauro.com, and they can be found on Twitter @LauraNMauro.

Edward Cox is the author of *The Wood Bee Queen*, *The Song of the Sycamore*, the Relic Guild trilogy, and *The Bone Shaker*. Originally from Colchester in Essex, he now resides in a haunted forest where he hunts old ghosts and tortures them for story ideas. You can find his poorly maintained website at edwardcox.net or catch up with him on Instagram and Twitter (@HerbertCloggs).

Kirsty Logan is a professional daydreamer and the author of novels, story collections, chapbooks, audio fiction, memoirs, and collaborative works with musicians and illustrators. "The Lost Boys Monologues" is based on characters from her Audible Original novel *The Sound at the End*, an Arctic ghost story recorded with a full cast and original music. Her work has been optioned for TV, adapted for stage, recorded for radio and podcasts, exhibited in galleries and distributed from a vintage Wurlitzer cigarette machine. She lives in Glasgow with her wife, baby and rescue dog. Kirsty's website is at kirstylogan.com, and she can be found on Twitter as @kirstylogan.

Claire North is a pseudonym for Catherine Webb, whose first novel was published when she was fourteen years old. Her first novel as Claire was *The First Fifteen Lives of Harry August*, which became a word-of-mouth bestseller and was shortlisted for the Arthur C. Clarke Award, while her subsequent novel *The Sudden Appearance of Hope* won the World Fantasy Award. Her most recent book is *Ithaca*, published September 2022. She lives in London and also works as a live music lighting designer and teaches women's self-defence. Her website can be found at clairenorth.com, and she's on Twitter as @clairenorth42.

Cavan Scott is the *New York Times* bestselling author of *Star Wars: The High Republic – The Rising Storm*, *Star Wars: Dooku – Jedi Lost*, *Shadow Service*, *The Ward*, *Sleep Terrors* and *Dead Seas*. One of the five story architects for Lucasfilm's bestselling multimedia initiative, *Star Wars: The High Republic*, Cavan has written comics for Marvel, DC Comics, Dark Horse, IDW, *2000 AD* and more. He is currently developing a number of new properties for both comics and television. A former magazine editor, Cavan lives in the United Kingdom with his wife and daughters. His lifelong passions include folklore, audio drama, the music of David Bowie and scary movies. He owns far too much LEGO. Cavan's website is cavanscott.com, and he can be found on Twitter as @cavanscott, and Instagram as cavanscottwriter.

Anna Smith Spark is the author of the grimdark epic fantasy series *The Court of Broken Knives, The Tower of Living and Dying* and *The House of Sacrifice,* and the forthcoming *A Woman of the Sword.* Her writing has been described as "a masterwork" by *Nightmarish Conjurings,* "an experience like no other series in fantasy" by *Grimdark Magazine,* and "howls like early Moorcock, converses like the best of Le Guin" by the *Daily Mail.* Her favourite authors are Mary Renault, R. Scott Bakker and M. John Harrison. She's aspie, dyslexic and dyspraxic; a petty bureaucrat and a former fetish model. You may know her by the heels of her shoes. Her website can be found at courtofbrokenknives.com, and she can be found on Twitter @queenofgrimdark, or on Facebook as Anna Smith Spark.

Rio Youers is the British Fantasy and Sunburst Award nominated author of *Westlake Soul* and *Lola on Fire.* His 2017 thriller, *The Forgotten Girl,* was a finalist for the Arthur Ellis Award for Best Crime Novel. He is the writer of *Refrigerator Full of Heads,* a six-issue comic series from DC Comics, and *Sleeping Beauties,* a graphic novel based on the number-one bestseller by Stephen King and Owen King. Rio's latest novel, *No Second Chances,* was published by William Morrow in

February 2022. He can be found online at rioyouers.com, and on Twitter as @Rio_Youers.

As a ghost writer, **Guy Adams** has kicked heroin, robbed a casino, worked as a prison doctor and enjoyed the riches that come as part of being a hugely successful YouTuber.

When feeling more himself, he is the author of *The Clown Service* novels, the *Heavens Gate* trilogy and the famous sixties newspaper strip that never existed, *Goldtiger*. He also writes comics for various publishers, including *2000 AD*.

He has twice been a finalist in the BBC Audio Drama Awards, and as well as writing hundreds of hours of *Doctor Who*, is the co-author of *Arkham County* for Audible and *Children of the Stones* for BBC Sounds.

He also writes about and reviews and watches and watches and watches film.

He lives in Eastbourne with fellow author and live-in genius A. K. Benedict and their daughters (one hairy and canine, the other human) Verity and Dame Margaret Rutherford. His website can be found at guyadamsauthor.com, and he is on Twitter as @guyadamsauthor and Instagram as guyadams.

Premee Mohamed is a Nebula Award-winning Indo-Caribbean scientist and speculative fiction author based in Edmonton, Alberta. She is an Assistant Editor at the short fiction audio venue Escape Pod and the author of the *Beneath the Rising* series of novels as well as several novellas. Her short fiction has appeared in many venues and she can be found on Twitter at @premeesaurus and on her website at premeemohamed.com.

A. K. Benedict writes novels, scripts and short stories. She writes high concept novels such as the critically-acclaimed *The Beauty of Murder*, *The Evidence of Ghosts* and the forthcoming *Little Red Death*. She has twice been shortlisted for the Scribe Award for Audio Drama, winning it in 2019, and was shortlisted for the BBC Audio Drama Podcast Award 2020. Her short stories have featured in many anthologies, including *Best British Short Stories 2012*, *Great British Horror*, *New Fears*, *Best British Horror 2017*, *Phantoms*, *Exit Wounds*, *Invisible Blood* and *Black is the Night*. She also writes Golden Age inspired crime fiction under the name Alexandra Benedict. *The Christmas Murder Game* was an Amazon Fiction Bestseller and was longlisted for the Gold Dagger, and *Murder on the Christmas Express* came out late 2022. She is currently writing novels, TV scripts and a short story collection. Her website is at akbenedict.com, and she can be found on Twitter as @ak_benedict and Instagram as a.k.benedict.

Alison Littlewood's first book, *A Cold Season*, was selected for the Richard and Judy Book Club and described as "perfect reading for a dark winter's night". Other titles include *Mistletoe*, *The Hidden People*, *The Crow Garden*, *Path of Needles* and *The Unquiet House*. She wrote *The Cottingley Cuckoo* as A. J. Elwood, along with *The Other Lives of Miss Emily White*. Alison's short stories have been picked for a number of year's best anthologies and published in her collections *Quieter Paths* and *Five Feathered Tales*. She has won the Shirley Jackson Award for Short Fiction.

Alison lives with her partner Fergus in a house of creaking doors and crooked walls in deepest darkest Yorkshire, England. She has a penchant for books on folklore and weird history, Earl Grey tea, fountain pens and semicolons. She can be found online at alisonlittlewood.co.uk, and on Twitter as @ali_l.

Gama Ray Martinez is a computer programmer and avid writer, author of multiple middle grade fantasy series: *Pharim War*, *Goblin Star*, *The Oranges of Kurnugi* and *Nylean Chronicles*. He is a student of Brandon Sanderson, who has called Gama "an excellent writer." He lives near Salt Lake City, Utah, collects antique weapons in case he ever needs to supply a medieval battalion, and greatly resents when work or other real-life things get in the way of writing. His adult fantasy debut, *God of Neverland*, was published by HarperVoyager in 2022, and its sequel *Queens of Wonderland* will be published in 2023. His website can be found at gamaraymartinez.com, and he can be found on Twitter as @gamaraymartinez.

Juliet Marillier was born and raised in Aotearoa, New Zealand. She is a graduate of the University of Otago and has had a varied career that included music teaching and performing. She now lives in a historic cottage in Western Australia.

Juliet's historical fantasy novels and short stories are published internationally and have won numerous awards, including five Aurealis Awards, four Sir Julius Vogel Awards, the American Library Association's Alex Award, and the Sara Douglass Book Series Award. She is the author of twenty-four novels, including the Blackthorn & Grim series, the Sevenwaters series, and most recently the Warrior Bards series, well as two collections of short fiction. Juliet loves mythology, folklore and strong, complex characters.

Juliet is a member of the druid order OBOD (the Order of Bards, Ovates and Druids). When not writing, she is kept busy by a small crew of rescue dogs. She can be found online at julietmarillier.com, and on Instagram as julietmarillier.

Paul Finch is an ex-cop and journalist turned bestselling author. He first cut his literary teeth penning episodes of the *The Bill,* and has written extensively in horror and fantasy, including for *Doctor Who.*

He is also known for his crime/thriller novels, of which there are twelve to date, including the Heckenburg and Clayburn series.

Paul lives in Lancashire with his wife and business partner, Cathy. His website is at paulfinch-writer.blogspot.com, and he's on Twitter as @paulfinchauthor.

Muriel Gray has had a forty-year career in the media. She has written three horror novels and many short stories. She is currently the joint vice chair of the board of trustees of the British Museum, and a non-executive board member of the British Broadcasting Corporation. Despite her beginnings as an artist and punk, she has so far, quite demonstrably, failed in bringing down the establishment. Muriel can be found on Twitter as @artybagger, and on Instagram as muriel_gray.

Marie O'Regan is an Australian Shadow, British Fantasy and Shirley Jackson Award-nominated author and editor based in Derbyshire. She won the British Fantasy Society's Legends of FantasyCon Award in 2022, and has been nominated for several other BFS awards both as a writer and editor. Her first collection, *Mirror Mere*, was published in 2006 by Rainfall Books; her second, *In Times of Want*, came out in September 2016 from Hersham Horror Books. Her third, *The Last Ghost and Other Stories*, was published by Luna Press early in 2019. Her short fiction has appeared in a number of genre magazines and anthologies in the UK, US, Canada, Italy and Germany, including *Best British Horror 2014*, *Great British Horror: Dark Satanic Mills* (2017), and *The Mammoth Book of Halloween Stories*. Her novella, *Bury Them Deep*, was published by Hersham Horror Books in September 2017. She was shortlisted for the British Fantasy Society Award for Best Short Story in 2006, Best Anthology in 2010 (*Hellbound*

Hearts) and 2012 (*The Mammoth Book of Ghost Stories by Women*). She was also shortlisted for the Shirley Jackson Award for Best Anthology in 2020 (*Wonderland*). Her genre journalism has appeared in magazines like *The Dark Side, Rue Morgue and Fortean Times,* and her interview book with prominent figures from the horror genre, *Voices in the Dark*, was released in 2011. An essay on "The Changeling" was published in PS Publishing's *Cinema Macabre*, edited by Mark Morris. She is co-editor of the bestselling *Hellbound Hearts, The Mammoth Book of Body Horror, A Carnivàle of Horror – Dark Tales from the Fairground, Exit Wounds, Wonderland, Cursed,* and *Twice Cursed*, as well as the charity anthology *Trickster's Treats #3*, plus editor of the bestselling anthologies *The Mammoth Book of Ghost Stories by Women* and *Phantoms*. Her first novel, the internationally bestselling *Celeste*, was published in February 2022. A former chair of the British Fantasy Society, she was also co-chair of the UK Chapter of the Horror Writers' Association as well as co-chair of ChillerCon UK. Visit her website at marieoregan. net. She is on Twitter as @Marie_O_Regan and Instagram as marieoregan8101.

Paul Kane is the award-winning (including the British Fantasy Society's Legends of FantasyCon Award 2022), bestselling author and editor of over a hundred books – such as the *Arrowhead* trilogy (gathered together in the sellout *Hooded Man* omnibus, revolving around a post-apocalyptic version of Robin Hood), *The Butterfly Man and Other Stories, Hellbound Hearts, Wonderland* (a Shirley Jackson Award finalist) and *Pain Cages* (an Amazon #1 bestseller). His non-fiction books include *The Hellraiser Films and Their Legacy* and *Voices in the Dark*, and his genre journalism has appeared in the likes of *SFX, Rue Morgue* and *DeathRay*. He has been a Guest at Alt.Fiction five times, was a Guest at the first SFX Weekender, at Thought Bubble in 2011, Derbyshire Literary Festival and Off the Shelf in 2012, Monster Mash and Event Horizon in 2013, Edge-Lit in 2014 and 2018, HorrorCon, HorrorFest and Grimm Up North in 2015, The Dublin Ghost Story Festival and Sledge-Lit in 2016, IMATS Olympia and Celluloid Screams in 2017, Black Library Live and the UK Ghost Story Festival in 2019, plus the WordCrafter virtual event 2021 – where he delivered the keynote speech – as well as being a panellist at FantasyCon and the World Fantasy Convention, and a fiction judge at the Sci-Fi London festival. A former British Fantasy Society Special Publications Editor, he has served as co-chair for the UK Chapter of the Horror Writers' Association and co-chaired ChillerCon UK in May 2022.

His work has been optioned and adapted for the big and small screen, including for US network primetime television, and his novelette "Men of the Cloth" has just been turned into a feature by Loose Canon/Hydra Films, starring Barbara Crampton (*Re-Animator, You're Next*): *Sacrifice*, released by Epic Pictures/101 Films. His audio work includes the full cast drama adaptation of *The Hellbound Heart* for Bafflegab, starring Tom Meeten (*The Ghoul*), Neve McIntosh (*Doctor Who*) and Alice Lowe (*Prevenge*), and the *Robin of Sherwood* adventure *The Red Lord* for Spiteful Puppet/ITV narrated by Ian Ogilvy (*Return of the Saint*). He has also contributed to the Warhammer 40k universe for Games Workshop. Paul's latest novels are *Lunar* (set to be turned into a feature film), the YA story *The Rainbow Man* (as PB Kane), the sequels to *RED* – *Blood RED* & *Deep RED* – the award-winning hit *Sherlock Holmes & the Servants of Hell*, *Before* (an Amazon Top 5 dark fantasy bestseller), *Arcana* and *The Storm*. In addition, he writes thrillers for HQ/HarperCollins as PL Kane, the first of which, *Her Last Secret* and *Her Husband's Grave* (a sellout on both Amazon and Waterstones.com), came out in 2020, with *The Family Lie* released the following year. Paul lives in Derbyshire, UK, with his wife Marie O'Regan. Find out more at his site shadow-writer.co.uk, which has featured Guest Writers such as Stephen King, Neil Gaiman, Charlaine Harris, Robert Kirkman, Dean Koontz and Guillermo del Toro. He can also be found @PaulKaneShadow on Twitter, and paul.kane.376 on Instagram.

ACKNOWLEDGEMENTS

And now for the important bit – our opportunity to say thank you. Firstly, to all the authors for their contributions, and to George Sandison, Daniel Carpenter and all of the team at Titan Books for their support and tireless efforts on our behalf, as always. Finally, thanks to our respective families, without whom etc.

ISOLATION
EDITED BY DAN COXON

Lost in the wilderness, or alone in the dark, isolation remains one of our deepest held fears. This horror anthology from Shirley Jackson and British Fantasy Award finalist Dan Coxon calls on leading horror writers to confront the dark moments, the challenges that we must face alone: survivors in a world gone silent; the outcast shunned by society; the quiet voice trapped in the crowd; the lonely and forgotten, screaming into the abyss.

Experience the chilling terrors of Isolation.

Featuring stories by:

Nina Allan	Alison Littlewood
Laird Barron	Ken Liu
Ramsey Campbell	Jonathan Maberry
M. R. Carey	Michael Marshall Smith
Chịkọdịlị Emelumadu	Mark Morris
Brian Evenson	Lynda E. Rucker
Owl Goingback	A. G. Slatter
Gwendolyn Kiste	Paul Tremblay
Joe R. Lansdale	Lisa Tuttle
Tim Lebbon	Marian Womack

CURSED
EDITED BY MARIE O'REGAN AND PAUL KANE

ALL THE BETTER TO READ YOU WITH

It's a prick of blood, the bite of an apple, the evil eye, a wedding ring or a pair of red shoes. Curses come in all shapes and sizes, and they can happen to anyone, not just those of us with unpopular stepparents…

Here you'll find unique twists on curses, from fairy tale classics to brand-new hexes of the modern world – expect new monsters and mythologies as well as twists on well-loved fables. Stories to shock and stories of warning, stories of monsters and stories of magic.

TWENTY TIMELESS FOLKTALES, NEW AND OLD

Neil Gaiman	Jen Williams
Jane Yolen	Catriona Ward
Karen Joy Fowler	James Brogden
M. R. Carey	Maura Mchugh
Christina Henry	Angela Slatter
Christopher Golden	Lillith Saintcrow
Tim Lebbon	Christopher Fowler
Michael Marshall Smith	Alison Littlewood
Charlie Jane Anders	Margo Lanagan

WONDERLAND
EDITED BY MARIE O'REGAN AND PAUL KANE

Join Alice as she is thrown into the whirlwind of Wonderland.

Within these pages you'll find myriad approaches to Alice, from horror to historical, taking us from the nightmarish reaches of the imagination to tales that will shock, surprise and tug on the heart-strings. So, it's time now to go down the rabbit hole, or through the looking-glass or... But no, wait. By picking up this book and starting to read it you're already there, can't you see?

Brand-new works from the best in fantastical fiction

M. R. Carey	Laura Mauro
Mark Chadbourn	Cat Rambo
Genevieve Cogman	Lilith Saintcrow
Jonathan Green	Cavan Scott
Alison Littlewood	Robert Shearman
James Lovegrove	Angela Slatter
L. L. Mckinney	Catriona Ward
George Mann	Jane Yolen
Juliet Marillier	Rio Youers

TITANBOOKS.COM

AT MIDNIGHT: 15 BELOVED FAIRYTALES REIMAGINED

Fairy tales have been spun for thousands of years and remain among our most treasured stories. Weaving fresh tales with unexpected reimaginings, *At Midnight* brings together a diverse group of celebrated YA writers to breathe new life into a storied tradition. You'll discover . . .

Dahlia Adler, "Rumplestiltskin"
Tracy Deonn, "The Nightingale"
H.E. Edgmon, "Snow White"
Hafsah Faizal, "Little Red Riding Hood"
Stacey Lee, "The Little Matchstick Girl"
Roselle Lim, "Hansel and Gretel"
Darcie Little Badger, "Puss in Boots"
Malinda Lo, "Frau Trude"
Alex London, "Cinderella"
Anna-Marie McLemore, "The Nutcracker"
Rebecca Podos, "The Robber Bridegroom"
Rory Power, "Sleeping Beauty"
Meredith Russo, "The Little Mermaid"
Gita Trelease, "Fitcher's Bird"
and an all-new fairy tale by **Melissa Albert**

For more fantastic fiction, author events,
exclusive excerpts, competitions, limited editions and more

VISIT OUR WEBSITE
titanbooks.com

LIKE US ON FACEBOOK
facebook.com/titanbooks

FOLLOW US ON TWITTER AND INSTAGRAM
@TitanBooks

EMAIL US
readerfeedback@titanemail.com